The Best
AMERICAN
SHORT
STORIES
1977

The Best
AMERICAN
SHORT
STORIES
1977

And the Yearbook of the
American Short Story

Edited by Martha Foley

1977

Houghton Mifflin Company Boston

Library of Congress Catalog Card Number: 16-11387
ISBN: 0-395-25701-8
Printed in the United States of America

V 10 9 8 7 6 5 4 3 2 1

"The Trouble with Being Food" by Frederick Busch. First published in *Esquire*.
Reprinted from *Domestic Particulars* by permission of New Directions Publishing
Corp. Copyright © 1976 by Frederick Busch.

"Tarzan Meets the Department Head" by Price Caldwell. Reprinted from *The
Carleton Miscellany*. Copyright © 1977 by Price Caldwell.

"Falconer" by John Cheever. Originally appeared in *Playboy* Magazine. Copyright © 1976 by John Cheever.

"At Peace" by Ann Copeland. First published in *Canadian Fiction Magazine*,
Number 22 (August, 1976). Copyright © 1976 by Ann Copeland.

"Pleadings" by John William Corrington. Reprinted from *The Southern Review*.
Copyright © 1976 by John William Corrington.

"Growing Up in No Time" by Philip Damon. First published in *Hawaii Review*.
Copyright © 1976 by Hawaii Review.

"The Steinway Quintet" by Leslie Epstein. First published in *Antaeus*. Reprinted from *The Steinway Quintet: Plus Four* by permission of Little, Brown and
Company. Copyright © 1976 by Leslie Epstein.

"The Lover" by Eugene K. Garber. Reprinted from *Shenandoah:* The Washington and Lee University Review with the permission of the Editor. Copyright ©
1976 by Washington and Lee University.

"Look at a Teacup" by Patricia Hampl. First published in *The New Yorker*. Copyright © 1976 The New Yorker Magazine, Inc.

"Rider" by Baine Kerr. Originally published in the *Denver Quarterly* (Winter,
1976). Copyright © 1976 by the University of Denver.

"A Questionnaire for Rudolph Gordon" by Jack Matthews. Reprinted from *The
Malahat Review*, Number 39 (July, 1976). © Malahat Review 1976.

"A Passion for History" by Stephen Minot. First published in the *Sewanee Review* 84 (Spring, 1976). Copyright © 1976 by the University of the South. Reprinted by permission of the Editor.

"The Woman Who Thought Like a Man" by Charles Newman. Reprinted from
Partisan Review (Vol. XLIII, No. 4). Copyright © 1976 by P. R., Inc.

TO THE MEMORY OF
REX STOUT

Acknowledgments

GRATEFUL ACKNOWLEDGMENT for permission to reprint the stories in this volume is made to the following:

The editors of *The American Review, Antaeus, The Atlantic, The Canadian Fiction Magazine, The Carleton Miscellany, The Denver Quarterly, Esquire, The Hawaii Review, The Malahat Review, The New Yorker, Partisan Review, Playboy, Ploughshares, The Sewanee Review, Shenandoah, The Southern Review;* and to Frederick Busch, Price Caldwell, John Cheever, Ann Copeland, John William Corrington, Philip Damon, Leslie Epstein, Eugene K. Garber, Patricia Hample, Baine Kerr, Jack Matthews, Stephen Minot, Charles Newman, Joyce Carol Oates, Tim O'Brien, Tom Robbins, William Saroyan, John Sayles, Anne Tyler, William S. Wilson.

Foreword

THE MOST IMPORTANT literary event in the United States of America in the past year was not the writing of a great poem, story, play, essay, or history. It was writing of an entirely different kind but one that protects literary works and their authors. It was the legal wording of this country's first real copyright law, which finally was passed by Congress and signed by the President, after many years of struggle and needless hardship for our writers. The new law will become fully effective January 1, 1978. Because many short stories are first published in magazines and later appear in books or are made into plays, the law has double value for short story authors.

Away back in 1909, the ladies and gentlemen of the American Authors' Society, an organization long defunct in 1977, felt affronted when the "Big Six," as the typographical unions were called, asked the Society to help them draw up a joint copyright law. The law then in effect was an 1891 rudimentary one, based on an American act of 1790, which in turn had copied an English statute of 1710. None of those laws, of course, foresaw modern printing and reproduction methods. Queen Victoria was dead in 1909 but Victorian genteelism still influenced Anglo-American attitudes. The Authors' Society told the printers that association with a labor union was beneath a writer's professional dignity. Not knowing what writers needed, the typographical unions went ahead by themselves and put through the 1909 copyright law, which took care of their interests while those of writers were unspecified.

That pretty piece of snobbery by the Authors' Society resulted in years of terrible deprivation for American writers. Many authors, some great geniuses, went hungry, their children shoeless, and wound up in a destitute old age while their writings made money for other people. Readers would be shocked if they knew the names of some of the famous American authors whose children had to be helped from the limited funds of the Authors' Guild.

American writers were not the only ones victimized by lack of an adequate copyright law. When I was a correspondent in Europe, some foreign authors were so bitter at the pirating of their work in the United States that they refused to give interviews to American journalists. In turn, because the United States did not belong to the International Copyright Union, which gave literary works protection during the author's entire lifetime and for fifty years after death, thus ensuring benefit for his children, American writers were cheated in foreign publishing.

One of the most pernicious clauses in the 1909 American law was that which gave writing a copyright for twenty-eight years only. It could be renewed for another twenty-eight years *if* the author remembered to renew it before the end of the twenty-eighth year. How many authors, belonging to the most unbusinesslike of all human species, did remember? Or instruct their families to watch out for that twenty-eighth-year expiration date? How many literary agents, even, kept track after a first, initial sale? When a copyright lapsed, a work went into the public domain, free for anyone to use.

When I founded *Story* in Vienna, in 1931, I saw to it that it carried a notice, as permitted by Austrian copyright law, that all rights to the stories printed in it belonged to the authors. When the magazine was moved to Spain, that policy still prevailed. But when the magazine came to New York in 1933, we were told that only a blanket copyright, covering all the contents in a magazine as a unit, was allowed under American law. This bestowed on the publisher of a periodical ownership of all the rights to a story. Reprint, dramatic, book, or foreign rights could be obtained by the author only if he wrote to the magazine publisher and asked that they be transferred to him and if the request was recorded at the Copyright Office in Washington. Some publishers granted the request, some asked to share in the proceeds, some refused, but many were never asked. When *Collier's* magazine, which had published thousands of short stories during its long history, discontinued publication in 1957, I asked Ramona Stewart, a frequent contributor, who now owned the rights to her stories. "I have no idea," she said, looking surprised.

In 1947, the students in my Columbia University fiction-writing classes, many of whom are today well-known authors, brought out *Stateside*, a publication to introduce their work, not to the public, but to publishers, editors, and literary agents. I tried again to have magazine short stories individually copyrighted. My correspondence with Washington was terminated by the statement "We are sorry you do not like our copyright law."

There were plenty of others who did not like the law. One of the most remarkable was Rex Stout, to whom should go great credit for his part in ending long copyright injustice to authors. Rex and I were friends. His was an extraordinary variety of abilities. He was a banker and a liberal activist, a publisher and an author, and an expert carpenter and a farmer. I met him in 1928 when he was forty-two years old and came to Paris to keep a promise he had made himself when he was twenty-two, trying to be a writer. The promise, he told me, was that he would devote twenty years solely to making enough money so that he could devote the rest of his life to writing the way he wanted to write. Because banks are where money is, he had gone into banking. Now he was ready to write his books.

For his first evening in Paris I took Rex to dinner at Pharamond's, a small restaurant in the ancient market district, infinitely superior to the much-touted Maxim's. Eugène Rossetti, a rambunctious Romanian gourmet who covered the Police Prefecture for the Paris *Herald,* on which I also worked, was there. I introduced him to Rex. It was a historic literary moment.

"Would you like a cocktail?" Rex asked me after we all had sat down together at a table. Before I could answer, Rossetti burst out at him, "Barbarian! Cocktails and Coca-Cola! Americans are savages!" Rossetti turned to me protectively. "You will have some good red Mâcon wine." He glared at Rex. "You put sugar in your salad dressing!" "I do not!" Rex protested, but a twinkle came into his eye. He was enjoying this. "And eat food out of cans," Rossetti went on. "Americans don't cook food; they manufacture it."

Without consulting either Rex or me, Rossetti ordered the dinner. It was sublime. I will not describe it because a foreword is no place to make a reader hungry for anything but literature. Rex was enthralled by Rossetti. As friends, they shared many Lucullan feasts. When Rex returned to the United States, he took the gastronomic tyrant back with him. Not, of course, in the flesh. Rossetti, the Paris police reporter from Romania, arrived in America in the guise of a detective genius from Montenegro with a passion for orchids. Today he is famous as Nero Wolfe, the gourmet detective hero of Rex Stout's long series of mystery stories.

As president for many years of the Authors' Guild, Rex used financial canniness gained during his years as drop-out writer and successful banker to benefit all writers. His liberal principles never would have permitted him to turn away a labor union as did the long-ago Authors' Society. He had too much respect for work with one's hands. He made beautiful furniture out of rare woods, helped in the actual construction of his contemporary Brewster, New York, home, and cultivated a successful small farm. Guild members, galvanized into action by a booklet entitled "Do You Let Dollar Bills Lie Around Like Your Copyrights?" undertook action to reform the law.

It was a tough fight. The Authors' Guild and its sister organization, the Dramatists' Guild, had to overcome a multitude of obstacles. The tangle of archaic laws was further complicated by modern reproduction techniques of literary work in films, radio, and television. Particularly difficult to solve was the situation created by photocopying of printed works without payment to, or permission of, the writers who had worked hard to compose them. Public apathy was appalling. Americans, unlike the citizens of many other countries, failed to understand that if a Marshall Field founded a department store, it belonged to him and his heirs, whereas if an American writer founded a book, his ownership quickly evaporated. Such unawareness still continues. A *New York Times* Washington correspondent, reporting on the copyright law's passage, commented that it was of interest only to legal specialists, an opinion the *Times* corrected in later accounts. Typical was a headline in another paper: OF ALL THINGS, CONTROVERSY OVER COPYRIGHT LAW.

The authors won. January 1, 1978, will mean a Happy New Year indeed for American writers. The new law extends copyright protection of their work for their lifetime, plus fifty years thereafter. It terminates long-term assignment of copyrights. Public broadcasters are forbidden to use works of writers without their permission, and librarians forbidden the routine photocopying of them. Details of these and other of the law's provisions may be obtained free of charge by writing to the Copyright Office, Library of Congress, Washington, D.C. 20559. Especially informative is Circular R 99, giving highlights of the law in simple language. I have two regrets about the new law. One is that it took so long to win it. The other is that Rex Stout is not alive to see its adoption. I dedicate this year's *Best American Short Stories* to his memory.

It never occurred to me to be anything so practical as a banker when I was young. I did what most young people of my time who wanted to write did; I went into newspaper work. Today young writers join college faculties. To compare the two approaches to literature is interesting. Teaching is no lotus land, as I know from experience, but I vote for Academe. This year, as for many years past, more fine stories are written by teachers than journalists, as this present collection attests. It is sad to think that you can open the bottom desk drawers of countless newspapermen and find there the manuscript of a half-finished novel or a sheaf of rejected short story manuscripts. John Gunther, the foreign correspondent, who was author of the best-selling *Inside* books, spoke for many of his fellow journalists when he said, as quoted in his *New York Times* obituary, "I would rather have written one good short story than all my books!"

The ideal life for a writer would be that provided for those lucky enough to stay at the MacDowell Colony in the beautiful Mount Monadnock country of New Hampshire. Anna MacDowell founded the retreat in memory of her husband, the composer Edward MacDowell, because he told her he wished every artist could have the uninterrupted peace and privacy he himself enjoyed. The colonists have bedrooms in the main cluster of buildings, but after breakfast they leave for the woods and the widely separated, comfortably furnished individual studios where until evening they can compose music, write, or paint without a single interruption. Lunch is quietly hung in a basket from a hook on a studio wall, too high for animals to reach. Not allowed is any "visitor from Porlock," as Coleridge called the man who interrupted him in the middle of "Kubla Khan," causing that glorious poem to remain forever unfinished. Edwin Arlington

Robinson, Hervey Allen, Thornton Wilder, and Willa Cather are some of the many writers who have done their best work at the Colony.

Anna MacDowell was still alive the summer of 1950, when I was there. She was a lively, laughing woman in her nineties, unhandicapped by her deafness. When she welcomed me, I told her I was very tired and was afraid I could not accomplish much writing. She said, "That is all right. You just sit and rest and daydream. A writer has to have a lot of thoughts before he writes, you know, and you can't get them in the hurly-burly of everyday life."

Mrs. MacDowell's "hurly-burly," intensified, is what cripples the journalist's ability to write fiction. Thoughts about writing — the daydreaming so important as a matrix for creative work — are swamped by the never-ceasing onslaught of daily news events about which a newspaperman must write factually.

Until this year, good humorous stories have been few and far between in American fiction. Perhaps our writers have not been unhappy enough. Our two most important humorous short story writers were Ring Lardner and James Thurber. Both were miserable. Lardner was so depressed while writing that he would rent a hotel room, pull down all the shades, and hide from the world. James Thurber told me, when he gave me permission to reprint his hilarious story, "The Catbird Seat," that he had to use four hundred sheets of paper to write it because of his growing blindness.

Surprise is a vital part of humor. Unless he is Charlie Chaplin, do you laugh when a poor, old tramp slips on a banana peel? But if a dignified, well-fed, top-hatted gentleman stumbles in his strut! There are some very funny stories in this year's collection but I won't tell you which. Surprise!

I am grateful to all the editors who have kept this anthology supplied with copies of their magazines and to their authors for generously granting reprint rights. The editor of any new magazine is urged to send copies to me.

The editors and staff of Houghton Mifflin are entitled to gratitude for their help. Finally, tribute is paid to the memory of Edward J. O'Brien, who founded this anthology in 1915.

MARTHA FOLEY

Contents

The Best
AMERICAN
SHORT
STORIES
1977

FREDERICK BUSCH

The Trouble with Being Food

(FROM ESQUIRE)

I WAS a very fat boy and always had to tolerate mezzanines in clothing stores called Big Guys and Muscle Builders, and in smaller shops in our neighborhood I would suffer comments from little men and women, spoken at my parents from between my legs, such as, "He needs a lot of room in the seat, huh?" Then, in college, I grew thin without trying, and loved it, and wore as little as I could to show as much of my smallness as was possible. When I left school, I ballooned again — and as I've wandered, I've swelled.

But Katherine, whom I travel to in Montpelier, Vermont, where she lives with her kids, from Cicero, New York, where I live with myself and little income, says she loves my stomach, which stays round when I lie down. She holds it sometimes between her hands. I try to cram it all inside her cold palms.

I'm not in good health. I try not to pant on the pillow after love.

On the pillow after love at night in Vermont I hear my heart knock, and it wakes me. Katherine snores. My pillow is a drum; I hear my heart. It haunts me out of sleep.

Katherine stops snoring and says, "What is it?"

I say, "Me."

She says, "Oh." Then: "I thought it was one of the kids." Then: "Or Marlon Brando." Then she snores.

I say it to myself: tomorrow morning I'm going on a diet. I'm losing seventy-five pounds. I'll become superb. Because when I have the heart attack I don't want my nurses making jokes about me.

I fold the pillow so it hurts the back of my neck, and I lie against my rock, a holy man, impressed that I'm not afraid, but earnest about staying up all night so as not to hear my heart do what it does in the darkness: surge to the base of my throat and rap like fists, race my pulse up, cover my forehead and neck with sweat. I am no longer impressed, and I *am* afraid, and I wonder if Katherine will wake to find my body in bed in her home but no one home in the skin.

This is not a fertile pursuit. I consider her sons — slender like her, like their long-gone crazy father whom we often discuss, matter-of-factly, because Katherine and I are adults and this is her history: what can we do but discuss? (We can burn his clothing, cauterize her cervix of his trace, defile his name in the children's ears, and hire assassins to hunt him into terror and death.) But we discuss — it's what she needs. And in her old farmhouse surrounded by potato fields, wind with the smell of snow lying up against our breathing, I lie against Katherine, blink against sleep and the dreams of my fat body, and consider her sons.

The question is whether Sears, Roebuck will question my lie that Rocky and Bob are my sons, too. They're listed on the application I returned, which came to tell her about life insurance for less than seven cents a day, which everyone needs because in America there's death by accident every five minutes. It said, "Think what a check for $100,000 can mean to your loved ones at such a time."

All right: a fertile pursuit.

What I'm waiting for, of course, is the burst of pain up my neck, the tingling fingers. What I'm waiting for is a way to fall beneath a truck before that happens: accidental death, and an end, by the way, to nighttime snacks and the sneaking of seventh helpings — the ultimate diet.

So here I am now, insured but still breathing, though not awfully well, at Katherine's living room window. The coffee is made, the house is in its early Saturday morning ease. Upstairs, Bob rolls against the bars of his crib and they rattle, but everyone sleeps. The light swings through the town. It squeaks over fog frozen onto cornstalks that flap, and over the telephone wires fencing in the leafless trees on either side of the road. Everything had just been blue, and then it was ashen with cold sun on houses and fields. And now it's morning, the truck is idling at the trees beside Purdy's Bridge while the hydraulic hoist lifts a workman up to prune the branches that in winter might fall under snow loads and snap the telephone cable into silence.

While one man from the telephone company uses his chain saw and hooks, another in an orange safety vest gathers fallen branches and throws them into the back of the truck. Then he waits for the hoist to come down, then gets inside and drives to the next stand of trees, gets out and places the yellow sign in its metal frame on the road in front of the truck. It says: MEN WORKING IN TREES, and he gathers more gray wood as the saw tears. I think of men in the crotches of all the trees everywhere, repairing shoes, restringing guitars, mitering wood, filing down ignition points. All of them are loved by fine women, everyone is smiling, and chamber music makes the shape of a room above the road and fills it. Yellow light from the top of the cab, in its squeaky swinging bubble, jumps through the town. And here comes Katherine, softly through the cold morning in her wooden house while children breathe upstairs and flatter us with their serenity. By keeping silent, we pretend to give them cause for calm sleep: that lie of family love.

Think what a check for $100,000 can mean to your etc.

Heart disease makes you look *in*. So as Katherine walks across her living room — tall in a fleecy blue bathrobe that ties beneath the breasts, big of foot in slippers of fleece, long-faced, shining, glad — I hear my heart rock wetly in my chest. The pulse feels fast; I want to clock it.

She watches my eyes; she feels me sliding in and hooks me out as the light of the truck creaks by: "Good morning, good morning. Are you leaving us for good?"

I shake my head and smile.

She says, "Are you leaving us for a quickie back home?"

Shake.

"Are you tired of older women? Am I scary-looking in the morning?"

Shake again. Reach for her furry front and pet it.

"So why are you sneaking around the house? You make coffee at dawn like a husband. Pad-pad-pad in your bare feet. Clank the pot like a cymbalist."

"That's me. Your community orchestra. Music to get laid by."

She pushes into my palm, we hug in until our crotches dock through cloth. We spill coffee, chunk the mugs onto the white-painted windowsill, back off and circle around the sofa, which is at right angles to the window: she goes her way around, and I go mine, and we meet at adjacent cushions. When I sit, my stomach presses up inside my body and squeezes my lungs. It feels like that. I pant, looking at the framed prints, cherry wood and clear-grained maple, textures that want to be touched. The hope, I guess, is that she'll look where I do, instead of at me. Or do I want her to watch me and say, *What's wrong?* so I can be brave and start a fight in defense of not complaining — and thus complain while chalking credits up for courage, strength, great pain?

She looks at the walls and I grunt up onto my feet — a lesser stegosaurus in glasses and corduroy trousers — and then I walk around, breathing. I bring our coffee from the windowsill and hand a cup over her shoulder. When she bends to drink, I bow to graze on her long neck. She puts her cup on the mahogany table, but I can't reach there and, bending as I am to chew on the back of her neck, I can't set down the cup. So I hang as if fastened by my teeth at great height. She feels this, then she feels the coffee droplets, then she turns — her face knocks my glasses from one ear — and when she laughs she wakes the children up.

Think what a check for etc. can mean.

So we go upstairs and get hugged by sleepy kids. Rocky is talking already: he wonders if we can find an Indian longhouse or at least a war canoe buried in the backyard field that goes to the looping river. Bob's trying to climb from his crib. Washcloths, turtleneck jerseys, miniature dungarees, small shoes, and all the time, "No, honey, put this hand through *here,*" as I help to dress someone else's children in a house he signed a mortgage for, and there is a two-room apartment in Cicero, New York, where I am not listening to good opera on a bad record player while starting my survey of the week's *TV Guide* to see what films I'll watch at nine and then eleven-thirty and then one-fifteen.

Downstairs, Bob watches Katherine fill a bowl with cereal and milk. He drops his spoon on the floor, smiles a sly one at me, bends to his bowl, saying, "More?" Rocky drinks orange juice and says, "Mommy, I have dripping sinuses. I can't eat. Okay?"

Katherine says, "No."

I say, "Perhaps this isn't wise . . ."

Katherine, looking at my face, says, "No to you, too."

"I would like to marry this."

Rocky says, "I'll *up*chuck if I eat."

Katherine says, "You better not, boy."

"Which one, Kath?"

"Both of you."

Which leads us to stacking the dishes, brushing our teeth — Bob chews a small brush ropy with ancient Crest — and the zipping of quilted jackets. Then, Katherine towing Bob in a wagon with wooden sides, we walk down the road toward the postal substation, Rocky speculating on what happened to the Indians: "Then, after the settlers shot their buffaloes, they got extinct? Like dinosaurs? They went into the ground?"

"No," I tell him, "there are lots of Indians left. A lot of them live near Syracuse. A lot live everywhere."

"Then where's their spears and bow and arrows?"

"No, they're like us now, hon. They wear the same kind of clothes and work in offices . . ."

"Do you have any in your office, Harry?"

"Oh, sure. Chiefs, too. Chiefs all over the place."

"Do they got any knives?"

"*Knives?* Listen . . ."

Katherine says, "Let's be quiet for a while, Rocky, okay? Let's listen to the morning for a while."

Bob, in his wagon, is a motor pukketing to the motion of his ride. Rocky and I keep still. We hear woodpeckers and the snarl of jays, local dogs, cars on distant roads that are aimed for the Saturday errands I crave: the lumberyard drive, haul to the local dump, the station wagon mission with kids in the back and no hurry, and then home to soup and soda and the wind blowing from the river.

At the post office, which is someone's garage, Katherine and Rocky go in for the mail while I stand with my legs apart and, holding Bob's wrists, swing him below me and back and forth. He shouts and laughs his laugh: he's a lump of heavy cloth and knitted cap and scarf, his breath, small white smoke puffs. Then I put him back in the wagon — "More?" he says, holding his hands up. "More?" — and I listen to the knock in my chest, the steamwhistle noises.

I work at my breathing. I have eaten no breakfast and promise to starve all day. I breathe.

Rocky stoops at the post office door and plays with a cat. The cat doesn't want to play, but Rocky nails it down with his hand, crushing the soft neck to the ground, cooing, "Ah, ba-by."

Katherine comes out with some magazines and an opened letter. Her eyes are like the eyes in a drawing: almost like life. She sends Rocky ahead with the wagon, weaving in the road toward home, Bob an impossible engine.

"Dell's coming," she says. She shakes the letter out: it crackles and refolds. "He'll be here tonight or tomorrow. He wants to see the kids. Sure he does."

We walk back. We say nothing.

Her face is nearly not familiar, like the palm of someone else's hand.

Which leads us to the long lunchtime — I eat three sandwiches — and then we carry the boys upstairs for early naps. Bob's resigned; Rocky is angry and wants to dig up Indians. The sky is smoky with early snow, and through Rocky's window I see the black field hands nod their heads and tighten up. They come from Burlington to work for thirty-five cents a bag. The farmer comes from his truck and lays a row of brown burlap bags beside a quarter-mile furrow the tractor has made. Now the snow comes down, a fine fast grainy fall, and Katherine and I lie down on her very historical double bed and listen to her children bounce around as the tractor changes gears and returns from the river over the field toward the road, pulling earth and potatoes up.

We're dressed. She's under the quilt, waiting. I say, "Kath? You think I ought to go home?"

She doesn't answer.

I'm still breathing heavily from climbing the stairs, and I know she's listening to that, too — to my lungs, and perhaps to my heart in its damp wrappings. "Listen," I tell her, "you should decide about this. It'd be easier, wouldn't it?"

She says, "Easier for Rocky and Bob, I guess. Less embarrassing for me. Weaker."

"No. What weak? It's your *life*."

"By now I should be able to deal with him. And you're a fact now, Harry. I don't have to get married for you to be a fact."

"But you *could*."

"I don't want to be married anymore. Shut up."

"Katherine — I want to be married anymore."

She doesn't answer, the tractor roars, a field hand's voice comes up. When I look over, her eyes are closed. I think of her driving

me to the bus stop, and then the ride to Burlington with travelers
and their old suitcases, shopping bags, cigars, then the wait in the
terminal, the longer ride to Albany, then Syracuse, in darkness,
and the half-lighted Greyhound station, all the people there not
knowing me or that I've left a New England farmhouse and a
family and people grunting over food dug up from cold soil.

I tell her, "I don't want to go back."

"What?"

"Go back. Leave."

After a while she moves on the bed, says, "Then that's the
decision."

She turns over and with one hand unbuttons my shirt, puts her
icy hand inside, draws her knees up and becomes a small girl
falling into sleep. We lie like that, and I reach to the bedside table
for something to read — an old *New Yorker* with a long profile of
the Metropolitan Opera's new director, who is recently dead in a
car crash.

Think what a check for $100,000 can mean to your loved ones
at such a time.

And then four o'clock in the far western corner of the field, the
burlap sacks in their rows, the tractor cutting the porridge of
snow — it still falls lightly — and the hands, in their thin jackets
or only shirts, pulling up potatoes with the curved metal long-
handled forks, making deep noises, talking sometimes. We are
near the river, its rich cold smell comes through the dense little
forest on its bank, and Rocky, with a shovel impossibly long for
him, is digging with total seriousness through snow and hard
ground to find an Indian longhouse or a fallen warrior's skull.
Bob is on my back in a baby-carrier, solid and happy and still,
swathed in woolen cap and long scarf. I pant as I move with him;
he listens to my rhythms and pants to my time.

A short coal-gleamy field worker in an aqua-colored Wind-
breaker stands, stretches his back, blows on his hands. He calls
over, "You got yourself a burden, now."

I nod, smile. I have what I want for a minute, and he knows
that. I say, "Not as bad as yours."

He shakes his head. He calls, "You want some of these for the
missus?"

"Do I look like I need potatoes?"

He laughs and shakes his head. Bob laughs, too.

Rocky comes over with a small lump of limestone. "Harry, is this from the bones of someone?"

I say, "Probably. But put your *mittens* on, will you? Aren't you cold?"

His lecturing face comes on as he ignores mere weather to say, "See this mark over here? This is where the bullet from the settler's gun went in. Isn't it, Harry? Here. You hold this while I go back to find the bullet. It probably fell out when his brains got rotten."

The field worker drinks from a pint of something dark. The cracks on his hard hands are white. Wind comes across the river to blow him into motion again. The tractor rips slowly past and Bob says, "Choo!"

Then the man who harvests potatoes nearby says, "This is a bad-ass day for living. You give me some other day for that."

Down the row a heavier man who is drunker — he slips whenever he moves from his knees — says, "Pick the day with care, son. They coming bad more often. I noticed that."

The short one says, "Your cold black ass told you that, isn't that right?"

The drunker one says, "My cold black *life,* son."

The snow is thicker — Bob says, "Rice!" — and Katherine's house moves farther away, diminishes. Rocky pokes with the tall shovel. An old green truck with snow chains in the southeast corner, near the road, is loaded with filled brown sacks. Bob says, "Rice!" and then pants to my rhythms. The tractor starts toward us.

Then, far away, at the distant house, a small red car is in the drive, a man beside it. I see Katherine on the back porch. The man comes up the steps, stands below her, and they talk. She points toward us in the field. The tractor comes closer, Bob in the backpack stirs to watch. The man raises his hand, drops it, walks past the clothesline in the backyard, then past the swings the wind has set drifting on their chains, then over the chewed land in a fog of blown snow, toward Rocky and Bob and me.

Arms across her chest, Katherine watches.

I look at the field hands and their long lives and think of *TV Guide.* Rocky digs for dead Indians, Katherine watches from her distance, the tractor comes closer, its steel fork tears up food and huge stones, and think what a check for $100,000 can mean.

But the people in the story include that baby tied to the fat man's back.

Everyone stands still, including Dell at the edge of his former freehold. Then Rocky drags his shovel toward the man who waits, not looking any place but down, and I lug Bob back, too, walking in the path the shovel makes. The tractor is past. There has been no accidental death. And Katherine watches us all come home.

Now there are the usual backstage noises: clatter of stainless steel and crockery, the battle of the kids being fed, the utter politeness of conversation among adults who cannot imagine how to survive the hours flat ahead of them — stony field they have to somehow work. When the children offer a chance, we drop all over them like sudden snow. There is the sound of corks being pulled and the tops of beer cans exploding. Now here are the grownups at the kitchen table (it's a litter of chicken death and vessels), and here are the sounds of Bob in his crib too early to sleep and Rocky upstairs playing Indians.

There is one partly nibbled drumstick on my pottery plate and the wreckage of some servings of salad. My wineglass shows the scallops of many pourings. Dell, who has removed his sport coat and tie and rolled up his sleeves, drinks ale from a can — he has stowed a case in the refrigerator. His ironed-in shirt creases are still firm, and in his oxford cloth he looks like Katherine's date, warming up for the evening's abandon. I feel as if I look like me: an ocean of rumples. Katherine drinks more wine. Some of it has run onto her thick tan sweater, and her hair is up, and I consider how important it is that I lick the wine that has gotten through to her front.

Lean pale Dell, with his left eye bloodshot, his large hand wrinkling empty Red Cap cans, his legs jiggling up and down, a smile on his long face — I sneak my looks at him.

He says, "Harry, you didn't eat much." The host.

"Well."

"I *know* you tend to put away more than that."

"Well, I've got big bones."

Katherine, now my mother or my aunt, says, "He ate a lot of salad. Didn't you, Harry?"

"Yes, ma'am. A good deal of salad."

Two wall lamps light the big room and Dell inspects the shadows. He says, "You forget how intimate the kitchen looks."

"*You* forget," Katherine says. And then she says, "I didn't mean to be rotten," and pours more wine for her and me. My stomach cheers for political triumph, since Dell is excluded by his ale. But he pours water from his goblet into mine and holds the glass out for Katherine to fill, and she does. She looks at my plate. I slump in the chair and stretch my legs for better breathing; it doesn't work, and I sit up straight.

"So I'm a success," Dell says. "I'm a dean of students. What do you think of that? I'm into administration and right guidance." He drinks ale. "I will deftly guide them through the thickets of life."

"And along the abyss, don't forget," I say.

"Absolutely. Abyss, and crumbling ledge. *And* gorse and hawthorn and virulent ivies. Never ignore the virulent ivies. You get really fucked over if you fail to keep the virulent ivies in mind. I've always found that to be true — haven't you, Harry?"

"It's a safe rule to live by, Dell."

Katherine pours us more wine, and Dell holds his goblet up for more, too, though he hasn't drunk any.

She says, "So here we are. The extended family." This is supposed to be humorous, so we do our duty, laugh.

Katherine puts her glass down and pushes at the stem with one finger, which suggests that she's about to suggest something. She says, "I wonder why you came here, Dell."

I say, "I think I'll take a walk. I'm taking a walk."

As I get my coat from the wall hook, not looking at Katherine, Dell stands up and takes his long black tweed dean's overcoat down.

Katherine says, "No."

Dell says, "But it's your answer — that's why I came. I wanted to address the gentleman currently in your life."

"And see the children, of course," she says.

He says, "Of course."

She says, "Let's all stay inside."

But he is pushing my arm at the door and we go, not drunk enough yet, but going, and then already down the back steps and into the snow in our street shoes, which fill with slush, walking past the swings and onto the field. There's a shape out there I wonder about, and a bright white moon, strong wind.

"Dell, don't you think someone should keep Katherine company?"

He strolls a little ahead of me, says, "Why, someone always does, you see."

Now even though he's a dean, he's a dangerous man. He has beaten Katherine with his hands and once with a rolled-up newspaper they were using to train a Dalmatian that was later killed by an electrician's truck. Of course, she's beaten him, too — he's a dean. But Dell is drunk in a gaseous loose-jointed way that thin men have which frightens me. And he hates the history of their house. And he has to hate me, too — unless he thrives by dining on pain. He grips my sleeve as we walk toward the river and — the moon turns it on like a lamp now — the stubby chipped station wagon snuggled into hard mud.

Dell says, "I don't think my wife hates me anymore, do you?"

"Me? No. No, I don't think so, Dell."

"Did you ever get divorced, Harry?"

"No, I never got married, actually."

"So you couldn't have gotten divorced, then."

"Right."

"Yeah. You're pretty young, still. So you don't know what me and Katherine are talking about."

"Well . . ."

"Unless you think playing house's the same thing as what Katherine and me're talking about."

"Look, Dell. This is very embarrassing."

"It *is?* Oh, I'm sorry there, Harry. It was not my intention to drive all the way here at risk to life and limb just to throw shadows on your soul."

"Dell, you want us to go back inside and have some more to drink, maybe? I don't know what to *say* to you. Maybe if we all got very drunk I would find it easier."

"Actually, old Harry, I am fairly well drunk at the present time. And I don't honestly give two pounds of llama shit what makes anything in the whole world easier on you." He lets my sleeve loose so he can indicate the whole world. "You got shadows on your soul because I'm a long-term cuckold on account of you. You put the shadows on your own soul, Harry."

Near the station wagon I stop and he stops, too. Around us the wide white field spins out, and the furrowed potatoes, the unfilled bags, curved forks. I decide not to discuss the logistics and amenities of divorce, or the question of when precisely a woman is allowed to need the presence of someone without being digested by the major figures of her history. I do consider the gleaming points of potato forks, and Dell's deep craze, and how much, at a time like this, a check for $100,000 can mean. Does homicide count as an accident if you really don't want to die? My chest is shaking at my clothes: breathing is a serious business again.

Dell comes closer, stands before me, takes my glasses off, and puts them in his pocket. "Being in the academic trade," he says, "I appreciate what these could mean to you."

I have watched too many TV shows of violence to be unwary. I am on my wet cold toes, moving backward, squinting at her blurry husband. And when he moves in again, I scream a judo–kung-fu–karate noise to paralyze his reflexes; I spin on my left foot and kick backward with my right for the nerve complex just below his sternum. I strike nothing, something collapses in my ankle, I go down. He cries, "You terrific bag of weakness, you don't snort the scraps off my plate!" And his knees or elbows land on my chest, my face is opening up beneath his hands. I push up, strike up, swinging wide loose powdery punches, get lucky, and something other than mucus streaks on my hand. He shouts — no words — and I stick up fingers as if I were a maddened typist. He screams, and then his breath is in close, his teeth on my cheekbone: he bites down — and though I roll and kick and punch on his skull, he bites in harder.

I scream in his ear.

He's off. I'm helped to my feet by people I can't see. I stand on one leg and hold to someone's hard shoulder. There's a smell of deep cold and whiskey, sweat. Dell sits before me on the field, blurred face. I see the tailgate of the station wagon open — courtesy light, I remind myself. There are brown unfocused faces in the light and much commentary.

Dell says, "Like it's an academic situation, brother, dig? Much as I appreciate your interest, I don't think you see the subtleties here."

A deep voice near him says, "I don't believe we your brother, *man.*"

The potato picker I hold to says, "You own one chewed face, you know that, mister? I don't wonder if you got yourself some rabies."

The one with the deep voice far away says, "Yeah, well that's the trouble with being food, son."

I listen to my body breathe and I whisper, "Are my glasses broken?"

"If not, they the only things that's whole now. So come on to your home."

We slide and lurch to the house I can't see, me thanking and him saying never-you-mind, and then, by the time we reach the drifting swings, I am gasping in the cold air, silent.

In the window above the back porch there's a dim brown light. I say, "Who is that? Upstairs?"

"A small kind of Indian. Red and yellow feathers. Watching you drag home."

The clicking of the storm door, and Katherine's — fury? fear? — and alcohol on the eaten face, an elastic bandage on the ankle, Rocky's wagging headdress, the hobble upstairs, the weight of blankets, Katherine's insistence on silence, sleep, the sound of Dell's car starting down the drive: they wash into morning, the gray and golden early light in her still house, the curl of her body on the bed.

Rather than consider, I twist down.

Rather than consider that an accident — by civil law, papal bull, Torah, or the New York Builders' Code — is what you don't make plans for. Rather than consider that the final sentence of the Sears, Roebuck contract no doubt says, *In the event that the Insured is counting on this Policy for a measure of design in his little story, the Contract is nullified* — it becomes just one more *Voided Petition to end whatever pickle, puzzle, plot, or unofficial war Insured can't deal with.* Rather than consider, truly, whether I heard Dell whine away. Rather than consider that I first heard Dell and Katherine yowl and sigh, make a long silence, and maybe leathery love, before he rode for home with part of my face in his war bag. Rather than consider shadows on my soul, or the thickets and abysses and the crumbling ledge.

My cheek feels wrong, the ankle complains, but I twist down, slowly diving, and nose beneath the covers for her flesh. I push at the nightgown, kiss her cool thigh and crotch, then stomach, as she stirs. I come up onto her chest and suck a nipple, turn at it.

She slams me, under the covers, and I sit up, the quilt like a shawl all over me.

"Goddamnit! Will you stop biting me!"

I wait. Because here it comes.

She pushes her nightgown down. And then she covers her eyes with her hand, whispers, "I don't want to live with *any*one, Harry. Not even weekends for a while. All right? I think just *alone* right now. All right?"

I cover her with the blanket and put a pillow over my lap and bellymound and hold it with a hugging arm.

She squeezes her eyes with her fingers.

We wait.

Bob bangs his crib slats to start the day.

It will not be a fertile pursuit. It will finish with a ride to Syracuse, the bullet-whipped fragment of a Mohican's skull, another truth and trophy wrapped in my clothes. It will finish with an elevated leg, some great living stack of sausages and eggs and chocolate milk, and lean men on the TV screen easily breathing. It will finish with the extra pair of glasses, an old prescription, nearly strong enough, which I've kept in a drawer with my socks for emergencies.

Katherine says, "All right?"

Sure.

PRICE CALDWELL

Tarzan Meets the Department Head

(FROM THE CARLETON MISCELLANY)

HE PICKS UP HIS MAIL once a week, on Wednesday afternoons, when the Department Head plays golf. Now it is Tuesday. Bulk-rate envelopes and periodicals are stacked three inches high on the shelf above his pigeonhole in the departmental office.

It is 12:05. Everyone has gone to lunch. Tarzan emerges from his office, where he has been reading Mallarmé. With one eye he peeks both ways from the outer doorway. Catlike, he moves across the hall to the stairs, thence to the side entrance at ground floor, thence to the cafeteria. Only students eat there. He has the special: turnip greens, potatoes, fried pork. He watches, as he eats, the conveyor belt, which runs across the side of the long room, carrying the dirty dishes to the kitchen, and tries to measure the speed of his own metabolism against it. He is approached, at coffee, by a student who asks him to explain the assignment in this morning's class, which he missed.

"Piss off," Tarzan explains.

Seven minutes into his lecture on Tennyson, the classroom door abruptly opens. He stops. It is Ms. Harris. She smiles familiarly and moves toward her seat in the front row. She is wearing her blue-flowered dress and carries no books. She belongs to a sorority. As she slides into her desk she allows opportunity for Tarzan to examine her panties and tanned legs. The panties are pink, also with flowers. He does not ascertain whether the flowers of her panties are identical to the flowers of her dress. "We are reading the 'Flower in the Crannied Wall,' " he admits. The whites of his eyes show, denoting suffering. Her knees slide shut. She smiles again. "We must distinguish quite carefully between the sentimentality of transcendentalism and the bathos of pantheism. But Tennyson had no qualms, after all, about plucking the flower . . ."

Examining the top of the Jim Beam bottle, he ponders a question: "Am I an alcoholic?"

"Surely no one who knows that I never drink more than twice a week would say so. Surely the strength of my constitution stands in my favor. My body is solid muscle. I have fantastic energy. I eat prodigiously and never gain weight. My teeth have no cavities. I can fuck Jane three times a night, three nights in a row, and have, several times. I have climbed high mountains in my day, and built log cabins. Given my fantastic metabolism, however, I will have to drink half of this bottle before I begin to feel anything at all. If I drink it all I will of course be shitfaced, but that is another story. I may not have a headache tomorrow, but since my gall bladder has been removed I will suffer from the drizzling trots for thirty-six hours."

During the first week of every semester he writes a new *vita* to accompany his letter of application to Harvard. This time he includes a new category: Avocations. "My favorite pastime is big-game hunting. I have a four-wheel–drive vehicle and a quilted jacket filled with goose down. My favorite big-game animal is the caribou. Caribou, in summer, have hair on their antlers. Damn!"

The walls of his apartment are covered with photographs of him standing, in his quilted jacket, next to the huge carcasses of caribou and moose. "Although I own nineteen different firearms," he says, "I hunt caribou only with the bow and arrow. The arrows are tipped with 800 milligrams of succinylcoline chloride. It immobilizes the heart muscles, among others, within sixty seconds. I feel that is more sporting." Asked why he has a 12-gauge Browning Automatic shotgun mounted on the rear window of his truck, he replies, humorously, "For people."

The Department Head says: "Why does he hate me? Have I persecuted him? Have I given him eight o'clock classes? No.

Have I given him low sections of freshman comp? No. As a matter of fact I have been very good to him. So why does he hate me?" Between phone calls he paces the floor. The Department Head's work consists, mainly, in phone calls, incoming and outgoing. He has two secretaries, one of whose job is to monitor his calls and keep him abreast of which are incoming and which outgoing. "I have invited him to cocktails at my house. I have invited him to dinner at my house: roast venison . . . I have even instructed my wife to call that woman he lives with, and be friendly. Nevertheless he has declined each time. Maybe he thinks I will put him on a committee if I see him. Nothing could be further from the truth. I just want to *see* him. I have not *seen* him since October." One of the secretaries hands him a cup of coffee. He stops and sips. "My informants tell me that Dr. Tarzan is a brilliant man, that he delivers provocative lectures and frequently writes articles on Tennyson. I have heard that several of them have been accepted for publication. That is very fine. As long as he publishes I do not give a damn what he does with his private life. But I would like to *see* him on occasion." He notices that Dr. Tarzan's mailbox contains a letter from the Head of the Department at Harvard. "Perhaps if I steamed it open I would find out what in hell is going on. But my professional ethics will not allow it. I will assign him to work at registration next semester. He will hate me even more, but at least I will get to *see* him.

He likes to answer questionnaires. To the question from the Instructional Improvement Committee, which reads, "Do you favor the current policy of exempting graduating seniors from final exams if they are making a B in the course?" he writes: "Current policy is inadequate in almost every case, as are almost all current policies. Policy, in my own case, has ever pricked my perquisites, entangled my tenders, and circumscribed my holy offices. Despite my having humbled myself to a fatuous nincompoop at the University of Pennsylvania in order to acquire a Ph.D., I have, in the main, made my own way, sneakily as was necessary, amongst the policies of institutional assholes like you. I was conceived miraculously in the sphincter of a Protestant mother, smothered by a policy of love and forbearance when I was a child, raised up strong and dedicated by a father who wanted me to be a professional shortstop, and was in all respects spoiled for questions like yours. Why don't you ask me something reasonable, like where did I piss away my poor gall bladder?"

He has been in a bad mood. Now Jane is taking him to the city. An evening of entertainment to cheer him up. They have dressed in their party clothes, matching see-through blouses and floppy pants. The tone for the evening is to be Pathos. As they ride, Jane prepares his make-up: large electric blue tears are made to well up under his eyes, and to drip, with perfect symmetry, down his cheeks. Rhinestones are pasted in each teardrop as a highlight. When she is finished he admires himself in the rearview mirror.

At the restaurant he orders the meal for Jane and himself. "Margueritas while we are waiting. Then oysters, en brochette, a dozen each. Then the flounder with crabmeat, and the broccoli. Perhaps, later, the crêpes with blueberries, and coffee." The waiter stands with pencil poised, but writes nothing. When he has gone, Tarzan removes from a paper sack the large dildo which they purchased at a souvenir store on their way to the restaurant. They examine it with pleasure. It has symbolic value, they feel: it bespeaks Pathos. Presently they are approached by the manager of the restaurant, who requests their departure. Two policemen stand behind him, smirking.

On the street, Tarzan explains: "I was in a bad mood. But now, having seen all that good food on the menu, I feel good again. Let's go to Felix's and have a dozen raw and some gumbo."

It is six o'clock on Friday afternoon. Tarzan is taking notes on Baudelaire: "The sensuousness is cloying sometimes. Am I getting old?" He hears someone knocking out of the corner of his ear. He continues taking notes: "Is that my Death knocking at my door? If so, why does it sound, when it calls, like the Assistant Department Head? Quite possibly it is, merely, the Assistant Department Head, and he only wants to come in and look at me. Probably he will say that he is making sure that all the lights are off in all of the offices; but in actuality, of course, he wants to look at me. That is what they all want to do. Perhaps their intentions are not really malevolent but I keep thinking of how it was in Alaska. You could not go to a party where you couldn't find, somewhere near the exit, an Assistant Dean taking notes in a small black notebook: Who is drinking more than one drink. Whose wife is being danced with, and by whom. Who goes frequently to the john. Whose voice rises above the general din. These memories make me paranoid. What I should do, of course, if the Assistant Department Head comes in, is smile broadly and pretend to have been preoccupied. He will understand that: after all, Baudelaire . . . I will say, Oh I'm sorry, I didn't hear you knock, and then, of course, the burden of apology will be upon him. Then . . ."

Tarzan looks up. The Assistant Department Head is standing in the doorway, smiling. Tarzan swings rapidly back through the 1000 zones of reality, but he cannot find the right one. His eyes fix on the Assistant Department Head's abdomen. He stares and stares, smiling broadly . . .

Ms. Phillips, of Intro to Lit 1203–09, says: "My professor, Dr. Tarzan, is a very warm person. Wow, does he know a lot about English literature, all the authors and everything. His lectures are about a lot of stuff I can't even write down, much less remember. (Who in the world, by the way, is Mr. Mollogy? He's not in our book.) I probably don't have a very high grade in this course — I don't ever say anything in class and Dr. Tarzan probably thinks I'm dumb or something. But really, I try very hard to at least read the material. Maybe if I talked to him *in person* it would help. How can he tell anything about me, after all, if he's never once heard me open my mouth? I am, after all, a warm, open, loving human being who has a great deal to offer, and surely he can't deny . . ."

Among twenty cartoons, posters, and signs on his office door, a white sheet of paper catches her eye:

ATTENTION STUDENTS

BEFORE YOU KNOCK ON MY DOOR PLEASE READ THIS:

1. *If you have cut class, do not think to take up one instant of my time with questions about the assignment or the content of the lecture.*
2. *Do not seek to discuss with me any of your silly personal or emotional problems. I do not pretend to be a shrink. Go see your adviser, who does.*
3. *Do not present me with beatific countenances and vacuous pam-*

*phlets on Christianity or other religions, or otherwise try to convert
me to any of the value-systems you may think you have in your
"philosophy."*

4. *If you wish to discuss the content of the course, or to challenge any
   issue in the lecture, you are welcome during the posted office hours.
   Please be prepared with a knowledge of the texts involved. I am not
   willing to explain things which a simple reading of the assigned
   material should have already explained.*

5. *If you cannot confer with me during office hours, I will be glad to
   make an appointment (during office hours) for another time mutually convenient. Do not, under any circumstances, call me at
   home.*

"Hmmmm," says Ms. Phillips. "That gives me pause."

His praise for Jane is very high. "She has a somewhat *different*
outlook on life. Once, after she was married, she worked in the
geriatrics ward of the state hospital, in Alaska. Mostly, I think,
she gave enemas and emptied bedpans. She was a specialist in
physical therapy. She ingratiated herself with several of the patients there, those who still had prostates. One of them left her
twenty thousand dollars in his will. I met her in a men's room in
Fairbanks. My wife was fucking her boy friend and she was distraught. I never could pee in front of other people . . ."

He explains his philosophy of drinking: "When I get shitfaced
it is as if my body abandons its normal public personality. Perhaps it is because it does not *like* its normal public personality.
However, I am not convinced that the change is altogether for the
better. I want to do many things that people consider wicked, or
perhaps in bad taste, when I am shitfaced. Like use vivid language or piss, discreetly, under the table. Sobriety, for most people, implies a somewhat limited point of view. Else why would
Paula react the way she did when I spilled beer in her lap?
Doesn't she appreciate the grammar of body language? Must she
cut herself off from all the more interesting forms of social communication just because she is married to whatshisface? In Fairbanks things were different. Besides, there were mountains to
climb. How did I get stuck in this flatland town anyhow?"

*

Jane's praise for him is very high: "You ought to see his thighs. Wow! I guess it was all that mountain-climbing he did in Alaska. He was kind of going to fat before, but now I think he's got muscles enough to climb anything. His wife fucked him over something awful, though, which is partly why he is the way he is. He has been very sweet to her but I don't think he could ever get back in with her and his kids now. He never had the kind of rotten life I did though so he thinks things ought to be better. I get so pissed off at him when he gets in these moods, I don't know why I stay here. I've never been with just one guy for so long, I mean without screwing other men, even including when I was married. But wow, is he a good fuck. Except, of course, when he is writing. When he is writing he doesn't want to fuck, he doesn't want to drink, he doesn't want to do anything. And then he goes for two or three weeks like that and writes two or three fucking articles on Tennyson or some such fart and he won't say shit to me until he's finished. Damn, I bet even Tennyson's wife didn't have to put up with that, if he had a wife . . ."

Tarzan and Jane are conducting research on Aesthetic Theory at the drive-in movie. Two young men and a young lady occupy a bed in a motel room. The young lady has dirty feet. All of her orifices are filled with various appendages of the two young men. Tarzan checks his watch. The camera has lingered on the scene for 11½ minutes.
  "Now that's love," he says. "Except, of course, that it's not real."
  "It's real enough, but it's not love," Jane says.
  "Love fulfills like that."
  "No, but reality is bareass like that."
  "Love is boring like that."
  "No, reality is boring like that."
  "Reality is boring when everyone always has his clothes on."
  "No, love is boring when everyone always has his clothes off."
  "Fiction is boring when everyone always has his clothes off."
  "Love is fiction, then."
  "Right."
  "Oh, shit," Jane says.
  The scene changes. "Wow, look at that!" Tarzan says. "She's got her clothes on! Wow! She's out on the street where everybody can see her! Everybody's got his clothes on! Hey, honey!

Get your skirt up a little higher! Yeah! Put your foot up on the fireplug and check your stockings! Fondle your panties! Get your rocks off! Get my rocks off! Yeah! Art! Art!"

The Department Head loiters in the hall. He is just outside room 210, which contains Dr. Tarzan's office. He looks at his watch. "Tee, hee," he says craftily. "Here it is twelve–0-five and everyone gone to lunch." He listens for the sound of footsteps within. Or the creaking of a swivel chair. Or the clicking off of a desk lamp. He waits.

There are many signs on the window of the door. There are many more inside, on the doors to the individual offices and the walls. Periodically he lets himself in, at night, to read them. They are asinine, blasphemous, contumacious, disgusting, egregious, freaky, gross, hideous, insane, juvenile, kitschy, lurid, malignant, nihilistic, obscene, priapic, queer, ridiculous, scurrilous, treasonous, unreasonable, vicious, wicked, xenophobic, and . . . youthful. "What the hell," the Department Head says. "The place is like a zoo."

The Department Head looks at his watch. He paces three steps away from the door. His foursome will be teeing off at one-fifteen sharp. He paces three steps back toward the door. A shadow moves briefly across the glass. He looks up, sees nothing. A door clicks shut within. Too late. The Department Head thinks of the roast beef buffet at the club. His stomach growls.

Tarzan is reading term papers for En 4473/6673, Modern English Prose. It is very late at night. He reads very rapidly, very interestedly. He looks anxiously for insight. In the margins he makes critical comments: "You have not fully assimilated your sources." "See *M.L.A. Style Sheet*." "This sentence is ill-formed, ill-considered, and crappy."

He does not put grades on papers. Grades, he feels, stifle creativity. Only the unfettered application of mind to critical problems can stimulate the growth of insight. His own lectures demonstrate that, he feels. But after reading twelve papers, he perceives no *growth*.

The present paper belongs to Mr. Curry, a graduate student. Mr. Curry has a great deal of personality and warmth. His paper, however, is morose, condescending, cynical, and indulgent. Its last paragraph reads: "We must conclude, therefore, that Marlow is not so much a spokesman for Conrad's insight into the natives of disadvantaged cultures, as for the Victorian stupidity and blindness of Colonial Englishmen. Unfortunately that blindness seems too often to be Conrad's as well."

In the margin Tarzan writes: "I'd like to beat the shit out of you."

Tarzan has escaped his last class of the day. It is a warm and sunny afternoon. He and Jane are on the motorcycle, riding westward out of town at a high rate of speed. "Goddamn!" Jane shrieks joyfully. "Slow this motherfucker down!" They stop in a grove of pine trees, beside a lake, and lie on the grass. Tarzan looks up to where the pine needles interlace against the sky. He explains: "I like to go fast, by motorcycle, and feel the aether against my body. It is also very nice to lie on the leaves and watch the aether between the pine needles. Very few know what the aether is. Those who know it do not speak of it, and those who speak of it do not know it. Aether is that which cometh behind but no one sees its face. Aether is that which goeth before but no one sees its rear end. Aether is the origin of inspiration, expiration, exasperation. Aether cometh below, above, and in the cracks. The way of aether is broad but difficult to find. Once found, the way of aether is narrow but difficult to fall off of. To seek the aether one must not-seek all that is not-aether. Aether is not the Me in It or the It in Me. Or you. However, the aether about your left tit maketh a perfect halo. Hmmm."

The Department Head, 110 yards out in the rough on the eighteenth hole, addresses the ball. "It is as if he doesn't exist. Perhaps, for that matter, the fact that I haven't seen him is proof that he doesn't exist. If that is the case, why has the Comptroller's office been sending him his paychecks? Perhaps if his paycheck is withheld, and he does in fact exist, he will come looking for it. Then I will get to *see* him. Ahah!" His backswing is perfect. The nine-iron bites the turf just behind the ball. The ball arcs high in a perfect line, bounces once and digs in. A two-foot putt for a birdie. His opponents, two down already at ten dollars a hole, despair. The Department Head exults. He envisions Tarzan existing on berries.

JOHN CHEEVER

Falconer

(FROM PLAYBOY)

THE MAIN ENTRANCE to Falconer — the only entrance for convicts, their visitors, and the staff — was crowned by an escutcheon representing Liberty, Justice and, between the two, the power of legislation. Liberty wore a mobcap and carried a pike. Legislation was the Federal eagle, armed with hunting arrows. Justice was conventional; blinded, vaguely erotic in her clinging robes and armed with a headsman's sword. The bas-relief was bronze but black these days — as black as unpolished anthracite or onyx. How many hundreds had passed under this — this last souvenir they would see of man's struggle for coherence? Hundreds, one guessed, thousands, millions was close. Above the escutcheon was a declension of the place names: Falconer Jail, 1871, Falconer Reformatory, Falconer Federal Penitentiary, Falconer State Prison, Falconer Correctional Facility, Falconer Rehabilitation Center and the last, which had never caught on: Phoenix House. Now cons were inmates, the assholes were officers and the warden was a superintendent. Fame is chancy, God knows, but Falconer — with its limited accommodations for 2000 miscreants — was as famous as Old Bailey. Gone were the water torture, the striped suits, the lock step, the balls and chains, and there was a softball field where the gallows had stood; but at the time of which I'm writing, leg irons were still used in Auburn. You could tell the men from Auburn by the noise they made.

Loomis (fratricide, zip to ten, number 734-508-32) saw none of this from the catwalk of an abandoned water tower where he goldbricked with his friend Jody. He had seen the escutcheon and would not, he thought sadly, ever see it again. After less than a year, he was still sad. What he could see were the old cell blocks and, beyond those, a two-mile stretch of river with cliffs and mountains on the western shore. This was best seen from the old death house and was known as The Millionaire's View. It was a warm afternoon in July and Jody was telling his story. Jody was crowding thirty, claimed to be twenty-four and could pass. He had an American face — very clean, princely in some of its angles and responses, but without a hair, a grain, a trace of nostalgia. It was charming, easy and as persuasive as a poster, but peel it off the hoarding and there was nothing left but the hoarding. He had told his story piecemeal to Loomis, but patched together, the definitive version — and there were many — went like this: "It's really in the past. I don't have any future and I'm heavy on the past. I won't see the parole board for twelve years. What I do around here doesn't matter much, but I do like to stay out of the hole. I know there's no medical evidence for brain damage, but after you've hit yourself about fourteen times, you get silly. Anyhow, I was indicted on fifty-three counts. I had a forty-five thousand–dollar house in Levittown, a lovely wife, and two great sons, Michael and Dale. But I was in a bind. I don't think people with your kind of lifestyle understand. I hadn't graduated from high school, but I was up for a vice-presidency in the mortgage department of Fiduciary Trust. Nothing was moving, my lack of education was a drawback and they were laying people off. I just couldn't make enough money to support four people and when I put the house up for sale, I discovered that every house on the block was on the market. I thought about money all the time. I dreamed about money. I picked dimes, nickels and pennies off the sidewalk. I was bananas about money. I had a friend named Howie and he had a solution. He told me about this old guy — Massman — who ran a stationery store in the shopping center. He had two pari-mutuel tickets worth seven thousand dollars each. He kept them in a drawer beside his bed. Howie knew this because he used to let the old man blow him for a fin. Howie had a wife, kids, a wood-burning fireplace but no money. We decided to go after the tickets. In those days, you didn't have to register them. It was fourteen thousand dollars in cash and no way of tracing it. So we watched the old man for a couple of nights. It was easy. He closed up the store at eight, drove home, got drunk, ate something and watched TV. One night, when he closed the

store and got into his car, we got in with him. He was very
obedient, because I was holding a loaded gun against his head.
The gun was Howie's. He drove home and we lock-stepped him
up to the front door, poking the gun into any part of him that was
convenient. We marched him into the kitchen and handcuffed
him to this big, goddamned refrigerator. It was very big, a very
recent model. We asked him where the tickets were and he said
they were in the lockbox. If we pistol-whipped him, like he said
we did, it wasn't me. It could have been Howie, but I didn't see it.
He kept telling us that the tickets were in the bank. So then we
turned the house upside down looking for the tickets, but I guess
he was right. So we turned on the TV for the neighbors and left
him chained to this ten-ton refrigerator and took off in his car.
The first car we saw was a police car. This was just an accident,
but we got scared. We drove Massman's car into one of those car
washes where you have to get out of the car when it hits the
shower. We put the car in the slot and took off. We got a bus
into Manhattan and said goodbye at the terminal. You know
what that old son of a bitch Massman did? He wasn't big and he
wasn't strong and he wasn't young, but he started inching this big,
fucking refrigerator across the kitchen floor. Believe me, it was
enormous. It was really a nice house, with lovely furniture and
carpets, and he must have had one hell of a time with all those
carpets bunching up under the refrigerator, but he got out of the
kitchen and down the hall and into the living room, where the
telephone was. I can imagine what the police saw when they got
there: this old man chained to a refrigerator in the middle of his
living room with hand-painted pictures all over the walls. That
was Thursday. They picked me up the following Tuesday. They
already had Howie. I didn't know it, but he already had a record.
I don't blame the state. We did everything wrong. Burglary,
pistol-whipping, kidnaping. Kidnaping's a big no-no. Of course,
I'm the next thing to dead, but my wife and sons are still alive.
She sold the house at a big loss and went on welfare. She comes
to see me once in a while, but you know what the boys do? First
they got permission to write me and then Michael, the big one,
wrote me a letter saying that they would be on the river in a
rowboat at three on Sunday afternoon and they would wave to
me. I was out at the fence at three on Sunday and they showed
up. They were way out in the river — you can't come too close to
the prison — but I could see them and feel my love for them and

they waved their arms and I waved my arms. Oh, shit! That was in the autumn and they stopped coming when the place where you rent boats shut down, but they started again in the spring. They were much bigger, I could see that, and then it crossed my mind that for the length of time I'm here, they'll get married and have children and I know they won't stuff their wives and their children into a rowboat and go downriver to wave to Daddy . . ."

"734-508-32, you got a visitor." It was the public address.

"That's you," said Jody. "Who do you think it is?"

"My wife, I guess. She hasn't been here for three months. It could be someone selling subscriptions or encyclopedias. It could be my lawyer. It might be my son."

Loomis climbed down the ladder, rust on his hands, jogged up the road past the fire house and into the tunnel. It was four flights up to cell block F. "Visitor," he said to the guard, who let him into his cell. He kept a white shirt for visits. This was dusty. He washed his face and combed his hair with water.

"Don't take nuttin' but a handkerchief," said the guard.

"I know, I know, I know . . ." Down he went to the door of the visitors' room, where he was frisked. Through the glass, he saw that his visitor was Marcia.

There were no bars in the visitors' room, but the glass windows were chicken-wired and open only at the top. A skinny cat couldn't get in or out, but the sounds of the prison moved in freely on the breeze. She would, he knew, have passed three sets of bars — clang, clang, clang — and waited in an anteroom, where there were pews or benches, soft-drink machines and a display of the convicts' art with prices stuck in the frames. None of the cons could paint, but you could always count on some wet-brain to buy a vase of roses or a marine sunset if he had been told that the artist was a lifer. There were no pictures on the walls of the visitors' room, but there were four signs that said: NO SMOKING. NO WRITING. NO EXCHANGE OF OBJECTS. VISITORS ARE ALLOWED ONE KISS. This was also in Spanish. NO SMOKING had been scratched out. The visitors' room in Falconer, he knew, was the most lenient in the East. There were no obstructions — nothing but a three-foot counter between the free and the unfree. While he was being frisked, he looked around at the other visitors — not so much out of curiosity as to see if there was anything there that might offend Marcia. A con was holding a baby. A weeping old woman talked to a young man. Nearest to Marcia was a Chicano couple. The woman was beautiful and the man was caressing her bare arms.

Loomis stepped into this no man's land and came on hard, as if he had been catapulted by circumstance into the visit. "Hello, darling," he exclaimed, as he had exclaimed "Hello, darling" at trains, boats, airports, the foot of the driveway, journey's end; but in the past, he would have worked out a timetable, aimed at the soonest possible sexual consummation.

"Hello," she said. "You look well."

"Thank you. You look beautiful."

"I didn't tell you I was coming because it didn't seem necessary. When I called to make an appointment, they told me you weren't going anywhere."

"That's true."

"I haven't been here sooner because I've been in Jamaica with Gussie."

"That sounds great. How's Gussie?"

"Fat. She's gotten terribly fat."

"Are you getting a divorce?"

"Not now. I don't feel like talking with any more lawyers at this point."

"Divorce is your prerogative."

"I know." She looked at the Chicano couple. The man had stroked his way up to the hair in the girl's armpits. Both their eyes were shut.

"What," she asked, "do you find to talk about with these people?"

"I don't see much of them," he said, "excepting at chow, and we can't talk then. You see, I'm in cell block F. It's sort of a forgotten place. Like Piranesi. Last Tuesday, they forgot to spring us for supper."

"What is your cell like?"

"Twelve by seven," he said. "The only things that belong to me are the Miró print, the Descartes and a colored photograph of you and Peter. It's an old one. I took it when we had a house on the Vineyard. How is Peter?"

"Fine."

"Will he ever come to see me?"

"I don't know, I really don't know. He doesn't ask for you. The social worker thinks that, for the general welfare, it's best at the moment that he not see his father in jail for murder."

"Could you bring me a photograph?"

"I could if I had one."

"Couldn't you take one?"

"You know I'm no good with a camera."

Someone on cell block B struck a five-string banjo and began to sing: "I got those cell-block blues / I'm feeling blue all the time / I got those cell-block blues / Fenced in by walls I can't climb . . ." He was good. The voice and the banjo were loud, clear and true, and brought into that border country the fact that it was a summer afternoon all over that part of the world. Out of the window Loomis could see some underwear and fatigues hung out to dry. They moved in the breeze as if this movement — like the movements of ants, bees and geese — had some polar ordination. For a moment, he felt himself to be a man of the world, a world to which his responsiveness was marvelous and absurd.

Marcia opened her bag and looked for something. "The Army must have been a good preparation for this experience," she said.

"Sort of," he said.

"I never understood why you so liked the Army."

He heard, from the open space in front of the main entrance, a guard shouting: "You're going to be good boys, aren't you? You're going to be good boys. You're going to be good, good, good boys." Manacled in groups of ten, looking utterly bewildered and (if they were young) gazing up at the blue sky with an innocence that seemed divine, they would go under the escutcheon, under Liberty, Justice and Legislation. He heard the dragging ring of metal and guessed they'd come from Auburn.

"Oh, damn it," she said. Peevishness darkened her face. "Oh, goddamn it," she said with pure indignation.

"What's wrong?" he asked.

"I can't find my Kleenex," she said. She was foraging in the bag.

"I'm sorry," he said.

"Everything seems to fight me today," she said, "absolutely everything." She dumped the contents of her bag onto the counter.

"Lady, lady," said the turnkey, who sat above them on an elevated chair like a lifeguard. "Lady, you ain't allowed to have nothing on the counter but soft drinks and butt cans."

"I," she said, "am a taxpayer. I help to support this place. It costs me more to keep my husband in here than it costs me to send my son to a good school."

"Lady, lady, please," he said. "Get that stuff off the counter or I'll have to kick you out."

She found the small box of paper and pushed the contents of her handbag back to where they belonged. Then Loomis covered her hand with his, deeply thrilled at this recollection of his past. She pulled her hand away, but why? Had she let him touch her for a minute, the warmth, the respite would have lasted for weeks. "Well," she said, regaining her composure, her beauty, he thought.

The light in the room was unkind, but she was equal to its harshness. She had been an authenticated beauty. Several photographers had asked her to model, although her breasts, marvelous for nursing and love, were a little too big for that line of work. "I'm much too shy, much too lazy," she had said. She had accepted the compliment, her beauty had been documented.

"You know," his son had said. "I can't talk to Mummy when there's a mirror in the room. She's really balmy about her looks."

Narcissus was a man and he couldn't make the switch, but she had, maybe twelve or fourteen times, stood in front of the full-length mirror in their bedroom and asked him: "Is there another woman of my age in this county who is as beautiful as I?" She had been naked, overwhelmingly so, and he had thought this an invitation; but when he touched her, she said: "Stop fussing with my breasts. I'm beautiful." She was, too.

He knew that after she'd left, whoever had seen her — the turnkey, for instance — would say: "If that was your wife, you're lucky. Outside the movies, I never seen anyone so beautiful."

If she was Narcissa, did the rest of the Freudian doctrine follow? He had never, within his limited judgment, taken this very seriously. She had spent three weeks in Rome with her old roommate, Maria Lippincot Hastings Gugliemi. Three marriages, a fat settlement for each, and a very unsavory sexual reputation. They then had no maid and he and Peter had cleaned the house, laid and lighted fires, and bought flowers to celebrate her return from Italy. He met her at Kennedy. The plane was late. It was after midnight. When he bent to kiss her, she averted her face and pulled down the floppy brim of her new Roman hat. He got her bags, got the car and they started home. "You seem to have had a marvelous time," he said.

"I have never," she said, "been so happy in my life." He

jumped to no conclusions. The fires would be burning, the flowers gleaming. In that part of the world, the ground was covered with dirty snow.

"Was there any snow in Rome?" he asked.

"Not in the city," she said. "There was a little snow on the Via Cassia. I didn't see it. I read about it in the paper. Nothing so revolting as this."

He carried the bags into the living room. Peter was there in his pajamas. She embraced him and cried a little. The fires and the flowers missed her by a mile. He could try to kiss her again, but he knew that he might get a right to the jaw. "Can I get you a drink?" he asked, making the offer in a voice that rose.

"I guess so," she said, dropping an octave.

"*Limone?*" he asked.

"*Si, si,*" she said, "*un spritz.*"

He got the ice and the lemon peel and handed her the drink. "Put it on the table," she said. "Campari will remind me of my lost happiness." She went into the kitchen, wet a sponge and began to wash the door of the refrigerator.

"We cleaned the place," he said with genuine sadness. "Peter and I cleaned the place. Peter mopped the kitchen floor."

"Well, you seem to have forgotten the refrigerator door," she said.

"If there are angels in heaven," he said, "and if they are women, I expect they must put down their harps quite frequently to mop drainboards, refrigerator doors, any enameled surface. It seems to be a secondary female characteristic."

"Are you crazy?" she asked. "I don't know what you're talking about."

His cock, so recently ready for fun, retreated from Waterloo to Paris and from Paris to Elba. "Almost everyone I love has called me crazy," he said. "What I'd like to talk about is love."

"Oh, is that it?" she said. "Well, here you go." She put her thumbs into her ears, wagged her fingers, crossed her eyes and made a loud farting sound with her tongue.

"I wish you wouldn't make faces," he said.

"I wish you wouldn't look like that," she said. "Thank God you can't see the way you look." He said nothing more, since he knew that Peter was listening.

It took her that time about ten days to come around. It was

after a cocktail party and before a dinner. They took a nap, she in his arms. They were one, he thought. The fragrant skein of her hair lay across his face. Her breathing was heavy. When she awoke, she touched his face and asked: "Did I snore?"

"Terribly," he said. "You sounded like a chain saw."

"It was a lovely sleep," she said. "I love to sleep in your arms." Then they made love. His imagery for a big orgasm was winning the sailboat race, the Renaissance, high mountains. "Christ, that felt good," she said. "What time is it?"

"Seven," he said.

"When are we due?"

"Eight."

"You've had your bath, I'll take mine."

He dried her with a Kleenex and passed her a lighted cigarette. He followed her into the bathroom and sat on the shut toilet seat while she washed her back with a brush. "I forgot to tell you," he said. "Liza sent us a wheel of Brie."

"That's nice," she said, "but you know what? Brie gives me terribly loose bowels."

He hitched up his genitals and crossed his legs. "That's funny," he said. "It constipates me."

That was their marriage then; not the highest paving of the stair, the clatter of Italian fountains, the wind in the alien olive trees, but this, a jay-naked male and female discussing their bowels.

One more time. It was when they still bred dogs. Hannah, the bitch, had whelped a litter of eight. Seven were in the kennel behind the house. One, a sickly runt that would die, had been let in. Loomis was awakened, around three, from a light sleep by the noise of the puppy vomiting or defecating. He slept naked and naked he left the bed, trying not to disturb Marcia, and went down to the living room. There was a mess under the piano. The puppy was trembling. "That's all right, Gordo," he said. Peter had named the puppy Gordon Cooper. It was that long ago. He got a mop, a bucket, and some paper towels and crawled bare-assed under the piano to clean up the shit. He had disturbed her and he heard her come down the stairs. She wore a transparent nightgown and everything was to be seen. "I'm sorry I disturbed you," he said. "Gordo had an accident."

"I'll help," she said.

"You needn't," he said. "It's almost done."

"But I want to," she said. On her hands and knees, she joined him under the piano. When it was done, she stood and struck her head on that part of the piano that overlaps the bulk of the instrument. "Oh," she said.

"Did you hurt yourself?" he asked.

"Not terribly," she said. "I hope I won't have a bump or a shiner."

"I'm sorry, my darling," he said. He stood, embraced her, kissed her and they made love on the sofa. He lighted a cigarette for her and they returned to bed.

But it wasn't much after this that he stepped into the kitchen to get some ice and found her embracing and kissing Sally Midland, with whom she did crewel work twice a week. He thought the embrace was not platonic and he detested Sally. "Excuse me," he said.

"What for?" Marcia asked.

"I broke wind," he said. That was nasty and he knew it. He carried the ice tray into the pantry. She was silent during dinner and for the rest of the evening. When they awoke the next day — Saturday — he asked: "Good morning, darling?"

"Shit," she said. She put on her wrapper and went to the kitchen, where he heard her kick the refrigerator and then the dishwasher. "I hate you broken-down, fucking, second-rate appliances!" she shouted. "I hate, hate, hate this fucking, dirty, old-fashioned kitchen! 'I dreamt that I dwelt in marble halls.'" This was ominous, he knew, and the omens meant that he would get no breakfast. When she was distempered, she regarded the breakfast eggs as if she had laid and hatched them. The egg, the egg for breakfast! The egg was like some sibyl in an Attic drama.

"May I have eggs for breakfast?" he had once asked, years and years ago.

"Do you expect me to prepare breakfast in this House of Usher?" she had asked.

"Could I cook myself some eggs?" he asked.

"You may not," she said. "You will make such a mess in this ruin that it will take hours for me to clean it up."

On such a morning, he knew, he would be lucky to get a cup of coffee. When he dressed and went down, her face was still very dark and this made him feel much more grievous than hungry.

How could he repair this? He saw, out of the window, that there had been a frost, the first. The sun had risen, but the hoarfrost stood in the shadow of the house and the trees with a Euclidean preciseness. It was after the first frost that you cut the fox grapes she liked for jelly. Not much bigger than raisins, black, gamy, he thought perhaps that a bag of fox grapes would do the trick. He was scrupulous about the sexual magic of tools. This could be anxiety or the fact that they had once summered in southwestern Ireland, where tools had been male and female and the west meant death. He would, carrying a basket and shears, have felt like a transvestite. He chose a burlap sack and a hunting knife. He went into the woods — half or three quarters of a mile from the house — to where there was a stand of fox grapes against a stand of pines. The exposure was due east and they were ripe, blackish purple, and rimed with frost in the shade. He cut them with his manly knife and slapped them into the crude sack. He cut them for her, but who was she? Sally Midland's lover? Yes, yes, yes! Face the facts. What he faced was either the biggest of falsehoods or the biggest of truths, but, in any case, a sense of reasonableness enveloped and supported him. But if she loved Sally Midland, didn't he love Chucky Drew? He liked to be with Chucky Drew, but standing side by side in the shower, he thought that Chucky looked like a diseased chicken with flabby arms like the arms of those women who used to play bridge with his mother. He had not loved a man, he thought, since he had left the Boy Scouts. So, with his bag of wild grapes, he returned to the house, burs on his trousers, his brow bitten by the last flies of that year. She had gone back to bed. She lay there with her face in the pillow. "I picked some grapes," he said. "We had the first frost last night. I picked some fox grapes for jelly."

"Thank you," she said, into the pillow.

"I'll leave them in the kitchen," he said.

He spent the rest of the day preparing the house for winter. He took down the screens and put up the storm windows, banked the rhododendrons with raked and acid oak leaves, checked the oil level in the fuel tank, and sharpened his skates. He worked along with numerous hornets that bumped against the eaves, looking, even as he, for some sanctuary for the coming ice age.

"It was partly because we stopped doing things together," he said. "We used to do so much together. We used to sleep together, travel together, ski, skate, sail, go to concerts; we did everything together; we watched the World Series and drank beer together, although neither of us likes beer, not in this country. That was the year Lomberg, whatever his name was, missed a no-hitter by half an inning. You cried. I did, too. We cried together."

"You had your fix," she said. "We couldn't do that together."

"But I was clean for six months," he said. "It didn't make any difference. Cold turkey. It nearly killed me."

"Six months is *not* a lifetime," she said, "and anyhow, how long ago was that?"

"Your point," he said.

"How are you now?"

"I'm down from forty-four cc's to thirty-seven. I get methadone at nine every morning. A pansy deals it out. He wears a hairpiece."

"Is he on the make?"

"I don't know. He asked me if I liked opera."

"You don't, of course."

"That's what I told him."

"That's good. I wouldn't want to be married to a homosexual, having already married a homicidal drug addict."

"I did not kill my brother."

"You struck him with a fire iron. He died."

"I struck him with a fire iron. He was drunk. He hit his head on the hearth."

"All penologists say that all convicts claim innocence."

"Confucius say . . ."

"You're so superficial, Loomis. You've always been a light —"

"I did not kill my brother."

"Shall we change the subject?"

"Please."

"When do you think you'll be clean?"

"I don't know. I find it difficult to imagine cleanliness. I can claim to imagine this, but it would be false. It would be as though I had claimed to reinstall myself in some afternoon of my youth."

"That's why you're a lightweight."

"Yes."

He did not want a quarrel, not there, not ever again with her. He had observed, in the last year of their marriage, that the lines of a quarrel were as close to ordination as the words and the sacrament of holy matrimony. "I don't have to listen to your shit anymore!" she had screamed. He was astonished, not at her hysteria but at the fact that she had taken the words out of his mouth. "You've ruined my life, you've ruined my life!" she screamed. "There is nothing on earth as cruel as a rotten marriage." This was all on the tip of his tongue. But then, listening for her to continue to anticipate his thinking, he heard her voice, deepened and softened with true grief, begin a variation that was not in his power. "You are the biggest mistake I ever made," she said softly. "I thought that my life was one hundred percent frustration, but when you killed your brother, I saw that I had underestimated my problems."

When she spoke of frustration, she sometimes meant the frustration of her career as a painter, which had begun and ended by her winning second prize at an art show in college, 25 years ago. He had been called a bitch by a woman he deeply loved and he had always kept this possibility in mind. The woman had called him a bitch when they were both jay-naked in the upper floor of a good hotel. She then kissed him and said: "Let's pour whiskey all over each other and drink it." They had, and he could not doubt the judgment of such a woman. So bitchily, perhaps, he went over Marcia's career as a painter. When they first met, she had lived in a studio and occupied herself mostly with painting. When they married, the *Times* had described her as a painter and every apartment and house they lived in had a studio. She painted and painted and painted. When guests came for dinner, they were shown her paintings. She had her paintings photographed and sent to galleries. She had exhibited in public parks, streets and flea markets. She had carried her paintings up 57th Street, 63rd Street, 72nd Street, she had applied for grants, awards, admission to subsidized painting colonies, she had painted and painted and painted, but her work had never been received with any enthusiasm at all. He understood, he tried to understand, bitch that he was. This was her vocation, as powerful, he guessed, as the love of God, and like some star-crossed priest, her prayers misfired. This had its rueful charms.

Her passion for independence had reached into her manipulation of their joint checking account. The independence of women was nothing at all new to him. His experience was broad, if not exceptional. His great-grandmother had been twice around the Horn, under sail. She was supercargo, of course, the captain's wife, but this had not protected her from great storms at sea,

loneliness, the chance of mutiny and death or worse. His grandmother had wanted to be a fireman. She was pre-Freudian but
not humorless about this. "I love bells," she said, "ladders, hoses,
the thunder and crash of water. Why can't I volunteer for the
fire department?" His mother had been an unsuccessful business-
woman — the manager of tearooms, restaurants, dress shops,
and, at one time, the owner of a factory that turned out handbags,
painted cigarette boxes and doorstops. Marcia's thrust for independence was not, he knew, the burden of his company but the
burden of history.

He had caught on to the checkbook manipulation almost as
soon as it began. She had a little money of her own but scarcely
enough to pay for her clothes. She was dependent upon him and
was determined, since she couldn't correct this situation, to conceal it. She had begun to have tradesmen cash checks and then
claim that the money had been spent for the maintenance of the
house. Plumbers, electricians, carpenters, and painters didn't
quite understand what she was doing, but she was solvent and
they didn't mind cashing her checks. When Loomis discovered
this, he knew that her motive was independence. She must have
known that he knew. Since they were both knowledgeable, what
was the point of bringing it up unless he wanted a shower of tears,
which was the last thing he wanted?

"And how," he asked, "is the house?" He did not use the pos-
sessive pronoun — my house, your house, our house. It was still
his house and would be until she got a divorce. She didn't reply.
She did not draw on her gloves, finger by finger, or touch her
hair or resort to any of the soap-opera chestnuts used to express
contempt. She was sharper than that.

"Well," she said, "it's nice to have a dry toilet seat."

"Goodbye," he said to her back. He jogged out of the visitors'
room and up the stairs to cell block F. He hung his white shirt on
a hanger and went to the window, where, for the space of about a
foot, he could focus on two steps of the entrance and the sidewalk
the visitors would take on their way to cars, taxis, or the train. He
waited for them to emerge like a waiter in an American-plan hotel
waiting for the dining room doors to open, like a lover, like a
drought-ruined farmer waiting for rain but without the sense of
the universality of waiting, that waiting was the human condition.

They appeared — one, three, four, two — twenty-seven in all.
It was a weekday. Chicanos, blacks, whites, his upper-class wife

with her bell-shaped coif — whatever was fashionable that year. She had been to the hairdresser before she came to the prison. Had she said as much? "I'm not going to a party, I'm going to jail to see my husband." He remembered the women in the sea before Sally Ecbatan's coming out. They all swam a breast stroke to keep their hair dry. Now some of the visitors carried paper bags in which they took home the contraband they had tried to pass on to their loved ones. They were free, free to run, jump, fuck, drink, book a seat on the Tokyo plane. They were free, and yet they moved so casually through this precious element that it seemed wasted on them. There was no appreciation of freedom in the way they moved. A man stooped to pull up his socks. A woman rooted through her handbag to make sure she had the keys. A younger woman, glancing at the overcast sky, put up a green umbrella. An old and very ugly woman dried her tears with a scrap of paper. These were their constraints, the signs of their confinement, but there was some naturalness, some unself-consciousness about their imprisonment that he, watching them between bars, cruelly lacked.

This was not pain, nothing so simple and clear as that. All he could identify was some disturbance in his tear ducts, a blind, unthinking wish to cry. Tears were easy; a good ten-minute hand job. He wanted to cry and howl. He was among the living dead, but that was a chestnut. There were no words, no living words to suit this grief, this cleavage. He was primordial man confronted with romantic love. His eyes began to water as the last of the visitors, the last shoe disappeared. He sat on his bunk and took in his right hand the most interesting, worldly, responsive and nostalgic object in the cell. "Speed it up," said the Cuckold. "You only got eight minutes to chow."

The night that followed would go down in the memory of Falconer as deeply as the night of the last executions. Loomis queued up for supper. They had rice, franks, bread, oleomargarine, and half a canned peach. He palmed three slices of bread for his cat and jogged up to cell block F. Jogging gave him the illusion of freedom. Tiny was sitting down to his supper of outside food at his desk at the end of the block. He had on his plate a nice London broil, three baked potatoes, a can of peas, and on another plate a whole store cake. Loomis sighed loudly when he smelled the meat. Food was a recently revealed truth in his life.

He had reasoned that the Holy Eucharist was nutritious if you got enough of it. In some churches, at some times, they had baked the bread — hot, fragrant and crusty — in the chancel. "Eat this in memory of Me." Food had something to do with his beginnings as a Christian and a man. To cut short a breast-feeding, he had read somewhere, was traumatic, and from what he remembered of his mother, she might have yanked her breast out of his mouth in order not to be late for her bridge game; but this was coming close to self-pity and he had tried to leach self-pity out of his emotional spectrum. Food was food, hunger was hunger, and his half-empty belly and the perfume of roast meat established a rapport that it would take the Devil to cut in two. "Eat good," he said to Tiny. A telephone was ringing in another room. The TV was on and the majority had picked, through a rigged ballot, some game show. The irony of TV, played out against any form of life or death, was superficial and fortuitous.

So as you lay dying, as you stood at the barred window watching the empty square, you heard the voice of a man, a half-man, the sort of person you wouldn't have spoken to at school or college, the victim of a bad barber, tailor and make-up artist, exclaim: "We present with pleasure to Mrs. Charles Alcorn of 11235 275th Boulevard the four-door cathedral-size refrigerator containing two hundred pounds of prime beef and enough staples to feed a family of six for two months. This includes pet food. Don't you cry, Mrs. Alcorn, oh, darling, don't you cry, don't you cry . . . And to the other contestants, a complete kit of the sponsor's product." The time for banal irony, the voice-over, he thought, is long gone. Give me the chords, the deep rivers, the unchanging profundity of nostalgia, love and death.

Tiny had begun to roar. He was usually a reasonable man, but now his voice was high, shattering, crazy. "You rat-fucking, cocksucking, ass-tonguing, sneaky, stinking fleabag."

Obscenities recalled for Loomis the long-ago war with Germany and Japan. "In a fucking line rifle company," he or anyone else might have said, "you get the fucking, malfunctioning M-1s, fucking '03s instead of fucking carbines, fucking obsolete BARs and fucking sixty-millimeter mortars, where you have to set the fucking sight to bracket the fucking target." Obscenity worked on their speech like a tonic, giving it force and structure, but the word fucking, so much later, had for Loomis the dim force of a recollection. Fucking meant M-1s, sixty-pound packs, landing nets, the stinking Pacific island with Tokyo Rose coming over the radio. Now Tiny's genuine outburst unearthed a past, not very vivid, because there was no sweetness in it, but a solid, memorable four years of his life.

The Cuckold passed and Loomis asked: "What's wrong with Tiny?"

"Oh, don't you know?" said the Cuckold. "He had just begun his dinner when the deputy called him on the outside phone to check on work sheets. When he got back, a couple of cats, big cats, had finished off his steak and potatoes, shit in his plate, and were halfway through his cake. He tore the head off one of them. The other got away. When he was tearing off the cat's head, he got very badly bitten. He's bleeding and bleeding. I guess he's gone to the infirmary."

If prisons were constructed to make any living thing happy, it might have been cats, although the sententiousness of this observation made Loomis irritable. But the fact was that trained men with drawing boards, hod carriers, mortar, and stone had constructed buildings to deny their own kind a fair measure of freedom. The cats profited most. Even the fattest of them, the sixty-pounders, could ease their way between the bars, where there were plenty of rats and mice for the hunters, lovelorn men for the tender and the teases, and franks, meatballs, day-old bread and oleomargarine to eat.

Loomis had seen the cats of Luxor, Cairo and Rome, but with everybody going around the world these days and writing cards and sometimes books about it, there wasn't much point in linking the shadowy cats of prison to the shadowy cats of the ancient world. As a dog breeder, he had not much liked cats, but he had changed. There were more cats in Falconer than there were convicts, and there were 2000 convicts. Make it 4000 cats. Their smell overwhelmed everything, but they checked the rat-and-mice population. Loomis had a favorite. So did everybody else — some had as many as six. Some of the men's wives brought them Kitty Chow — stuff like that. Loneliness taught the intransigent to love their cats as loneliness can change anything on earth. They were warm, they were hairy, they were living, and they gave fleeting glimpses of demonstrativeness, intelligence, uniqueness and sometimes grace and beauty. Loomis called his cat Bandit,

because — black and white — it had a mask like a stagecoach robber or a raccoon. "Hi, pussy," he said. He put the three pieces of
bread on the floor. Bandit first licked the margarine off the
bread and then, with feline niceness, ate the crusts, took a drink
of water out of the toilet, finished the soft part and climbed onto
Loomis' lap. Its claws cut through the fatigues like the thorns of a
rose. "Good Bandit, good Bandit. You know what, Bandit? My
wife, my only wife came to see me today and I don't know what in
hell to think about the visit. I remember mostly watching her
walk away from the place. Shit, Bandit, I love her." He worked
behind the cat's ears with his thumb and third finger. Bandit
purred loudly and shut its eyes. He had never figured out the
cat's sex. He was reminded of the *Chicanos* in the visiting room.
"It's a good thing you don't turn me on, Bandit. I used to have
an awful time with my member. Once I climbed this mountain in
the Abruzzi. Six thousand feet. The woods were supposed to be
full of bears. That's why I climbed the mountain. To see the
bears. There was a refuge on the top of the mountain and I got
there just before dark. I went in and built a fire and ate the
sandwiches I'd brought and drank some wine and got into my
sleeping bag and looked around for sleep, but my goddamned
member was not in the mood for sleep at all. It was throbbing
and asking where the action was, why we'd climbed this mountain
with no rewards, what was my purpose, and so forth. Then
someone, some animal, started scratching at the door. It must
have been a wolf or a bear. Excepting for me, there wasn't anything else on the mountain. So then I said to my member, 'If
that's a female wolf or a female bear, perhaps I can fix you up.'
This made it thoughtful, for once — pensive — and I got to sleep,
but —"

Then the general alarm rang. Loomis had never heard it before and didn't know what it was called, but it was a racket, obviously meant to announce fires, riots, the climax and the end of
things, but it rang on and on, long after its usefulness as an announcement, a warning, an alert, an alarm, it sounded like some
approach to craziness, it was out of control, it was in control, in
possession, and then someone pulled a switch and there was that
brief, brief sweetness that comes with the cessation of pain. Most
of the cats had hidden and the wiser ones had taken off. Bandit
was behind the toilet. Then the metal door rolled open and a

bunch of guards came in, led by Tiny. They wore the yellow waterproofs they wore for fire drill and they all carried clubs.

"Any of you got cats in your cells, throw them out," said Tiny. Two cats, at the end of the block, thinking, perhaps, that Tiny had food, went toward him. One was big, one was little. Tiny raised his club, way in the air, and caught a cat on the completion of the falling arc, tearing it in two. At the same time, another guard bashed in the head of the big cat. Blood, brains and offal splattered their yellow waterproofs and the sight of carnage reverberated through Loomis' dental work; caps, inlays, restorations, they all began to ache. He snapped his head around to see that Bandit had started for the closed door. He was pleased at this show of intelligence and by the fact that Bandit had spared him the confrontation that was going on between Tiny and Chicken Number Three. "Throw that cat out," said Tiny to Chicken.

"You ain't going to kill my pussy," said Chicken.

"You want six days cell lock," said Tiny.

"You ain't going to kill my pussy," said Chicken.

"Eight days cell lock," said Tiny. Chicken said nothing. He was hanging on to the cat. "You want the hole," said Tiny. "You want a month in the hole."

"I'll come back and get it later," said one of the other men.

It was half and half. Half the cats cased the slaughter and made for the closed door. Half of them wandered around at a loss, sniffing the blood of their kind and sometimes drinking it. Two of the guards vomited and half a dozen cats got killed eating the vomit. The cats that hung around the door, waiting to be let out, were easy targets. When a third guard got sick, Tiny said, "O.K., O.K., that's enough for tonight, but it don't give me back my London broil. Get the fire detail to clean this up." He signaled for the door to open, and when it rolled back, six or maybe ten cats escaped, giving to Loomis some reminder of the invincible.

The fire detail came in with waste cans, shovels and two lengths of hose. They sluiced down the block and shoveled up the dead cats. They sluiced down the cells as well and Loomis climbed onto his bunk, knelt there and said: " 'Blessed are the meek,' " but he couldn't remember what came next. " 'For theirs is the Kingdom of Heaven'?"

ANN COPELAND

At Peace

(FROM THE CANADIAN FICTION MAGAZINE)

BY SHEER ACCIDENT I happened to be passing through Saddleburg when the obituary columns listed Barney's death. Even more accident that I happened to pick up a paper that night and read of it. But for the CN breakdown, I'd have charged right through that godforsaken burg and left it behind forever. As luck would have it, though, our ailing train gasped to a halt about twenty miles outside town. After the usual apologies, reassurances, official explanations, and unofficial speculations, they hauled us off, baggage and all, and left us huffing and puffing in the frost, a band of about fifty derailed passengers thrust on the bleak bosom of a November night in Maritime Canada. It was every bit as chilling as I remembered it.

Small pockets of human frustration clustered alongside the track, here and there a cigarette lighter briefly illuminating anxious eyes or a stoic jaw, intermittent mutters uselessly rehearsing our impotence as we waited to be rescued. The surge of rhythmic power that had so effortlessly borne us past hamlets, shacks, straggling ends of villages, vacant sagging barns, wintering maple and evergreen forests, miles of unpeopled marsh, standing cows, and scattered workhorses — was still. For hours we had sat in the overheated cars staring vaguely out at the darkening landscape that passed us, lulled and rocked by the mechanical song of our train; or we had turned away from that mesmerizing window to the comforts of the inside: a drink, dinner, conversation, a snooze. But now our instinctive balances of cold observed and warmth enjoyed had been exploded. We were on the other side of that glass, we were out there, ourselves impossibly part of the desolate landscape with which we had felt so tenuously connected, if connected at all. *We* were in the moving picture, but we weren't even moving.

There was no inside to turn to, no way to shut this out, turn it off. The best distraction I could find from gradually numbing toes and buzzing irritation all round me was to stare straight up. I could remember that from before. It wasn't the old cliché of finding solace in the sky. Not that sky. It was simply that there was no sky like it anywhere else I'd been. There was nothing else to do with it but look. It was a sky that reduced one to staring. Going blank. A sky whose vast darkness somehow inverted and restated those vacant stretches of landscape it shrouded by day. Neither a pillar of fire nor a manned rocket seemed to have anything to do with those heavens. Stars were everywhere in the black, patterned holes cutting through — to what? No trace of that pinkish rainbow that arches over a large city at night, the almost sickening glow of darkness's covenant with urban hustle-bustle. I can remember seeing, once, the night sky over the steel-works in Gary, Indiana — puffed with swiftly merging forms of billowing gray-yellow above belching flames: gorgeous. Faced with that one might come to believe in apocalypse. But this sky yielded nothing to human desires; it remained barren and silent even with studding stars and subtle wisps of whiteness graining through its black. I stared and felt again what I remembered feeling long before about the marsh sky: it was neither reassuring nor warming. It was silencing.

Eventually, as is usually the way with such human inconveniences, we were taken care of. They stuffed us all into a bus and transported us to a Holiday Inn just outside town from which they would collect us next morning and put us on the ten o'clock train they promised would leave promptly. When I finally lugged my loaded suitcase and parcels into that plastic world, even the blank surfaces of chartreuse and mauve in the predictable lobby and the equally opaque surface of the desk clerk were welcome. At times vacuity disguised as the familiar can seem to give warmth. This was such a time. I was relieved to be inside. In no time, I had squared away my belongings, freshened up, picked up a paper in the lobby, and headed for the dining room. One thing I remembered about Maritime food: their fish chowder was usually fabulous. This was the perfect night for a bowl of it.

When the waitress disappeared with my order I settled down with the paper. I'd had enough of enforced socializing and people-watching for that night, and soon enough I'd be back in my own nest of domestic wear and tear. For those few final hours, at least, I cherished my solitude. And so the unfailing defense: I folded back the evening paper and began to read.

By the time dessert came, I was to the obituary page. It didn't take long to reach the obits; papers in that section of the country are notoriously slim. And then, there it was.

Died

Sister Barnabas MacLean, 64, daughter of Angus and Genevieve MacLean of Scotland, coadjutrix sister of Order of St. Gertrude. Funeral from the Church of Our Savior, Saturday, November 28. Friends may call at the convent between the hours of 3:00–5:00 and 7:00–9:00 P.M. *on November 27. Donations may be made to the Heart Fund.*

Barney, it had to be Barney. There could be only one lay sister in Maritime Canada named Sister Barnabas MacLean. Reading that notice seemed to paralyze all my responses momentarily. I didn't want Barney to be dead. Not, mind you, that I'd seen her in twenty or more years. But Barney had a corner in my consciousness that was carpeted, furnished, mythologized, and turned to in moments both secret and articulate. I had told many stories about her to dear friends. There were others I would tell no one because she trusted me not to. There was a pact of secrecy and trust between Barney and me, had been since I left the Order and even well before that. Barney belonged to life, the life of memory and mind that was mine. I didn't want her buried.

I remembered our first encounter with a spasm of discomfort still. I was new to Our Savior's community, fresh from the novitiate, impressionable, earnest, conscientious — not to say scrupulous — about keeping untarnished and pure the vows I had just made. I realize now how hard it is to convey to an outsider what strange beings we were when we finally completed our three years of novitiate-training and went to live in community. We were filled with ideals, many as yet untested, schooled to the observance of details we believed would become the measure of sanctity in a world that denied us more obvious martyrdom, committed to a daily round of prayer and meditation that was taxing, time-consuming, and, we fervently hoped, eternally efficacious. Anyhow, there I was, assigned that first year to help Sister Barnabas in the kitchen during my "free time" — of which there was none. (At using such euphemisms we all became unwittingly expert.) I had some vague notion that I was a victim. When I'd innocently told a few sisters what charge Reverend Mother had given me for the year, they rolled their eyes expressively, charity notwithstanding, and wished me luck.

So I found my way to the kitchen on my third day in the community. There she was, Sister Barnabas, puttering slowly around. It was ten o'clock in the morning, a Saturday.

"Good morning, Sister Barnabas," I said from the doorway, timid of crossing the premises without her clear sanction.

"Hrumph." It was barely audible. She kept moving about, grunting and sniffing, opening the refrigerator, shuffling to the sink, slamming cupboard doors, effectively communicating to me without so much as a word that she wished I was at the opposite end of the house, if not of the world.

"Reverend Mother told me I might be of some help to you in the kitchen."

She stopped dead. Then she looked at me, scowled, and snorted. "Help! So that's her idea, is it? Never *has* liked the way I run this kitchen. So she sent a spy, eh?"

She slammed the drawer behind her with her broad rump and grabbed the broom. Sister Barnabas was lame. Like most people who have lived long years with a handicap, she compensated amazingly well. When she really wanted to move quickly, she did. Now she hobbled over to about two inches in front of me.

"Well, you can get right out o' here an' find yourself somethin' else to do to pass yer Saturday mornin's more in keepin' with the education the likes o' you has had." She started to sweep vigorously, covering my feet with the broom, forcing me back out of the doorway. "An' that's that!"

I left.

Something kept me from telling anyone about it. I held my peace and mentioned nothing to Reverend Mother. Not that at that point I wanted to conceal; it was some deeper instinct I couldn't name that said: let her be. So I did. But the next Saturday morning, promptly at ten, I appeared again in the doorway. This time I saw that the kitchen floor had been scrubbed and was glistening wet. Sister Barnabas was nowhere to be seen. It was understood that one didn't disturb her in her room, a tiny cell just across the hall from the kitchen. That week again I felt a bit guilty but decided nonetheless to leave her a note that I'd been there, let time pass, and try just once more the next Saturday.

At ten o'clock I appeared. There she was, hobbling about. Grumbling. Apparently oblivious that I was in the doorway. I waited. Then cleared my throat. She turned immediately, but it was clear that she was not about to help me.

"Good morning, Sister Barnabas."

She scowled at me once more. "Well, I got yer note." Not another word. No indication of how she felt. No explanation.

"Is there anything I could do to help you this morning, Sister?"

"Wash the floor." She pointed silently to the mop and pail she had left in the corner by the doorway. As she did that, she was loosening her apron, obviously not intending to be around while I helped.

"Fine." I held my tone as absolutely neutral as I could. Perhaps I did have a charge, after all.

She left and I moved about, sloshing the linoleum and hoping it would suit her. One thing worked in my favor: I knew she was not a fussy housekeeper. In fact, the prioress at that time kept away from the kitchen just because she couldn't stand the mess. The food Sister Barnabas fed us was excellent, the best in the province I later realized, after I'd moved around a bit. But the kitchen — a godawful mess. Pots within pots, nothing sized, jars and containers here and there with leftovers and promises dripping or hardening in various colors and shapes, a conglomeration only she could keep straight. Thick greasy dust coated the top of the refrigerator. The oven window was crusted with a baked glaze that resisted repeated applications of Easy-Off. I learned that later, when the oven came to be my special task, one I loathe even now.

And plants. Where there wasn't dirt or pots or pans or food, there was a plant. Counter space seemed to disappear almost before it existed. Ivy trailing all over the kitchen windows, even though the convent was poorly insulated and the windows were frosty. A jade tree growing from a sodded wash basin in the corner, *impatiens* blooming fiery red on the edge of the butcher block in the center of the kitchen, a tuberous begonia on the flour barrel, shifted about during the day as baking proceeded. And — who would believe it? — African violets thriving on the corner of the kitchen counter.

It made no sense; her plants were always in danger. But they were a precious part of her mess and she was scrupulous about their care. Talked to them, long before plant nuts were telling us that was the secret. Vented her spleen on them, too. Perhaps it was simply that she had no one else living with whom she felt she could communicate, so the plants got it — whole. And she had spleen aplenty. But they rooted and grew and flowered and trailed in that atmosphere of hostility and harangue. To this day I can't keep an ivy from dying, not even with the advantages of mild climate, peat moss, plant food, sun, water, and a library of How-To books. All she did was mutter and growl, and this in a part of the world whose climate spoke of death. My milder skies of the Pacific northwest, the long growing season, the abundant rain — none of this has made my thumb green. But nothing green seemed to wither in Barney's kingdom.

Apparently my floor passed muster, for she let me in each Saturday morning thereafter, usually muttering some direction to me and leaving immediately for her room. When I left the kitchen and headed down the hall an hour or so later, I'd often hear her cell door click as she shuffled back to inspect. We went on like this for some time.

Then one Saturday morning she paused as she was leaving the kitchen. She seemed to be making a more elaborate knot in the apron strings she was about to dangle from the hook behind the door.

"Sister," she grunted in my direction. I was busy pouring water into a pail and turned off the tap quickly to hear. "How come you never told Reverend Mother I wouldn't let you in my kitchen?"

"Because I figured you must have your own good reasons." The answer was true and it was uncalculated. As sometimes happens with such responses, unfortunately only sometimes, it went right to the mark. She didn't let on then.

"Hrumph." She hung up the apron and hobbled out.

The next Saturday, though, before I started my work, she offered a comment, as if a whole week hadn't intervened, as if we were just continuing our conversation. "Yer the first one has ever done that fer me here." She jabbed the apron onto the hook and left. I mopped away that morning with the distinct sense that in some queer way I'd made a difference in her feeling about the place, about me, or about I didn't know what.

I came to know what, of course, as months passed and our weekly punctuated exchanges grew into what couldn't properly be called conversations, ever, but limping dialogues that seemed to erupt, almost unwilled, out of some inexpressible need in her. For my part, I came to see certain things about Sister Barnabas.

First of all, somewhere, somehow, and it was probably many years before, she had been badly hurt. I was never sure just how. I could read the many subsequent hurts that resulted from her being the only lay sister in an Order of highly educated women, who willed to deal charitably with her but found it hard to absorb her thorns without the flower of articulate acknowledgment. For Sister Barnabas never admitted guilt. Nor did she speak easily or grammatically — nor even, sometimes, coherently. Before she could get a statement out, she had to feel she could trust you. Most of the time she made do with monosyllables and grunts delivered with a scowl. By the time I met her she trusted literally no one. Except, for some strange reason as our history bore out, me.

Secondly, she was basically bright. She had had no schooling to speak of — just grades one and two in a little country schoolhouse. (I observed with fascination her self-taught methods of calculating proportions for enlarging recipes.) Then, when she was eight, she had lost both parents: first her father was killed in a freak accident by his own tractor, then her mother, a month later, died in childbirth. She was farmed out to a distant uncle who was none too happy to have another mouth to feed and body to clothe, but saw to it that she redeemed the burden on him by taking care of his four children, all younger than she.

She had known little about the sisters when she first came to them, had merely passed their convent whenever she went into the nearest town, some fifteen miles from her uncle's farm. As she grew older she occasionally saw them moving about in town and she understood — because she had her depths of uneducated piety — that they lived for God. She was about seventeen when her uncle told her one day that the sisters were looking for someone to help with the work in their convent. She took the hint, went timidly to investigate, and shortly thereafter went to live with the sisters. She had a place and she had a job.

"I felt I'd found a home," she put it to me simply, in one of her many narrations about life in the old days. "They needed an' wanted me. There wasn't many of 'em, but some very good souls. As well as one or two *divils!*" With this, she'd swat an invisible fly or rub her hands energetically against her crusty apron for emphasis and relief, her dark eyes snapping beneath heavy disorderly brows. "But most of us got along real well. The superior fer years was Sister Alphonsus. She didn't put on airs." Here, a pause with a meaningful sniff. "None o' this bowin' an' scrapin' from here to eternity. We showed her proper respect, but she was one of us. Did the dishes, taught in the classroom like the rest. No stayin' in her office, seein' people an' hearin' their reports on others from dawn to dusk." Again, she would italicize her complaint with a physical gesture — kick a box, slam a drawer, or perhaps, if we were chatting in her cell as later came to be our habit, she'd just slap her knee hard once or twice.

It was a particularly sore point with Barney while I was there that our prioress, as the superior was then called, was somewhat reserved and set great store by her dignity. She made no attempt to hide her disapproval of the way Barney kept, or didn't keep, her kitchen. She despised mess; her own office seemed dust-resistant, the top of her desk tediously neat. She and Barney lived in a state of cold war. But meals must go on: the status quo was maintained.

In any case, when Barney first went to live with the sisters in town, she found one substantial change in her lot: she felt valued. There was no great change in her material situation. As she herself put it, "We was all from that area an' most of us already knew what poor farm livin' was all about. So we worked hard an' didn't think much about it. Got mighty cold sometimes, tho', in midwinter. That's always what bothered me most. *Cold.*"

Then the world began to change, even that world we may think of as so unchanging. Their convent grew poorer and poorer. In the late twenties and thirties they were largely dependent on alms, their school income having dropped to virtually nothing. They skimped and prayed — and went on teaching.

"We'd peel an orange for breakfast," she told me, "an' even that was an effort, our hands would be so cold. After breakfast I went

round and started the wood stoves in the three classrooms so by
the time the children arrived those rooms, the kitchen, an' the
little chapel would be warm." To me, her kitchen in Saddleburg
was always stifling.

When Barney told them to me, I heard stories of those days
with the fascination that attaches to some far-distant era, for in
my time we were snug in a convent that was spacious, orderly, and
well appointed if plain. In the fifties the superiors could afford to
debate whether floors in a new convent would be hardwood or
linoleum, whether the chapel would have a pipe organ or electric.
But the times Barney spoke of were long before such affluence,
and the nuns in that little community came to know the meaning
of the poverty they had vowed. Barney cooked for them as best
she could, gradually mastering the secrets of the kitchen and the
soil. Her hands, swollen with arthritis when I knew her, had the
look of hands that were friends of earth.

"I'd always grown vegetables, even as a child," she boasted early
one summer morning in Saddleburg, when she took me out behind our convent to admire her flourishing garden. "I surprised
'em all when I managed to stock enough vegetables to take us
clear through the winter."

Her secret was a method of storing in shallow holes out behind
the convent, lined and covered with hay. It was in one of her
early morning trips out to such a hole that she caught her foot in
a crevice hidden by snow and turned her ankle badly. It never
healed properly. She tried to keep the pain to herself; there was
enough to worry about without doctors' bills. Somehow she hobbled about and managed to borrow first crutches, then a cane.
When I came to know her in Saddleburg years later, she still had
that same cane — horny, worn smooth — the proverbial Irish
walking stick.

Their little group managed to survive in that state for several
years, perplexed as to their future but, one supposes, living day
by day and pluckily trusting to Providence. I see them in my own
imagination as a small band of valiant women committed to the
task of hanging on. They were receiving no subjects. Except for
Sister Barnabas, as she came to be called, after she finally decided
to become one of the group at the age of twenty-six or so.

"I wasn't so sure they'd take me," she admitted to me in a rare show of humility once. "Especially since I couldn't help out in the school. Most of 'em had been through grade six at least. But they liked my cookin' an' they'd grown used to my ways. I felt right good they was so pleased to have me."

She always felt her lack of education. Even when I was in Saddleburg I'd come upon her trying furtively to improve herself. She kept a tattered pocket dictionary on a secret shelf and eventually she asked me to read and correct any notes she sent to Reverend Mother. For their communication was chiefly by notes, even though they lived in the same house.

So that was how she spent her early years in the convent. Her job was to scrape the pot as creatively as she could, but the bottom looked emptier and emptier. Their end seemed inevitable: gradual extinction. They were an autonomous house in the rural periphery of a particularly slack diocese. Times were hard all over and little help was forthcoming from ecclesiastical authorities, who no doubt saw the hopelessness of wasting resources on a dying group.

Chance rescued them. I was on the other side of that chance. But for the improbable, I would never have met Barney. As it turned out, my own Order — highly organized, international, strictly monastic as it was — reached out the sisterly hand. Officially it was called amalgamation. Perhaps interment would have been a more accurate term. Anyhow, Barney's little group of nuns was absorbed by us.

"No way we could know what we was in fer," she'd ruminate as she poked around the kitchen after our work was done, shifting the arbutus, checking the violets, or easing herself onto the rickety high stool near the sink. "But I'm tellin' you, Sister, I'm tellin' you — I never wants to live through seein' a house closed again. Not one I've been livin' in and thinkin' of as home. Not one I knows like the back o' my hand an' loves. It was awful, it was awful." Intense in memory for a moment, then she'd shuffle off, jostling herself back to present practicalities.

I could imagine the world she had left. It's the same today, only more so. This was an early version of the very scene I'd stared at for hours through the train window that later November night. But in her time the whole area was just *beginning* to depopulate, people moving away to greener pastures — which to Maritimers generally meant Upper Canada, if they could get that far.

Somewhere they felt they'd have a chance. Farms — always a precarious source of livelihood in this rugged area of the country — were straggling into anonymous dereliction. The sagging gray barn with loose siding was becoming a landmark everywhere. Wherever you turned there were signs of village life that once had been but now was gone: vacant buildings with broken windows, abandoned tarpaper shacks, junked wagons, rusting car parts, mounds of debris, litter. Stragglers lingered on — the old-timers who blended tobacco, tall stories, and repetitive wit as they stood staring out at the vacant landscape; the lounging adolescents. But it was improbable that any ambitious school would stand a chance of success here. And our Order was committed to education.

"We gathered fer one final party in the old house," Barney told me. "Even the old students, many of 'em now grown with children of their own, came. I made a great cake — we all sang, then ended with Benediction together fer the last time. We had it outdoors, the chapel was too small fer the crowd. I'll never forget that final hymn, 'Holy God' it was. Next mornin' they split us up an' shipped us out to the communities that had agreed to take us, by twos and threes. Sister Alphonsus and I came here. I wanted to bring my mutt, but they said NO." I thought of her kitten litter at the back door.

"Here" was Saddleburg, where the Order had a flourishing elementary school and was about to start the private girls' high school to which I was assigned. Thus — chance. There were about twenty-five in the community when she came. They desperately needed a cook; there were no lay sisters in this Order. The job was hers. They soon saw, I'm sure, that she had already developed her crotchets, but she was tolerated easily since the convent was large enough that they could leave her alone.

That was just it: they could leave her alone. From my perspective, Barney had come from a world one might almost call cozy: where convent and school were in one building, where in the midst of her morning a youngster from grade three might run into her kitchen to sneak a fresh doughnut, if their pungent odor had seeped down to the hallway toward the classrooms. Occasionally, even in their hardest days, Barney would prepare a treat for one of the primary grades and the children would greet her appearance at the classroom door with a cheer, for they knew it meant doughnuts, candy, or the succulent candied cherries she turned out by the dozen at Christmas time. When she went to town, limping along with her perpetual frown, people nodded, or children darted up to her to introduce their parents. She was an institution. I'm not minimizing the hardships she must have known, but it was all within a context that had some human warmth for her. She knew where she fit.

Now all that was gone. There was *no* going to town: these nuns were strictly cloistered. The school itself was an acre away. She saw the children only in the distance, lining up for classes or at recess time. They had never heard of her, much less smelled her doughnuts or tasted her candied cherries. Parents' Day was catered and held in the school; she never met the families. The convent itself was shaped like a Y: refectory and kitchen in one wing, chapel in the other, nuns' cells and community room in the third. In chapel the nuns chanted Divine Office in Latin. To her it might as well have been Hindustani.

She fit in only one place: the kitchen. And that place was cut off from the others. Seculars were not allowed within the cloister; the sisters stayed away from the kitchen. So she was structurally cut off from the others, to say nothing of the fact that she had no history or training in common with the rest of us. Everyone in the order had at least a B.A. and, as the years passed and our training was upgraded, the younger nuns were sent on to graduate school. Sister Barnabas might have pronounced the same vows as we had, but in terms of everyday living that language of shared aspiration was delusion. All the tongues we spoke in the course of a day were to her foreign, even threatening: it was a living babel called community life.

Just about that time I came to the house and went through my Saturday morning trial period before gradual acceptance came. Just why it came was never clear to me. Maybe not to her. Perhaps it was just that conjunction of person, need, and time in one's life that worked, as it sometimes can, for the most unlikely reasons.

"Sister," she'd say to me as I was about to leave on Saturday morning, "do you have a minute?" I dared not say I was rushed, had to prepare a class, had papers to do. Instead we'd go across the hall to her small cell, the only one in that wing. Outside — the silent polished corridors, glistening Formica-topped tables in the long refectory, the spotless community room, the tidy cells of the older nuns. Everywhere the house reflected order, an order understood to mirror timeless higher realities. Inside Sister Barnabas' room — clutter, glorious clutter. I understood why she never let anyone in.

First of all, the bed had on it no standard white cotton spread of the kind that reduced our cells to facelessness. Her bed was covered with an old quilt carefully patched in places.

"A variation on the Dresden plate," she told me, patting it with her swollen hands and then plopping down in the middle of it as she motioned me to the one small chair.

"In the old days we spent winter evenin's workin' quilts with pieces o' cotton the parishioners brought us. Turned out 'bout two a winter, mostly local favorites: Dresden Plate, the Bear's Paw, Double Irish Chain, Maltese Cross. They brought patterns with 'em from their families." ("Patterens" she said, I can still remember.)

Her words conjured up a homey rural scene to my stereotyping imagination: a group of nuns gathered round the quilting frame by the Franklin stove. Snow outside. Currier and Ives in the Maritimes. No doubt there was tedium in it, I thought, but there must have been steady delight, as well, in working with such beautiful designs and colors. Once a year, for their bazaar, they always raffled one or two quilts.

"One year Orville Landry took a chance in my name," she gleamed. "He was our jack-of-all-trades, a handyman. Loved my cookin'. I used to send him home with a batch o' fresh doughnuts every Saturday night. Anyhow, didn't he win the quilt an' give it to me."

It may sound like a trifle but just such a detail represented the gulf between these two worlds: her old convent world and the one she and I were now in, the only model I had known, in fact, until I met Barney. For we, trained — with some pride, I always felt — to revere the austerities of monastic observance, had eliminated color from the mind's horizon. And gifts. Whatever we received we turned in to the superior, and we soon learned to warn family and friends not to give anything that was colorful. I can still remember the gaily striped towels I brought with me to the novitiate. On my second day there they disappeared and were quietly replaced by thin white ones. Towels in the convent were white, bedspreads were white, nightgowns were white, one is tempted to say now that the mind went white. The possibility of snuggling down under a colorful quilt that was your very own, a gift from someone you knew, was simply anathema to our highly conditioned virginal imaginations.

The abundance of things to look at in her room! Tacked to her walls was a hodgepodge of fraying snapshots, all from the past: squinting squatting youngsters crowded together in a photo that was all background and taken on the slant; an aging tintype, glued to cardboard backing, of a broad-bosomed woman sitting sternly in front of her little cottage.

"My grandmother," she told me, "on my mother's side."

A dog, several shots of the dog, the cheerful mutt who had his own warm spot next to the wood stove in the kitchen of the old house. Her walls were covered with these photos larded in between with holy cards of the saints: St. Teresa of Avila in ecstasy; St. Joseph holding a lamb and a staff; the Child Jesus, heart and halo glowing; Mary, decorous in blue and white, grinding the serpent; Blessed Margaret Mary Alacoque receiving the promises; and, of course, the children of Fatima. The small table by her bed held a plastic Madonna that lighted in the dark. Sister Barnabas couldn't stand the modern austere décor of our renovated chapel. She loved plaster statues, vigil lights, tabernacles decorated in gold leaf with little doors that opened, processions with strewers, the Lourdes hymn: that whole world of disappearing and comforting Catholicism we had been trained to regard as theologically and esthetically suspect. She hated the revised liturgy. Having mastered, with great pride, the Latin responses at Mass, she had no interest in reverting from *Et cum spiritu tuo* to "And with you, too." Her thumb-worn *Imitation of Christ* was there on the desk, next to the piled-high travel magazines the milkman brought her.

That first day, my initiation into her world of clutter and comfort brought me a feeling of release tinged with guilt: guilt because we chatted away in her cell, which was forbidden by the rule of silence; guilt because we stood in a world of clips from the past and I had been trained to let that past go, to forget, or suppress, or sublimate — whatever word a more sophisticated secular analyst might apply — the strands that had brought us to where we were. Leaving home meant to me *leaving* home: "He who having once put his hand to the plow looketh back . . ." We accepted, with some perverse pride, the cold absolute that we never would see home again. "Not even if there is a death in the family." That was the way they put it to us. Such a peak of detachment from home represented to us an achievement.

Yet there we stood surrounded, held, and (I felt it consciously even then) warmed by colorful fraying strands from a past of hardship that were gathered as best they could be into a whole skein of life: the effort to hold what had spoken, warmed, and comforted her in a world which was obviously now for Sister Barnabas cold, austere, and fundamentally incomprehensible. I began to understand the litter of her kitchen; I began not to see litter so much as composition, to grasp why she worked so hard at each original piece she produced.

For that too was special about Barney. She had in her a touch of the artist. It showed in a variety of unexpected turns: she baked gorgeous, extravagant birthday cakes, quite unasked, and sent them into the refectory on the appropriate day for Sister So-and-So. The prioress disapproved visibly (we were to celebrate not birthdays but baptismal days) but found it futile to argue. I was assigned to keep track of the birthdays, to discover them by some means and let her know. She usually got a thank you. She was wounded to the quick if she didn't, though she'd never let on to the sister in question.

When I came into the kitchen one Saturday morning, I found her muttering and kicking an empty carton about fiercely. I waited a moment, wondering whether I ought just to leave (she valued her privacy passionately), then said as if I'd noticed nothing: "Anything special for me to do today?"

She booted the carton a good six feet till it struck a wall and, turning, slammed in an offensive drawer.

"Think all that matters round here is sayin' yer prayers, saying yer prayers, doin' yer work. Can't tell me God Hisself don't like birthday cakes!"

She had just received a note from Reverend Mother urging that she at least adopt more religious motifs for her cakes, not the usual dogs, cats, houses, flowers, etc. The one the evening before had been particularly offensive, it seemed. So Sister Barnabas growled and kicked and scowled her way through the next twenty-four hours, simmering with resentment. The next sister to be so honored got a cake with a bleeding heart on it.

She made her own Christmas cards. I don't think Reverend Mother ever knew. It was quite possible she didn't, for Sister Barnabas, down there in her wing of the convent, had her own world. She kept kittens out near the back door and her Christmas cards were rough drawings of a kitten or two with a red ribbon, colored not painted, and a conventional little message written inside. These she started to create in her spare hours sometime in October, and she would give them to the milkman, the deliveryman, the bread man, the garbage collector, the string of people who came to her back door during the year. I liked to think of the circuit of relationships that emanated from Sister Barnabas' back door: a network of people who spoke her language and read her scowls, were not put off, brought her little treats and favors which she never turned in but hoarded in her cell. She had her favorites and she played them. What I got from her treasure hoard on my birthday was positively embarrassing but there was no getting around it.

It is extremely difficult to try to re-create now the texture of our relationship during those three years I spent at Saddleburg. It settled into a kind of tacit complicity which she herself never fully understood as complicity, for she simply disregarded impossible restrictions she couldn't see the sense of, and went her way. I was a different breed; I had to balance two kinds of consciousness. Trained to much more rigid ideals, I had my twinges. But through it all, Sister Barnabas' obdurateness, her persistent passionate grasp at the bits of life she could still hold, her rage at what had been lost and her inability to say what — for in some ways she had never even known what; she could only feel its loss — these realities touched me more deeply than the hours of teaching, of living with that community, of doing what was expected and trying to fathom its meaning.

When I left Saddleburg, having been transferred to another house several hundred miles away, Sister Barnabas wept. She did it in the privacy of her room; she was nowhere in evidence the next morning when I left officially, the whole community standing around outside the front door to say the prayers for travelers and then good-bye.

At supper the night before, she sent me a note by the server, scrawled on the back of an envelope in her childish hand: "*Come see me after nite prayer.* B."

There was no denying it. Great Silence or not, she would have her private farewell.

So, after night prayer, when the others were padding off to study hour or to get ready for bed, I went to Sister Barnabas' cell and knocked.

"Sister?" a whisper from behind her door.

"It's me."

She opened the door. Inside seemed strangely dim and shadowy. Then I saw what she had done. The cluttered little cell was aglow with dozens of candle stubs, sacristy butts no doubt, lighted and stuck anywhere she could perch them. I suppressed my instant urge to warn against fire: the holy cards, photos, papers, old magazines seemed to be leaping toward the flames, in my excited imagination. She took my hand and pulled me inside.

Sister Barnabas ("Barney," I called her to myself even then) had prepared for me a party. Her own kind of party. It was like a child's birthday party. Red, pink, and purple balloons hovered up against the ceiling. Flickering candles cast huge blobs of dancing shadows on her white walls. The house outside her room was absolutely still. She had her small transistor radio that the garbageman had given her three Christmases before going softly on FM. By some miraculous effort, she had cleared her desk and set on it a masterpiece. On the cake, built high above the top layer, stood a replica of the convent we were in. A light on in one window, the kitchen. And underneath the replica: "Good-bye." Sister Barnabas was almost speechless herself at the effect of her efforts on me.

That passed quickly, however, and we settled down to cake and Coke. I asked no questions. She had her ways. Her gesture made me want to cry, but I didn't. There was some steel impulse in me that said, "Hold on; it will be too much." It would have been. Instead, we gorged ourselves on Barney's seven-layer cake. She had wrapped several small presents for me and I was expected to open these, one by one.

"Do you like it?" she asked with childlike eagerness as I'd barely finished opening the can of Johnson's Baby Powder. Then the new toothbrush. Then a little box of Christmas cards she had saved for me. And the most touching, perhaps, a bookmark for my Office book: the cut-out head of the Virgin pasted on a small strip of leather she had found somewhere and trimmed with pinking shears. I have it still.

Our party lasted about an hour. That was all the time I could manage, with packing yet to finish. But Barney had made her point. At the door to her cell she hugged me and bristled her black whiskers against my cheek, then turned brusquely back into her cell, hiding tears.

Life has a way of simply going on. The large hurdles like good-byes are risen to and then gradually fade before the onslaught of daily tasks, deadlines, and expectations to be met in the ordinary business of getting through twenty-four hours. It was the same in the convent, only perhaps more so for us for we never had those upholstered pauses I now recognize as part of a normal rhythm of day-to-day living "outside": the evening when you choose to forget the outer world and curl up before the fire once the children are in bed; the latch is on the door, and the tentacles of encroaching minutiae are temporarily at bay. In the convent as I knew it, there were no such pauses. We moved from task to task, recreation itself was a task, staying awake in chapel could be a task, trusting the validity of one's own responses became a task — especially when they were at variance with what was expected. Days passed. Years passed. We worked. We prayed. We did our best to survive intact.

Through those years during which I moved about from house to house I never once heard from Barney. Of her I would hear, periodically, just enough — usually conveyed in guardedly judgmental words — to convince me that her life went on as I had known it, fringed with dust and decaying strands, built on the bits of human contact she could elicit in an environment that was basically hostile to her. And to which she herself was hostile. Now and then a friend who had spent time at Our Savior's would mention some anecdote about Barney. I gleaned that she was still cooking creations for birthdays, that her kitchen was still messy beyond description, that she was still so grouchy that the prioress found it virtually impossible to assign anyone to help her — that she was still, that is, herself as life had made her.

Five years passed before I decided to leave the Order for good. That is not part of this story really, except that my leave-taking made possible our final meeting. I left, moved far away, worked, eventually married. The shape and feeling of different periods of our lives is mysterious. I passed through several phases of feeling about that chunk of my life, but ultimately came to hold it all at a distance. It ceased to be as living or as painful as it once had been, before the growing realities of husband, family, time passing, gray hairs, and all that whispers to us that regrets are a waste of time. Still, somewhere quite alive in my fading memory of detail there was a short, stumpy, grouchy, affectionate face and figure: Barney.

I didn't know how living that figure was until her letter came. The first one arrived shortly after my second baby was born. We were still in the welter of two sets of diapers, sibling jealousy, and house clutter that says life has exploded in colossal disregard for tidiness and order. It was fitting that into this world of fraying nerves and sharp edges muted by the welcome of loving affection that underlay our fatigue, Barney's letter came. She would have understood and responded to the mess. I remember sitting down in the midst of unfolded diapers, a mountain of them, while Jeffrey finally settled into Play-Doh and the baby was building up for a good yell. I wanted to indulge immediately the unexpected surge of feeling that had risen at this sudden link with a world that had seemed so far off. I hadn't known I would be so glad to hear. I had spoken often of Barney, and with affection. But I had *placed* her in my imagination; her spot was fixed in my memory. Now she was dislodging herself, refusing to be put away neatly, asserting her living right to be as she wanted to be.

"*Dear One,*" it read. I had to struggle to make out that childish scrawl, large letters on small pages of what looked like her own card, a kitten on the front. "*I have not forgot u. u no I did luv u. Life hear is worse than it was tho I no u suffered. i did see it even tho i never sed so. i so u have a good husband now and a baby.*" She had not heard of the recent addition. "*i want u to no i still think of u. if i cud i wud send u sweets. think of me. B.*"

Then began our correspondence. It had the same character as our old Saturday-morning eruptions had had. I tried to write regularly over the next four years despite our many moves, our growing family, and my own work. She had awakened some sense of loyalty that I wanted to keep alive. Her notes came spasmodically, almost as if some moment in her life that laid claim on

her with a particular stranglehold forced her to choke out a letter
to a faraway friend.   One came, two years ago now, which read in
part: *"u no, dear one, that if i cud, i wud have left myself. but where
wud i go?"*

It saddened me.   Where would she go?   She could never at this
point — for she was well over sixty, I thought — go anywhere.
And she suffered so there.   That was clear from her notes, almost
illegible and illiterate as they were.

Then this.   "Sister Barnabas MacLean."

There was something offensive and compelling in it.   I had had
no plan ever to revisit that convent.   I had been going to pass
right through Saddleburg with no train stop at all that night because I was at the tail end of my journey, at that point of fatigue
that leaves the traveler with only one desire: to get back to the
warm comforts of home.   I still had a distance to go.   At Montreal
Tom would meet me and we would fly from there back to Vancouver to collect the children from the grandparents before heading home.   Home.   Somehow, sitting over the last of the chocolate
sundae in the Holiday Inn that night in November, I wanted desperately to be back home, fast.

But first this.   Barney.   I reread the notice several times.   There
was no way around it.   If I chose to, thanks to the breakdown of
the good old CN, I could see Barney for one last time.   If I chose
to.   That was the hitch.   There wasn't likely to be anyone there
that I knew except Barney.   What kept me sitting over the second
and then the third cup of coffee that night was not any fear that
familiar faces would awaken old discomforts; it was simply the
question of whether I wanted to see Barney that way.

But there was something else that stirred me, that finally made
me gather up the check and head for the room to ready myself
and call a cab.   It wasn't quite the banality of paying one's last
respects but, to be honest, it had something of that in it.   Mixed
with the need, perhaps, to confirm in my own sensibilities the fact
that Barney was dead.   My going had something to do with her
and something to do with me.   For her it seemed somehow right,
foolish as it is to suppose our visits of final deference have a thing
to do with the dead themselves.   But what exactly was that feeling?   That someone coming, someone from the outside who had
known her on the inside, who had understood her own alienation

and perhaps re-enacted it in another way, that my coming was —
what is the word — "fitting"? Right. Somehow a circle come
complete. For me the meaning was clear. It cut a continuity.
Not at all a physical continuity like the loss of a child or a parent.
A spiritual continuity. That point of common understanding in
this world was gone. Just that. Gone. I had to be sure. And
honor its reality.

So I went. The taxi was about five minutes late, time enough
for me to stand in front of the Holiday Inn stamping my feet as I
tensed myself against that November air, time enough to lose myself for a few moments in that resplendent sky. There really is
nothing like it elsewhere: of that I'm convinced. By day the
scenery there would have to be called bleak: the long low marshes,
few sloping hills, forests of evergreens, stubbly farmlands, gray
barns — a littered landscape of indigence and lack of imagination.
But by night that disappears. It was years — twenty-one to be
exact — since I had felt my neck grow stiff as I strained to follow
this design, then that, in the fluffing Milky Way. Orion. The Big
Dipper. A night world of pattern revealed by depthless black.
The world above. Barney up there?

The taxi came and I slammed in, gathering my inner forces for
this last visit. It had about it that character and I was sensitive to
it. How often in this life was I likely to find myself alone, traveling, away from family and friends, driving through a landscape
that once had held me, revisiting it almost as if I were someone
else? It was a privileged moment. I felt that.

I asked the taxi driver to wait. The convent was the same. I
could just make out the familiar dimensions in the darkness: the
heavy front door, the wing with the cells and the community
room in it to the left, the chapel wing to the right. Extending out
back, invisible from the front, would be Barney's wing, the
kitchen. Who, I wondered, took over?

"Good evening." The sister was politely inquiring as she
opened the door and held it ajar for me to explain myself. She
was middle-aged, rather nondescript. Her face had that blond
look that ages poorly, pale shading into paler. Her modernized
habit was unflattering.

"Good evening. I've come to pay my respects to Sister Barnabas." I didn't even stumble over the formula. It came with the
mechanicalness that gets us through some of life's worse mo-

ments. I was caught up in a sensation I hadn't expected: utter familiarity. For one brief instant I had the urge to say to the sister, *"And if you'll just stand aside, I'll find my way to her cell and the kitchen."* But I didn't. I behaved. There was something indescribably strange in that moment of unintended masquerade. Strange — and comic.

"Come in." She smiled faintly, then turned wordlessly as I shut the door behind me and, ignoring the heavy inner doors that read CLOISTER, led me through another door to the right into a small parlor. Of course. I had forgotten that. They would wake her in one of the outside rooms so the public could come. *The public.* The garbageman? The milkman? I wondered who had come. That barrier of inside-outside had been so thoroughly obscured in my mind that it was a momentary shock to come smack up against it. The Cloister Door. I had lived on the other side of that. But here, Barney and I re-met on the outside. Had we been there all along?

There was no one in the visitors' parlor except the casket with Barney in it and one nun praying. This I dreaded. I hate corpses. I hate going to look. Why on earth this compulsion to see Barney again? Then, steeling inner responses, I walked over and knelt automatically at the priedieu before her.

It wasn't Barney. Of course it was, but it wasn't Barney. She was in the habit, hands folded, rosary through them. I had never seen her look neat. Her headdress was straight. Her whiskers were gone. Whoever prepared the corpse had shaven the chin smooth, removing one of Barney's most characteristic marks. She was smiling — that pasty, waxen smile meant to reassure us that wherever she was, things weren't that bad. I had never seen that smile on Barney. Her forehead was smooth. No scowl. She lay in a simple box, as was the custom, with a white lining. There were no flowers. Those I didn't miss. But I wanted ivy, arbutus, philodendron, African violets, *impatiens* — the plant that always seemed to fit Barney. I wanted them all there, surrounding her indiscriminately. I wanted the scowl. Maybe a big cake on the casket saying "Goodbye," with a kitten on the top. Something colorful. The quilt as a lining for the casket. I didn't want this effigy of nunhood, of dedication and service. I wanted the real thing: screaming dissonances in that sterile setting.

Nowhere could I find it. I could imagine her kitchen. Someone would have cleaned it already. Of her room I hated to think. What had happened to the bosomy lady in front of her cottage? Was the plastic Madonna already at the dump? The nun behind me went on praying. The silence was oppressive. A tall beeswax taper at the end of the bier sent flickers of shadow across the still form. It wasn't Barney.

I nodded to the sister and headed for the door. There, Sister Poker-Face was waiting for me and she noiselessly opened the outer door. I could see the exhaust from the taxi billowing pale gray in the darkness. He had kept the engine idling against the cold.

"Thank you for coming. She is at peace."

I nodded. I wanted to rage. I wanted to scream, "You don't know me, but I know you. You didn't know Barney, but I knew her!" What was the point? There was no way. Could any scream penetrate it?

As I walked down the path I heard the heavy door click behind me. Then, one look up. I was grateful for the cold air. And stars. The vast Milky Way. The sky that turned all this dark and illumined its own shuddering spaces with something not warm but clear. Cold. It cleansed. I breathed deep and looked for a long moment. Goodbye, sky. Then I heard the motor revving. The cabbie leaned over and opened my door.

At first in the halting spasms, then with that satisfying surge of power that says all connections have been made, our engine built up to a steady rhythm. Spent, I leaned back against the seat and closed my eyes, grateful to be borne away in the dark.

JOHN WILLIAM CORRINGTON

Pleadings

(FROM THE SOUTHERN REVIEW)

DINNER was on the table when the phone rang, and Joan just stared at me.

— Go ahead, answer it. Maybe they need you in Washington.

— I don't want to get disbarred, I said. — More likely they need me at the Parish Prison.

I was closer than she was. It was Bertram Bijou, a deputy out in Jefferson Parish. He had a friend. With troubles. Being a lawyer, you find out that nobody has trouble, really. It's always a friend.

— Naw, on the level Bert said. — You know Howard Bedlow?

No, I didn't know Howard Bedlow, but I would pretty soon.

They came to the house after supper. As a rule, I put people off when they want to come to the house. They've got eight hours a day to find out how to incorporate, write a will, pull their taxes down, or whatever. In the evening I like to sit quiet with Joan. We read and listen to Haydn or Boccherini and watch the light fade over uptown New Orleans. Sometimes, though I do not tell her, I like to imagine we are a late Roman couple sitting in our atrium in the countryside of England, not far from Londinium. It is always summer, and Septimus Severus has not yet begun to tax Britain out of existence. Still, it is twilight now, and there is nothing before us. We are young, but the world is old, and that is all right because the drive and the hysteria of destiny is past now, and we can sit and enjoy our garden, the twisted ivy, the huge caladiums, and if it is April, the daffodils that plunder our weak sun and sparkle across the land. It is always cool in my fantasy, and Joan crochets something for the center of our table, and I refuse to think of the burdens of administration that I will have to lift again tomorrow. They will wait, and Rome will never even know. It is always a hushed single moment, ageless and serene, and I am with her, and only the hopeless are still ambitious. Everything we will do has been done, and for the moment there is peace.

It is a silly fantasy, dreamed here in the heart of booming America, but it makes me happy, and so I was likely showing my mild irritation when Bert and his friend Howard Bedlow turned up. I tried to be kind. For several reasons. Bert is a nice man. An honest deputy, a politician in a small way, and perhaps what the Civil Law likes to call *un bon père du famille* — though I think at Common Law Bert would be "an officious intermeddler." He seems prone to get involved with people. Partly because he would like very much to be on the Kenner City Council one day, but, I like to imagine, as much because there lingers in the Bijou blood some tincture of piety brought here and nurtured by his French sires and his Sicilian and Spanish maternal ascendants. New Orleans has people like that. A certain kindness, a certain sympathy left over from the days when one person's anguish or that of a family was the business of all their neighbors. Perhaps that fine and profound Catholic certainty of death and judgment which makes us all one.

And beyond approving Bert as a type, I have found that most people who come for law are in one way or another distressed: the distress of loss or fear, of humiliation or sudden realization. Or the more terrible distress of greed, appetite gone wild, the very biggest of deals in the offing, and O, my God, don't let me muff it.

Howard Bedlow was in his late forties. He might have been the Celtic gardener in my imaginary Roman garden. Taller than average, hair a peculiar reddish gold more suited to a surfing king than to an unsuccessful car salesman, he had that appearance of a man scarce half made up that I had always associated with European workmen and small tradesmen. His cuffs were frayed and too short. His collar seemed wrong; it fit neither his neck nor the thin stringy tie he wore knotted more or less under it. Once, some years ago, I found, he had tried to make a go of his own Rambler franchise, only to see it go down like a gutshot animal, month by month, week by week, until at last no one, not even the manager of the taco place next door, would cash his checks or give him a nickel for a local phone call.

Now he worked, mostly on commission, for one used-car lot or another, as Bert told it. He had not gone bankrupt in the collapse of the Rambler business, but had sold his small house on the west bank and had paid off his debts, almost all of them dollar for dollar, fifty here, ten there. When I heard that, I decided against offering them coffee. I got out whiskey. You serve a man what he's worth, even if he invades your fantasies.

As Bert talked on, only pausing to sip his bourbon, Bedlow sat staring into his glass, his large hands cupping it, his fingers moving restlessly around its rim, listening to Bert as if he himself had no stake in all that was passing. I had once known a musician who had sat that way when people caught him in a situation where talk was inevitable. Like Bedlow, he was not resentful, only elsewhere, and his hands, trained to a mystical perfection, worked over and over certain passages in some silent score.

Bedlow looked up as Bert told about the house trailer he, Bedlow, lived in now — or had lived in until a week or so before. Bedlow frowned almost sympathetically, as if he could find some measure of compassion for a poor man who had come down so far.

— Now I got to be honest, Bert said at last, drawing a deep breath. — Howard, he didn't want to come. Bad times with lawyers.

— I can see that, I said.

— He can't put all that car-franchise mess out of mind. Bitter, you know. Gone down hard. Lawyers like vultures, all over the place.

Bedlow nodded, frowning. Not in agreement with Bert on his own behalf, but as if he, indifferent to all this, could appreciate a man being bitter, untrusting after so much. I almost wondered if the trouble wasn't Bert's, so distant from it Bedlow seemed.

— I got to be honest, Bert said again. Then he paused, looking down at his whiskey. Howard studied his drink, too.

— I told Howard he could come along with me to see you, or I had to take him up to Judge Talley. DWI, property damage, foul and abusive, resisting, public obscenity. You could pave the river with charges. I mean it.

All right. You could. And sometimes did. Some wise-ass tries to take apart Millie's Bar, the only place for four blocks where a working man can sit back and sip one without a lot of hassle. You take and let him consider the adamantine justice of Jefferson Parish for thirty days or six months before you turn him loose at the causeway and let him drag back to St. Tammany Parish with what's left of his tail tucked between his legs. Discretion of the Officer. That's the way it is, the way it's always been, the way it'll be till the whole human race learns how to handle itself in Millie's Bar.

But you don't do that with a friend. Makes no sense. You don't cart him off to Judge Elmer Talley, who is the scourge of the working class if the working class indulges in what others call the curse of the working class. No, Bert was clubbing his buddy. To get him to an Officer of the Court. All right.

— He says he wants a divorce, Bert said. — Drinks like a three-legged hog and goes to low-rating his wife in public and so on. Ain't that fine?

No, Bedlow acknowledged, frowning, shaking his head. It was *not* fine. He agreed with Bert, you could tell. It was sorry, too damned bad.

— I'm not going to tell you what he called his wife over to Sammie's Lounge last night. Sammie almost hit him. You know what I mean?

Yes I did. Maybe, here and there, the fire is not entirely out. I have known a man to beat another very nearly to death because the first spoke slightingly of his own mother. One does not talk that way about women folk, not even one's own. The lowly, the ignored, and the abused remember what the high-born and the wealthy have forgotten.

— Are you separated, I asked Bedlow.

— I ain't livin with the woman, he said laconically. It was the first time he had spoken since he came into my house.

— What's the trouble?

He told me. Told me in detail while Bert listened and made faces of astonishment and disbelief at me. Bert could still be astonished after seventeen years on the Jefferson Parish Sheriff's squad. You wonder that I like him?

It seemed that there had been adultery. A clear and flagrant act of faithlessness resulting in a child. A child that was not his, not a Bedlow. He had been away, in the wash of his financial troubles, watching the Rambler franchise expire, trying hard to do right. And she did it, swore to Christ and the Virgin she never did it, and went to confinement carrying another man's child.

— When, I asked. — How old is . . . ?

— Nine, Bedlow said firmly. — He's . . . it's nine . . .

I stared at Bert. He shrugged. It seemed to be no surprise to him. Oh, hell, I thought. Maybe what this draggle-assed country needs is an emperor. Even if he taxes us to death and declares war on Guatemala. This is absurd.

— Mr. Bedlow, I said. — You can't get a divorce for adultery with a situation like that.

— How come?

— You've been living with her all that . . . nine years?

— Yeah.

— They . . . call it reconciliation. No way. If you stay on, you are presumed . . . what the hell. How long have you lived apart?

— Two weeks and two days, he answered. I suspected he could have told me the hours and minutes.

— I couldn't take it anymore. Knowing what I know . . .

Bedlow began to cry. Bert looked away, and I suppose I did. I have not seen many grown men cry cold sober. I have seen them mangled past any hope of life, twisting, screaming, cursing. I have seen them standing by a wrecked car while police and firemen tried to saw loose the bodies of their wives and children. I have seen men, told of the death of their one son, stand hard-jawed, with tears running down their slabby sunburned cheeks, but that was not crying. Bedlow was crying, and he did not seem the kind of man who cries.

I motioned Bert back into the kitchen. — What the hell . . .

— This man, Bert said, spreading his hands, — is in trouble.

— All right, I said, hearing Bedlow out in the parlor, still sobbing as if something more than his life might be lost. — All right. But I don't think it's a lawyer he needs.

Bert frowned, outraged. — Well, he sure don't need one of . . . them.

I could not be sure whether he was referring to priests or psychiatrists. Or both. Bert trusted the law. Even working with it, knowing better than I its open sores and ugly fissures, he believed in it, and for some reason saw me as one of its dependable functionaries. I guess I was pleased by that.

— Fill me in on this whole business, will you?

Yes, he would, and would have earlier over the phone, but he had been busy mollifying Sammie and some of his customers who wanted to lay charges that Bert could not have sidestepped. It was short and ugly, and I was hooked. Bedlow's wife was a good woman. The child was a hopeless defective. It was kept up at Pineville, at the Louisiana hospital for the feebleminded, or whatever the social scientists are calling imbeciles this year. A vegetating thing that its mother had named Albert Sidney Bedlow before they had taken it away, hooked it up for a lifetime of intravenous feeding, and added it to the schedule for cleaning up filth and washing, and all the things they do for human beings who can do nothing whatever for themselves. But Irma Bedlow couldn't let it go at that. The state is equipped, albeit poorly, for this kind of thing. It happens. You let the thing go, and they see to it, and one day, usually not long hence, it dies of pneumonia or a virus, or one of the myriad diseases that float and sift through the air of a place like that. This is the way these things are done, and all of us at the law have drawn up papers for things called "Baby So-and-so," sometimes, mercifully, without their parents' having laid eyes on them.

Irma Bedlow saw it otherwise. During that first year, while the Rambler franchise was bleeding to death, while Bedlow was going half-crazy, she had spent most of her time up in Alexandria, a few miles from the hospital, at her cousin's. So that she could visit Albert Sidney every day.

She would go there, Bert told me — as Bedlow had told him — and sit in the drafty ward on a hard chair next to Albert Sidney's chipped institutional crib, with her rosary, praying to Jesus Christ that He would send down His grace on her baby, make him whole, and let her suffer in his place. She would kneel in the twilight beside the bed stiff with urine, and stinking of such excrement as a child might produce who has never tasted food, amidst the bedlam of chattering and choking and animal sounds from bedridden idiots, cretins, declining mongoloids, microcephalics, and assorted other exiles from the great altarpiece of Hieronymus Bosch. Somehow, the chief psychologist had told Howard, her praying upset the other inmates of the ward, and at last he had to forbid Irma coming more than once a month. He told her that the praying was out altogether.

After trying to change the chief psychologist's mind, and failing, Irma had come home. The franchise was gone by then, and they had a secondhand trailer parked in a run-down court where they got water, electricity, and gas from pipes in the ground and a sullen old man in a prewar Desoto station wagon picked up garbage once a week. She said the rosary there, and talked about Albert Sidney to her husband who, cursed now with freedom by the ruin of his affairs, doggedly looking for some kind of a job, had nothing much to do or think about but his wife's abstracted words and the son he had almost had. Indeed, did have, but had in such a way that the having was more terrible than the lack.

It had taken no time to get into liquor, which his wife never touched, she fasting and praying, determined that no small imperfection in herself should stay His hand who could set things right with Albert Sidney in the flash of a moment's passing.

— And in that line, Bert said, — she ain't . . . they . . . never been man and wife since then. You know what I mean?

— Ummm.

— And she runs off on him. Couple or three times a year. They always find her at the cousin's. At least till last year. Her cousin won't have her around anymore. Seems Irma wanted her to fast for Albert Sidney, too. Wanted the cousin's whole family to do it, and there was words, and now she just takes a room at a tourist court by the hospital and tries to get in as often as that chief psychologist will let her. But no praying, he holds to that.

— What does Bedlow believe?

— Claims he believes she got Albert Sidney with some other man.

— No, I mean . . . does he believe in praying?

— Naw. Too honest, I guess. Says he don't hold with beads and saying the same thing over and over. Says God stands on His own feet, and expects the same of us. Says we ain't here to shit around. What's done is done.

— Do you think he wants a divorce?

— Could he get one . . .?

— Yes.

— Well, how do I know?

— You brought him here. He's not shopping for religious relics, is he?

Bert looked hurt. As if I were blaming him unfairly for some situation beyond his control or prevention.

— You want him in jail?

— No, I said. — I just don't know what to do about him. Where's he living?

— Got a cabin at the Bo-Peep Motel. Over off Veterans Highway. He puts in his time at the car lot and then goes to drinking and telling people his wife has done bastardized him.

— Why did he wait so long to come up with that line?

— It just come on him, what she must of done, he told me.

— That's right, Bedlow said, his voice raspy, aggressive. — I ain't educated or anything. I studied on it and after so long it come to me. I saw it wasn't *mine*, that . . . thing of hers. Look, how come she can't just get done mourning and say, well, that's how it falls out sometimes and I'm sorry as all hell, but you got to keep going. That's what your ordinary woman would say, ain't it?

He had come into the kitchen where Bert and I were standing, his face still wet with tears. He came in talking, and the flow went on as if he were as compulsive with his tongue as he was with a bottle. The words tumbled out so fast that you felt he must have practiced, this country man, to speak so rapidly, to say so much.

— But no. I tell you what: she's mourning for what she done to that . . . thing's real father, that's what she's been doing. He likely lives in Alex, and she can't get over what she done him when she got that . . . thing. And I tell you this, I said, look, honey, don't give it no name, 'cause if you give it a name, you're gonna think that name over and over and make like it was the name of a person and it ain't, and it'll ruin us just as sure as creaking hell. And she went and named it my father's name, who got it after Albert Sidney Johnston at Shiloh . . . look, I ain't laid a hand on that woman in God knows how many years, I tell you that. So you see, that's what these trips is about. She goes up and begs his pardon for not giving him a fine boy like he wanted, and she goes to see . . . the thing, and mourns . . . and goddamnit to hell, I got to get shut of this . . . whole *thing*.

It came in a rush, as if, even talking, saying more words in the space of a moment than he had ever said before, Bedlow was enlarging, perfecting his suspicions — no, his certainty of what had been done to him.

We were silent for a moment.

— Well, it's hard, Bert said at last.

— Hard, Bedlow glared at him as if Bert had insulted him. — You don't even know hard . . .

— All right, I said. — We'll go down to the office in the morning and draw up and file.

— Huh?

— We'll file for legal separation. Will your wife contest it?

— Huh?

— I'm going to get you what you want. Will your wife go along?

— Well, I don't know. She don't . . . think about . . . things. If you was to tell her, I don't know.

Bert looked at him, his large dark face settled and serious. — That woman's a . . . Catholic, he said at last, and Bedlow stared back at him as if he had named a new name, and things needed thinking again.

A little while later they left, with Bedlow promising me and promising Bertram Bijou that he'd be in my office the next morning. For a long time after I closed the door behind them, I sat looking at the empty whiskey glasses and considered the course of living in the material world. Then I went and fixed me a shaker of martinis, and became quickly wiser. I considered that it was time to take Zeno seriously, give over the illusion of motion, of sequence. There are only a few moments in any life and when they arrive, they are fixed forever and we play through them, pretending to go on, but coming back to them over and over, again and again. If it is true that we can only approach a place but never reach it as the Philosopher claims, it must be corollary that we may almost leave a moment, but never quite. And so, as Dr. Freud so clearly saw, one moment, one vision, one thing come upon us, becomes the whole time and single theme of all we will ever do or know. We are invaded by our own one thing, and going on is a dream we have while lying still.

I thought, too, mixing one last shaker, that of the little wisdom in this failing age, Alcoholics Anonymous must possess more than its share. I am an alcoholic, they say. I have not had a drink in nine years, but I am an alcoholic, and the shadow, the motif of my living is liquor bubbling into a glass over and over, again and again. That is all I really want, and I will never have it again because I will not take it, and I know that I will never really know why not.

— It's bedtime, Joan said, taking my drink and sipping it.

— What did they want?

— A man wants a divorce because nine years ago his wife had a feeble-minded baby. He says it's not his. Wants me to claim adultery and unclaim the child.

— Nice man.

— Actually, I began. Then no. Bedlow did not seem a nice man or not a nice man. He seemed a driven man, outside whatever might be his element. So I said that.

— Who isn't, Joan sniffed. She is not the soul of charity at two-thirty in the morning.

— What? Isn't what?

— Driven. Out of her . . . his . . . element?

I looked at her. Is it the commonest of things for men in their forties to consider whether their women are satisfied? Is it a sign of the spirit's collapse when you wonder how and with whom she spends her days? What is the term for less than suspicion: a tiny circlet of thought that touches your mind at lunch with clients or on the way to the office, almost enough to make you turn back home, and then disappears like smoke when you try to fix it, search for a word or an act that might have stirred it to life?

— Are you . . . driven, I asked much too casually.

— Me? No, she sighed kissing me. — I'm different, she said. Was she too casual, too?

— Bedlow isn't different. I think he wants it all never to have happened. He had a little car franchise and a pregnant wife ten years ago. Clover. He had it made. Then it all went away.

Joan lit a cigarette, crossed her legs, and sat down on the floor with my drink. Her wrapper fell open, and I saw the shadow of her breasts. — It always goes away. If you know anything, you know that. Hang on as long as you can. 'Cause it's going away. If you know anything . . .

I looked at her as she talked. She was as beautiful as the first time I had seen her. It was an article of faith: nothing had changed. Her body was still as soft and warm in my arms, and I wait for summer to see her in a bathing suit, and to see her take it off, water running out of her blond hair, between her breasts that I love better than whatever it is that I love next best.

— Sometimes it doesn't go away, I said. Ponderously, I'm sure.

She cocked her head, almost said something, and sipped the drink instead.

What made me think then of the pictures there in the parlor? I

went over them in the silence, the flush of gin, remembering
where and when we had bought each one. That one in San Francisco, in a Japanese gallery, I thinking that I would not like it
long, but thinking too that it didn't matter, since we were at the
end of a long difficult case with a fee to match. So if I didn't like
it later, well . . .
   And the Danish ship, painted on wood in the seventeenth century. I still liked it very much. But why did I think of these
things? Was it that they stood on the walls, amidst our lives, adding some measure of substance and solidity to them, making it
seem that the convention of living together, holding lovely things
in common, added reality to the lives themselves. Then, or was it
later, I saw us sitting not in a Roman garden in Britain, but in a
battered house trailer in imperial America, the walls overspread
with invisible pictures of the image of a baby's twisted unfinished
face. And how would that be? How would we do then?
   Joan smiled, lightly sardonic. — Ignore it, and it'll go away.
   — Was there . . . something I was supposed to do, I asked.
   The smile deepened, then faded. — Not a thing, she said.

   The next morning, a will was made, two houses changed hands,
a corporation, closely held, was born, seven suits were filed, and a
deposition was taken from a whore who claimed that her right of
privacy was invaded when the vice squad caught her performing
an act against nature on one of their members in a French Quarter alley. Howard Bedlow did not turn up. Joan called just after
lunch.
   — I think I'll go over to the beach house for a day or two, she
said, her voice flat and uncommunicative as only a woman's can
be.
   I guess there was a long pause. It crossed my mind that once I
had wanted to be a musician, perhaps even learn to compose. —
I can't get off till the day after tomorrow, I said, knowing that my
words were inapposite to anything she might have in mind. — I
could come Friday.
   — That would be nice.
   — Are you . . . taking the children?
   — Louise will take care of them.
   — You'll be . . . by yourself?
   A pause on her side this time.
   — Yes. Sometimes . . . things get out of hand.

— Anything you want to talk about?

She laughed. — You're the talker in the family.

— And you're what? The actor. Or the thinker?

— That's it. I don't know.

My voice went cold then. I couldn't help it. — Let me know if you figure it out. Then I hung up. And thought at once that I shouldn't have, and yet glad of the minuscule gesture because, however puny, it was an act, and acts in law are almost always merely words. I live in a storm of words: words substituting for actions, words to evade actions, words hinting of actions, words pretending actions. I looked down at the deposition on my desk and wondered if they had caught the whore *talking* to the vice squad man in the alley. Give her ten years: the utterance of words is an act against nature, an authentic act against nature. I had read somewhere that in Chicago they have opened establishments wherein neither massage nor sex is offered: only a woman who, for a sum certain in money, will talk to you. She will say anything you want her to say: filth, word-pictures of every possible abomination, fantasies of domination and degradation, sadistic orgies strewn out in detail, oaths, descriptions of rape and castration. For a few dollars you can be told how you molested a small child, how you have murdered your parents and covered the carcasses with excrement, assisted in the gang rape of your second-grade teacher. All words.

The authentic crime against nature has finally arrived. It is available somewhere in Chicago. There is no penalty, for after all, it is protected by the first amendment. Scoff on, Voltaire, Rousseau, scoff on.

My secretary, who would like to speak filth to me, buzzed.

— Mr. Bijou.

— Good. Send him in.

— On the phone.

Bert sounded far away. — You ain't seen Howard, have you?

— No, I said. — Have you?

— Drunk somewhere. Called coughing and moaning something about a plot to shame him. Talking like last night. I think you ought to see Irma. You're supposed to seek reconciliation, ain't you?

— I think you're ripe for law school, Bert. Yes, that's what they say do.

— Well, he said. — Lemme see what I can do.

I was afraid of that. When I got home there was a note from Louise, the childrens' nurse. She had taken them to her place up in Livingston Parish for a day or two. They would like that. The house was deserted, and I liked that. Not really. I wondered what a fast trip to the Gulf Coast would turn up, or a call to a friend of mine in Biloxi who specializes in that kind of thing. But worse, I wasn't sure I cared. Was it that I didn't love Joan anymore, that somewhere along the way I had become insulated against her acts? Could it be that the practice of law had slowly made me responsive only to words? Did I need to go to Chicago to feel real again?

I was restless and drank too many martinis and was involved so much in my own musings that time passed quickly. I played some Beethoven, God knows why. I am almost never so distraught that I enjoy spiritual posturing. Usually, his music makes me grin.

I tried very hard to reckon where I was and what I should do. I was in the twentieth century after Christ, and it felt all of that long since anything on earth had mattered. I was in a democratic empire called America, an officer of its courts, and surely a day in those courts is as a thousand years. I was an artisan in words, shaping destinies, allocating money and blame by my work. I was past the midpoint of my life and could not make out what it had meant so far.

Now amidst this time and place, I could do almost as I chose. Should it be the islands of the Pacific with a box of paints? To the Colorado mountains with a pack, beans, a guitar, pencils, and much paper? Or, like an anchorite, declare the longest of nonterminal hunger strikes, this one against God Almighty, hoping that public opinion forces Him to reveal that for which I was made and put in this place and time?

Or why not throw over these ambiguities, this wife doing whatever she might be doing on the coast of the Gulf, these anonymous children content with Louise up the country, contemplating chickens, ducks, and guinea fowl. Begin again. Say every word you have ever said, to new people: hello, new woman, I love you. I have good teeth and most of my mind. I can do well on a good night in a happy bed. Hello, new colleagues, what do we do this time? Is this a trucking firm or a telephone exchange? What is the desideratum? Profit or prophecy?

Bert shook my arm. — Are you okay? You didn't answer the door.

I studied him for a moment, my head soft and uncentered. I
was nicely drunk, but coming back. — Yeah, I said. — I'm fine.
What have you got going?
— Huh? Listen, can I turn down that music?
— Sure.
He doused the Second Symphony, and I found I was relieved,
could breathe more deeply. — I brought her, he said. — She's
kinda spaced out, like the kids say.
He frowned, watched me. — Are you sure you're all right?
I smiled. — All I needed was some company, Bert.
He smiled back. — All right, fine. You're probably in the best
kind of shape for Irma.
— Huh?
He looked at the empty martini pitcher. — Nothing. She's
just . . .
His voice trailed off and I watched him drift out of my line of
sight. In the foyer, I could hear his voice, soft and distant, as if
he were talking to a child.
I sobered up. Yes, I have that power. I discovered it in law
school. However drunk, I can gather back in the purposely
loosed strands of personality or whatever of us liquor casts apart.
It is as if one were never truly sober, and hence one could claim
back from liquor what it had never truly loosed. Either drunken-
ness or sobriety is an illusion.
Irma Bedlow was a surprise. I had reckoned on a woman well
gone from womanhood. One of those shapeless bun-haired middle-aged creatures wearing bifocals, smiling out from behind the
secrecy of knowing that they are at last safe from any but the most
psychotic menaces from unbalanced males. But it was not that
way. If I had been dead drunk on the one hand, or shuffling up
to the communion rail on the other, she would have turned me
around.
She was vivid. Dark hair and eyes, a complexion almost pale, a
lovely body made more so by the thoughtless pride with which she
inhabited it. She sat down opposite me, and our eyes held for a
long moment.
I am used to a certain deference from people who come to me
in legal situations. God knows we have worked long and hard
enough to establish the mandarin tradition of the law, that circle
of mysteries that swallows up laymen and all they possess like a
vast desert or a hidden sea. People come to the law on tiptoe,

watching, wishing they could know which words, what expressions and turns of phrase are *the ones* which bear their fate. I have smiled remembering that those who claim or avoid the law with such awe have themselves in their collectivity created it. But they are so far apart from one another in the sleep of their present lives that they cannot remember what they did together when they were awake.

But Irma Bedlow looked at me as if she were the counselor, her dark eyes fixed on mine to hold me to whatever I might say. Would I lie, and put both our cases in jeopardy? Would I say the best I knew, or had I wandered so long amidst the stunted shrubs of language, making unnatural acts in the name of my law, that words had turned from stones with which to build into ropy clinging undergrowth in which to become enmeshed?

I asked her if she would have a drink. I was surprised when she said yes. Fasts for the sake of an idiot child, trying to get others to do it, praying on her knees to Jesus beside the bed of Albert Sidney, who did not know about the prayers and who could know about Jesus only through infused knowledge there within the mansions of his imbecility. But yes, she said, and I went to fix it.

Of course Bert followed me over to the bar. — I don't know. I think maybe I ought to take care of Howard and let *her* be your client.

— Don't do that, I said, and wondered why I'd said it.

— She's fine, Bert was saying, and I knew he meant nothing to do with her looks. He was not a carnal man, Bert. He was a social man. Once he had told me he wanted either to be mayor of Kenner or a comedian. He did not mean it humorously and I did not take it so. He was the least funny of men. Rather he understood with his nerves the pathos of living and would have liked to divert us from it with comedy. But it would not be so, and Bert would end up mayor trying to come to grips with our common anguish instead of belittling it.

— I never talked to anyone like her. You'll see.

I think then I envisioned the most beautiful and desirable Jehovah's Witness in the world. Would we try conclusions over Isaiah? I warn you, Irma, I know the Book and other books beyond number. I am a prince in the kingdom of words, and I have seen raw respect flushed up unwillingly in the eyes of other lawmongers, and have had my work mentioned favorably in appellate decisions which, in their small way, rule all this land.

— Here you are, I said.

She smiled at me as if I were a child who had brought his mother a cool drink unasked.

— Howard came to see you, she said, sipping the martini as if gin bruised with vermouth were her common fare. — Can you help me . . . help him?

— He wants a divorce, I said, confused, trying to get things in focus.

— No, she said. Not aggressively, only firmly. Her information was better than mine. I have used the same tone of voice with other attorneys many times. When you know, you know.

— He only wants it over with, done with. That's what he wants.

Bert nodded. He had heard this before. There goes Bert's value as a checkpoint with reality. He believes her. Lordy.

— You mean . . . the marriage?

— No, not that. He knows what I know. If it *was* a marriage, you can't make it be over. You can only desert it. He wouldn't do that.

I shrugged, noticing that she had made no use of her beauty at all so far. She did not disguise it or deny it. She allowed it to exist and simply ignored it. Her femininity washed over me, and yet I knew that it was not directed toward me. It had some other focus, and she saw me as a moment, a crossing in her life, an occasion to stop and turn back for an instant before going on. I wondered what I would be doing for her.

— He *says* he wants a divorce.

She looked down at her drink. Her lashes were incredibly long, though it was obvious she used no makeup at all. Her lips were deep red, a color not used in lipsticks since the forties. I understood why Bedlow drank. Nine years with a beautiful woman you love and cannot touch. Is that your best idea?

— He told you . . . I'd been unfaithful.

Bert was shaking his head, blushing. Not negating what Howard had said, or deprecating it.

— He said that, I told her.

— And that our baby . . . that Albert Sidney wasn't . . . his?

— Yes, I said. Bert looked as if he would cry from shame.

She had not looked up while we talked. Her eyes stayed down,

and while I waited, I heard the Beethoven tape, turned down but
not off, running out at the end of the "Appassionata." It was a
good moment to get up and change to something decent. I found
a Vivaldi Chamber Mass, and the singers were very happy. The
music was for God in the first instance, not for the spirit of frater-
nity or Napoleon or some other rubbish.

— What else, she asked across the room. I flipped the tape on,
and eighteenth-century Venice came at us from four sides. I cut
back the volume.

— He said you . . . hadn't been man and wife for nine years.

— All right.

I walked back and sat down again. I felt peculiar, neither
drunk nor sober, so I poured another one. The first I'd had since
they came. — Howard didn't seem to think so. He said . . . you
wouldn't let him touch you.

She raised her eyes then. Not angrily, only that same firmness
again. — That's not true, she said, no, whispered, and Bert nodded as though he had been an abiding presence in the marriage
chamber for all those nine long years. He could contain himself
no more. He fumbled in his coat pocket and handed me a crumpled and folded sheet of paper. It was a notice from American
Motors canceling Howard Bedlow's franchise. Much boilerplate
saying he hadn't delivered and so on. Enclosed find copy of
agency contract with relevant revocation clauses underlined. Arrangements will be made for stock on hand, etc.

It was dated 9 May 1966. Bert was watching me. I nodded. —
Eight years ago, I said.

— Not ten, Bert was going on. — You see . . .

— He lost the business . . . six months after . . . the . . . Albert
Sidney.

We sat looking at the paper.

— I never denied him, Irma was saying. — After the baby . . .
he couldn't. At first, we didn't think of it, of anything. I . . . we
were lost inside ourselves. We didn't talk about it. What had we
done? What had gone wrong? What were we . . . supposed to
do? Was there something we were supposed to do?

— Genes went wrong . . . hormones, who knows, I said.

Irma smiled at me. Her eyes were black, not brown. — Do you
believe that?

— Sure, I said, startled as one must be when he has uttered

what passes for a common truth and it is questioned. — What else?

— Nothing, she said. — It's only . . .

She and Bert were both staring at me as if I had missed something. Then Irma leaned forward. — Will you go somewhere with me?

I was thinking of the Gulf Coast, staring down at the face of my watch. It was almost one-thirty. There was a moon and the tide was in, and the moon would be rolling through soft beds of cloud.

— Yes, I said. — Yes I will. Yes.

It was early in the morning when we reached Alexandria. The bus trip had been long and strange. We had talked about east Texas, where Irma had grown up. Her mother had been from Evangeline Parish, her father a tool-pusher in the Kilgore fields until he lost both hands to a wild length of chain. She had been keeping things together working as a waitress when she met Howard.

On the bus, as if planted there, had been a huge black woman with a little boy whose head was tiny and pointed. It was so distorted that his eyes were pulled almost vertical. He made inarticulate noises and rooted about on the floor of the bus. The other passengers tried to ignore him, but the stench was very bad, and his mother took him to an empty seat in back and changed him several times. Irma helped her once. The woman had been loud, aggressive, unfriendly when Irma approached her, but Irma whispered something, and the woman began to cry, her sobs loud and terrible. When they had gotten the child cleaned up, the black woman put her arms around Irma and kissed her.

— I tried hard as I could, miss, but I can't manage . . . oh, sweet Jesus knows I wisht I was dead first. But I can't manage the other four . . . I *got* to . . .

The two of them sat together on the rear seat for a long time, holding hands, talking so softly that I couldn't hear. Once, the boy crawled up and stopped at my seat. He looked up at me like some invertebrate given the power to be quizzical. I wondered which of us was in hell. He must have been about twelve years old.

In the station, Irma made a phone call while I had coffee. People moved through the twilight terminal, meeting, parting. One elderly woman in a thin print dress thirty years out of date even among country people kissed a young man in an army uniform good-bye. Her lips trembled as he shouldered his duffel bag and moved away. — Stop, she cried out, and then realized that he could not stop, because the dispatcher was calling the Houston bus. — Have you . . . forgotten anything? The soldier paused, smiled, and shook his head. Then he vanished behind some people trying to gather up clothes which had fallen from a cardboard suitcase with a broken clasp. Somewhere a small child cried as if it had awakened to find itself suddenly, utterly lost.

Irma came back and drank her coffee, and when we walked outside it was daylight in Alexandria, even as on the Gulf Coast. An old station wagon with a broken muffler pulled up, and a thin man wearing glasses got out and kissed Irma as if it were a ritual and shook hands with me in that peculiar limp and diffident way of country people meeting someone from the city who might represent threat or advantage.

We drove for twenty minutes or so, and slowed down in front of a small white frame place on a blacktop road not quite in or out of town. The yard was large and littered with wrecked and cannibalized autos. The metal bones of an old Hudson canted into the rubble of a '42 Ford convertible. Super deluxe. There was a shed which must have been an enlarged garage. Inside I could see tools, a lathe, workbenches. A young man in overalls without a shirt looked out at us and waved casually. He had a piece of drive shaft in his hand. Chickens ambled stupidly in the grassless yard, pecking at oil patches and clumps of rust.

We had eggs and sausage and biscuits and talked quietly. They were not curious about me. They had seen a great deal during the years and there was nothing to be had from curiosity. You come to learn that things have to be taken as they come and it is no use to probe the gestations of tomorrows before they come. There is very little you can do to prepare.

It turned out there had been no quarrel between Irma and her sister's family. Her sister, plain as Irma was beautiful, who wore thick glasses and walked slowly because of her varicose veins, talked almost without expression, but with some lingering touch of her mother's French accent. She talked on as if she had saved everything she had seen and come to know, saved it all in exhaustive detail, knowing that someone would one day come for her report.

— It wasn't never any quarrel, and Howard had got to know better. Oh, we fussed, sure. My daddy always favored Irma and so I used to take after her over anything, you know. Jesus spare me, I guess I hated my own little sister. Till the baby come, and the Lord lifted the scales from my eyes. I dreamed He come down just for me. He looked like Mr. Denver, the station agent down to the L and N depot, and He said "Elenor, I had enough stuff out of you, you hear? You see Albert Sidney? You satisfied now? Huh? Is that enough for you? You tell me that, 'cause I got to be getting on. I don't make nobody more beautiful or more smart or anything in this world, but I do sometimes take away their looks or ruin their minds or put blindness on 'em, or send 'em a trouble to break their hearts. Don't ask why 'cause it's not for you to know, but that's what I do. Now what else you want for Irma, huh?"

Tears were flowing down Elenor's face now, but her expression didn't change. — So I saw it was my doing, and I begged Him to set it right, told Him to strike me dead and set it right with that helpless baby. But He just shook His head and pushed up His sleeves like He could hear a through-freight coming. "It's not how it's done. It ain't like changing your mind about a hat or a new dress. You see that?"

— Well, I didn't, but what could I say? I said yes, and He started off and the place where we was began getting kind of fuzzy, then He turned and looked back at me and smiled. "How you know it *ain't* all right with Albert Sidney," he asked. And I saw then that He loved me after all. Then, when I could hardly see Him, I heard Him say, "Anything you forgot, Elly," but I never said nothing at all, only crossed myself the way Momma used to do.

Elenor touched her sister's shoulder shyly. Irma was watching me, something close to a smile on her lips. — Well, Elenor said, — we've prayed together since then, ain't we, hon? Irma took her sister's hand and pressed it against her cheek.

— We been close since then, Charlie, Elenor's husband said. — Done us all good. Except for poor Howard.

It seemed Howard had hardened his heart from the first. Charlie had worked for him in the Rambler franchise, manager of the service department. One day they had had words and Charlie quit, left New Orleans which was a plague to him anyway, and set up this little backyard place in Alex.

Why the fight, I asked Charlie. He was getting up to go out to
work. — Never mind that, he said. — It . . . didn't have nothing
to do with . . . this.

Elenor watched him go. — Yes it did, she began.

— Elenor, Irma stopped her. — Maybe you ought not . . .
Charlie's . . .

Elenor was wiping her cheeks with her apron. — This man's a
lawyer, ain't he? He knows what's right and wrong.

I winced and felt tired all at once, but you cannot ask for a
pitcher of martinis at seven-thirty in the morning in a Louisiana
country house. That was the extent of my knowledge of right
and wrong.

— A couple of months after Albert Sidney was born, I was at
their place, Elenor went on. — Trying to help out. I was making
the beds when Howard come in. It was early, but Howard was
drunk and he talked funny, and before I knew, he pulled me
down on the bed, and . . . I couldn't scream, I couldn't. Irma had
the baby in the kitchen . . . and he couldn't. He tried to . . . make
me . . . help him, but he couldn't anyhow. And I told Charlie,
because a man ought to know. And they had words, and after
that Charlie whipped him, and we moved up here . . .

Elenor sat looking out of the window where the sun was beginning to show over the trees. — And we come on up here.

Irma looked at her sister tenderly. — Elly we got to go on over
to the hospital now.

As we reached the door, Elenor called out. — Irma . . .

— Yes . . . ?

— Honey, you know how much I love you, don't you?

— I always did know, silly. You were the one didn't know.

We took the old station wagon and huffed slowly out of the
yard. Charlie waved at us and his eyes followed us out of sight
down the blacktop.

Irma was smiling at me as we coughed along the road. — I feel
kind of good, she said.

— I'm glad. Why?

— Like some kind of washday. It's long and hard, but comes
the end, and you've got everything hanging out in the fresh air.
Clean.

— It'll be dirty again, I said, and wished I could swallow the
words almost before they were out.

Her hand touched my arm, and I almost lost control of the car. I kept my eyes on the road to Pineville. I was here to help her, not the other way around. There was too much contact between us already, too much emptiness in me, and what the hell I was doing halfway up the state with the wife of a man who could make out a showing that he was my client was more than I could figure out. Something to do with the Gulf. — There's another washday coming, she whispered, her lips close to my ear.

Will I be ready for washday, I wondered. Lord, how is it that we get ready for washday?

The Louisiana State Hospital is divided into several parts. There is one section for the criminally insane, and another for the feeble-minded. This second section is, in turn, divided into what are called "tidy" and "untidy" wards. The difference is vast in terms of logistics and care. The difference in the moral realm is simply that between the seventh and the first circles. Hell is where we are.

Dr. Tumulty met us outside his office. He was a small man with a large nose and glasses which looked rather like those you can buy in a novelty shop — outsized nose attached. Behind the glasses, his eyes were weak and watery. His mouth was very small, and his hair thin, the color of corn shucks. I remember wondering then, at the start of our visit, whether one of the inmates had been promoted. It was a very bad idea, but only one of many.

— Hello, Irma, he said. He did not seem unhappy to see her.

— Hello, Monte, she said.

— He had a little respiratory trouble last week. It seems cleared up now.

Irma introduced us and Dr. Tumulty studied me quizzically.
— A lawyer . . . ?

— Counselor, she said. — A good listener. Do you have time to show him around?

He looked at me, Charon sizing up a strange passenger, one who it seemed would be making a round trip. — Sure, all right. You coming?

— No, Irma said softly. — You can bring him to me afterward.

So Dr. Tumulty took me through the wards alone. I will not say everything I saw. There were mysteries in that initiation that will not go down into words. It is all the soul is worth and more to say less than all when you have come back from that place where, if only they knew, what men live and do asleep is done waking and in truth each endless day.

Yes, there were extreme cases of mongolism, cretins and imbeciles, dwarfs and things with enormous heads and bulging eyes, ears like tubes, mouths placed on the sides of their heads. There was an albino without nose or eyes or lips, and it sat in a chair, teeth exposed in a grin that could not be erased, its hands making a series of extremely complicated gestures over and over again, each lengthy sequence a perfect reproduction of the preceding one. The gestures were perfectly symmetrical and the repetition exact and made without pause, a formalism of mindlessness worthy of a Balinese dancer or a penance — performance of a secret prayer — played out before the catatonic admiration of three small blacks who sat on the floor before the albino watching its art with a concentration unknown among those who imagine themselves without defect.

This was the tidy ward, and all these inventions of a Bosch whose medium is flesh wore coveralls of dark gray cloth with a name patch on the left breast. This is Paul, whose tongue, abnormally long and almost black and dry, hangs down his chin, and that, the hairless one with the enormous head and tiny face, who coughs and pets a filthy toy elephant, that is Larry. The dead-white one, the maker of rituals, is Anthony. Watching him are Edward and Joseph and Michael, microcephalics all, looking almost identical in their shared malady.

— Does . . . Anthony, I began.

— All day. Every day, Dr. Tumulty said. — And the others watch. We give him tranquilizers at night. It used to be . . . all night, too.

In another ward they kept the females. It was much the same there, except that wandering from one chair to another, watching the others, was a young girl, perhaps sixteen. She would have been pretty — no, she was pretty, despite the gray coverall and the pallor of her skin. — Hello, doctor, she said. Her voice sounded as if it had been recorded — cracked and scratchy. But her body seemed sound, her face normal except for small patches of what looked like eczema on her face. That, and her eyes were a little out of focus. She was carrying a small book covered in imitation red leather. My Diary, it said on the cover.

— Does she belong here, I asked Tumulty.

He nodded. — She's been here over a year.

The girl cuddled against him, and I could see that she was trying to press her breasts against him. Her hand wandered down toward his leg. He took her hand gently and stroked her hair. — Hello, doctor, she croaked again. — Hi, Nancy, he answered. — Are you keeping up your diary?

She smiled. — For home. Hello, doctor.

— For home, sure, he said, and sat her down in a chair opposite an ancient television locked in a wire cage and tuned, I remember, to "Underdog." She seemed to lose interest in us, to find her way quickly into the role of Sweet Polly, awaiting the inevitable rescue. Around her on the floor were scattered other of the less desperate cases. They watched the animated comedy on the snow-flecked, badly focused screen with absolute concentration. As we moved on, I heard Nancy whisper, — There's no need to fear . . .

— Congenital syphilis, Tumulty said. — It incubates for years, sometimes. She was in high school. Now she's here. It's easier for her now than at first. Most of her mind is gone. In a year she'll be dead.

He paused by a barred window, and looked out on the rolling Louisiana countryside beyond the distant fence. — About graduation time.

— There's no treatment . . . ?

— The cure is dying.

What I can remember of the untidy wards is fragmentary. The stench was very bad, the sounds were nonhuman, and the inmates, divided by sex, were naked in large concrete rooms, sitting on the damp floors, unable to control their bodily functions, obese mostly, and utterly asexual with tiny misshapen heads. There were benches along the sides of the concrete rooms, and the floors sloped down to a central caged drain in the center. One of the things — I mean inmates — was down trying slowly, in a fashion almost reptilian, to lick up filthy moisture from the drain. Another was chewing on a plastic bracelet by which it was identified. Most of the rest, young and older, sat on the benches or the floor staring at nothing, blubbering once in a while, scratching occasionally.

— Once, Dr. Tumulty said thoughtfully, — a legislator came. A budgetary inspection. We didn't get any more money. But he complained that we identified the untidy patients by number. He came and saw everything, and that's . . . what bothered him.

By then we were outside again, walking in the cool Louisiana summer morning. We had been inside less than an hour. I had thought it longer.

— It's the same everywhere. Massachusetts, Wyoming, Texas. Don't think badly of us. There's no money, no personnel, and even if there were . . .

— Then you could only . . . cover it.

— Cosmetics, yes. I've been in this work for eighteen years. I've never forgotten anything I saw. Not anything. You know what I think? What I really *know?*

— . . . ?

Tumulty paused and rubbed his hands together. He shivered a little, that sudden inexplicable thrill of cold inside that has no relationship to the temperature in the world, that represents, according to the old story, someone walking across the ground where your grave will one day be. A mockingbird flashed past us, a dark blur of gray, touched with the white of its wings. Tumulty started to say something, then shrugged and pointed at a small building a little way off.

— They're over there. One of the attendants will show you.

He looked from one building to another, shaking his head. — There's so much to do. So many of them . . .

— Yes, I said. — Thank you. Then I began walking toward the building he had indicated.

— Do . . . whatever you can . . . for her, Dr. Tumulty called after me. — I wish . . .

I turned back toward him. We stood perhaps thirty yards apart then. — Was there . . . something else you wanted to say, I asked.

He looked at me for a long moment, then away. — No, he said. — Nothing.

I stood there as he walked back into the clutter of central buildings, and finally vanished into one of them. Then, before I walked back to join Irma, I found a bench under an old magnolia and sat down for a few minutes. It was on the way to becoming warm now, and the sun's softness and the morning breeze were both going rapidly. The sky was absolutely clear, and by noon it would be very hot indeed. A few people were moving across the grounds. A nurse carrying something on a tray, two attendants talking animatedly to each other, one gesturing madly. Another attendant was herding a patient toward the medical building. It was a black inmate, male or female I could not say, since all the patients' heads were close-cropped for hygienic purposes, and the coverall obscured any other sign of sex. It staggered from one side of the cinder path to the other, swaying as if it were negotiating the deck of a ship in heavy weather out on the Gulf. Its arms flailed, seeking a balance it could never attain, and its eyes seemed to be seeking some point of reference in a world awash. But there was no point, the trees whirling and the buildings losing their way, and so the thing looked skyward, squinted terribly at the sun, pointed upward toward that brazen glory, almost fell down, its contorted black face now fixed undeviatingly toward that burning place in the sky which did not shift and whirl. But the attendant took its shoulder and urged it along, since it could not make its way on earth staring into the sun.

As it passed by my bench, it saw me, gestured at me, leaned in my direction amidst its stumblings, its dark face twinkling with sweat.

— No, Hollis, I heard the attendant say as the thing and I exchanged a long glance amidst the swirling trees, the spinning buildings, out there on the stormy Gulf. Then it grinned, its white teeth sparkling, its eyes almost pulled shut from the effort of grimace, its twisted fingers spieling a language both of us could grasp.

— Come on, Hollis, the attendant said impatiently, and the thing reared its head and turned away. No more time for me. It took a step or two, fell, and rolled in the grass, grunting, making sounds like I had never heard. — Hollis, I swear to God, the attendant said mildly, and helped the messenger to its feet once more.

The nurse in the building Tumulty had pointed out looked at me questioningly. — I'm looking for . . . Mrs. Bedlow.

— You'll have to wait . . . she began, and then her expression changed. — Oh, you must be the one. I knew I'd forgotten something. All right, straight back and to the left. Ward Three.

I walked down a long corridor with lights on the ceiling, each behind its wire cover. I wondered if Hollis might have been the reason for the precaution. Had he or she or it once leaped upward at the light, clawing, grasping, attempting to touch the sun?

The walls were covered with an ugly pale yellow enamel which had begun peeling long ago, and the smell of cheap pine-scented deodorizer did not cover the deep ingrained stench of urine, much older than the blistered paint. Ward Three was a narrow dormitory filled with small beds. My eyes scanned the beds and I almost turned back, ready for the untidy wards again. Because here were the small children — what had been intended as children.

Down almost at the end of the ward, I saw Irma. She was seated in a visitor's chair, and in her arms was a child with a head larger than hers. It was gesticulating frantically, and I could hear its sounds the length of the ward. She held it close and whispered to it, kissed it, held it close, and as she drew it to her, the sounds became almost frantic. They were not human sounds. They were Hollis' sounds, and as I walked the length of the ward, I thought I knew what Tumulty had been about to say before he had thought better of it.

— Hello, Irma said. The child in her arms paused in its snuff-lings and looked up at me from huge unfocused eyes. Its tongue stood out, and it appeared that its lower jaw was congenitally dislocated. Saliva ran down the flap of flesh where you and I have lips, and Irma paid no mind as it dripped on her dress. It would have been pointless to wipe the child's mouth because the flow did not stop, nor did the discharge from its bulging, unblinking eyes. I looked at Irma. Her smile was genuine.

— This is . . . I began.

— Albert Sidney, she finished. — Oh, no. I wish it were. This is Barry. Say hello.

The child grunted and buried its head in her lap, sliding down to the floor and crawling behind her chair.

— You . . . wish . . . ?

— This is Albert Sidney, she said, turning to the bed next to her chair.

He lay there motionless, the sheet drawn up to what might have been the region of his chin. His head was very large, and bulged out to one side in a way that I would never have supposed could support life. Where his eyes should have been, two blank white surfaces of solid cataract seemed to float, lidless and intent. He had no nose, only a small hole surgically created, I think, and ringed with discharge. His mouth was a slash in the right side of his cheek, at least two inches over and up from where mouths belong. Irma stepped over beside him, and as she reached down and kissed him, rearranged the sheets, I saw one of his hands. It was a fingerless club of flesh dotted almost randomly with bits of fingernail. I closed my eyes and then looked once more. I saw again what I must have seen at first and ignored, the thing I had come to see. On Albert Sidney's deformed and earless head, almost covering the awful disarray of his humanity, he had a wealth of reddish golden hair, rich and curly, proper aureole of a Celtic deity. Or a surfing king.

We had dinner at some anonymous restaurant in Alexandria, and then found a room at a motel not far from Pineville. I had bought a bottle of whiskey. Inside, I filled a glass after peeling away its sticky plastic cover that pretended to guard it from the world for my better health.

— Should I have brought you, Irma asked, sitting down on the bed.

— Yes, I said. — Sure. Nobody should . . . nobody ought to be shielded from this.

— But it . . . hasn't got anything to do with . . . us. What Howard wants to do, does it?

— No, I said. — I don't think so.

— Howard was all right. If things had gone . . . the way they do mostly. He wasn't . . . isn't . . . a weak man. He's brave, and he used to work . . . sometimes sixteen hours a day. He was very . . . steady. Do you know, I loved him . . .

I poured her a drink. — Sometimes, I said, and heard that my voice was unsteady. — None of us know . . . what we can . . . stand.

— If Howard had had just any kind of belief . . . but . . .

— . . . He just had himself . . . ?

— Just that. He . . . his two hands and a strong back, and he was quick with figures. He always . . . came out . . .

— . . . ahead.

She breathed deeply, and sipped the whiskey. — Every time. He . . . liked hard times. To work his way through. You couldn't stop him. And very honest. An honest man.

I finished the glass and poured another one. I couldn't get rid

of the smells and the images. The whiskey was doing no good. It
would only dull my senses prospectively. The smells and the images were inside for keeps.

— He's not honest about . . .

— Albert Sidney? No, but I . . . it doesn't matter. I release him
of that. Which is why . . .

— You want me to go ahead with the divorce?

— I think. We can't help each other, don't you see?

— I see that. But . . . what will you do?

Irma laughed and slipped off her shoes, curled her feet under
her. Somewhere back in the mechanical reaches of my mind,
where I was listening to Vivaldi and watching a thin British rain
fall into my garden, neither happy nor sad, preserved by my in-
difference from the Gulf, I saw that she was very beautiful and
that she cared for me, had brought me to Alexandria as much for
myself as for her sake, though she did not know it.

— . . . do what needs to be done for the baby, she was saying.

— I've asked for strength to do the best . . . thing.

— What do you want me to do?

— About the divorce? I don't know about . . . the legal stuff. I
want to . . . how do you say it . . . ? Not to contest it?

— There's a way. When the other person makes life insupportable . . .

Irma looked at me strangely, as if I were not understanding.

— No, no. The other . . . what he says.

— Adultery?

— And the rest. About Albert Sidney . . .

— No. You can't . . .

— Why can't I? I told you, Howard is all right. I mean, he
could be all right. I want to let him go. Can't I say some way or
other that what he claims is true?

I set my glass down. — In the pleadings. You can always accept what he says in your . . . answer.

— Pleadings?

— That's what they call . . . what we file in a suit. But I can't
state an outright . . . lie . . .

— But you're his counsel. You have to say what he wants you
to say.

— No, only in good faith. The Code of Civil Practice . . . if I
pleaded a lie . . . anyhow, Jesus, after all this . . . I couldn't . . .
Plead adultery . . . ? No way.

— Yes, Irma said firmly, lovingly. She rose from the bed and came to me.
— Yes, she whispered. — You'll be able to.

The next evening the plane was late getting into New Orleans. There was a storm line along the Gulf, a series of separate systems, thin monotonous driving rain that fell all over the city and the southern part of the state. The house was cool and humid when I got home, and my head hurt. The house was empty, and that was all right. I had a bowl of soup and turned on something very beautiful. *La Stravaganza.* As I listened, I thought of that strange medieval custom of putting the mad and the demented on a boat, and keeping it moving from one port to another. A ship full of lunacy and witlessness and rage and subhumanity with no destination in view. *Furiosi,* the mad were called. What did they call those who came into this world like Irma's baby, scarce half made-up? Those driven beyond the human by the world were given names and a status. But what of those who came damaged from the first? Did even the wisdom of the Church have no name for those who did not scream or curse or style themselves Emperor Frederic II or Gregory come again? What of those with bulbous heads and protruding tongues and those who stared all day at the blazing sun, all night at the cool distant moon? I listened and drank, and opened the door onto the patio so that the music was leavened with the sound of the falling rain.

It was early the next morning when Bert called me at home. He did not bother apologizing. I think he knew that we were both too much in it now. The amenities are for before. Or afterward.

— Listen, you're back.
— Yes.
— I got Howard straightened up. You want to talk to him?
— What's he saying?
— Well, he's cleared up, you see? I got him to shower and drink a pot of coffee. It ain't what he says is different, but he *is* himself and he wants to get them papers started. You know? You want to drop by Bo-Peep for a minute?
— No, I said, but I will. I want to talk to that stupid bastard.
— Ah, Bert said slowly. — Uh-huh. Well, fine, counselor. It's cabin ten. On the street to the right as you come in. Can't miss it.
I thought somebody ought to take a baseball bat and use it on

Howard Bedlow until he came to understand. I was very tight about this thing now, no distance at all. I had thought about other things only once since I had been back. When a little phrase of Vivaldi's had shimmered like a waterfall, and, still drunk, I had followed that billow down to the Gulf in my mind.

There were fantasies, of course. In one, I took Irma away. We left New Orleans and headed across America toward California, and she was quickly pregnant. The child was whole and healthy and strong, and what had befallen each of us back in Louisiana faded and receded faster and faster, became of smaller and smaller concern until we found ourselves in a place near the Russian River, above the glut and spew of people down below.

Acres apart and miles away, we had a tiny place carved from the natural wood of the hills. We labored under the sun and scarcely talked, and what there was, was ours. She would stand near a forest pool, nude, our child in her arms, and the rest was all forgotten as I watched them there, glistening, with beads of fresh water standing on their skin, the way things ought to be, under the sun.

Then I was driving toward Metairie amidst the dust and squalor of Airline Highway. Filling stations, hamburger joints, cut-rate liquor, tacos, wholesale carpeting, rent-a-car, people driving a little above the speed limit, sealed in air-conditioned cars, others standing at bus stops staring vacantly, some gesticulating in repetitive patterns, trying to be understood. No sign of life anywhere.

The sign above the Bo-Peep Motel pictured a girl in a bonnet with a shepherd's crook and a vast crinoline skirt. In her lap she held what looked from a distance like a child. Closer, you could see that it was intended to be a lamb, curled in her arms, eyes closed, hoofs tucked into its fleece, peacefully asleep. Bo-Peep's face, outlined in neon tubing, had been painted once, but most of the paint had chipped away, and now, during the day, she wore a faded leer of unparalleled perversity, red lips and china blue eyes flawed by missing chips of color.

Bert sat in a chair outside the door. He was in uniform. His car was parked in front of cabin 10. The door was open, and just inside Howard Bedlow sat in an identical chair, staring out like a prisoner who knows there must be bars even though he cannot see them. He leaned forward, hands hanging down before him, and even from a distance he looked much older than I had remembered him.

Bert walked out as I parked. — How was the trip?
We stared at each other. — A revelation, I said. — He's sober?
— Oh, yeah. He had a little trouble last night down at the Kit-
Kat Klub. Bert pointed down the road to a huddled cinderblock
building beside a trailer court.
— They sent for somebody to see to him, and luck had it be me.
Howard looked like an old man up close. His eyes were
crusted, squinting up at the weak morning sun, still misted at that
hour. His hands hung down between his legs, almost touching
the floor, and his forefingers moved involuntarily as if they were
tracing a precise and repetitious pattern on the dust of the floor.
He looked up at me, licking his lips. He had not shaved
in a couple of days, and the light beard had the same tawny
reddish color as his hair. He did not seem to recognize me for a
moment. Then his expression came together. He looked almost
frightened.
— You seen her, huh?
— That's right.
— What'd she say?
— It's all right with her.
— What's all right?
— The divorce. Just the way you want it.
— You mean . . . like everything I said . . . all that . . . ?
— She says maybe she owes you that much. For what she did.
— What she did?
— You know . . .
— What I said, told you?
— Wonder what the hell that is, Bert put in. He walked out
into the driveway and stared down the street.
Bedlow shook his head slowly. — She owned up, told you
everything?
— There was . . . a confirmation. Look, I said. — Bert will line
you up a lawyer. I'm going to represent Ir . . . your wife.
— Oh? I was the one come to you . . .
I took a piece of motel stationery out of my pocket. There was
a five-dollar bill held to it with a dark bobby pin. I remembered
her hair cascading down, flowing about her face. — You never
gave me a retainer. I did not act on your behalf.
I held out the paper and the bill. — This is my retainer. From
her. It doesn't matter. She won't contest. I'll talk to your lawyer.
It'll be easy.

— I never asked for nothing to be easy, Bedlow murmured.

— If you want to back off the adultery thing, which is silly, which even if it is true you cannot prove, you can go for rendering life insupportable . . .

— Life insupportable . . . ? I never asked things be easy . . .

— Yes you did, I said brutally. — You just didn't know you did.

I wanted to tell him there was something rotten and weak and collapsed in him. His heart, his guts, his genes. That he had taken a woman better than he had any right to, and that Albert Sidney . . . but how could I? Who was I to . . . and then Bert stepped back toward us, his face grim.

— Shit, he was saying, — I think they've got a fire down to the trailer court. You all reckon we ought to . . .

— If it's mine, let it burn. Ain't nothing there I care about. I need a drink.

But Bert was looking at me, his face twisted with some pointless apprehension that made so little sense that both of us piled into his car, revved the siren, and fishtailed out into Airline Highway almost smashing into traffic coming from both directions as he humped across the neutral ground and laid thirty yards of rubber getting to the trailer court.

The trailer was in flames from one end to the other. Of course it was Bedlow's. Bert's face was working, and he tried to edge the car close to the end of it where there were the least flames.

— She's back in Alex, I yelled at him. — She's staying in a motel back in Alex. There's nothing in there.

But my eyes snapped from the burning trailer to a stunted and dusty cottonwood tree behind it. Which was where the old station wagon was parked. I could see the tailpipe hanging down behind as I vaulted out of the car and pulled the flimsy screen door off the searing skin of the trailer with my bare hands. I was working on the inside door, kicking it, screaming at the pliant aluminum to give way, to let me pass, when Bert pulled me back. — You goddamned fool, you can't . . .

But I had smashed the door open by then and would have been into the gulf of flame and smoke inside if Bert had not clipped me along side the head with the barrel of his .38.

Which was just the moment when Bedlow passed him. Bert had hold of me, my eyes watching the trees, the nearby trailers whirling, spinning furiously. Bert yelled at Bedlow to stop, that there was no one inside, an inspired and desperate lie — or was it a final testing.

— She is, I know she is, Bedlow screamed back at Bert.

I was down on the ground now, dazed, passing in and out of consciousness not simply from Bert's blow, but from exhaustion, too long on the line beyond the boundaries of good sense. But I looked up as Bedlow shouted, and I saw him standing for a split second where I had been, his hair the color of the flames behind. He looked very young and strong, and I remember musing in my semiconsciousness, maybe he can do it. Maybe he can.

— . . . And she's got my boy in there, we heard him yell as he vanished into the smoke. Bert let me fall all the way then, and I passed out for good.

It was late afternoon when I got home. It dawned on me that I hadn't slept in over twenty-four hours. Huge white thunderheads stood over the city, white and pure as cotton. The sun was diminished, and the heat had fallen away. It seemed that everything was very quiet, that a waiting had set in. The evening news said there was a probability of rain, even small-craft warnings on the Gulf. Then, as if there were an electronic connection between the station and the clouds, rain began to fall just as I pulled into the drive. It fell softly at first, as if it feared to come too quickly on the scorched town below. Around me, as I cut off the engine, there rose that indescribable odor that comes from the coincidence of fresh rain with parched earth and concrete. I sat in the car for a long time, pressing Bert's handkerchief full of crushed ice against the lump on the side of my head. The ice kept trying to fall out because I was clumsy. I had not gotten used to the thick bandages on my hands, and each time I tried to adjust the handkerchief, the pain in my hands made me lose fine control. My head did not hurt so badly, but I felt weak, and so I stayed there through all the news, not wanting to pass out for the second time in one day, or to lie unconscious in an empty house.

— Are you just going to sit out here, Joan asked me softly.

I opened my eyes and looked up at her. She looked very different. As if I had not seen her in years, as if we had lived separate lives, heights and depths in each that we could never tell the other. — No, I said. — I was just tired.

She frowned when I got out of the car. — What's the lump? And the hands? Can't I go away for a few days?

— Sure you can, I said a little too loudly, forcefully. — Anytime at all. I ran into a hot door.

She was looking at my suit. One knee was torn, and an elbow was out. She sniffed. — Been to a fire sale, she asked as we reached the door.

— That's not funny, I said.

— Sorry, she answered.

The children were there, and I tried very hard for the grace to see them anew, but it was just old Bart and tiny Nan trying to tell me about their holiday. Bart was still sifting sand on everything he touched, and Nan's fair skin was lightly burned. Beyond their prattle, I was trying to focus on something just beyond my reach.

Their mother came in with a pitcher of martinis and ran the kids back to the television room. She was a very beautiful woman, deep, in her thirties, who seemed to have hold of something — besides the martinis. I thought that if I were not married and she happened by, I would likely start a conversation with her.

— I ended up taking the kids with me, she said, sighing and dropping into her chair.

— Huh?

— They cried and said they'd rather come with me than stay with Louise. Even considering the ducks and chickens and things.

Hence the sand and sunburn. I poured two drinks as the phone rang. — That's quite a compliment, I said, getting up for it.

— You bet. We waited for you. We thought you'd be coming.

No, I thought as I picked up the phone. I had a gulf of my own. It was Bert. His voice was low, subdued.

— You know what, he was saying, — he made it. So help me Christ, he made it all the way to the back where . . . they were. Can you believe that?

— Did they find . . .

Bert's voice broke a little. — Yeah, he was right. You know how bad the fire was . . . but they called down from the state hospital and said she's taken the baby, child . . . out. Said must have had somebody help . . .

— No, I said. — I didn't, and as I said it I could see Dr. Tumulty rubbing his hands over nineteen years of a certain hell.

— Never mind, listen . . . when the fire boys got back there, it was . . . everything fused. They all formed this one thing. Said she was in a metal chair, and he was like kneeling in front, his arms . . . and they . . . you couldn't tell, but it had got to be . . .

I waited while he got himself back together. — It had got to be the baby she was holding, with Howard reaching out, his arms around . . . both . . .

— Bert, I started to say, tears running down my face. — Bert . . .

— It's all right, he said at last, clearing his throat. There was an empty silence on the line for a long moment, and I could hear the resonance of the line itself, that tiny lilting bleep of distant signals that you sometimes hear. It sounded like waves along the coast. — It really is. All right, he said. — It was like . . . they had, they was . . .

— Reconciled, I said.

Another silence. — Oh, shit, he said. — I'll be talking to you sometimes.

Then the line was empty, and after a moment I hung up.

Joan stared at me, at the moisture on my face, glanced at my hands, the lump on my head, the ruined suit. — What happened while I was gone? Did I miss anything?

— No, I smiled at her. — Not a thing.

I walked out onto the patio with my drink. There was still a small rain falling, but even as I stood there, it faded and the clouds began to break. Up there, the moon rode serenely from one cloud to the next, and far down the sky in the direction of the coast, I could see pulses of heat lightning above the rigolets where the lake flows into the Gulf.

PHILIP DAMON

Growing Up in No Time

(FROM THE HAWAII REVIEW)

THERE WAS A MOUND of shrimp six feet high in the reception room and a ragtime band composed of seven shriveled up old black musicians. The string quartet was on the patio. "My father-in-law tried to get Lester Lanin," Rob was saying, "but he was all booked up."

"Your father-in-law?" Malcolm asked.

"Lester Lanin."

"That's good. It'd be a hell of a wedding if your father-in-law couldn't make it."

Malcolm was having a hard time eating shrimp. He had a glass of champagne in each hand and in order to eat some shrimp he had to balance one of the glasses on the pile. It was a very delicate process, considering just how stoned he was. The reception was being held at the Hackensack Country Club (at no small expense to Rob's father-in-law) and Malcolm had spent some time earlier out by the first tee smoking a fat number of something called elephant weed a friend of his had brought back from Vietnam. It had put a whole new perspective on the game of golf.

Rob was trying to get Malcolm's mind back onto something they had been discussing earlier. "Now about that wedding gift," Rob was saying.

"How's your golf game?" Malcolm asked.

"Pretty good. Around a two or a three handicap."

"Never could get the hang of it myself," Malcolm said. "I guess I'm just not rich enough."

"The wedding gift," Rob said.

"What are you talking about?" Malcolm said. "We're having a

conversation about golf. What do wedding gifts have to do with golf?"

"Malcolm," Rob said. "Are you upset because I didn't ask you to be an usher?"

"I always wanted to be an usher," Malcolm said. "I think it was the uniform."

"I wanted you in the wedding. You know that. But Renee was afraid to let you. You know how she is. She thought you might do something like put a tack under somebody as you were seating them."

"I would've made sure everybody kept his feet off the seats. That's one of the most important jobs an usher has."

Rob reached out and took the two glasses of champagne from Malcolm's hands. "Can we get back to the subject of the wedding gift?"

Now that his hands were free, Malcolm took two handfuls of shrimp. They were three inches long and delicious. He had tried to keep track of how many he'd eaten, but had lost count once at fifteen, and, starting over, again at nine. "Do you remember that night when we were juniors and had that beer at your place and you wouldn't let us swear?" Every time any of Rob's friends had sworn he had taken the offender's beer away for five minutes. For most of them it had been an amusing way to relieve boredom, but Malcolm had never been certain of Rob's motives.

Rob looked down at the champagne glasses in his hands. "We're not seventeen now, Mal," he said. "We're twenty-seven. We're grown up."

"Give me my champagne back then," Malcolm said.

Rob handed him the two glasses. "Mal," he said. "I wish you would tell me what you gave us as a wedding gift."

Malcolm took a sip of champagne and remembered enough of the earlier conversation to know why Rob was so upset now. He had told Rob it was an electric dildo. "Rob, old buddy. You know it's against the rules for me to divulge that information until the bride opens the package."

Rob's face grew stern above the wide groom's necktie, and Malcolm's shattered mind flashed on that look, ten years ago at a teen-age beer party. Had either one of them grown up, he suddenly wondered. Or, perhaps, had Rob always been grown up?

"Mal, a lot of people are going to be watching Renee open those packages. Family, friends, business associates of mine. I don't want her embarrassed."

Mal smiled. "Hey, Rob, don't sweat it. Let's you and I go out to the first tee and tee off on some super grass."

"Listen, Mal, I've got to know. Now."

"Now, huh?" said Malcolm.

"Now."

"Later isn't soon enough, right?"

"Right."

"It's going to ruin the surprise for you, man."

"Now, Malcolm."

"Okay, man, if that's the way you want it." Malcolm placed a hand on Rob's shoulder and leaned over to whisper in his ear. "It's a Sports Illustrated Football Game."

Rob gazed at him for a long moment and then started to say something. "Mal . . ."

"Yeah, I know, old buddy. Renee's going to love it."

Mal left the new bridegroom/old friend standing there and made for the waiter with the champagne tray, liberated two fresh glasses and made for the first tee. On the way he bumped into Abelard Oates.

"Malcolm, is that you?" said Oates. "I didn't recognize you with all that hair."

"It's someone else," Malcolm said and started for the first tee again.

"No, it's you, I can tell. You haven't changed a bit."

"What are you, kidding?" Malcolm said. "I'm twenty-seven years old. You trying to tell me I look like a goddamn high school kid?"

Abelard Oates was rumored to have seduced a practice teacher named Miss Abercrombie one day after detention. Malcolm had never believed it and had preferred to believe that Oates had started the rumor himself, to deflect attention from the real truth: that he liked boys.

"Hey, Abbie," Malcolm said now. "It was nice seeing you and everything but I've got a date waiting out in the bushes behind the first tee and she's waiting for me to bring her some champagne. See?" And he held up the two glasses as corroboration.

"Not so fast, Malcolm, not so fast. *Uno momento, por favor,*" and Malcolm flashed on what a stupid shit Oates had been in Spanish I.

Malcolm rolled his eyes to the top of his head and heaved a great sigh and grimaced and did everything else that could possibly put Oates at a lack of ease, then said, "What is it, Abbie?" in very resigned tones.

"Who's handling your investments?"

"My what?"

"Your investments. Who's handling them?"

"Abbie, I don't have any investments."

"Well what are you doing with your money?"

"I don't have any money either."

"Where are you working, Malcolm?"

"I substitute teach a couple days a week, once in a while."

"That's all?"

"Yeah."

"Wow. That's all, huh?"

"That's the whole ball of wax, Abbie."

"Wow. Well look, Malcolm. Let me give you my card and in the event you have some available capital in the future and you feel the need of some professional advice . . ."

"Thanks, Abbie," Malcolm said. "I'll call you."

At the first tee he lit up a number and wondered if he should have put Abbie on a bit. It must have come as a pretty heavy jolt to find out that Malcolm wasn't investment material. He should have told him he was making it big in advertising and had around ten thou he could afford to speculate a little on. Nothing too crazy, but none of that AT&T crap either. Something with growth. Abbie would have had a chance to give his spiel and would have felt a hundred percent better, except Malcolm hadn't wanted him to feel better, had just wanted to get rid of him. He felt in his pocket for the card and pulled it out with a handful of other ones. There were nine, altogether, nine goddamn cards he had in his pocket as souvenirs of this day, his old friend's wedding. He looked at the names on the cards. There was Clayton Thomas, who in high school was famous for having only one testicle, and whenever anyone said something like, "I really laughed my balls off," someone would always say, "If Clayton was here he'd have to say I laughed my *ball* off," and everyone would laugh. He was listed on his card as a Certified Public Accountant. There was Barnaby Braille, who had gotten caught cheating on the written exam to get his driver's license and had been made to take it over again, alone, with a policeman in the room. He was listed on

his card as a Life Insurance Underwriter. And so on. All kinds
of guys that Malcolm had known in high school, guys that picked
their noses and farted surreptitiously in class and scratched their
balls when they didn't think any girls were looking, even a guy
named Honey Boy Heine who once actually shit in another guy's
mitt after a baseball practice, all these guys were walking around
serious as hell with a little card that said they were somebody
other than the kid Malcolm remembered. It was too much for
him and he started to take great big lung-breaking tokes off the
joint to try to forget. As he watched the Saturday afternoon
golfers teeing off he wondered if maybe Benjy Compson wasn't
stoned that afternoon he watched the golf game out behind where
his pasture used to be. He looked down at the fistful of cards in
his hand again and thought of Jason Compson and knew that *he*
would have had a business card to show to people and then somehow Quentin and Caddy got into the picture and he was flashing
on Caddy and *caddy* and was almost ready to holler out one
when Rob's father strolled up and sat down next to him on the
bench.

Robert Oliver Babcock, Senior. Robber Babcock they called
him, golfer/businessman. He had always been pleasant to Malcolm, never openly disapproving as Rob's proud and stately
mother often had been, and now, in his slightly drunken state, he
was inclined to be very friendly. Malcolm slipped the roach into
his pocket.

"It's a lovely wedding," Malcolm said.

"Yes, it is," Mr. Babcock said. He was watching the golfers tee
off. "Do you think it'll rain?"

"I don't know," Malcolm said. "I've never been very good at
predicting the weather."

"It's about time Rob was getting married," Mr. Babcock said.

Malcolm wasn't sure how to respond to that. He was watching
the way one of the golfer's buttocks and thigh muscles flexed beneath the sheen of his golf slacks and wondering if maybe he
instead of Abbie wasn't . . . but no, it was the grass, it made you
notice things like that. If he wanted to he could just pull a switch
in his mind and shoot the golfers into slow motion, slowing their
swings down so that every single individual move of the muscles
was accentuated just so and . . .

"You haven't gotten married yet, have you Malcolm?" He

didn't hear Mr. Babcock's voice at first. It was slurred with wedding-reception booze and for a moment had seemed to be in perfect synch with the slow-motion picture of the golfers.

"No, I haven't."

"Well, there's plenty of time."

"I'm not sure I want to."

"Not sure you want to get married?" Mr. Babcock appeared ready to launch into a speech. He took a long pull from what looked like a tall Scotch on the rocks, started to speak again, then simply said, "Well of all the damn fool ideas. Not get married."

With that Mr. Babcock turned his attention to the golfers. Malcolm sat there for a while, next to the man they called Robber Babcock, and tried to think. It was impossible. The graying golfer had just said something about marriage, but he couldn't remember what it was. He decided to return to the party.

The first girl he came across was a tall brunette. He'd never seen her before. "Excuse me," he said. "I was wondering if you'd like to get married."

"Of course," she said with a tilt of the head. "Wouldn't you?"

Malcolm was getting ready to say that was why he asked her. It must have taken him a long time because she finally said, "How do I compare with the rest of the girls?"

Malcolm looked around. Her legs were better than most but she was on the flat side. He was trying to make up his mind about her face when she said, "Aren't you taking a survey?"

"Not exactly," he said.

"Well then why'd you ask if I'd like to get married?"

"To me," Malcolm said.

"Oh! To *you!* But I don't even know you."

Malcolm took one of the cards from his pocket and handed it to her. "Frank D. Fleece," she read, "Attorney-at-Law. Well, Mr. Fleece, I'm very flattered. Tell me, what's the *D.* stand for?"

"Darrow," Malcolm answered.

"Darrow! That's appropriate. I really am flattered, but I've never been proposed to by someone with his eyes closed before."

Malcolm hadn't even noticed that his eyes were closed. "Sorry," he said, and he walked away with the girl still holding the card.

He went from girl to girl, exhausting the cards. To one girl he handed a shrimp, wondering just how the hell that had gotten into his pocket. It was covered with lint. The girl he handed

Clayton Thomas' card to was ugly as sin. "I should tell you in all honesty," he said, "that I only have one testicle. But the doctors assure me that it won't have any effect on my ability to father children." As he walked away from her he felt vaguely guilty.

He was proposing to a freckled but still attractive redhead when he discovered the cards were gone. "They used to call me Mal," he told her. "But now they call me Ben. It has a nice ring, don't you think?"

"One means bad and one means good," she said.

"Yes. I'm sorry I'm all out of cards," he said, feeling as though he liked this girl.

"That's all right," she said with a smile. "What do you do, Ben?"

"I'm on the professional golf tour."

"Like Ben Hogan," she said.

"Sort of."

He really did like the redhead but somewhere along the way he lost her. He tried to find her in the crowd but the beat of the ragtime music was hurting his head. He went to the shrimp mound and they were all gone. A waiter told him they were all out of champagne. He looked for someone to propose to but all the girls looked so familiar he couldn't remember who he'd asked already and who he hadn't. He didn't think anyone had said yes.

He was in the men's room when Rob caught up to him, trying to remember if he'd already urinated or if he still had to.

"Malcolm," Rob said.

"Robber," Malcolm said. "Robber Babcock. Congratulations."

"Mal, Clay Thomas is all upset. Did you tell some girl he only had one testicle?"

"Of course not, Rob, you know me better than that. I told her *I* only had one testicle."

"Open your eyes, Mal."

Malcolm nodded. "I know it's impolite as hell. I've been trying to keep them open, but they just keep closing."

Rob reached out and shook him. It struck him that perhaps he hadn't come in here to urinate at all. Perhaps he'd come here to throw up. "Malcolm, when the hell are you going to grow up?"

Malcolm opened his eyes now and looked his old friend square in his. "What do you think I've been trying to do ever since I got here?"

"Look," Rob said. "I don't want to have you thrown out. You and I are old friends. Can I trust you to behave until the reception is over?"

"Trust me, Rob," he said. "I'm growing up fast."

Rob shook his head and returned to his bride and their guests. Malcolm shook *his* head and put it in his hands and sat on a toilet. He had the strangest feeling that he might fall in and drown and wished the toilet had a seat cover. He decided to sit on the edge just to be on the safe side. He was trying to remember something and it was the subject of throwing up and when he remembered it he wondered if he should stand up just in case. But he hadn't the energy. The trouble with this elephant weed was what it did to time. If he could have some idea how long he'd been sitting there he might have a better idea if he needed to throw up or not. If he'd been sitting there for an hour the chances were he didn't need to. On the other hand if he'd only been there a few minutes then he might. It was a real problem.

There was another problem. He couldn't remember his name. He was so stoned he couldn't remember his own goddamn name. He knew that it had been bad and now it was good. Or maybe it had been good and now it was bad. That was a horrifying thought. But how about his business cards; *they'd* tell him who he was. He rose from the toilet and started going through his pockets. First his pants pockets, then his coat, inside and out, and all he could find in how many, ten pockets, counting the change pocket, was one measly little half-crushed roach. Not a card in sight. Not even a handkerchief. Then the thought struck him that perhaps something was wrong with his sense of touch, and so, with eyes wide open this time, he methodically turned each pocket inside out and watched to see if anything dropped. Nothing but lint.

He was becoming a little panicky. He was going to have to leave the safety of the toilet stall and return to the party. It was his only chance. He had given all his business cards away, to female wedding guests, and he had to find one of those guests and get one of his cards back. But could he leave? What if he walked out into the reception room and promptly threw up? Or worse, urinated in his pants? Or even worse still?

He leaned against the stall door and took stock of himself. He checked all his parts, bowels, bladder and belly, and pronounced himself empty. He was as empty as his inside-out pockets. He was as empty as the Hackensack Country Club men's room. He was as empty, in fact, as the reception room.

Which he discovered upon opening the door. There was nobody in sight. He lurched into the great room, his dangling pockets flapping madly, and forced his tired eyes to remain open as he searched every corner for some sign of life. There was nobody. Not the testicle girl. Not the redhead he had liked. Not Rob or Renee. Not even a waiter. The room was as silent as someone's mausoleum; the ragtime band had packed it in. They had all gone and they had taken his cards with them.

He ran to the french doors opening out onto the first tee and saw that it had become dark. Dark and cold. And Robber Babcock and the golfers were there no longer. He returned to the reception room and stood for a moment near where the great mound of shrimp had been, wondering for God's sake what time could it possibly be, then, quickly shoving his pockets back right side in, he walked to the ladies' room and opened the door. Easing his head inside he said, in a tone that was as polite as possible, "Does anyone in there want to get married?"

LESLIE EPSTEIN

The Steinway Quintet

(FROM ANTAEUS)

> Be not afeard; the isle is full of noises,
> Sounds and sweet airs that give delight and hurt not.
> — *The Tempest*

GOOD EVENING, my name is L. Goldkorn and my specialty is woodwind instruments, the oboe, the clarinet, the bassoon, and the flute. However, in 1963, on Amsterdam Avenue, my flute was stolen from me by a person I had not seen before, nor do I now own any other instrument of the woodwind classification. This is the reason I play at the Steinway Restaurant the piano, and not clarinet, on which I am still proficient, or flute, with which my career began at the Orchester der Wiener Staatsoper. Examples of my work on the latter instrument may be found on recordings of the NBC Orchestra, A. Toscanini conducting, especially the last movement of the Mendelssohn-Bartholdy Fourth Symphony, in which exists, for the flute, a wonderful solo passage.

I wish to say that I am an American citizen since 1943. My wife is living, too. These days she spends most of her time in bed, or on the sofa, watching the television; it is rare that her health allows her to walk down the four flights of stairs that it takes to the street. In our lives we have not been blessed with children. Although the flute was in a case, and the case was securely under my arm, a black man took it from me and at once ran away. It was a gift to me from the combined faculty of the Akademie für Musik und Darstellende Kunst, when I was fourteen. Only a boy.

1963. That is what Americans call ancient history. Let us speak of more recent events.

It was at the Steinway Restaurant a quiet night, a Tuesday night, raining, only four tables, or five tables, occupied. The opinion of experts was that sometime in the night the rain would turn into snow. Mosk, a waiter, came to the back of the room.

"I got a request," he told Salpeter, our first violinist.

"Yes?" Salpeter replied.

"From the lady. Purple dress. Pearls. A bowl of schav."

This lady was a nice-looking young person, a nice purple dress, her hair a mixture of red and brown. She smiled at the orchestra members.

"Yes?"

" 'Some Enchanted Evening.' "

Salpeter picked up his bow. Murmelstein, also a violinist, put his instrument under his chin. Also present were Tartakower, a flautist, and the old 'cellist, A. Baer. For an instant there was silence. I mean not only from the Steinway Quintet, which had not yet started to play, but from the restaurant occupants, who ceased conversation, who stopped chewing food; silence also from Margolies, Mosk, Ellenbogen, still as statues, with napkins over their arms. You could not see in or out of the panes of the window, because the warmth had created a mist. Around each chandelier was a circle of electrical light. Outside, on Rivington Street, on Allen Street, wet tires of cars made a sound: *shhhh!* Salpeter dipped one shoulder forward and drew his bow over the strings. The sweet music of Hammerstein's partner filled the room.

It was during the performance of this selection that the door opened and two men, a tall Sephardic Jew and a short Jew, also of Iberian background, came in. Their hats and the cloth of their shoulders were damp. They walked through the tables to the bar, which is located directly opposite the platform where the musicians are seated. It is possible for my colleagues and me to see ourselves in the mirror of this bar while we are playing. Without removing their hats, the two men ordered some beer to drink.

After a time a party of four, who had dined on roast duck and Roumanian broilings, stood up, then departed; as they did so snowflakes came in the door. The night in the crack looked very dark. Murmelstein, who had wonderful technique, received a specific request: "September Song." Of course from *Knickerbocker Holiday.* When this selection came to an end, the lady in the purple dress put on her coat and, with a gentleman companion, went out to Rivington Street. Eleven o'clock. The members of the Steinway Quintet had then some tea. The figs and the cakes were removed from the window. At a side table Martinez, the cook, was eating a plate of potatoes. Tartakower smoked. The heat went off, the temperature dropped. It helped to warm clumsy fingers on the outside of a glass. At eleven-fifteen Salpeter nodded. We played selections from Mister Sigmund Romberg's *The Student Prince.*

At this moment the mouth of Ellenbogen's wife, who served liquors at the bar, dropped completely open and her hands rose into the air. The explanation for this was in the mirror behind her: both Sephardim were holding big guns. Out of the open mouth of Mrs. Ellenbogen came a loud scream. The music, except for the violoncello, ceased. The tall man stood up and put his hand over the barmaid's face. Ellenbogen himself allowed a tray of something, strudel perhaps, to tip slowly onto the floor. Tartakower leaned toward the old musician:

"Mister Baer, time to stop."

The short man climbed to the top of the bar. "We don't want no trouble and we don't want nobody hurt. But you gotta cooperate with us. Anybody who don't cooperate completely is gonna be hurt very bad." This man had still his hat low over his eyes. However, it was possible to see that he had a thin moustache on his lip and at the end of a long chin were a few added hairs, just wisps. A young man then. In profuse perspiration.

"The first thing is to cut out that music."

This was a reference to A. Baer, who had come to the end of the vigorous "Drinking Song," and was now beginning again.

"Psssst! Psssst! Mister Baer!" said Tartakower, pulling on the 'cellist's shoulder.

"Mister Baer!" Salpeter echoed. "I ask you to stop!"

"No! No! Reprise!" said A. Baer, and hunched farther forward, peering at the music on the music stand.

The tall man — it was now possible to see that he had also a moustache; yet he was older, not so slight in his physique, with eyes that seemed almost sad, that is, they were close-set, drooping, filled with liquid — this man came quickly toward us, seized the bow from the aged musician and broke it over his knee.

"*Er hat gebrochen de strunes fin mein fiedl!*"

Murmelstein stood up. "That ain't right what you done. He don't hear."

"*Er hat gebrochen mein boigenhaar!*"

"I am the conductor here," Salpeter said. "What is it you want? Why have you done this? Why, please? Never has such a thing happened before! Do you know what Goethe said about music?"

"Raising the hands! Up! Up! Onto the wall!" The sad-eyed man held his pistol in front of the face of the first violinist. Salpeter turned, he joined Tartakower, who was already leaning against the famous murals, by Feiner, of classical Greece. And I? I stood up, I too turned about. From the corner of my eye I observed the first man, the young one, still standing on the bar-top, motioning with his gun. He was making the others, the waiters and patrons, face the wall, too. "Oh! Oh!" a woman, the wife of Ellenbogen — "Oh! Oh!" she was saying. In front of my eyes was Socrates — Feiner was an artist who put real people into his paintings — with a group of young men beneath a tree. Murmelstein turned around. Behind our backs A. Baer was talking.

"Young man! You have broken my bowstring. *Mein boigenhaar!* Now how can I play? Do you know what it costs such a bowstring? The horsehairs? I paid for this thirteen dollars. I am Rothschild? I have such a sum in the bank? *Ai! Ai! Er reist mein bord!*"

Without thinking, Murmelstein, Salpeter, Tartakower, and I, we all turned our heads. Terrible vision! The tall individual had taken our colleague by the hair of his beard. In only a moment he pulled the old man off his chair onto his knees. What happened next is almost too painful to speak of. The gunman released his hold upon A. Baer and leaped into the air and came down with both feet through the back of his violoncello.

"I am an American citizen since nineteen forty-three!" some person cried. The voice was familiar. It was certainly that of Leib Goldkorn.

"This was no accident! No, no, it was a purposeful act!" Tartakower speaking.

Murmelstein, a young man, not even sixty, began to advance on the terrorist, who, still with sad eyes, was smiling with bright, white, shining teeth. "You done that to an old man. You got no idea how old this man happens to be. Ain't you ashamed? A venerable man? To pull his beard!"

Salpeter reached out his hand. "No, stay, Mister Murmelstein, what is the use? He does not appreciate music."

"There is a hole in it. A hole in it." A. Baer held his instrument in his lap as if it had been an injured child.

"What's so funny? What's the joke here? This is a tragedy. A tragedy!" The second violinist stepped in front of the man, who, under his hat, still smiled; then that villain raised his pistol so that it pointed straight at young Murmelstein's chest.

Suddenly from across the room his partner cried out in Ladino: "¡Jesús! ¡El cocinero! ¡Está tratando de usar el teléfono!"

The gunman whirled about to where his colleague was pointing. There, next to the door to the kitchen, Martinez was dropping nickels and dimes into the box of the pay telephone. The next thing we knew the hoodlum was flying in the air, Martinez was shouting, the weapon was raised and — in front of everyone's eyes — brought down upon the cook's head. More than once. Twice. And the victim fell to the floor. Is this not in many ways an act as terrible as the destruction of a violoncello? To attack a man's head, where great thoughts often are born? Everyone was still. No person dared to breathe. Then Tartakower spoke:

"Friends, these two are not Jews."

I felt a chill on my neck. Like a cold hand. Then Salpeter said what we dreaded to hear:

"Hispanics!"

From Murmelstein: "Puerto Ricans!"

The tall man's hat had fallen onto the floor. He put it back on his head, which was pomaded. Without difficulty, with a swipe of his hand, he tore the phone box off of the wall.

Greetings! L. Goldkorn once again. I have paused for some time. It was necessary to mix medicaments for my wife. Now she is sleeping, my life's companion, with no obstruction of nasal passages. Sweetly. Also, it is sometimes desirable to settle the nerves. I am too old to speak of such terrible things, the destruction of property, attacks to the head, without becoming myself upset. This is to explain the presence of Yugoslavian schnapps. Alcohol is good for you; it allows to breathe the hundreds of veins which surround the heart.

Now I will confess that this lengthy delay was not due to what I have already described; no, it is rather a hesitation over what remains to be said. Such abominations! There, out the window, over Columbus Avenue, the huge night sky is growing lighter. Like color returning to the cheeks of a patient. Yet at the Steinway Restaurant, where the temperature continued to fall, it was not yet even midnight. A storm of snow. I shall speak briefly of Tartakower, my successor in our orchestra. He is a cultured man, born in Bialystok, and like all Bialystokers he possesses a full, a rich, an unwavering tone. But he has no breath. We do not permit him a single cadenza. The reason for this is cigarettes. It is a disgusting habit that has stained his fingers permanent yellow.

Tartakower! Tartakower is not the point!

To understand what happened next you must know a detail of the Steinway Restaurant, which is that when you come through the door the men's water cabinet and the ladies' water cabinet are together down the stairs to the right. Many times Hispanic people, colored people, Ukrainians even, would descend this stairway in order to move their bowels upon the toilets below. Such freedom is now and has always been the policy of this dining spot, since the day it was founded by M. P. Stutchkoff, the belletrist, in 1901. Nineteen o-one, by a coincidence, is also the year of my birth. Of course Vienna then had many such Jews, young Zweig, young Schoenberg; and the head of the Hof-Operntheater was Mahler himself: thus no one looked twice when a fresh little flautist arrived in the city. Finished, Vienna. Kaputt. In America, too, on Rivington Street, have occurred similar changes. I have been told there was once throughout the neighborhood of this restaurant a lively Jewish culture: opera houses, concert stages, recital halls, an Academy of Musical Art. Now there is nothing but Pipe, a bedding merchant, and the fish store of Scheftelowitz. Even A. Baer, one year ago, moved away. Living here now are the colored peoples I have already mentioned, poor as poor Jews, downtrodden, silent, without even plumbing.

Also downstairs, between the two water cabinets, is the room of the son of M. P. Stutchkoff, V. V. Stutchkoff, a room whose door is perpetually closed. From the time that I joined the orchestra of the Steinway Restaurant in 1959 until the snow-filled night I have described, no more than ten greetings, or fifteen greetings, had been exchanged between myself and my employer. What I know of this man I have learned from others.

They say he was a pale child, a pious child, a non-eater, so thin that he would blow on Allen Street like a leaf, a feather, and not a person. When he was just seven years of age people would come from north of Fourteenth Street in order to sit with him, to listen to him, to ask his advice. Stutchkoff's son! Only a boy! I am the contemporary of O. Klemperer and Bruno Walter. We all read the *Fackel* of Karl Kraus. I have attended a lecture by Otto Rank. Impossible to believe in wonder-working rabbis, *zadikim*, whiz-kids, and such. But the others believed whatever he told them, and finally it was decided to send him to Europe to study. The year, I think, was 1930. They sent him to Godiadz. A town in Poland. Young Stutchkoff was then eighteen.

What occurred in the war years is not precisely clear. It is certain that in spite of his American passport the young scholar was put by the German invaders into a Jewish district, they say in the Lubartowsky quarter of Lublin. After that everything is confused. According to Margolies, the waiter, a miracle happened. One day stormtroopers came to shoot him, only when they fired they missed. He fell into a hole and other Jews fell on top. He waited beneath those bodies until the night and then he got up and walked away. Let us assume this account of events is a true one. Is it a miracle? The gift of life to a scholarly child? In my opinion it is a weakness of human nature to think such a thing. Many died. A few escaped. That is all. If you want to know more, ask Margolies. Ask Ellenbogen.

What is known for a fact is that after the war M. P. Stutchkoff died and V. V. Stutchkoff returned, not quite so thin as he had been before. Also, he took at this time a blond-headed wife. We see the sensualist element here. Yes, he was eating, he put on weight. Even in the sixteen years I have been at the Steinway Restaurant, he developed from a man of average size into a corpulent figure. In the recent past I have seen him only rarely. He remained in his room, and on occasion sent up a request for the music of Meyerbeer, or potted meatballs. By his wish everything here has remained the same, with the window divided in little panes, the chandeliers each with one dozen bulbs, the bar-top zinc, a chip on the leg of my Bechstein, and, in the mural of Feiner, ladies in togas, the figure of Archimedes at rest in his bath. The pay telephone, the register — these are new. Every man has heard some story in which a wild and profligate youth

reformed himself and led in his manhood an exemplary life. It
must be said of V. V. Stutchkoff, the pious boy, the man of flesh,
that he had reversed the traditional tale.

I return to the events of Tuesday night. The door opened.
Who then came in? The lady in purple! "I left my handbag," is
what she said. Thus the many events that occurred — selections
of Romberg, A. Baer's persecution, the blow to the head of Martinez — which seemed to take hours, had gone by in only five or six
minutes, just long enough for this woman to walk away, to discover the loss of her handbag, to return.

"This it, lady?" The speaker was the young gangster. He had
in his hand a leather purse, whose contents he then emptied onto
the bar.

The woman did not reply. She looked quickly around, saw the
patrons with their hands on the wall, saw the two Puerto Ricans
holding guns, saw, on the floor, with red blood in his hair, Martinez: and she uttered a scream. *Eeeeee,* and then, *eeeeeee!*

Now others began also to shout. "Help! Help!" "They will kill
us!" Such things as that. The young man with the wisps of hair
on his chin jumped down from the bar; his older companion put
his pistol into his belt. In my opinion they were on the point of
taking flight. But at that instant we all heard, upon the stairs, a
tremendous reverberation. It was a kind of snorting, snorting
through the nose, and crashing against things, and the thud and
bang of heavy feet from stair to stair. Everyone became motionless. There was the sound of whistling breath, a boom, a further
snort, and then the rounded dome and then the fierce red face of
V. V. Stutchkoff appeared on the stairs.

"WHAT THE FUCK IS GOING ON HERE?"

With one hand on a banister railing and another hand braced
against the wall, Stutchkoff pulled himself higher. He was wearing a black bowtie and a white shirt. It was possible to see the
pink skin through it. His mouth was open. Into it he sucked the
air.

"I SAID WHAT THE FUCK IS GOING ON?"

The tall Puerto Rican, called Jesús by his colleague, fell to his
knees with his arms held before him. In my confused condition
of mind I believed he was beginning a Spanish prayer. But I soon
saw the gun in his hands. It was pointed at the spot where
Stutchkoff was pulling himself out of the stairwell. Higher and

higher, the air rushing into and out of his mouth, he rose. It seemed as if there would be no end to him. With his white shirt he wore shiny black pants, in size large enough to cover the top of my Bechstein grand. The gun went off and a bullet emerged. One of the extreme left panes of the window suffered a hole. Stutchkoff brushed his right ear with the back of his plump hand. It was a bee, an annoyance, to him.

The second Hispanic crouched on the floor. He rested his gun-arm on the seat of a chair, tilted his head, narrowed his eye. His weapon detonated with a terrific report. The ceiling above Stutchkoff's head splintered and pieces of plaster fell on his shoulders. But Stutchkoff himself continued climbing the last of the stairs. To the men on the floor he must have seemed like a figure in one of Feiner's murals, like some ancient deity rising out of the water, or the god of the sun appearing over the hills.

Both robbers shot once again. Unbelievable fulmination. Salpeter with his hands over his ears. Screams. Screaming. Sulphuric smells. Yet the consequences were not of great moment. Additional plaster dropped from the ceiling. A glass of tea on a table broke in two. Stutchkoff, however, who had emerged from the stairwell and was moving rapidly in front of the window, had not been touched. When he reached the aisle between the tables he paused, he swung himself around: then he descended upon the assassins.

The shooting stopped. Both Puerto Ricans, the young man with the wisps of a beard, and his bright-toothed colleague, crawled backward, got to their feet, and with wild eyes ran toward the rear kitchen door. Stutchkoff took two or three steps, and halted. His mouth fell. His hands went to his chest. He stood there a time, like a basso singing an aria; then his red face went white, and he hauled himself about in the other direction. He lurched toward the front of the room.

"HILDA! HILDA!" he shouted.

His wife ran from behind the cash register counter. She had a red mouth painted over thin lips, and wore a feather boa because of the cold.

"Vivian!" she cried. "Vivian!"

"HILDA!" said her husband and sought to take her in his arms. But he staggered, he missed her, he clutched only the air as he

fell slowly and ponderously, the way a great tree falls to the
earth.

In that room, after that crash, there was silence. Slowly Salpeter lowered his hands. A. Baer looked up from his violoncello.
One hatted figure, a second hatted figure, peered around the
edge of the kitchen door. Then, into this stillness, this hush,
came two extraordinary sounds. By this I do not mean they were
in any way noises removed from the course of everyday life. On
the contrary, what could be more common than this rip-rip-rip?
This rattle-rattle? But after the bang and roar of the gunshots (in
my lifetime the only pistols I have heard fired, even during the
adventure of my journey from Vienna to Basel to Lisbon), no one
was able to imagine the existence of such simple sounds. People
were looking about. "What's that?" they whispered. "What could
it be?" Then Margolies started to move.

"Hildegard," he said. "You shouldn't do it." He came up to
where Mrs. Stutchkoff was standing alone, tearing the sleeve of
her dress.

"Why not to do it? How come why not?"

"But this is only a fit. A spell. Something to do with the nerves.
You see, there is no blood. I will revive him. Mister Stutchkoff!
Mister Stutchkoff!"

At my side the flautist started to laugh, a thin, high, hysterical
laugh. "Look, look," he gasped, pointing toward Margolies. "He
still has his napkin over his arm!" It struck him as something
amusing.

"Mister Tartakower, control your emotions." This was
Salpeter.

"Not moving! I knew not moving! Not blinking his eyes! Is
finish! Is the end!" Hildegard Stutchkoff resumed, in the ortho-
dox manner, ripping her clothes.

But what was that noise like a rattle? At first I believed it came
from the throat of our stricken employer. Then a movement
above him drew my attention. The gold-colored doorknob was
twisting around. The door itself shook back and forth inside its
frame. A person was attempting to enter; however, the body of
Stutchkoff, with the belly upward, was blocking the way. Now
somebody actually pounded.

"Beverly! For Christ's sake, Beverly! I'm double-parked!"

"Eeeeee! Eeeeee!"

In a windowpane of the Steinway Restaurant the face of a man appeared. The lady in purple saw him, screamed once again, and then the short Hispano-American, the one who had promised that no harm would befall us, snatched the napkincloth from the forearm of Mosk, and stuffed it into her mouth. The gentleman companion stared an instant, and then he vanished. Just disappeared.

"¡Ay, Dios! ¡Nos van a cojer! ¡Vámonos de aquí!"

"¡Un momento! ¡La registradora!"

The young man, in truth only a boy, the perspiration flying from him, leaped to the front counter. He opened the cash register and swept the money from the drawer into his own jacket pockets. No person attempted to stop him. Then he and his colleague ran through the restaurant into the kitchen.

"Are you well, Mister Baer? Mister Goldkorn, are you calm? They are gone. They will escape through the door in the rear."

"No they won't, Mister Salpeter. You forgot that door is locked."

"Mister Murmelstein, where is the key?"

The second violinist pointed to where Margolies was shaking the shoulder of the great black and white form. "In Stutchkoff's pocket."

"Oh, no! ¡Demonios! Locked! They got bars on it!"

"¡Empuja! ¡Empujemos a La Vez!"

Mosk, meanwhile, climbed on a Steinway Restaurant chair. "We need a medical doctor! Doctor Fuchs! How about you?"

A bald man in a nice brown herringbone suit turned around, although he kept his hands on the wall. "Freudian analyst. Sorry."

Mosk persisted. "You're a distinguished man. You could make an examination."

"Doctor Fuchs! I am asking, too!"

At the appeal of the grief-stricken woman the alienist dropped his arms and went toward the prostrate restaurateur.

Now the Ellenbogens, the man and wife, ran to each other. Mosk got down from his chair and began to mop up the pool of spilled tea. Salpeter and Tartakower sought to help A. Baer to his feet. He waved them away. "Azah teire zach!" The violoncello, a priceless item, was still rocked in his arms. "This was from Genoa, Italy. This was made by Italian hands."

Trotting fiercely, yes, like yellow-eyed wolves, the intruders

burst out of the kitchen and went to the blockaded front door.
The tall one started to take hold of Stutchkoff's feet, stopped,
then said to his junior colleague:

"*¡Jala!*"

"*¿Yo?* No. *You* pull."

"*¡Ha! ¡Ha! ¡Cobarde! El muchachito es cobarde.*"

"*¿Yo?* You are the coward. *You!*"

"*¡Espera! Tengo una idea.*"

The last speaker turned toward the two elderly men. To Mosk,
the Lithuanian. To Margolies, a Steinway Restaurant waiter fifty-
five years. "Hey! You mothas! Legs! Legs! Pulling the legs!"

Just then Doctor Fuchs, who had been snapping his fingers by
the ear of his patient, got up. "A moment, please," he said, and
went to where Hildegard Stutchkoff was standing. He plucked a
feather from her stole and turned back to V. V. Stutchkoff. With
care he laid the fluff upon his lips. It was pink in color. A flamingo feather. It did not stir.

"Dead," the alienist declared.

From the waiters, an echo: "Dead."

"Blessed be the True Judge!"

From outside, from far off, came a sound of many sirens.

"*¡Los policías!*"

Each of the killers then jumped for the doorknob and pulled
energetically at it; but the son of M. P. Stutchkoff still barred the
way. The sirens, already louder, were approaching from several
directions. The tall hoodlum, the one with the liquid-filled eyes,
abandoned his effort to open the door, and began striking his
own head, through his hat, with his hands. The other pulled with
even more vigor, so that his whole body trembled. Then, on Rivington Street, the police forces arrived. Brake sounds and tire
sounds, sirens so grudgingly fading. Now it was possible to see
through the Steinway Restaurant window the fall of the snowflakes: red snow, blue snow, holiday snow, lit up by the flashing
lights of the cars.

"Chino! Tell me! What to do?"

"Wait a minute! Give me a minute!"

"*Unschätzbar! Unschätzbar! Eine Antike!* What will I play on?
I'm supposed to whistle? To hum? Next they will sew on a yellow
star. *Zei hoben gebrochen meine boigenhaar! Zei hoben gerissen mein
bord! Ich volt bedorfen zein* a Rothschild? A J. P. Morgan?"

At just this moment of tremendous tension — police outside,

inside the guns — the widow Stutchkoff dropped to the floor and began to untie the laces on her late husband's shoes. As soon as she had completed this she crawled to his head and with her long fingers loosened the knot of his tie.

"What's going on, man? What's she doing?"

Doctor Fuchs answered: "She is undoing the knots that might hinder the release of her husband's soul. His *anima*. It's Jungian psychology."

"No, no," said Margolies in a hoarse whisper. "Not his soul. The Angel of Death! Otherwise it would be tempted to linger. You can look it up in Zev Wolf of Zbarazh."

"In that case," Ellenbogen added, "you must open the window as well. This is according to the Maggid of Mezritch himself!"

"Maggid, schmaggid!" Mosk, a skeptical man, declared.

The tall hooligan waved his gun as ex-Mrs. Stutchkoff got to her feet. "Crazy lady! Black magic! She got the eye! Jewish lady! Jewish! Viva Puerto Rico!"

But the cashieress ignored him. She began to walk — from her eyes tears were dropping — through the restaurant tables toward the back of the room.

"Stop, lady! Nobody moves! Stop! You gonna make me kill you!" Chino, the wispy-chinned lad, aimed his pistol at her back: the Steinway Quintet dropped to the floor.

There are those who maintain that this Hildegard Stutchkoff was not a Jew at all. I have already described how a red mouth was painted on top of her own. Yes, and her long fingers. In addition she curled her hair, her blond hair, until it looked like small sausages. Her eyes were plain Polish blue. It was necessary to look away from her bust, both parts of which were young, strong, and well developed. I did not think she had a musical nature until one night, three years in the past, it was also a Tuesday, she sat beside me on the bench of the Bechstein and played the bass, while I played the melody, of "Stout-Hearted Men." Perhaps I did not mention that the nails of her toes were painted, too? After the piety with which she mourned her husband, the rumors on the subject of her Polishness, her youthfulness, her fox furs, have ceased at last.

The murderer did not, however, fire his gun. The fresh widow stopped and removed a tablecloth from a table. With this she began to cover the surface of the bar area mirror.

"The Spola Grandfather!"

"No, Shmelke of Nikolsburg! The dead man must not see his own spirit depart!"

"Mister Ellenbogen, am I not correct in assuming that the purpose of this action is to prevent the Angel of Death from becoming entrapped in the glass?"

"That is a valid interpretation, Mister Margolies."

"Pfui!"

Doctor Fuchs spoke from the viewpoint of science: "I agree with the negative opinion of our friend Mister Mosk. These are Jungian daydreams. A regression to primitive thinking. Even children —"

"Look, gentlemen! She has finished!" It was Salpeter, our first violinist, who was speaking. "Now dear V. V. Stutchkoff, patron of the arts, may depart!"

Every person's eyes swung back to the corpse. The pink feather remained attached to its lips. It did not stir. It did not tremble.

"THIS IS THE POLICE DEPARTMENT SPEAKING. YOU ARE SURROUNDED. COME OUT WITH YOUR HANDS IN THE AIR. YOU MUST SURRENDER."

That voice came from an amplified horn. One of the gangsters, an adolescent, a boy, shouted back:

"We ain't going nowhere! We got hostages! We're cold killers! You gonna find out, because we going to kill them one by one!" He threw a blue-colored pill into his mouth. His colleague smiled, and swallowed a red one.

"Mama!" The cry came from the rear. "Mama!" Martinez, the cook, raised his bloody head from the floor.

Hello? Hello? Leib Goldkorn here. What a poor memory! Have I mentioned my performance of the *Italienische Symphonie?* Or have I not? Only a short time ago I happened to hear this same recording on radio station WQXR. The difficult aspect of playing in the orchestra of A. Toscanini — of course there were also many joys — was tempi, tempi, always the tempi! An artist went as fast as he could and — "No, no, no, no: Allegro! Allegro *vivace!*" The key to the final movement, this thrilling passage, is breath control: whether I possessed it or whether I lacked it you will judge for yourself.

Now the radio is off; this is because of the television for the

entertainment of my wife. She is watching from the sofa, with
her medicaments on the table. A red cotton nightdress and a
white lace cap: adorable, the little mouse! You will pardon me? I
am sipping hot milk with hot coffee. No sugars. I am fond of
sugars. However, Clara has diabetes. I think now we are having
a spring morning. The tree on the street has birds in it and the
buds of leaves. The clouds are not serious clouds. I have suffered since February from a disturbance in sleeping. A result of
the events in the Steinway Restaurant? A sign of advancing age?
Brandy from plums is good for this condition. Yes, but the bottle
is nearly empty. An inch at the bottom is all that remains.

I remember from the night not so much fear, but the cold
instead. No heat, and outside a sudden wind: snowflakes went
from the left hand to the right. The tall Puerto Rican took Salpeter's waterproof, his silk muffler, his fur-lined gloves. Salpeter is
two years older than I: precisely seventy-six. Chino, the young
man, took the coat of a middle-aged patron, an eggplant eater,
who then rolled himself into a tablecloth and fell asleep. This
others did too, lying so that they touched, it did not matter about
men and women. But Mosk, Margolies and Ellenbogen walked
up the aisle and down the aisle wearing black coats. Their breath
came out in clouds. Tartakower suffered. He is a thin man, with
a thin face, on which there are prominent bones. He wore an
orange and black colored muffler and a topcoat which had, in the
place of buttons, clips, paper clips, and pins. Widower. He sat in
his orchestra chair with his knees together and a lit cigarette in his
mouth. The whole platform shook when he trembled.

I too sat at my place and my toes were burning. That is the
sensation of extreme cold, a fire in parts of the body, in kneecaps
and earlobes and nose, and the wish to sleep was the same as the
wish to put it out. I then had a dream of Hildegard Stutchkoff. I
must say that in this dream she was on the seat of a toilet, and I
must say she was not wearing clothes. The feeling that accom-
panied this sight was one of familiarity and friendliness. My life
has been such that I have never seen in this way any woman, not
even Clara, my wife. I looked down of course and felt great pity
for her uncovered feet. I removed my greatcoat and laid it upon
them. "You are getting warm," she said, and at once things returned to normal: I heard china piled upon china, and the clink
of waiters carrying plates. I woke. It was still night. From the

four corners of the Steinway Restaurant came the fierce sound of chattering teeth.

The chandeliers were no longer shining. But the light was on at the bar, and so were the illuminations for types of beer. Both villains sat there, facing the room, with their hats pulled to the level of their eyes. They were laughing together, and slapping each other's cheeks. I rose from my Bechstein. I left my colleagues, who now were sleeping. Tartakower's face was white as dishes. I walked alone to the counter of the bar. A row of red pills and blue pills were lined up on the zinc top. There was Scotch whiskey in glasses, and both the gray guns.

"A French cognac, please." This was L. Goldkorn speaking, but the voice itself belonged to a young piping child.

The hooligans looked at each other. They blinked their eyes.

"Courvoisier. V.S.O.P."

"What you want, you little man?"

"*Un brandy,* Chino. *¡Un cognac,* ha, ha!"

"Oh, sure; you wanna have a little drink!" The youth opened the fine champagne and filled to the brim a tall highball glass. "So, Mister Weinberg, Steinberg, Feinberg! You wanna drink to one hundred thousand dollars?"

"Ha! Ha! Ha! Weinstein, Feinstein, Steinstein! Ha! Ha! Ha!" The tall man, the man with the successful moustache, slapped the face of his younger colleague. "Names of Jews!"

"Ha! Ha! Listen, Mister Greenberg —"

"Mister Goldberg!"

"Ha, ha! Drink it down!"

Only once before in my life, thirty-two years in the past, have I tasted a liquor of this class. The Hispano-Americans continued to slap one another. They each swallowed a pill. They put more of the cognac into my glass.

"My name is L. Goldkorn, specialist in —"

"Ha! Ha! Ha! We gonna get a hundred thousand American dollars!"

"No. No. *¡Un cuarto de millón! Y despues aceptamos cien mil. ¿Verdad?*"

"Ha! Ha! Jesús is smart! We gonna demand a quarter million! Or more! Maybe a million! Then they gonna say, we don't got that kinda money and then we gonna say, okay, two hundred thousand, and then they gonna say we don't got that either, and then we say, okay, okay, one hundred and fifty, and when they say, no, no, that's too much too, we gonna say one hundred thousand in tens and twenties and fifties or we gonna shoot every dude in the room! Ha! Ha! Goldkorn! It's gonna be a negotiation!"

"*¡El avión! ¡El avión!* Goldkorns! In air! In sky! Like a bird! Tell him! *¡El avión!*"

"Yeah, we gonna have a plane, a big silver plane. No other passengers. Just me and Jesús. And maybe we gonna go to Cuba, and maybe we gonna go to Egypt, to China —"

"*¡La China!* Ha! Ha!"

"We gonna look down from the window and see the ocean, you know, Goldkorn, with ships on it, a blue ocean, and I heard that from a jet you can tell the world is round, like a ball, and the millions of people on it are just like a bunch of ants."

"*Pantalones de* silk! In China I am *un héroe! ¡Il revolucionario! ¡Sí!* Is true! *Pantalones de* silk!"

"What's that?" The adolescent hurled his body forward and picked up his pistol. The whiskey spilled from the glass. The weapon was aimed at the front of the room, where something black moved before the window glass.

"*¡Espíritus malos!*" shouted Jesús, and he also leaped for his gun.

"No! Please! This is Margolies!"

It was in truth the aged waiter. He walked slowly to where the corpse of V. V. Stutchkoff was lying and sat down beside it. He put his head on his ex-employer's chest.

"Goldkorn, man! What's the mothafucka doing? Is he talking to that fat-ass's ghost?"

"Ha-ha! Is only a jokes! The mirror! *¡La corvata!* Stunts, no? Is no *Espíritu malo!* Listen, little Jewish man. *Un hombre es solamente un hombre. No tiene alma. No tiene nada. No es nada. El resto es superstición.* Chino, tell it to him!"

"He said a man don't have no soul."

"Right? Right, Goldkorns? Right?"

I did not at that moment answer. In faint light, which came through the window as well as from the bar, I saw Margolies listening for his master's heart. Nearby was Hildegard Stutchkoff, with open eyes. Among the patrons one person cried out, as if some terrible vision oppressed him. A woman whimpered: had

she seen it, too? A. Baer lay upon his back on the floor of the
platform. There was his beard, his brow, the curled end of his
violoncello. It looked like the head of a sleeping bird. The
widow Stutchkoff wore shoes. I wished to ask her if she were
comfortable, if there was something I, Leib Goldkorn, might do.
Instead that same Goldkorn, a Viennese of some culture, an athe-
ist during his youth, spoke exactly as follows:

"Well, gentlemen, but what if he does have a soul?"

Margolies rose to his feet and passed once again, in his black
coat, in front of the window. The snow was now blowing in the
opposite direction, from the right hand to the left, although after
a time it seemed to drop down in the normal way, and still later it
stopped. Then that night, in some respects no different from any
other, came to an end.

Rivington Street in the morning was covered with snow. It was
on top of everything, sweet-looking, like *Schlagsahne* in a cup of
coffee. From the window of the Steinway Restaurant it was possible to see a crowd standing behind the barriers that had been
erected at either end of the block. But the street before us was
smooth, without even a footprint.

"Pam!" said the kidnapper with the perpetual smile. "Ha!
Ha!"

He was simulating a gunshot at a tan-colored spaniel that ran
down the street, stopping at one sugary curb, then the other.

"Pam! Pam! Pam!"

The dog disappeared. Across the street a window opened. A
person shook out a duster. The window closed. The gangsters
each drank a Ballantine Beer.

The small group of patrons, the musicians, and the wife of
Ellenbogen sat at the tables. The waiters put plates of hot kasha
before them. Nobody ate. Tartakower had something wrong
with his neck. A. Baer was flushed with a fever. Hildegard
Stutchkoff, her gown in tatters, did not leave her chair. The heat,
which worked automatically, by some kind of clock, came on, and
the windowpanes filled up with steam. The two Hispanics rubbed
constantly a clear place on the glass. Vivian Stutchkoff, looking
alive, started to thaw.

"Goldkorns! *¡Atención! ¿Qué pasa?*"

"A gypsy! A Checker cab! Okay, Goldkorn, you stand in front
of the window. You wave."

The automobile which came slowly across the snow was a Checker brand, but no longer a taxi. Taxis are yellow. This car was black, with black tires, a black grill, and black curtains over all of the windows. At a speed of perhaps one mile in an hour it approached the front of the restaurant, then stopped. Nothing happened. No person got out. The engine appeared to be off. It was not possible to see any movement inside.

"I don't like it," Chino said. "I don't like the looks of it. Why's it sitting there, huh? What's it want? How come you can't see inside?"

"Pam! Pam!"

Margolies came up with a tray and three bowls of kasha. He peered through the misted glass. "A hearse," he said.

The tall man, Jesús, vigorously rubbed the window. "Where? *¿Una carroza fúnebre? ¡Sí!* The covered windows! Same like the covered mirror! Ghosts! Ha! Ha! Ha!" He took a bowl from the waiter's tray.

The plumpish widow rose from her seat to look. She wore a Polish perfume and the back of her shoulders was rounded. "Mister Margolies, we must to make preparations."

"Nobody moves, got it? Nobody touches him!"

"But he must be buried by sundown," said the old man, and bent over Stutchkoff's unlaced shoes. The woman kneeled by his head.

Jesús spit varnishkas upon the Steinway Restaurant floor. "In China! Mu-shoo pork!"

"I like the smooth feeling of killing. Old man, to me you're just a fly." Chino pointed his gun at the head of the waiter. At that instant, with astounding volume, the black hearse broke into "La Cucaracha," and followed this with a medley of Latin American tunes.

"Ay! Ay! Ay! Ay!" Martinez, with a soup-cabbage and of course in need of a shave, was singing in the door of the kitchen. "Come to your window!"

The two killers swayed slightly and made their fingers snap. They too sang the words of the songs: the hardly-haired man did so poorly; but the tall man, what a surprise, was a light and elegant tenor. Then the music stopped. The black Checker-brand car, which had been trembling, as though from its exertions, was now silent, was now perfectly still.

"More!" cried the desperados, and as a matter of fact the auto, or rather some person in it, a woman with a low, soft, flavorful voice, began to speak:

"*¡Oigan, muchachos!* Is it lonely in there? No one to talk to? No one who understands? *Sí,* I know you have troubles, such big, sad troubles. You can tell them to me. I am listening. Come on, yankee-boys, put your head in my lap and tell me all about it. My big, brave soldier-boys!"

"Womans! Real womans! *Quiero llevarla a la cama. Tengo que mamarle las tetas.* Tell him, Chino. About the tits. Tell Goldkorns this."

But the adolescent's eyes had rolled up in his head. "Ooooo, I feel like she was blowing those words in my ear."

"Mama!" This from the cook, still in the kitchen door.

"Cold, boys? And hungry? Guess what I am going to cook for you? Hot honey plantains! Vegetable soup! *¡Especialidades cubanas! ¡Ay!* My hero-boys! What about a nice hot bath? Would you like that? That's for me, *muchachos!* Lots of hot steam! Then you can sleep. How tired you are, how much you want to sleep. *Sí. Sí.* I know. I understand. You don't want to hurt anybody. You want a lullaby. Who wants to die because of some Jews? Come on, yankee-boys! Come over to my side! Put your heads here, on my warm breasts!"

The older villain had climbed onto the belly of V. V. Stutchkoff and was in an insane manner pulling the handle off of the door.

"Surrender! Okay! Surrender!"

"No, man, listen, man, I think the whole gig's a trap. You cats — start playing! Play long! Play loud!"

This was an instruction to the membership of the Steinway Quintet, who, with a lively selection from Offenbach, tried to obey. But it must be remembered, first, that our orchestra possessed no means of amplification and, second, that A. Baer, although he sat in his place and moved his arms, had no instrument inside them. Thus, even in the passages of the *Can-Can,* the voice of the Siren was all too clearly heard:

> *Duerma, duerma mi niñito.*
> *Duerma, duerma mi amor.*
> *Su mami lo está cuidando*
> *Y lo besa con amor.*

Ladies and gentlemen, we are adults here. There is not a great deal left in this modern world to cause us surprise. Yet even those with the most experience among us might wish, from the present scene, to turn aside their eyes. The tall man, his name was actually Jesús, took by the arm the lady with the pearls, the lady with the reddish-brown hair, and rubbed his body against her. Then he put his hand inside her nice purple dress and pushed a part of her bosom. I cannot tell you how strenuously our orchestra played the *Barcarole*. Even Tartakower with his twisted neck produced a full-bodied tone. But we, and all our art, did not prevail.

For there then began the process which each one of us had held, perhaps, in fearful suspension at a dark spot in his mind. By this I mean that here after all were men with great power, but lacking the voice of conscience: and such men were in a room with desirable women. Otto Rank once remarked that — no, no, it is not necessary to recall his statement. We know, do we not, what men are? From my position at the Bechstein I saw the crazed man lower his victim — she did not resist, perhaps she had fainted? — to the Steinway Restaurant floor.

Here the poorest boy may rise to the highest position in the nation. Many have done so: many more will do so in the years to come. From what source, and from what distant time, had this thought come to my mind? At once I knew. These were the words of Judge Solomon Gitlitz, spoken to me, as they have been spoken to thousands of others, upon the occasion of my American naturalization. I stopped playing Offenbach then. I stood up on my feet. Murmelstein, nearby, pulled my clothing:

"Don't make trouble. Sit. Sit down."

I thought of myself as I had once been, young, proud, with the thick lips of a woodwind player. 1943. Dark days for the United Nations, and for international Jewry. But the spectacles of Solomon Gitlitz were shining, shining like coins, and so, too, were each of his words: *For you, policemen walk the streets, firemen are always ready to save you, doctors are trying to make the land healthful, brave soldiers and sailors are guarding the coasts.* The song of the temptress had ended. The black automobile drove away. One by one the other members of the Steinway Quintet put their instruments down. A. Baer alone continued silently bowing. Everything was still. The only sound to be heard came from the lips of the

despoiler. Panting. He had his hat on. And therefore Leib
Goldkorn, a citizen you see, a person who had for thirty years
every benefit, every blessing, he stepped off the platform and
went up to the Puerto Rican.

"Listen, young man, you must not do this. You have a fine
tenor voice."

But it was as if I were addressing a figure of stone. No person
spoke a word. The eyes of the woman in purple stared up into
mine. Two small lines, signs of anguish, appeared on her brow.
What were the possibilities in such a situation? I tapped the
shoulder of her attacker, who slowly turned toward me his head.

"You are dragging the flag of your country in the dust."

Still, he did not respond. A film was over his eyes. His trousers
dropped by themselves to his knees. Little time to lose. The
younger assassin was staring out of the Steinway Restaurant window, with his hand up, extending the brim of his hat. In a few
steps I stood before him, this child, with the wisps of hair for a
beard, with his nearly pupil-less eyes, with his dreams of an airship, of stars, clouds, and sky. "Young man, I believe I understand you and your companion. I was young once, like you. I,
too, wore a moustache over my lip. Nor was I always a city-
dweller, a cultured man; no, I once spoke a language that no one
about me could understand. It is an error to think I was actually
born in Vienna. The truth is I first saw the light in Gloggnitz,
which is over two hundred kilometers away. There was in our
town only a single paved street, although it was a part of the
Austrian-Hungarian Empire. Is there not a similarity in our destiny? Both of us colonial peoples? I came to the imperial capital
when I was six years of age, holding my sisters' hands. The sun at
that time was setting. People were sitting in cafés. Drinking
drinks of a raspberry color. The glass of the shop windows reflected the evening lights. Everyone was speaking the German
tongue. I saw a man in a turban."

I confess that my own words had carried me away. I heard
gasping. Behind my back Jesús had risen on all fours. The foot
of the woman had lost a shoe. It was at this point not possible to
look longer. "Young man, one thing more. My dream on that
day was to ride on a tramcar. These went through the streets of
Vienna, throwing out sparks, and each was equipped with a musical bell. If you work hard, if you learn to speak American En-

glish, you will be able to ride in a silver airship. I guarantee this to you! We have a land of opportunity! Do not commit this terrible crime. Stop your colleague! It is nearly too late!"

"Oh! Oh! Oh!"

The second shoe of the lady was gone. Each of her legs was now forced into the air. What happened next was that Leib Goldkorn, I myself, had knocked the hat of the tall Puerto Rican off of his head onto the floor. Not only that; violently I was pulling his hair. Success! The man rolled aside, and the lady — she was missing her collar of pearls — began to adjust her purple dress. The degenerate then clutched my throat with his hand and narrowed his wolf's yellow eyes.

"¡Van a morir! ¡Judío sucio! ¡Judío cabrón! Chino, tell him. Say what I say!"

But it was not his colleague, it was A. Baer who translated: "The Jew is going to die."

"¡Sí! ¡Sí! Going to die! All Jew! ¡Judios sucios!"

This Puerto Rican, the one with the pomaded hair, then put the end of his pistol underneath Leib Goldkorn's chin. At precisely that moment, upon the point of my death, the telephone, with its wires every which way, rang. No? Not possible? But it rang.

Mosk got up — a plate of groats was before him — and picked up the receiver:

"Hello, Steinway. You don't need no reservation. He ain't here. Kaputt. Some kinda heart attack. Yeah, they're here. You wanna speak to them? Yeah. Hang on a minute." The old Lithuanian shuffled over to where the killer was pressing the trigger. "It's for you."

Jesús took the pay telephone and began to shout in an insane manner directly into the mouthpiece: "Kill! Ha! Ha! Ha! Kill all! Sundown time! I kill them myself!"

"Look, Goldkorn. There." The other youth was pointing outside, toward the intersection of Rivington Street and Allen Street. There was a phonebox there, with a dome of snow upon it. Inside were two men, crowded together, wearing brown hats and brown coats.

"It's them. Yeah. The Hostage Squad."

The tall one, still hatless, continued screaming: "¡Pantalones! Silk! ¡Pantalones! You bring it! Ha! Ha! By sundown! The pantalones!"

"Goldkorn, you gotta make the negotiation. You know what we want, the plane, the money. I got six clips, Goldkorn, six shots to a clip, Jesús got the same. It ain't just you. It's enough to shoot everyone here through the eyes, man, and the ears and the mouth. I see anyone move on that snow, anywhere from Eldridge to Allen, I open fire. You say anything wrong, like mentioning names, like giving descriptions, I fire, too. That's square business. Tell them tonight we got to be out of the city. Tell them we got to be high in the sky."

The boy raised his weapon to a spot near my heart. I looked again through the Steinway Restaurant window. The officers of the Hostage Squad were speaking earnestly into the public phone. I walked then to the back of the room, and took the other end of the line.

"Hello? Hello? This is Leib Goldkorn speaking, former graduate of the Akademie für Musik und Darstellende Kunst."

"Hello? This is Officer Tim of the Hostage Squad. I'm awfully sorry but we don't speak Spanish."

In the background, a different voice: "What are you apologizing for? Ain't this America? Ain't English the common tongue?"

"Ha, ha, Officer Tim again. Are you a hostage, actually? Or an armed bandito? Don't be ashamed to admit the latter. We are going to meet every reasonable demand. You'll be calm, won't you? You won't be rash?"

"Give me that. Hello! This is Officer Mike of the Hostage Squad. You won't get away with this. You're surrounded. If you don't come out we'll come in and get you. And it won't be with kid gloves! We're going to smoke your black butts!"

"Hello! I am the artist on pianoforte for the Steinway Quintet. A Bechstein grand. I am not —"

"Goldkorns! *¿Qué pasa? ¿Qué dice?*"

"Goldkorn, what do they say?"

"One officer asks for calm. He has promised to meet all demands. But I believe the second officer intends soon to attack."

"Aha," said Doctor Fuchs. "That's psychology! The gentleman and the bully. Carrot and stick. Superego and Id. Very clever, very sophisticated."

"Hello? Hello? Señor? Are you there? This is Officer Tim. We have gifts to offer you. First of all, there's actual cash, up to fifty dollars, and surely your wife would appreciate a toaster or a new electric broom. How about a loan for that new car? For your bedroom here's a pair of matching lamps."

"I will say what is needed. A medical doctor. There is a sick man here, a man aged in his nineties. It is a case of brain fever. Also warm blankets because of the cold of the night. For the same reason a bottle of cognac. Of French manu —"

Through the receiver of the telephone the second man, Officer Mike, was screaming: "Outrageous! Do you hear me, Bechstein? Those are outrageous demands!"

Chino took the instrument from my hand. "Listen good. I am a stone-cold killer. You don't do what I say just like I say it a lot of Jews are going to die. We got to have a plane to go to China. We got to have a 'copter to get to the plane. We want one million dollars. You two cats got to personally bring it right up to this door. In tens. In twenties. In fifties. Anybody else comes near this building we open fire. Get here by sundown. That's a non-negotiable demand. What do you say? Huh? Yes? Yes or no? Hello! Hello!"

Through the Steinway Restaurant window I saw the two officers, like men who had lost their senses, first pull inside out each one of their pockets, and then begin to crawl about in the snow.

"¡Chino! ¿Qué pasa? Dígame."

"¡El teléfono! ¡La operadora! She cut us off!"

"Ay! Yids will die!"

A patron — pitchai appetizer, and grilled kidneys after — came up to Jesús. He was a short fat man, with a rumpled shirt. "I think I shall now intend to be going. This is not after all a Greek restaurant. I made a simple mistake as I was passing by. Anybody could make it. I am not a Jew. I am a Greek and speak in a dignified manner. Well, farewell!"

The fat man went through the tables to the front of the room. Mosk, the waiter, walked toward him at an angle.

"Hey, Printzmettel, you forgot your coat."

"Yes, yes, foolish, of course." The patron, with one arm through a Chesterfield jacket, reached the door. His way was blocked by the corpse. He stopped there a moment. V. V. Stutchkoff was warm and somewhat maroon. There was a slight odor, too. The shoulders of Printzmettel dropped. His nice jacket dragged. He went and sat by the wall.

Pop! I believe everyone jumped: Then the sound, *pop!*, again.

The two desperate men had opened each a can of Ballantine Beer.

Greetings, friends! Leib Goldkorn returns! Look, ha ha, my hands are shaking! The reason for this is not cold weather. It is still warm in the house. No, not for twelve years have my fingers trembled like this, not since a man in green trousers took from me my flute, a Rudall & Rose, made a century before in London. Here is a bottle of Mission Bell, a wine of California manufacture. For this half of a pint the price is forty-nine cents. I have been, not more than a few moments ago, on the premises of the same liquor store from which it is my practice to purchase plum brandy. For the first time they would not allow me a bottle on credit. "Boss's orders." And where was this boss, a Jewish man named Herman I have known for thirteen or fourteen years? "Lunch." Returning when? Not returning. I pointed out there had been a mistake. "Look, young man, I am a citizen. I am a musical artist, until recently employed. Just a bottle of slivovitz. A small one. Herman does not have to know."

My friends, from the border of Spain until shortly before sailing from Lisbon I had to wear the most startling disguise: a striped shirt, a felt hat, and around my neck strings of garlic. Never, in the depths of these indignities, not even when I had to hop on one foot and hum folkish tunes, was I — a former member of the Orchester der Wiener Staatsoper — so humiliated as when I had to beg a favor from this youth in his Eisenhower jacket. From my pocket I took one quarter and change. It was just at this moment, when I put down each of four pennies, that my hands, by themselves, began to shake.

There is in this wine a strong taste of sulphur. *Mein Gott!* It is nearly opaque against the light of the sun! I would not drink it if I had not suffered, only one hour ago, a particular shock to my nerves. What was this shock? It was a fright brought on by Clara, my wife. I do not know what it was that indicated to me that something was wrong. When you live for many years with another person there develops intuition. I am speaking to you from a chair next to the kitchen window. From this position I am able to see through an open doorway the back of the television, and the end of the sofa. Everything seemed normal, except that in the heat of noontime Clara had kicked her coverlet to the floor. Somehow the sight of her bare feet disturbed me. I stood up and went through the door. The cap and the nightdress had been thrown off, too, and the bedclothes bound her body like ropes. Her mouth was open. Her eyes were open. A coma? Death? Actually death? For some reason — no, without a reason, it was simply madness — I turned around to see what was on the TV. It was some sort of film: men and women driving in an automobile, while speaking to one another. However, the horizontal and the vertical controls were poorly set on the appliance, and this caused the deformed heads of the actors to rise to the top of the screen and appear again at the bottom. With a terrible sound Clara took a breath. It was like a person drowning in air. With this rattle she breathed again. Croup! A case of croup! I am not a weak man. I carried my wife to the bathroom and turned the hot water tap of the tub. In a moment the room was filled with steam and the crisis, which is caused by a kind of dryness in the membranes, had ended.

On Columbus Avenue the trucks are following one after the other and I cannot easily hear my own words. The wine is burning my larynx, too. Of the events of three months ago I shall speak no longer. Why should I continue? What more do you want to know? There are not any surprises. How could there be surprises when I am here, alive, a survivor, speaking to you? The suspense element is gone. To listen to more is simply *sensationslust*. At the Steinway Restaurant bar there is a beer illumination in the shape of a windmill-clock. This we often consulted. *We* did not know the end of the story; for *us* suspense existed, and in our ignorance we thought that each passing hour brought us nearer to our doom. Terrible! During the night we prayed for the morning but when the morning came, with its threats, its insults, its fierce demands, we prayed again for the night.

At the middle of the day A. Baer took a turn for the worse. He spat on the floor. Dark spots appeared on the surface of his clothes. *"Naronim! Idiotim! Zei vellen tsushterin yiddishe gesheftin. Reissen yiddishe bord. Farnichten yiddishe Kultur. Loifts! Behaltzich! Doss iz a toit lager!"* By the time of my teens I had forgotten all of my Yiddish — instead we had Schnitzler, we had Karl Kraus — and this has remained a gap in my knowledge I have not rectified. However, if you are familiar with the German tongue you have certainly grasped that the aged gentleman had confused these Hispanic intruders with members of the Nationalsozialistische deutsche Arbeiterpartei. Now defunct.

The condition of others had deteriorated also. Do you remember that Salpeter had been forced to spend the night without his waterproof cloak? He now periodically sneezed, and there was a clear drop of liquid near the end of his nose. Catarrh. The neck of Tartakower, moreover, had locked in the position of a violinist supporting with his chin his violin. Patrons, even Doctor Fuchs, were forced to visit regularly the water cabinet for men or the water cabinet for women. Yet in my eyes the saddest situation was that of the woman in the purple dress, the same person who had that morning come so close to being the victim of an unmentionable act. Now she sat for long periods upon the zinc of the bar, with her hands touching, or seeming to touch, the pearls that were no longer around her neck. One leg was crossed over the other, and moved up and down; a shoe hung by only a strap from her foot. She smiled, she giggled, and — does this not wrench the heart? — made inviting moues in the direction of Jesús, whom, under the stress of circumstances, she took to be her former gentleman companion.

"All things get worse," remarked once Sigmund Freud, who lived at Berggasse 19, only a few blocks from my boyhood home; "they don't get better." Of course the famous alienist was referring to the condition of living persons, but at the Steinway Restaurant, on Wednesday afternoon, it applied to dead people, too. By this I mean the corpse of Vivian Stutchkoff, which now unmistakably smelled. It was not hot in the room, although it had grown uncomfortably warm. The problem was the airlessness. Not a fresh breath came to us from the world outside. The smoke of Tartakower's, and others', cigarettes hung in layers over our heads. And with every inhalation, even when done through the mouth, came the smell of — it is difficult to put the experience of one sense into the language of another: it was a thick, sweet smell, and a tangy smell, too. Like boots, partly, and partly like caraway seeds.

"He stinks!" said Mosk, the Lithuanian waiter. "P U!"

Also, he was for some reason swelling. Large already, an impressive man, Stutchkoff had begun to bulge even further — not dramatically, not all at once, but steadily, like bread that is rising. By two o'clock his buttons were straining, and several had burst. But perhaps the most painful of these transformations was the way in which his skin altered its color. It had been, that morning, pink and rosy, as if through some miracle he had been frozen alive. Think of the pain for Hildegard Stutchkoff, seated nearby at the window, as that complexion deepened to purple and then turned an absinthe green. He had become like a statue of V. V. Stutchkoff, with a statue's patina; and on this green figure the only tone that resembled life was that of the little feather that still clung to the lips of the restaurateur.

And what of this Hildegard Stutchkoff? Alas, the Polish beauty was also subject to the process of disrepair. Her blond hair was no longer curled on top of her head. The red lips on her mouth had entirely vanished. Her gown was torn in many places and on her shoulder was the white strap of an undergarment. She kept her eyelids lowered over her eyes, underneath which were blue semicircles. Slowly, not according to any plan, the staff of the Steinway Restaurant gathered around her. Although the clock said only two-thirty, her face was already in shadow. Moment by moment — how quickly this happens in winter — the light was leaving the visible part of the sky.

"And after?" This was Ellenbogen, a waiter, speaking first. "Hildegard, what about after?"

The cashieress lifted then her lids from her eyes. "Mister Margolies, what is 'after'? Is already 'after.' Is the finish already." She raised an arm toward the body of her former husband, and dropped it again in her lap.

"But the Steinway Restaurant, Mrs. Stutchkoff. Next year is seventy-five years at a single location. Leon Trotsky ate here; what about that? And the Attorney General of the State of New York."

"Also champion boxers. B. Leonard. B. Ross."

Hildegard blew for a moment cool air down the front of her bosom. "Steinway Restaurant is finished, too."

"Wait a minute!" cried waiter Mosk. "This is a money-maker! A gold mine!"

"Is losing eighty dollars, in cold weather ninety dollars, Mister Mosk, each day, this gold mine. Is five hundred each week, such American dollars, is each month two thousand —"

"That's all right, lady! Don't worry! Please you don't worry! Everything is all right! I make mamaliga!" There were real tears on Martinez's cheeks.

In a soft voice Margolies said. "We are old men here. It is not a good time in our lives to go on the street."

"I wish to remind everyone that music is an aid to digestion.

Schiller writes that harmony is a feast for the ears. A feast for the ears!"

"My good, dear friends! Mister Martinez! Mister Salpeter, please! What am I to be doing about modern times? About American peoples? Mamaliga? Pitchai? Who comes in such an expensive taxi so far for pitchai? They want Gershwin? Gershwin is on the radio, the TV, the movies — is not necessary to make a request from the Steinway Quintet."

"Look, I am going over here. Attention everyone, please." Margolies called to us from a table by the wall. "Who sat in this chair? This very chair? Here is where her elbows were on the table, and she put her chin on the back of her hands. Do you remember who sat in this pose, Mister Mosk?"

"Yeah. Sarah Bernhardt."

"Yes! It was Sarah Bernhardt who sat in this chair! And smoked a cigarette in a holder! Never mind if I am crying. It is nothing. Never mind."

"Is to pay Mister Margolies no money. Is no more time. Is no more Jews."

"*Zei vellen arois reissen unzere tzeine! Zei vellen arois nemen de gold!*" A. Baer was spitting onto the floor. "Yes, and lamps out of our skins!"

All at once Ellenbogen, a married man, sank to his knees and grasped his ex-employer by his black suspenders: "What will become of us now, Mister Stutchkoff? What are we to do?"

Everyone gasped and looked around at our captors. The tall one, Jesús, was seated at the bench of the Bechstein, where he played one note, two maddening B-flats over high C, a shrill note, over and over again. Chino, the youth with the immature beard, stood at the window, with his hand on his hat brim, shading his eyes. Outside there was a black crust, soot, shadows, on top of the white of the snow. The sun was falling like a stone out of the sky. Across Rivington Street the bars of the fire escapes were lighting up one by one, like filaments in a lamp. How long until the end of the day?

All the others now joined Ellenbogen next to the corpse.

"What to do, Mister Ellenbogen? Once I saw a grown man ask Mister Stutchkoff the very same question, and Stutchkoff — this was nineteen twenty-three, he was only a boy — he said, 'Floor coverings,' and this man went on to invent some kind of linoleum that made him rich. In those days he told everyone what to do."

"A coincidence," said Mosk.

"Once is a coincidence," Margolies replied, "but not twice, not three times. A woman came, this was even earlier, nineteen twenty-one, and she had a definite cancer. The doctor wrote a prescription which she brought to Stutchkoff. It had two items on it. Stutchkoff said, 'Take this but don't take that.' A month or two later the cancer was gone. Another time when a certain man was sick Stutchkoff told him to buy medicine, fill up a teaspoon with it, and pour it into the sink. This man also got well."

"It's a lotta hooey," said the Lithuanian waiter. "What about when they dropped dead?"

Salpeter was shaking his head. "No, Mister Mosk, what Margolies says is true. I will tell you a thing that occurred in nineteen twenty-eight, when I was in the position of Murmelstein, that is to say, when I was second violinist in the Steinway Orchestra. I was not then the leader. Perhaps for that reason I would often arrive early at the Steinway Restaurant in order to practice. Even before you would arrive, my dear Mister Margolies."

"I remember. Ragstatt was the first violin."

"One afternoon — I recall the bright sunshine — I was playing the Concerto Grosso of Ernst Bloch, when a man walked by in front of the window. 'Quick! Stop him! Bring him to me!' Rarely had I seen young Stutchkoff so exercised. I put down my instrument and ran into the street. It is not necessary to describe each detail. I brought him inside and Stutchkoff, who was then . barely sixteen, asked him where he was going; but the man would not say. Stutchkoff then refused him permission to leave. O'Brien, our cook, and I restrained him by force. At last the man began to weep and said, 'Rabbi, I want to confess. I had the intention of committing a sin. I was about to be baptized. But you held me back and now the evil hour has passed.' This same person went on to become a very pious man and a lover of music."

Tartakower said, "But that is a miracle!"

"Unbelievable! Amazing!"

From an inside pocket the Litvak took out a cigar, and lit it. His face seemed perplexed. It was difficult indeed to reconcile the tales we had heard with the sight of the green giant that lay before us. Even I, from Vienna, a free-thinker, found myself, in the mounting excitement, somewhat disturbed.

"Baloney," Mosk said.

Margolies then spoke: "I came to the Steinway Restaurant in the summer, nineteen twenty. This Stutchkoff was then aged seven or so. Just a boy. Mister Mosk, I advise you to listen and not blow disrespectful rings in the air. One day M. P. Stutchkoff, Stutchkoff himself, and I sat down to a meal of Roumanian broilings. He was then a thin child, with a thin face, a long face, and he had black eyes and black lashes. It's true, he never ate much; but on this particular occasion he would not even touch the food. In addition, he said we must not eat either. Everything was getting cold. A delicious platter of broilings. But Stutchkoff, with that thin face, insisted: he would not budge. On the other hand, he would not give a reason. Nothing. So M. P. Stutchkoff and I decided, all right, we'll eat by ourselves. Attention, please, everyone: you have not heard a thing like this before. The meat was on my fork, not an inch from my mouth, when Premisher, the butcher, rushes in screaming and waving his arms: 'Stop! Stop! It's not kosher!' It turns out there was a mix-up with a side of a cow. An inch, Mister Mosk! An inch!"

"Ooooo," said Tartakower.

"A Rabbi! A Prince!"

"Blessed be His name!"

The staff of the Steinway Restaurant began to rock back and forth. Suddenly I was knocked rudely to the side and someone rushed by and fell on top of V. V. Stutchkoff. It was Murmelstein, the second violinist.

"Boss! Boss!" he cried. "I'm asking a favor! I got a kid in school! In college! University of Wisconsin! Boss! You hear me? Boss!"

What could one think, except that young Murmelstein, in the course of this night and day of terror, had lost control of his senses? An act of a madman. We cried out, of course. We took hold of our colleague's shoes. But Murmelstein only wrapped his arms more tightly around the mound of the corpse and clung there, as if to the top of a wave.

"*¡Ay! ¡Ay!*" the Hispanics cried. "*¡No hablen! ¡No hablen!*"

The tall Puerto Rican grasped the back of Murmelstein's jacket and pulled upon it. The second violinist, with the strength of his mania, held on to Stutchkoff's waist.

"No talking! Talking not allowed! This is dead individuals! Talking to ghost? Ghost? Ha ha ha! No such thing! Ain't spirits! Jew! Listen! Ain't anything! Ain't anything! Ain't anything!" With the gun in his hand, Jesús was striking Murmelstein, a parent, on the back of his head.

"Hey, cut it out!"

"You are striking a trained musician!"

"No! No blows on the head!"

The staff of the Steinway Restaurant had become agitated. Someone restrained the hoodlum's arm. Someone else — this is true, I am an eyewitness — began to strike him upon the hip. Let people say what they wish; let them even deny it. We acted, friends! At that hour we fought them back!

There was then a gunshot and a cry of pain. A second shot; but no cry came after. Murmelstein rose from the body of Vivian Stutchkoff. He had a smile, an unusual smile, on his face. "Hee, hee, hee," he said, and walked away.

"I warned them, the mothafuckas! I told the mothafuckas I'd shoot if I saw anything move." Chino was standing by the window, from which two panes were now missing. He rubbed the mist from the rest of the glass. In the snow, between the two curbs, was the tan-colored spaniel. There was enough light from the low sun to see the blood on its fur. From this sight I turned away. I went to the rear of the room.

"Psst! Look, Mister Goldkorn." Murmelstein was waiting there. He had a thing in the palm of his hand. "Hee, hee, hee. I got it out of his pocket. The key! The back door key! Hee, hee, hee. It was all a plan!"

Yass! Yass! Goldkorns here! At the kitchen table. And the window is right over there. A moment, just a moment, while I breathe in some air. I am a vigorous man but the flights of stairs are now a problem. Breathlessness? No, no, it is fatigue. *A flight of stairs* — is not this a strange way to say it? For three months I have been unable truly to sleep. However, pills are not acceptable to me. Goloshes, M.D., gave me tablets in March of this year. With these tablets it was like falling down a long staircase with something dark, a black thing, at the bottom. In English you say *falling asleep.* Ha, Ha! What a language!

The reason I have mentioned Doctor Goloshes is that a short time ago I was speaking with him directly on the telephone. That is why I have gone down and up once again so many stairs. He told me he would come by for a visit after his dinner. Clara is not well, after all. I thought it was the croup but she is making a sound as though she meant to bring up her phlegm. There is also incontinence of the bowels. We treat this as a little joke between us, but if I dared, if it were not undistinguished, I would request that she wear rubber pants. Am I not speaking of a disgraceful human condition? What a scandal! And what is the point? Tell me! She does not even know that she is alive! "Am I living or dying?" she said. A better way to treat old people would be to kill them. Kill them off would be better! There is no mind in her. No mind left! And when does Doctor Goloshes eat his dinner? Already it is growing quite dark. But where was I? Yes, I remember. I would accept any employment in the woodwind area, if necessary even the saxophone. In the percussion group I have at times played the piano. Is that something you already know?

Four flights. Four. Tartakower, with his yellow fingers, would be unable to do it. Have you ever attempted to make a call from a phone box in this city? The kind where you insert a dime? We have not here the spotlessness of Vienna. Remember this was an emergency situation. A call to a doctor. I went to three kiosks, first one, then another, and each time the earpiece hung down, yes, like the neck of a butchered goose. And then, while speaking with Goloshes, M.D., a respectable man, my feet were in a person's urine! There was for me a moment of fear in that place. The darkening sky. A wind springing up. All phonebooks torn. I then saw myself as if I were outside the transparent glass, as if I were a second caller impatiently waiting: fearful to see the light bulb exposing my hands, my shoulders, my large ears, my hairless head. *Hello, hello, Doctor Goloshes? Clara is ill!* What is that telephone ringing? We have here no telephone. I see that already there is a full moon. What a joke! And stars! Do you know what I think? These are simply holes, just pinpricks, in a black cloth. Do not tell me they are proof of a vast universe. In the American language: do not make me laugh. But what is that ringing? A month ago the Bell Telephone Company came and removed from our flat the telephone. Ringing. Still ringing. Yass! If I remember correctly, Doctor Fuchs, the Freudian, picked up the Steinway Restaurant receiver.

It was the friendly Officer Tim. I was at that time examining the mural of Feiner and listened with only slight interest to the conversation. Of course there was a shout of joy, an outburst, when it was announced that both officers would soon arrive with the money, that all demands would be met. Before my eyes was a skillful depiction of the death of Aeschylus: an eagle, they say, dropped a tortoise upon his head. Thinking the latter was stone. The telephone rang once again. Naturally — this was their plan — it was Officer Mike. An attack was about to be launched. All hostages must at once lie on the floor. Here was the philosopher Anaxagoras, whom Feiner portrayed as middle-aged, explaining the theory of atoms to a boy with a squint in his eyes. Socrates?

You would like to ask, perhaps, why I showed such little interest? Such small concern? It was my belief that the specialists of the Hostage Squad, even if they were serious men, and sincere in what they said, canceled each the position of the other. I mean by this that the ransom funds would not be paid and there would be no airship to the People's Republic of China. Equally, there would be that night, or the next day, upon the Steinway Restaurant, no armed attack. The windmill had turned to quarter to four. The deadline was now approaching. The only question was, what would, at sundown, our captors do?

The tall kidnapper, the one who had stepped through the back of A. Baer's violoncello, was at that moment throwing a pill into his mouth. Somehow he missed; it flew over his shoulder.

"Benny! My last Benny!"

He fell to his hands and his knees and began inspecting the floor. The room full of Jews watched without a word as he threw down chairs, upended a Steinway Restaurant table, and knocked a cart of desserts onto its side. But the little red capsule had rolled into a crevice, a crack. Not to be found. Jesús was weeping. He was uttering curses and cries. He pounded with his fists, his forehead, his shoetips upon the floor. It was surely a dangerous moment. All at once he sat up, with his back straight and his legs crossed underneath him. His eyelids came down. His chin struck his chest. His hat fell into his lap. Sleeping? No soul dared move. Then he said, "Ah! Ah ha! ¡El jefe Mao!"

Chino, the youth, was no longer at the Steinway Restaurant window, whose panes were now partly rose-colored and partly gray. He was instead behind me, with a cognac glass in his hand.

"For you, Goldkorn."

"This is very good cognac. Imported."

"Turn on the lights, man. It's dark in here."

"Dark? On the contrary, young man. It is quite light in this room. The overhead chandeliers do not go on until five o'clock. It is so early."

"Don't be punk-hearted, man. It ain't personal. We ain't going to do this because of you. It's just the way the thing broke down. Hit the lights."

"Please. Take this. I am finished. Not thirsty."

I myself put the cognac glass, which was mostly full, back into his hand. I turned from him to the wall. Why? I do not know why.

"What are you looking at, man? What's this painting called? The one all over the wall."

"This is a mural by Feiner. Perhaps it is his finest work. I think the title is *The Golden Age*."

"Yeah. Uh huh. Which is when a country is at the top, right? At the peak of its glory."

"Yes, at the peak of its culture and influence. You have, for example, Vienna at the turn of this century. It was then that the young Schoenberg composed his *Verklärte Nacht*."

"What place is this? Is this a country? Is it Greece?" The youth with the ridiculous moustache pointed to a spot on the wall where workmen, it appeared, were laboring upon the Parthenon.

"Yes. Correct. I believe that the man sitting there is Pericles, the leading citizen of Athens. He encouraged art, literature, and philosophy, in addition to music."

"And what's that building? The one they're working on?"

"The Parthenon. It is where the Greeks worshipped Athena."

"Magnificent. Right, Goldkorn? Magnificent."

The temple rose above the mass of men. Its columns were fluted and gleaming. The bright marble shone.

"Feiner was a well-known artist."

"You know something funny? I needed two hundred dollars. I owed a couple of dudes."

At that moment, as if it had plunged into a pot of water, the light from the sun went completely out.

Before I, or the youth, or any other person could locate the switch for the chandeliers, the shadow of Salpeter appeared on

the musical platform. With a pencil he rapped sharply the lid of
the Bechstein.

"I shall ask the members of the Steinway Quintet to take their
places. Quickly, please! Gentlemen, quickly!"

From different parts of the room the musicians emerged.
A. Baer could not by himself climb onto the platform. We gave
him assistance by holding his arms. Through the cloth of his coat
his skin was hot to the touch. Salpeter, with a handkerchief under
his nose, continued speaking:

"Ladies and gentlemen, as you are certainly aware, our concert
last evening was unfortunately interrupted before it had reached
its conclusion. How long ago that seems, and not merely a matter
of hours! However, in spite of the vicissitudes that have crowded
upon us, we are still alive, and still here together. Therefore, I
am pleased to announce that the Steinway Quintet will present at
this time a special program. Our selection is dedicated to the
memory of our colleague and co-religionist, V. V. Stutchkoff, a
true friend of the arts."

"Play anything by Irving Berlin!"

"Thank you, Mister Mosk, for your suggestion. But I am sure
you agree that tonight is not an ordinary occasion, and for that
reason we shall not entertain the usual requests. The fact is,
throughout the long years of its existence, the Steinway Orchestra
has numbered among its members many distinguished compos-
ers, some of whom, like S. Romberg himself, or Maximilian Steiner, the winner of three Academy Awards, are known and loved
all over the world. Yes, Romberg played at the Steinway Restaurant the double bass for nearly one year. Other members of our
orchestra are appreciated more often by connoisseurs. I am
thinking, as I am sure you have guessed, of Rubin Goldmark, K.
Goldmark's nephew, whose difficult *Samson* was composed between these walls; and also of our dear friend Joseph Rumshinsky, our pianist until his untimely death in nineteen sixty-three.
It is the work of these men that we shall play tonight, beginning,
for artistic reasons, and for morale also, precisely at that point at
which our concert was suspended. Ladies and gentlemen, *The
Student Prince,* followed by 'The Indian Love Call!' "

Murmelstein took his seat. Tartakower took his seat. A. Baer
had his damaged instrument propped between his knees. And I,
Leib Goldkorn, Rumshinsky's successor, slid onto the bench of the

Bechstein. Salpeter sat, too. Then everyone noticed that there was a bare music stand among us, and one extra chair.

"Oh, yes," said Salpeter, and rose to his feet again. "I have placed here the chair of the late Albert Einstein, the recreational violinist, who once, in the year nineteen forty-nine, joined our little orchestra for a musical evening. In the entire history of our organization, he was the only guest soloist allowed such a privilege. However, he brought his own instrument, and of course to such a world figure it was not possible to say no. And the truth is he played quite well. We were not embarrassed at all."

Salpeter sat down a second time, picked up his bow. But for some reason Tartakower was standing. Because of the sprain to his neck he had to walk sideways. He came over to me.

"I'll sit here, Mister Goldkorn, and you take, please, my chair."

"What are you suggesting? What can you mean?"

Tartakower held out his instrument. Yes, he was holding it out to me.

"Here, take it. I want you to play it tonight. I shall attempt the piano. For the *Phantasie* by Rumshinsky I shall play only chords."

His silver flute was in my hands. It was a Powell model, only thirty years old, of American manufacture. But it was light, was balanced correctly, and seemed to float up, to spring up, toward my lips.

"Short of breath, Mister Tartakower?"

"No, no, please. You are the older man, a woodwind specialist. I beg you not to argue."

The first violinist rapped with his pencil the edge of a music stand. Tartakower abruptly sat down and I, I stood up, I walked to his place, I eased myself onto his chair.

"What's this? What's this?" Salpeter wanted to know.

"He — it is his neck, his neck, you know."

Salpeter looked at me closely. He wiped, with a white handkerchief, his nose. Then he dipped his shoulder and we started to play.

I have remarked that it was dark in the room. The music on the music stand was obscure and difficult to read. The instrument, after so many years, felt strange to my hands, my lips. It was as if I were again speaking German, a dear but in part a forgotten tongue. I made many mistakes. My breath seemed to whistle. And soon it became necessary, for a moment, to stop. I looked about me. The revival of the Romberg selection seemed to have brought A. Baer to his senses. He had no bow, but he hummed his part softly, and the violoncello produced a pizzicato in spite of its broken back. The Bialystoker, meanwhile, with his chin on his clavicle, had mastered the pianoforte. I could not rest longer. The melody of "The Indian Love Call" is played exclusively by the flute. The Powell model felt heavy. It nearly fell from my hands. Salpeter nodded. I believe that Murmelstein encouragingly smiled. I played a wrong note. A second wrong note. Something was smarting my eyes. "Stop! Stop!" Salpeter cried. "We shall begin once more."

This we did. From my instrument there came at last — as had happened on one other occasion, the Graduation Day Recital of the Akademie für Musik, at which my grandparents, and parents, and my two sisters were present — a series of perfect and lucid and golden-throated tones.

I cannot say how long our concert lasted. Less than one hour perhaps. The light in the room soon faded completely. Between selections there was no applause. Yet in the seventy-four years of the Steinway Orchestra there had not been such music as this. I am struggling to find words to describe it and I fear I shall fail in this task. Not, however, because music is, as some critics say, an abstract art. I have never believed such fantastic statements. Each note corresponds to a nuance of feeling, just as every word of a poem does, or the brushstrokes of a painting. Very well. I must then simply describe what these feelings were. This is taxing. Difficult. Yet my emotion that Wednesday night was not in essence different from that which I regularly experience upon hearing a broadcast — perhaps Bizet — on station WNYC. Only sharper. It was what we used to call *Zusammengehörigkeit*, a feeling of connectedness. Connectedness, in the first place, to the man whose music I was at that moment hearing or playing. In that final hour at the Steinway Restaurant I felt nearest, I think, during his *Concert Suite* and the score from *The Life of Émile Zola*, to Maximilian Steiner. The reason for this is perhaps that he was Viennese. And a former pupil of Gustav Mahler. Indeed, I soon felt this connection not only to the film composer, but, behind him, so to speak, the whole world of the imperial city, its streets, its river, the Kaiserliche und Königliche Hof-Operntheater, and even at light moments, when I, myself, was executing a difficult trill, the Wienerwald, with its trees and its birds.

As our program continued, this feeling of closeness — better to say an absence of division, of divisiveness — grew to include those with whom I was playing: Murmelstein, Tartakower, A. Baer, Salpeter. It was as if the Steinway Quintet were a single person, giving a solo performance, as if invisible threads bound us one to another, so that when Salpeter moved his arm upward I felt myself pulled ever so slightly in his direction. And at last there grew to be a similar bond with those who were listening below. We could at that time hardly see them — only the shine from a pair of eyeglasses, a white shirt collar, the napkin on Margolies' arm. Like heads bobbing in an ocean of darkness. Then I felt myself to be not this Leib Goldkorn, no longer the separate citizen, but also a part of that ocean, like a grain of salt, no different from those other grains, Mosk, or Ellenbogen, or the woman, Hildegard Stutchkoff, or the lifeless corpse of her husband, yes, even — do not be alarmed by what I now say — even the two murderers, for they were a part of that ocean, too. That ocean. That darkness, friends. We know what it is, do we not? And this is my feeling concerning the nature of music: that it connects those who have died, Stutchkoff and Steiner and before Steiner, Mahler, with those who are merely waiting to do so. All in the same boat, as Americans say.

The last notes of our concert sounded. The violoncellist plucked three times — C sharp, E, A — his violoncello; Tartakower removed his foot from the footpedal; both violinists drew simultaneously their bows across their strings. The flautist sealed his lips. There was a pause of a single moment. Then the lights came on and the world went to pieces.

The elder Puerto Rican, still cross-legged, cried out in a voice of despair, "O, Chino! Such dreams! *Un sueño. ¡Estaba en China, con dragones y el jefe Mao!*"

The youth helped him to rise. "I know. Come on. The time is up."

"In China! Eating lemons! Only a dream!"

The men stood under the light from the chandeliers and put bullets into their pistols. Several of the patrons began to whimper. A woman was weeping. Then Chino told us what we should do:

"All right! Okay! Everybody! The deadline is over. The stars

are already out. They ain't coming. Understand? They ain't
going to come. I want everybody down here. Everybody in the
middle of the room. Quick! Quick! Move quick!"
"Mister," said Mosk, "I ain't electric."
With his arm Chino motioned to the members of the Steinway
Quintet. We climbed down — A. Baer had now practically
fainted — and stood with the others, in the center of the
restaurant.
"Okay. Now, don't argue, don't think, just do it: you people
take off your clothes."
Immediately Printzmettel went to the sad-eyed tall killer. "I am
Greek. Greek! Bazouki! Metaxa! You must let me go!"
Jesús, with his free hand, ripped the patron's shirtfront, from
top to bottom. Each button was gone. "Off! Shoes! The socks!
Everything! Off!"
"Put your stuff in a pile. Pile it all up in the middle."
Printzmettel did this. We all did this. There were for some
moments only the sounds that persons make when they are removing their clothes. Not then even weeping. Not even sighs. I,
myself, felt embarrassment at the great amount of hair upon my
shoulders, which showed so clearly under the twelve bulbs of the
chandelier. Murmelstein, in his boxer shorts, was helping A. Baer
take off his shirt.
"Is it you, Mister Murmelstein? *Lust mir iber mein bord.*"
Slowly there grew a mound of coats, trousers, and, shame to
say, ladies' blouses, stockings of nylon, a feather boa. Shoes of all
types stuck out everywhere. We were not at that time, however,
entirely naked; before this could be demanded of us a shout went
up, I believe from Margolies, who was standing nearest the
window.
"Here they come! They are bringing the money! I can see
them!"
"We are saved!" Everybody started to shout this out. "We are
saved, hurrah!"
In an instant the taller of the two gangsters was at the window,
rubbing away the mist from the glass. "Goldkorns! Goldkorns!
¡Ven acá!"
I came to where I was called, and looked out. It was dark on
Rivington Street. Light fell through the panes of the Steinway
Restaurant window onto the snow. On Allen Street the lamps
were already burning. From the other direction, still in the shad-

ows, two figures approached. They were of the same height. Both wore brown trenchcoats, and, it seemed, brown-colored hats. "*¡Sí, sí! Son ellos. Tienen todo el dinero.* The money. Ha! Ha!" As they came nearer the rectangle of light we could see that one of these men carried, upon his shoulder, a large sack of some kind, and the other man had a pail in each of his hands. They walked steadily toward us, lifting their feet high out of the inches of snow.

Chino shouted from the center of the room. "Tell them that's close enough, Goldkorn! Tell them to leave the money and go!"

But before I could respond the two men walked directly into the light and stopped in front of our window. They stood restlessly, shifting the weight of their bodies from one foot to the other. I crouched low in order to call to them through the panes of broken glass. In that position I looked up under the brims of their hats: I knew them at once from their faces. These were not the officers of the Hostage Squad. One was Sheftelowitz. The other was Pipe.

"Fools! *Idioten!*" I hissed these words. "What are you doing here?"

The two men simply stood there, swaying a bit from side to side. I cried out once more: "What is it you want?"

Sheftelowitz answered: "What else! Pee-pee."

"We been waiting a long time," said Pipe.

I put my hands to my mouth: "Run! Run for your lives!"

"Run! Ha! Ha! Run, you policemans!" Jesús waved his gun in the window.

Both Jews dropped their burdens. They looked at each other. Then they fled into the shadows on the left and the right. Chino, with no more beard on his face than on the previous evening, came quickly over.

"Where's the money? How much is it?"

We three looked out the window. Both pails had turned over and spilled their contents onto the snow. Fish: for the most part perch. The bag had split open. Feathers.

"Ay! Ay! Ain't dollars!"

"A mockery! An insult to us! Now everybody will die!"

One of these villains grasped the waistband of my shorts and pulled them, what awful tomfoolery, down to my knees. To my ankles. I was then a naked person.

"Get your clothes off! Yids, move your asses!"

Our antagonists then stepped into the crowd of Jews and began to rip from their bodies the last shreds of their clothes. Now there were plentiful screams, wailing, and exclamations. But the two men went about their work grimly, and pushed us, bare, trembling, and sick with sudden fear, toward the open staircase that led to the floor below. Then they stepped back ten, or perhaps fifteen, paces. All of us, musicians, waiters, patrons, were huddled together, as if on the lip of some common grave. Our bodies in the light of so many bulbs were extremely white. Ghosts of ourselves when clothed. Above the prayers, the groaning, the heart-wrenching cries, the voice of Doctor Fuchs — even without his herringbone suit an imposing man — was calm and clear:

"What is the cause of this fear of death? Let us think of it in a rational manner. Is it not in reality the childish fear of losing the penis? Of being cut off from this source of guilty pleasure? Notice how when we recognize the source of our anxiety it at once disappears. Now we feel truly joyful."

The alienist went on in this manner a moment longer, but in truth I no longer heard his words. For, as chance had arranged it, I found myself standing next to and in fact pressing against the body of Hildegard Stutchkoff. There was a wrist of mine against the small of her rounded back. She turned about. There were two breasts that depended. It was impossible not to feel how life stirred in my member; at the same instant I felt come over me a red wave of shame. The reason for this was not my sexual excitement, for how could one not respond to the proximity of such a sportive figure? No, it was just that at that very moment, for the first time in all these hours of terror, I happened to think of Clara, my wife.

Like a child in a classroom I raised my free hand. "Please! I must call on the telephone! My wife! She needs injections!"

Chino, who had previously offered me cognac to drink, now pointed his gun toward my head:

"Goldkorn, you gonna be first to die!"

I closed my eyes. I shut from my ears the sound of screaming. I prepared for what lay at the foot of the stairs.

However, there was no gunshot. Instead I heard Ellenbogen declare, "Look! Stutchkoff!"

I opened my eyes and turned toward the base of the door. At

first I could make out nothing; then I saw, by the head of the corpse, a small pink blur. The fluff of the flamingo had lifted off Stutchkoff's lips, and was rising slowly into the air.

"Ooooo!"

From the open mouth of the restaurateur there now issued a thin gray-colored shadow, a mist, a kind of a cloud — impossible to know what precisely to call it. Steam perhaps. Perhaps smoke. Everyone saw it slowly rising, more and more of it, growing taller, spreading outward, almost the size of a person.

"Ghost!" Chino exclaimed, although in a whisper.

"*¡Un diablo!*"

The two assassins were of course standing nearest the dead man; the sight of them was, even to my eyes, to the eyes of their enemies, pathetic to see. They had dropped their weapons and thrown their arms around each other. Their mouths were open, their eyes rolled about, and, strangest of all, their legs kept moving, in the manner of dream figures who wish to run but cannot. The cloud, now as large as the man had been himself, detached itself from Vivian Stutchkoff and floated toward the two terrified Puerto Ricans.

"Ah! Ah!" they cried, and disappeared inside the mist. Even their hats were gone. Then the cloud passed away: the men were the same, clinging each to the other, except that tears in sheets flowed from their eyes.

Ellenbogen, who had socks on, ran down the center of the restaurant turning all of the chairs upside down.

"The Maggid of Mezritch!" the waiter cried. "So his soul won't be tempted to stay!"

And in truth the cloud followed behind him, moving from table to table, like an eager proprietor. At the end of the room, it covered the zinc top of the bar, and obscured the rows of glasses and bottles. It rose to the first chandelier, then to the second. It enveloped the Bechstein. It touched all the walls. I was not able to resist the thought that it was in some fashion saying to the Steinway Restaurant farewell. Then it descended onto my head. And onto the heads of the others. When it lifted we were all weeping.

"You see?" said Margolies, as he wiped his eyes. "What did I tell you? It's just like Zev Wolf says!"

Mosk, to whom this was addressed, replied in a gasping voice,

"Zev Wolf, my eye! It's what you call tear gas. Look there!" The Lithuanian pointed with a thin white arm to Stutchkoff, or rather to just behind Stutchkoff, where a second cloud was now materializing from under the crack in the door.

The Hispanics saw this as well. They let go of each other, and retrieved their guns.

"Pssst! This way! Follow me! Hee, hee, I have the key!" It was Murmelstein, beckoning us toward the rear of the room.

"Nobody move! Freeze!" The cruel youth shouted those words.

However, the gas had already grown thick in the air. It was difficult to see one another. We joined hands and, in this chain, moved slowly between the platform and the bar, toward the door to the kitchen. The second violinist had already gone through and was fumbling with the lock on the back exit. "I got it!" he cried. "Eureka!"

We all moved as fast as possible — Doctor Fuchs had A. Baer over his back — through the small kitchen to where the barred door was just swinging open. But before we went through, a mysterious sound made us stop wherever we stood. It seemed to be everywhere about us, a kind of a hum, a drone, growing steadily louder. Then the floor under our feet began to shake, the stacked dishes and pans rattled, and the whole building trembled through its foundations. We looked back through the gloom of the Steinway Restaurant proper. Strange lights were descending in beams from the sky. The snow had risen from the ground and was swirling in the air. The noise was now like fists beating upon a rooftop.

"¡Ay! ¡Ay! Angel of death!" the pair of doomed men were screaming. "¡Espíritus malos!"

"Ladies and gentlemen! Do not hesitate! Go quickly outside!" Salpeter was urging everyone through the open door. I, myself, the flautist of the Steinway Quintet, glanced one final time over my shoulder — the shafts of strange light, the thick clouds of gas, our tormentors crying out with their hands stretched high above them — and plunged with bare feet into the alley of snow.

This is Leib Goldkorn. You do not want Goldkorn. You want to know what happened next. Am I not able to convince you that it is over? Finished? Kaputt? Listen: I never, from that moment

in the snow until this moment — and it is now nearly midnight,
Doctor Goloshes has been here already an hour, more than an
hour — set foot inside the Steinway Restaurant again. Not even
to retrieve my shoes, my clothing. These Hildegard Stutchkoff
sent some time later in the public mail. For such a warm day,
almost like spring, it has become a cold night. Wind blowing. We
possess a small electrical heater, and the electric current is still
being supplied; but it is plugged into the socket by Clara's bed.
What is he doing there? Why is he taking so long?

I cannot describe adequately our journey — slipping on ice
patches, feeling blindly the person before us, unable to hear our
own anguished cries — through that narrow alley. Worst was the
noise. It struck at one. It blew one's thoughts away. It was like
the dum-dum-dum of waves on the outside of a ship's metal
plates. Inside which you are sleeping. The shock of such sounds
on my American voyage made me fear my own mind was splitting. I have always thought of myself as a rational man. Once, in
a cafe, I met L. Wittgenstein, and after we had spoken for a few
moments he made a remark about the quickness of my brain.
Not one of the violent, even bizarre actions in the twenty-four-
hour period I have been describing caused me to doubt for a
moment the nature of reality, or the stability of my mind. Everything could be explained. However, as our group of former hostages emerged from the passageway onto Rivington Street, I felt
that the familiar world, one of cause and effect, of physical laws,
had been left behind. It was like a new planet.

What we saw was that between us and the Steinway Restaurant
the snow was actually rising. It was a whirlwind. At the top of
this swirling storm, a black shape hung in the air. It neither rose
nor descended, but simply remained, roaring, in defiance of gravity, of physics, of reason itself. From the belly of this form columns of light shot downward and played over the surfaces of the
snow. In the tremendous thunder it was difficult to hear what
people were saying; but Salpeter pointed toward the Steinway
Restaurant door. This had swung open. Standing inside it was
Vivian Stutchkoff. He appeared to be stuck. He backed up, into
the light of the chandeliers, then came forward and once again
caught in the doorframe. It was at this point, naturally, that my
own sanity came into question. I was not able to suppress an
inappropriate desire to laugh. *Dum-dum-dum* came the sound

from the sky. The dead spaniel was, I noticed, only a few feet away. On the third attempt, by turning a few degrees sideways, Stutchkoff got through the door. He came then bobbing toward us. Our party retreated to the opposite curb. "Golem!" some person cried. Margolies and Ellenbogen were rocking in prayer. Still Stutchkoff came, enormous in size, rising and falling, skimming the snow, like a gas-filled balloon. I barked with laughter again.

From a spot nearby four figures, all clothed, in brown trench-coats and hats, rushed forward toward the abandoned door of the Steinway Restaurant. Two local merchants. And the two members, no doubt, of the Hostage Squad. They all went inside. Stutchkoff, meanwhile, had glided to the center of Rivington Street. There he paused, bouncing about, turning left and right; then he fell face down into the snow. A tall and a short Puerto Rican stood in his place. It had been some kind of trick! Yes! The restaurateur had been their shield!

Some person was pulling my arm. Mosk, the Lithuanian waiter:

"Whirlybird," he said.

Everything, for me, now fell into place. I had been guilty of an error in logic, and my confusion followed from that. You must remember that I had thought that the promises of the Hostage Squad, so contrary in nature, would in the course of things cancel each other out, that nothing at all would be done. False assumption. In truth both plans had been put simultaneously into action. The tear gas belonged to the adamant Officer Mike. What hovered above us was the rescue ship provided by Officer Tim. Indeed, I now saw that hanging from the bottom of this aircraft, nearly invisible in the snowdust around it, was a kind of ladder, perhaps made from rope. Chino had started to climb it, was in fact halfway to the top. Jesús was just getting on.

Then, from the direction of Eldridge Street, a man wearing clothes came running toward us. "Beverly! Beverly!" he cried. It was the gentleman companion of the lady in purple. He was staring wildly about him. "Has anyone seen Miss Bibelnicks?"

I, myself, pointed her out. She was standing alone, near to the curb. Her hands were clasped under her chin and she was peering into the center of the whirling storm, where Jesús had climbed to the top of the ladder. He paused there. His hat blew away.

With one hand he held the ladder and with the other he waved. Then he disappeared inside the airship. The gentleman friend of the lady put his wrap over her bare, wet shoulders. She seemed not to notice, only stared, and moved her lips. "Don't hurt him, don't hurt him," she said.

Suddenly the black shape, with an even greater volume of sound, began to rise straight up in the air. I resisted the impulse, an unusually strong one, also to wave farewell. A light came on in the bottom of the aircraft, and winked on and off. In only a moment this was all that we could see. The sound soon faded completely. The air became clear. There was only the single, silent, red jewel in the sky; and then this vanished, too. We remained, not speaking. Not sobbing either. The yellow light poured from the Steinway Restaurant window and door; but it did not quite reach the street center, where V. V. Stutchkoff lay buried under a mountain of snow.

Goldkorn. Did you know there was a well-known composer named Korngold? An artist, like Steiner, for films? These are the tricks that life plays. I could not, that Wednesday, return directly home. The police officers insisted that we follow certain procedures, and afterward there was a frostbite treatment in the emergency room. It was the middle of the night by the time I pulled myself up these four flights of stairs. My wife was, as I feared, on the floor, in a serious coma. Blood sugar too high. I gave her, as prescribed, injections of insulin; and when she regained consciousness she did not know it was Wednesday instead of Tuesday, that a whole day had gone. It was on this occasion that she remarked, "Am I living, or dying?" She is in a bad way, Clara. The day for her is the same as the night. What is the point of life under these conditions? And I must pay Goloshes, too! How? With what money? Let him obtain it from the government, since it is the government, with all its laws, which insists that such a creature, no spark in her, remain alive!

I shall tell you about the waiters of the Steinway Restaurant, which of course has been closed. Ellenbogen's wife has found part-time work, although Ellenbogen himself has not. Still, they manage to live on her salary alone. Margolies was for many weeks quite ill, with fever and a coating of phlegm. Inflammation. But I have recently learned that he has left the hospital and is living with his young son and his daughter-in-law. They say that Mosk has a small sum of money, in addition to a house of his own in Brooklyn. I believe this is true. Martinez I do not know about. I thought one month ago that I saw, on Broadway, Hildegard Stutchkoff, the cashieress. The same springy curls, and she had a handbag that swung by her side. I called out, but she did not hear me; before I could reach her she had gone into the express stop of the subway. It is possible that I saw somebody else. It might not have been she.

What of our tormentors? In China? Possibly. But it is more likely that the pilot of the airship simply maneuvered it to the roof of a nearby prison. In my opinion they are at this moment in jail.

I am sorry to announce the death of A. Baer. I saw this in the newspaper only one week after our adventure had been concluded. It was a complimentary obituary and contained an interesting description of his student days in Hannover and Paris, his Red Cross concerts, and of how his two little pieces, a sonata for pianoforte and violoncello, and a partita for violoncello alone, were once played by masters all over the world. Salpeter is in Florida. I have lost contact entirely with Murmelstein, as one does at times with younger people. He is in many respects a resourceful and original artist, wrongfully overlooked, and there of course remains the possibility he will yet find a place worthy of his talent. Tartakower. Tartakower has now a position with the celebrated Epstein Brothers Orchestra, and may be heard at weddings, Bar Mitzvahs, and special occasions, in addition to that organization's regular concerts. It is an amazing thing, really. Of course he is a nice man, a generous spirit, I rejoice he has obtained such prestigious work. But does he have the breath control for that type of music? The truth is, when you own your own instrument that kind of question becomes merely academic. It is beside the point.

I hear now noises, footsteps, from my wife's room. Yes. Goloshes is coming soon. "Well, and how is she, Doctor?" That is what I shall say. I shall smile, too. This is my address: 134 West 80th Street. By Columbus Avenue. I would appreciate knowing of even the smallest position, on any type of musical instrument. Oboe. Cornet. English horn. No matter which. I have not in this account attempted to hide any shortcomings, but, on the contrary, to present myself as I am. You know that I drink sometimes schnapps, for example, and that I do not possess a religious temperament. Yet I am speaking truthfully when I tell you I feel myself to be now the same person who received the gift of a Rudall & Rose many years in the past; and like that young boy I am still filled with amazement that merely by blowing upon such an instrument, and moving one's fingers, a trained person may produce such melodious, such lyrical sounds. You are no doubt aware that with the flute the breath passes over the opening, and not into a mouthpiece, as with other woodwinds. Its music is, therefore, the sound of breathing, of life. It is the most ancient of instruments, and the most basic, too. A boy can make one with a knife and a hollow twig. This is what shepherds did, playing to sheep.

EUGENE K. GARBER

The Lover

(FROM SHENANDOAH)

HERE IS A BEGINNING. I am a tow-headed boy in the depression South, walking a dusty road by a creek. I am with two other boys, brothers. The older and taller is Abner Ellis, Junior. The one my age and height is Frank. Abner is seventeen. Frank and I are fifteen. Their mother is thousand-eyed. In my dreams I see her beautiful ocellated face fan out and cover the stars. She knows me, knows that I desire Frank. Abner has no inkling. Frank himself does not understand it. But she knows.

If she had been of a higher caste she undoubtedly would have had a significant history. Maybe she forfeited celebrity when she married Dr. Ellis upon his graduation from Tulane medical school, but I don't think so. Marie Crevet. There are no socially prominent Crevets in New Orleans, not even a marginal family who might marry an extraordinarily beautiful daughter upward into the ruling classes.

Anyway, she came as a bride to Laurelie in south Alabama, melon capital of the world, a patchwork of loamy fields and red clay hillocks, rank with the sweat of blacks and raucous with the hymns of Baptist farmers. No apparent destiny here for her beauty. The doctor liked seclusion. Probably he didn't trust the gentlemen of larger towns. Who could blame him? He was an unlikely husband for such a bride — gangly, big-eared, deformed by an Adam's apple that rode under his collar like a thieved melon in the toils of a creek, and crack-voiced, as though his glottis were arrested in perpetual adolescence. Everyone knows the type, "raw-boned, Lincolnesque." Everyone has read dozens of such biographical sketches. He made the archetypal sacrifices of the poor country boy to secure his degree in medicine: scrimped to save his tuition while still helping to support a widowed mother, studied blear-eyed by midnight oil for his entrance examinations, etc. By the time I knew him he'd already had one heart attack. There was good reason for it, other than his youthful sacrifices — an exhausting practice among blacks bloated by fatback and cornmeal, among gnarled fundamentalist dirt farmers too guilt- and God-ridden to come in time with their ripe tumors. So I despised him from the first for the constant outpouring of his charity, which left us in his home only the rind of his love.

I was his nephew, sent down in the summers from a motherless home in the great city of steel, Birmingham, by a sodden coal-blackened father. And it was I finally who provided the occasion for the heroism which such beauty as my aunt's inevitably has exacted of it.

Marie Crevet Ellis bore to her husband two sons, Abner and Frank. Abner was his father's son — blue-eyed, willowy, an effortless charmer of girls. Frank was his mother's son, dark and beautiful. He was marvelously hirsute, his nostrils dark and densely tendriled, his face shadowed below high cheekbones. His chest and limbs and even his back bristled with hairs that made beautiful black rivulets when he rose like a young sea god from our creek. But such dark beauty was uncouth in those parts, and so he was lonely.

So was my aunt lonely, in constancy to her faith. She attended Mass every Sunday afternoon. It was celebrated for her and two old women by a circuiting priest at a side altar of the Episcopal church, rented no doubt for the occasion through an uneasy alliance of prelacies in that benighted stronghold of fundamentalism. In the dead heat of July and August she still put on her black dress, covered her head with a black mantilla, and walked through the downtown streets to her devotions. The ice-cream eaters in front of the drugstore and the old men on the hotel verandah stared, but they said nothing. I myself would have liked to ask: why this penitential black in the seasonless summer, Lent past and Advent yet to come? What was she guilty of? Failing to rear her sons as Catholics? Later she had more to confess.

I began to succeed in my advances toward Frank. But I can say this for myself: as unthinkable as were my desires in that time and place, I always kept in view his good. When his gentle loneliness began to unfold to me, I touched it always with delicate love. If he wanted to tell me that I was beginning to trespass on his feelings, he only had to speak my name with a hint of admonition and I would stop. Still, I confess, my yearning outstripped the slow melting of his reserve. I found it more and more difficult to guard my feelings, even in the presence of others. Once at supper my uncle, noting our silence, suddenly said, "All right, Frank and Joe, what's the big secret?" Caught completely off guard, I blushed hotly. "What are they up to, Marie?"

My aunt's dark eyes looked straight into mine. "Oh, I think they've found something at the creek."

"They spend enough time down there," said Abner. "It must be a mermaid." His own wit surprised him and he guffawed.

"We don't have any secret, Father," said Frank with a voice as clear as a bell.

"Good. Then let's talk to each other instead of acting like we're at a wake."

I don't know where the conversation went from there, but I do remember that when my frightening embarrassment had passed, I was suddenly suffused with great pity — for the man with the youthfully cracked voice and the dying body; for my beautiful aunt, whose dark eyes pleaded with me to spare her son; for Frank, who was forced now for the first time to lie to his father; and even for Abner in his innocent ignorance. I should have leaped up and cried that I was the serpent in their bosom, that they must scotch me or be ruined. Instead, I excused myself on pretense of nausea. And after that I made ready a face to meet any comment that might touch my relationship with Frank.

For a while I kept my distance from Frank, sensing his revulsion toward the lie he had told his father, though it was not a deep lie. After all, we had only feasted eyes, touched hesitatingly. So, a few days later I resumed my courtship, and I was overjoyed to discover that the lie had left no taint, that the warm promise of his slow yielding was still there. One day when we had swum a while nude in the Blue Hole, we lay together on a flat rock at the lip of the deep pool. We embraced. I felt the hairs of his back, exposed to the motley sun in the trees, dry and grow erect. But after a few moments he disengaged himself and rolled over on his back. I leaned beside him, my body intensely hot. He looked up through half-closed eyes. "What is this thing, Joe?"

Then I knew that he felt, as I did, a palpable presence embrac-

ing us. I might have called it the god of love. I actually thought
of that, but I only said, "I don't know. I don't have to know." I
leaned forward and kissed his teat in its nest of black hair and it
hardened against my lips.

"I do need to know," Frank said.

"Tell me when you find out."

Do I make it sound as though there were only these episodes of
pursuit? Not at all. We played American Legion baseball. Abner
was a star pitcher. We flew model airplanes. Frank's, the most
delicately balanced, stayed up longest. My aunt caught us and
made us mow, weed, shell peas. My forte was frogging. Many
nights we waded the creek. Frank carried the gunny sack. Abner
hypnotized the frogs with the flashlight, and I snared them in the
long net that I myself had woven, hooped, and secured to an oak
sapling. My uncle loved the legs breaded and fried, but he had to
cook them himself because my aunt could not bear to watch the
final contractions in the pan. Of course, we boys one night saved
out a hapless creature for the classic experiment. When it was
newly dead, we passed through it a small battery current. The
twitching of legs bewitched us. We tumbled over each other and
gyrated splay-legged about our bunk room — three adolescents
having a saurian orgy. But even in that crude prank, as in the
chores and play of every day, the current of my love for Frank
never for one moment ceased to galvanize my heart.

Besides my aunt's vigilance, there was one other threat to my
love for Frank — a series of monologues that Abner delivered in
the bunk room when he got home from dates. He would lie on
his back in his bunk and light up cigarettes that he had stolen at
the drugstore. In the morning the room would have a dreadful
smell, but Abner's nicotine crimes were never detected because
my aunt was forbidden by my uncle ever to set foot in the bunk
room. His motives were twofold, he explained. No lady should
have the offensive job of cleaning up after boys. Conversely, boys
must have their sanctuary. Every Saturday afternoon my uncle
himself inspected our quarters. For this we carefully spruced up,
or titivated, as the doctor was fond of saying. Otherwise, the
room remained a congeries of clothes, balls, bats, string, balsam
scraps, etc. So Abner would light up one cigarette after another.
He didn't inhale and probably didn't even like the taste. But he
obviously liked the big white plumes of smoke that rose up into

the moonlight at the window, bequeathing his words a ghostly presence and wreathing about them the wraith of eroticism and nocturnal mystery. Here was the essence of his story repeated over and over with little variation. He had two girl friends, Betty and Harriet. Betty, the hotel manager's daughter, was only a decoy, Abner said. Harriet, a rich farmer's daughter, was his true love. Frank and I had seen them often, of course, and they were true in appearance to the character that Abner assigned them in his midnight monologues. Betty was a saucy little thing with black hair and dark eyes. Harriet, on the other hand, was blond, the perfect Aryan match for Abner. Betty must have absorbed what little there was to learn of vice in Laurelie, living in a hotel suite and helping with the travelers, because a great number of Abner's narratives dealt with her innovations in kissing — frenching, the love-bite, the lobe-lolly, etc.

I found all this repulsive, but I wondered what Frank thought. He made no signs in the dark, no response until one night he pressed Abner for details of a rare kiss from Harriet. "It was a soul kiss, Frank. Our tongues never touched, but it was a soul kiss, better than all of Betty's kisses put together."

"What do you mean, a soul kiss?"

"I mean the kind of kiss that makes you feel like you aren't there any more. You feel like you left your old self behind, like snake slough."

"Where did you go, into Harriet?" A dense fountain of smoke shot up toward the ceiling. "It's hard to tell, Frank. I did sort of feel like I was dropping down into her mouth if you can think of a mouth as big as night. But I wasn't thinking *this is Harriet*. I was just . . . going out of myself."

The halting of Abner's ending was more eloquent than his words. Silence descended on us. But I lay awake thinking: what has Frank learned from this? That one kiss from a true love is infinitely better than all the inventions of promiscuity? That the only true love for a man is a woman? But I found that I could not imagine for myself Frank's thoughts or desires, probably because my own were so simple: I wanted him.

That night's exchange with Abner had a profound effect on Frank. The next afternoon, when we were alone at the Blue Hole lying in shoaling water on the lip of the pool, I caressed his thigh, but he set my hand aside. "Don't touch me, Joe, and don't talk to me about it for a while." I feared he meant forever. I feared it with a wintry contraction of the heart that numbed all my senses. And I felt helpless, forbidden to plead my case with the one I loved. He was determined to work things out alone. My uncle noticed Frank's abstraction and joshed him. "Any chance of you getting out of the dog days of August, boy?" Yes, the summer was almost over, and I knew in my bones that it was this summer or never. I knew that if I could possess Frank even once, I could go back to my smoky city and my sodden father and sing in my heart despite their sooty faces. But if I went back with my desire all locked up, I could not live until another summer.

My aunt watched. One night I overheard her say, "I know what it is, my Frank. I know you will choose the good way." They were in her sewing room. I couldn't see them, but I imagined her taking his hand, stroking his hair, speaking dark eyes to dark eyes, excluding me forever. My heart raged against her. But I made no sign. I knew that if anything caused Frank to suspect I did not love her he would shut me out of his heart forever. So I was the serpent under the flower, waiting for something to come my way. And just when my patience was wearing dangerously thin, I was rewarded. The one who had almost ruined me gave me new hope — dear crude Abner.

My good fortune came on a Tuesday night. Abner was eating with Betty at the hotel and then they were going to the movie. Later, Frank and I learned that her parents were out of town for the night. From Abner's excitement I might have guessed as much, but there was something else on my mind. At supper my uncle had revealed that a much loved fellow doctor over in Minnville was hopelessly ill.

"Physician, heal thyself," I said. The moment the words were out I was horrified. It was as though a demon had spoken through my mouth. My uncle lay down his knife and fork. "The reason he is dying, Joe, is that he has worked himself to the bone for the people of Minnville. He couldn't turn away a sick nigger on Christmas morning." He spoke sharply.

"That's what I meant, Uncle Ab, about small-town doctors. Their patients take everything."

"Joe's right, Abner. You all work too hard." Pity and love streamed out of my aunt's eyes: for the husband with the slightly ashen face whose death would not lag far behind his friend's, for the son in whose dark eyes toiled warring images of awakening sex, and, yes, even for the perverse nephew whose thwarted love tipped his tongue with involuntary malice. She was our *mater dolorosa*. But I couldn't love her, not even for redeeming in Frank's eyes my wayward remark.

After supper the house seemed full of gloom. Halfheartedly I suggested frogging. To my surprise Frank agreed. Down at the creek we waited for the deepening dark to bring the sound of the big croakers. I had one of Abner's cigarettes, which I lit as soon as we had settled ourselves on a rock. Frank must have been surprised because I had never smoked before, but he said nothing. The smoke made a pale image against the moonless sheen of the creek. "Want a drag?" Maybe I hoped that mixing spit on the cigarette paper would seal our lips.

"No."

A moment later I threw the cigarette into the creek and spat after it. "I don't know what Abner sees in those things."

We waded into the creek. Frank went ahead with the flashlight. I followed him closely with my net. The croaker sack was tied over my shoulder. One by one I dropped the big frogs into it. But when we had maybe a half dozen, I began to be invaded by a curious feeling of deep kinship with the frogs — slimy singers of unmelodious love songs flung into a hairy darkness to writhe hopelessly until a hammer delivered them from confusion. So strong became this projection that it grew almost hallucinatory. The flashlight beam did not hypnotize them more than their glistening eyes fixated me.

"Are you going to get this one or not, Joe?"

"No. It's a mama full of eggs. We got enough. Let's quit."

Back at the house I pretended to knot the neck of the sack before I dropped it outside the bunk room door. But I didn't. I knew the frogs would wriggle free. But could they find the creek a half-mile away? Could they follow its sound or smell? Or would the sun catch them struggling lost in the crab grass and thickets? It was do or die for them once more, just as it had been the moment before I netted them, when they made that last jump. Some had cleared the hoop and won freedom, but these had landed in my net. That's what I determined to do now, make my leap. In just a moment, when we were both naked, I would take Frank into my arms as gently but as strongly as I could — my fatal leap of love.

Abner saved me at the last possible moment, bursting in on our nakedness. We had been undressing in the near dark, by the small nightlight — like white-bellied frogs, I was thinking, when the edge of the flashlight beam first touches them. Abner's bunk was closest to the door. He went straight to his bed light, turned it on, and looked at us with an expression of wild triumph. I shook fearfully. Somehow, I thought, his dull eye had spied me out, detected the truth in our surprised nakedness. But it was quickly obvious that I had misunderstood. The wild triumph was something he brought from the hotel, where he had been in Betty's bed. He quickly flung off his clothes and stood before our tall mirror inspecting himself minutely.

"What's going on?" said Frank, his voice already touched with disapproval.

"I was in her, in her." I looked at Frank. Disgust narrowed his eyes and turned down the corners of his mouth. So I pressed Abner with pretended innocence.

"Who?"

"Betty." He was still admiring himself in the mirror.

"In the car?"

"In her room at the hotel." He turned around suddenly and threw himself with a groan face down on his bed as though onto some palpable afterimage of Betty's body. Frank turned away. I followed his lead. A moment later we sat simultaneously on our beds.

"You won't believe it when you finally get some," he said. A tone of coarse tutelage crept into his voice, but when he turned and looked at us, that changed radically. "What the hell's the matter with you two?" Neither of us answered. "You, Frank," he said, "what are you looking like that for?"

"Why don't you go take a shower?" I had never heard Frank's voice so hard.

"Take a shower!" He sat up suddenly. "Take a shower when I saved the perfume for you boys?" I would not have guessed that Abner could be so sardonic. But he had obviously seen the utter disgust in Frank's face, and it infuriated him. He leaped from his bed and threw himself on Frank. I saw the naked limbs of the two brothers writhing together strenuously as Abner deliberately smeared on his brother the secretions of love. Then there was suddenly a cry. Frank had driven his knee into Abner's groin. Abner fell to the floor with a groan and lay there doubled up.

Frank hurried into the bathroom. I heard the instant hiss of the shower. After a while he came back and put on his pajamas. Abner was now lying supine on his bunk with the back of his hand over his eyes. "Don't touch me," he said. I had been wondering which of them would say it first.

The next afternoon, as the two of us lay naked in the shallows of the edge of the Blue Hole, Frank allowed me to lave him with cool water. I touched him everywhere, chastely. I was consoling him, of course, and washing away Abner's bestiality. But I was also making him ready for my embrace. All my intuition assured me that on the next afternoon would come the full consummation of our love. Yet it was not to be. When we returned to the house we found my aunt and uncle making arrangements necessitated by the death of the doctor's colleague in Minnville. My aunt, who lay in bed, was saying, "I don't feel well enough to go, but you go, and take the boys. They ought to be there. Jep has been like an uncle to them."

"I can't leave you alone, Marie," said the doctor.

"It's nothing serious, Abner, and besides, I've got Joe."

I had even then an inkling of the truth about my aunt's illness, but I did not reflect on it because I was so upset by the prospect of being separated from Frank.

At last, at my aunt's insistence, my uncle agreed. They would have to spend one night away, no more. And before they drove off, my uncle laid upon me the usual charge: I was the man of the house in his place and must see that nothing happened to my aunt. I promised and then watched them leave. Abner assumed the older brother's prerogative and sat in the front seat beside his father. Frank sat alone in the back, keeping his eyes constantly on me as a kind of promise until the car turned out of the driveway.

I sat in the living room that afternoon as my uncle had instructed me. I was also to sleep in the guest room that night with the door open so that I would never be out of earshot of my aunt's voice. About three, an old black woman came to the kitchen door. A half-dozen sacks hung from her shoulders. "Field peas, crowders, black-eyed peas, snaps, butter beans," she sang through the screen.

I hurried out to the kitchen. "Be quiet," I said. "Mrs. Ellis is sick."

"Lemme see her then."

I had run into this old black before and she had always looked at me curiously out of her rheumy brown eyes. She was either addled or preternaturally wise. She made me nervous. "Didn't you hear what I said? Go away. If you wake her up, I'll tell the doctor when he gets back." Too late. I heard my aunt's bare feet on the floor behind me. "It's all right, Joe. I'll speak to her." I went off into the dining room but I hid behind the door and listened.

"Hello, Granny. What do you have today?"

"That one say you sick." Why did she say *that one?* It gave me a start. Was she pointing at the dining room doorway, knowing I was there? Or did she say *that one* because she considered me a creature unnameable? I listened.

"You want me to send Seth with some of the black pot?"

I almost burst out laughing. Obviously the hag regularly sent this concoction to my aunt, a doctor's wife and a Catholic still clinging to some old Creole superstition. But if I had known then what I know now, I would not have been tempted to laugh. I listened. My aunt said something in a hushed voice. All I caught was the insistent concluding phrase, "You remember."

"I remember, Miss Marie, if you sho' that's what you want." My aunt apparently was sure, because the old woman left. I retreated quickly to the living room, where my aunt now came instead of returning directly to her room. "I'm sorry," I said. "I tried to keep her from waking you up."

"I wasn't asleep. It's too hot." Her cheeks had a hectic flush, and pinpoints of perspiration moistened her upper lip. She stood before me as if dazed. The light from the window shone through her sheer nightgown except where the cloth folded upon itself, so that I saw the outline of her body broken only here and there by thin streaks of shadow. It was beautiful in silhouette. In the flesh it would have the same delicate ivory as the skin of her arms. But I didn't go far with this imagining. Something in her manner put me on guard. For the first time I got a definite intimation that she had contrived for the two of us to be alone so she could separate me from Frank permanently. She must have guessed the day after Abner's midnight abominations that our relationship had resumed with a passion. After a few moments, saying nothing further, she walked slowly and not quite steadily down the hall to her room.

Now my mind began to work with a fierce heat, assembling a jumble of possibilities. Yet even in those first stages of thought, chaotic as they were, I had no doubt that I could pierce my aunt's intentions. If that seems too precociously self-confident for a boy of fifteen, remember: I had a mother who had been beaten to death by poverty and abuse, a father who was a villainous drunk with the strength of an ox, and wretched schoolmates who watched for every opportunity to humiliate me because I learned fast and whetted my tongue on their stupidity. It was only quick perceptions that enabled me to escape the fate of my mother, the sister whom the doctor had not saved. So I sat in the chair in my uncle's living room with an unread book in my lap. Here is what I had to think about. What was it that my aunt had ordered from the old black? Was it more of the same potion that already was causing her to change — some vial of it left from a much earlier episode which the old black had to fetch up from memory? I thought it must be. But why? Why make herself woozy and strange? It must relate to Frank and me, but how?

I let the questions tumble about in my head. Meanwhile I listened carefully for any noise which would signal a secret delivery by Granny's Seth. I asked myself more questions. If behind the potion and the mysterious behavior was the intention of separating Frank and me, why hadn't she gone about it more directly? Why not plead with my uncle to send me home? He wouldn't refuse her. Or why not call Frank in and tell him that he must break off from me? There was such a strong bond between them that she would inevitably be persuasive. But even as I considered these possibilities, I understood why she wouldn't accept either. The separation must come from us somehow. Otherwise, Frank would be left with crudely detached emotions which later might attach themselves, even more tenaciously, to a similar partner. Perhaps she was also concerned in this way for me. That settled that. But if severance was her goal, how did the potion-induced change fit? Was she going to tell me that my perverse love of Frank was driving her to addiction? That would explain why she ordered from the hag not curative black pot but some potion of different effect. On the other hand, she would know that it would be very difficult to convince me that she was so suddenly and deeply stricken. And even if she could convince me, was that likely to separate me from Frank? She must have known that my passion was strong beyond virtually any compunction. Here I came to the end of my thinking. I was confronted by possibilities none of which seemed quite right. So there was nothing to do now but listen and watch. I would find the answer. I was confident.

For supper, at her request, I brought my aunt a dish of chilled consommé and a glass of iced tea. I tasted both before taking them to her. The dark consommé surprised my tongue. I had never tasted it before. Its rich saltiness suffused my mouth, startling me, bringing back a dim memory of the taste of blood.

"What are you having, Joe?" my aunt said, sitting up, setting the tray carefully on her lap. She seemed more alert, more herself, except that her solicitude for once sounded a false note.

"I already had a double-decker sandwich."

"Then you can sit with me."

I took a chair by the window. The sun was down, but the yard was still full of the gentle gray light of the long August dusk. I looked at my aunt, lovely in the failing light, her thin blue nightgown darker now against the white sheet and the pale ivory of her throat. But it was her eating that arrested me. She spooned up the consommé very slowly, allowing each globule to melt on her tongue before she took the next, hand and mouth moving as if in the slow rhythm of a trance. But the uncanny thing was that my own mouth began to salivate, to fill up with salty flavor. So powerful was the taste that I feared I was being hypnotized. All my other senses were dimmed by the rich sensation in my mouth. Then a bizarre thought came to me: the consommé contained the potion. Seth had somehow slipped it by me.

"I'm not much company, am I, Joe?" She smiled. "But the consommé was so good." She put the glass of iced tea on the table by the bed. "You can take the tray now please."

When I approached the bed, she sat forward. "Here. Give me a kiss, poor boy, left to take care of an ailing aunt." I bent down and took the tray, offering her my cheek. But she turned my chin gently with her fingers and kissed me lightly on the lips. I went away to the kitchen careful not to lick the trace of salty saliva her kiss had left on my lips. At the sink I washed my mouth out and scrubbed my lips roughly with the back of my hand. Then I went to the back door and breathed deeply, but the air was not cool yet though dark was descending rapidly.

I was just beginning to work again at unraveling my aunt's intentions, which were growing clearer now, when Seth suddenly appeared around the corner of the house and stopped at the foot of the steps. I looked down at him. "What took you so long? Mrs. Ellis needs the medicine." I held out my hand.

Seth shuffled. "My granny say give it to Miss Marie herself."

"All right then. You'll have to come back to her bedroom." Seth shook his head. "One way or the other," I insisted, continuing to hold out my hand but at the same time making room for him on the steps if he chose to enter the house. After a long pause he finally handed me the potion. It was a small glass vial about as big as my thumb. "I'll see that she gets it," I said. But he just stood there. "I said I'll see that she gets it." He left then. The fast falling dark swallowed him up — head, torso, and limbs first, then the colorless cotton of his short pants.

By the kitchen light I examined the potion. It was about the color and consistency of molasses. In fact I suspected that it really was mostly molasses. I unscrewed the cap and smelled it — saccharine and bitter at the same time. I smiled — ground bone of bird's leg, frog's eye, drop of woman's blood. You don't catch me, Aunt. I hurried to her bedroom, anxious to see her reaction to my knowledge of this folly.

"What is it, Joe?"

"Seth brought you something." I walked to the side of the bed and handed the vial to her. Then I stepped to the window and called, "You can go now, Seth. She has it." I had heard him rustle in the bushes. Now he burst out with a great thrashing and raced across the yard. I laughed and turned back to my aunt. She was smiling. I could barely see her face now. "You won't tell on me, will you, Joe?"

"What is it?"

She made a high girlish laugh that I had never heard from her before. She was holding the vial in both hands next to her bosom as though it were some tiny creature, a bird or a mouse. "It's a magic potion."

"What's it supposed to do?" I spoke harshly, feeling that I had a definite advantage now.

"It's dream medicine. It makes me dream wonderful dreams and wake up all new."

"Let's turn the light on and look at it," I said, dropping my words as heavily as I could on the songlike lilt of her voice. If the bed lamp were on, the light would reveal the lines in her face, the neck and arms beginning to go sinewy. It would show those simple hands with the unpainted nails foolishly clutching the old black's worthless concoction. It would be the end of her plot against Frank and me.

"No. The light would hurt my eyes." She spoke absently as though she had to fetch her mind back from distant imaginings. Then she sat forward a little on the bed, held the vial out, and unscrewed the cap.

"Molasses," I said disdainfully.

She put a little of the viscid fluid on her finger and touched it to her tongue. "Yes," she said. "Yes." Not, of course, assenting to me but affirming that the formula was correct according to taste. She took several more drops from finger to mouth.

"Molasses," I said.

"Take some, Joe. Taste it."

"Why? I'm not sick."

"It doesn't hurt anybody to dream, especially if things are out of tune."

"Nothing is out of tune with me."

"Yes there is, Joe. We know that, don't we?"

"No."

"What a bad trait in one so young." She tossed herself back and made a little bumping noise on the headboard.

"What?"

"Holding on to something you ought to let go of, especially when there's so much else."

"I never had much, Aunt Marie. So I hold on to anything I get."

"And being foolishly afraid of something nice, something different from anything you've ever had."

"I'm not afraid."

"Yes you are. You're afraid of me. You're afraid of my dream medicine. You say it's molasses, but you think it's a love potion."

That made me swallow hard because it showed that she already knew what I was thinking. So she was ahead of me. She had the advantage. "I'm not afraid," I repeated doggedly.

"Here then." She sat forward and streaked the end of a finger thickly with the black liquid. I hesitated. She licked it off herself, but quickly made a new smear. "If you're going to take him away from me, Joe — in a room that I can't even enter — don't be a common thief in the night, a low miner's son. You're better than that. Win your love. Have courage. Here." I stepped over, took her wrist, and licked the viscid fluid off her finger. It tasted like molasses. "Am I supposed to take more?" She shook her head, sadly I thought. I didn't feel any effect. Of course. It was just an old hag's silly concoction. I began to be a little sorry for my aunt, having to put on this stupid act with dim lights and a sheer nightgown. And suddenly the wrist I held felt as brittle as a bird's wing. I dropped it.

"Kiss me goodnight, Joe." I bent and kissed her lightly on the lips. "Now go to sleep. You will dream of me and I will dream of you. In our dreams we will settle with each other."

"I always dream of Frank," I said.

"If you dream of him tonight, then you have won, Joe." She spoke very simply.

I left then. I went straight to the back steps and sat down. This was my fixed resolve: if the potion did begin to work on me, I would run to the creek and throw myself in. But nothing happened. A high breeze in the moonless sky stirred the tops of the pines. The crickets made great bursts of chirruping and then sank into silence, on and off as they sometimes will, I don't know why. When I was sure that the potion was a fake, I went in to the guest room. I undressed and put on my pajamas and then opened the door as my uncle had instructed. Down the hall my aunt's door was closed and no light shone underneath. I lay in bed listening to the crickets and the passing of an occasional car along the road at the end of the long front walk. For a while I was too uneasy to sleep. But it was not fear. It was this — my aunt, self-hypnotized by her own curious behavior and by her irrational belief in the potion, might do something horribly embarrassing for us both. But the house remained quiet, and after a while I fell into a light and dreamless sleep.

Sometime much later I awoke to the sound of my aunt's crooning. It was like nothing I had ever heard before — high, piercing, unearthly, coming from no particular direction, and burring my head as though a fatal earwig were boring into my brain. It unnerved me badly. I got out of bed and stepped into the hall. My aunt's door was still shut and dark. The crooning was almost constant, but in the short silences I heard the stillness of the night.

The crickets were quiet. I went out into the kitchen and shut the door behind me. There was a moment during which I heard the comfortable low rattle of the refrigerator. But the crooning quickly resumed. I went out on the landing of the back steps and shut the kitchen door behind me. At last I heard only the mild susurrus of the pines. She wouldn't follow me there and I could doze until morning leaning safely against the door. As I grew drowsy, I began to fill my mind with sweet images of Frank lying naked in the creek, his penis wavering under the light current and the hair of his body slanting downstream like deep green water grasses. But soon I went into a black sleep where even my unconscious marked no time so that when I awoke, or thought I awoke, it was into the body of a borderless night. I was lying on my back looking up. The wind in the pines had become water among dark tresses. Frank was gone. My aunt was bending over me. Her mouth, even in the black night, was red. It came down on my lips hot and salty. I began to throb. I felt the creamy essence of my desire rise for her as she stroked me with hands as gentle as the water winds of my dream. So she had been right. Why cling to Frank when there was this? I slipped out of my pajamas, entered the kitchen, crossed it, and opened the hall door. The house was full of warm breath. I felt my desire quicken as I stepped down the hall to the door of my aunt's room, where I did not pause but immediately turned the knob. She was waiting for me there in the dark, I was sure, because the moist heat of her breathing was suddenly denser. I started to make a sound, her name or merely a moan, to show that I had come from my dream to answer her call. But at that moment, I will never know exactly why, my mouth filled up. I do not say with saliva because the liquid was saltier and denser even than my aunt's consommé. And when I swallowed it down, it almost made me gag, for I suddenly knew what it was like — the terrifying richness of a tongue-bitten mouth full of blood. So the door I had just opened was not into my aunt's bedroom but into the heart of a night three years before. It was the summer after my mother's death, the eve of my first visit to my uncle's house, the only time my father had driven me down. That day he came home from work and drank nothing. He bathed himself violently, sputtering and fuming. Then he put on the suit he had not worn since my mother was buried. We left a little before dark. For a while he drove in silence, then he began to talk almost as furiously as when he was drunk, stitching his words together in angry patches. "They'll talk about me like I was coal dust. That's all right. They'll say I'm a God-forsaken drunk and a demon. That's all right too. But if they come down on you, boy, if they start to give you chicken gizzards and nigger's work, you write me. I'll visit them." He laughed wickedly. "I'll have a set with that sawbones and his Cajun beauty." He ranted on. "Glorified vets and bayou belles don't lord it over me or mine." I had heard all this before. I stopped listening and went to sleep.

I woke up to the sound of my father's curses. At first I thought he must have had some whiskey in the glove compartment and had drunk himself into a black fury. Even in the pale dash light I could see the sweat standing on his forehead and the jaws tight around his clenched teeth. "Goddamned son-of-a-bitching suck-egg frogs," he hissed.

"What is it?" I cried out in alarm.

"Sucking frogs."

I sat up and looked out over the hood of the car. Frogs by the hundreds were making white arches in the headlights, thumping against the car and bursting under the tires. In the glare above the highway I saw their mad glazed eyes, saw the flat bodies and pallorous underbellies gliding toward death. "Stop!" I cried.

"Shut up! These suckers have been crossing ever since we left Harlow County." He beat on the horn. "No end to the sons-of-bitches, goddam 'em."

"Stop!" I hollered again.

"Shut up, you little peckerhead. I'll mash you same as I mash these sucking frogs." He stepped on the accelerator and howled out his execrations. The tempo of the thumping and popping of the frogs rose until I couldn't bear it. "Stop! Stop!" He hit me with the back of his hand and made me bite my tongue. My mouth filled with blood. I swallowed it. A moment later I threw up. "Stick your head out of the window, goddamit!"

When we got to my uncle's house, I was white and rank with the smell of vomit. "We passed through a frog migration twenty miles long," my father said grinning. "He'll live, though he is of the delicate kind."

Standing there in the door of my aunt's room, I saw again the doomed white frogs, heard the drum and hiss of their innumerable deaths, felt the weight of my father's blows, and smelled the acid odor of my own vomit. My aunt stirred. "Joe? Joe, is that you?" I ran. Wriggled out of the sack. Ran through the grass toward the creek. Ran for my life from the angry glaring light that raced across the gray morning toward the horizon.

I thought I would not make it. In my frenzy I missed the path. Blackberries snared me and bled me pitilessly. And soon the sun would blaze forth and cook me down to a dry parchment of brittle bones. I could feel its great heat poised behind the pines, ready to beat me down. But when I had fallen a dozen times and a dozen times been turned back by thickets, I at last heard the murmur of the creek. That gave me courage. I burst through the last barrier of underbrush and plunged into the shallow water. I cried out because the cold water at first burned my wounds. Even the creek, I thought, had betrayed me. But after a while the current became more soothing. So, sunrise did not catch me in the open after all. Even so, moved by a lingering fear of the heat, I made my way downstream to the Blue Hole. There I dove down into the dark water and for a while hung by roots in the shadow of the high cut bank. Underneath me wavered the image of my splayed, foreshortened body, the little frog that had miraculously made it across the sun's wide way.

After a time I paddled over to the lip of the Blue Hole and lay in the shoals looking at my body, which was lengthened and human again, though badly scratched. As I lay there, hope and fear divided my heart, but neither finally imaged itself beside me in the water — the black-haired body of Frank or the ivory body of his mother. I tried to think about that, but I couldn't just then. I got up and walked around to the sand bar and looked down at my image in the quiet backwater. My face was so scratched and puffy that it hardly seemed me. I'll tell you what it did look like though. It looked like the face of my father the morning after a particularly bad night, one in which he'd lost a fight. The thought made me smile. The smile was crooked like his because my bottom lip was torn. "Well, Father," I said to the image, "you were almost right. They didn't give me gizzards and nigger's work, but the Cajun beauty gave me nigger's medicine and it almost made me crazy and killed me." Then I spat on the image.

About that time Seth came down to the creek calling out my name in a quavering voice as if it were the name of a demon that might start up after him at any moment. "Here I am, Seth."

"Miss Marie say come back to the house." He kept his distance.

"Go get me some clothes."

When he came back with them, I put them on and went up to the bunk room and began to pack. My aunt came and stood in the door in her housecoat. "What are you doing, Joe?" I looked at her carefully. She seemed entirely herself. "I'm going now, Aunt Marie. The medicine worked."

"That's backward, Joe. It means it's safe for you to stay here now, as long as you want to."

"Yes, it's safe," I said. I kept packing.

"Come in the house and let me put some salve on those cuts."

"No. I don't need any, Aunt Marie. But I'll tell you what I could use is some money, for bus fare."

"Your uncle Ab would never forgive me if I let you go this way."

"You couldn't explain to Uncle Ab what way I went if you wanted to, Aunt Marie. So just tell him I ran off. I'll never tell him different. In fact, it's the truth. I am running off."

"Where are you going?" That surprised me a little, how obviously she knew I was not going home. When I didn't answer, she shook her head. "They'll take you back to him."

"Maybe once or twice, Aunt Marie. But I'm a smart boy. Everybody says so. I'll learn pretty quick how to get away for good."

"From us, too, Joe?" I nodded. "I never wanted that, Joe."

"I believe you, Aunt Marie, but you knew it had to be, even if you didn't want it."

She went off and got some money and brought it back to me, almost a hundred dollars. I gave half of it back to her. "It's too much, Aunt Marie. I have to start learning right away how to get it myself."

My aunt looked at me with a face so drawn in upon itself that I thought she would begin to weep. But all I wanted then was to get away from her. Before many years, though, I would pity her. This is how it must have been with her. There I stood destitute, having lost mother and cousin lover, having renounced father, uncle, and aunt. All I had was an old grip, forty-odd dollars, and a scarred face and body. But I was free. And there she was, twenty-five years older, with a dying husband, one son no more like her than day is to night, and another son separated from her by the perpetual secret of what she had just done for him. All she

had left was her God. Or had she even traded God for son that
night?

"Tell Frank I said good-bye."

My Aunt Marie was wrong. They never did take me back to my
father even once. I went straight from Laurelie to New Orleans.
I changed buses three times, traveled mostly at night, and never
talked to anybody.

My aunt laid upon me either a great blessing or a terrible curse.
Here is how it has been with me. For over thirty years I have
been absolutely free of desire. Remember? At the lip of the Blue
Hole that last day no image appeared, neither Frank's nor hers.
None has appeared since. Of all the beds I have slept in, I have
shared not one — all as clear as the limpid water of the imageless
creek. From what I have seen I would count this a blessing. But
I don't press the point. Each must be his own judge.

PATRICIA HAMPL

Look at a Teacup

(FROM THE NEW YORKER)

SHE BOUGHT the teacup in 1939, of all years. It was on sale downtown, because it was a discontinued pattern. Even on sale, it was an extravagance as far as her new in-laws were concerned; it set her apart. She used to say how she just put the money down on that counter and let Aunt Gert sigh as loud as she pleased. Nineteen thirty-nine. My mother was buying dishes that had come from Czechoslovakia, because they made the best china and she was marrying an American Czech. Most of the teacups are still unbroken. They're mine now, because I'm her daughter and she cleaned out her china cabinet last week. Each piece has a tiny "Czechoslovakia" stamped on the bottom. The cup is thin — you can almost see through its paleness when it's empty; right now, there's tea in it, and its level can be gauged from the shadow outside. The cup is the palest water-green imaginable. Sometimes, in certain lights, it is so pale it doesn't seem green at all, just something not white. It is shiny, and there are thin bands of gold around the edges of the saucer and cup, and again midway down the bowl of the cup and at its base, which is subtly formed into a semi-pedestal. There is also a band of gold on the inner circle of the saucer, but it has been worn away, after so many years, except for a dulled, blurred line. There is no other decoration on the outside of the cup — a bland precision of lines and curved light.

But inside the cup there are flowers, as if someone had scattered a bouquet and it had tumbled into separate blossoms, falling in a full circle around the inside. Some have fallen faster to the bottom of the cup, while some are still floating. The blossoms don't seem to be pasted on the surface like decals; they really appear to be caught in motion. And now, for the first time, alone in my own house (I've never been alone with one of these cups before; they were her company dishes), I see that no two flowers on the cup or the saucer are the same. Each a different flower — different colors, different altitudes of falling, nothing to create a pattern. Yet the cup and saucer together are pure light, something extremely delicate but definite. As refined as a face.

My mother's face, which has fallen into sadness. Nothing tragic ever happened to her — "nothing big," she'll say. I am the one who has wanted something big.

"I know the most important thing in the world," I told her when I was ten.

"Well, what is it?" she asked.

"Work. Work is the most important thing."

Her face showed fear. "Oh, no," she said quickly, trying to sweep away the thought. "No. Family is the important thing. Family, darling." Even then, her voice was sounding a farewell, the first of all those goodbyes mothers say to their daughters.

Or maybe our parting began one day when Dad came up behind her in the kitchen. He kissed her on the back of the neck. She thought they were alone, but my brother and I had followed him into the kitchen. He kissed her neck just where the hair stops. She turned from the sink like a swaying stem, with her hands all full of soapsuds, and put her stem arms around his neck. Her eyes were closed, her arms heavy and soapy. Pure and passionate soap arms of my mother. He drew her down suddenly in a swooping joke of an embrace — a Valentino bend, an antic pose for us giggling kids. He swept her in his arms and gave her lips a clownish kiss. We giggled, and our father laughed and turned to grin at his audience. "My dahling, I *luff* you!" he said to her soulfully. Her body struggled awkwardly, her eyes flew open, and she tried to rise from his clownish embrace.

"No, no," she said. No, no to any joke. She stood at the edge of her red-petaled life. There are buds that never open. "Just let me up," she said. "I've got these dishes to do. Let me *up*." And she plunged her hands back into the dishwater. Every night, she swam with her thoughts in that small sea.

In the cup, amid the bundle of pastel falling flowers at the bottom of the bowl, there is another firm, thin gold circlet. It

shines up just below the most deeply submerged flower, like a
shoreline submerged by a momentary tide of morning tea. The
engulfed flowers become oranges and violets — those colors.
Above the tea-line there are green leaves and several jots of blue
flowers, not deep and bright like cornflowers, but a powdery,
toneless blue, a monochrome without shadow or cloud. Also,
there is the shape of the flowers. Some are plump, all curve and
weight. There is a pale lavender rose on the saucer, with a
rounded, balled-up cabbage head of petals; and on the opposite
side a spiky, orange dahlia-like flower. None of the flowers looks
real. They are suggestions, pale, almost unfinished, with occasional sparks of brightness, like a replica of memory itself. There
is a slur of recollection about them, something imprecise, seductive, and foggy but held together with a bright bolt of accuracy —
perhaps a piercing glance from a long-dead uncle, whose face, all
the features, has otherwise faded and gone.

In 1939, in Chicago, my mother was a bride. That was the first
year of the war, when Europe began to eat itself raw. In the
newspaper picture announcing the marriage, her head had a
halo. A golden light was around her head.

"I wasn't one for buying a lot of stuff," she tells me. "You only
need so much. I bought what I needed when I got married." In
the past few years, she's been giving me many of those things,
piece by piece. Every time I go over to visit, she says, "Well, you
might as well take the yellow tablecloth." Or there will be a pile of
silverware she'll want me to have. These teacups. I'm always
walking off with something.

I try to get her to talk about her life, but she won't do that. It's
not that she thinks I'm prying. "Well, honey, what do you want to
know?" she says. "I mean, what's there to say?" And she pushes
her hair, which is still more blond than anything else, away from
her face, and she looks really beautiful. I start talking fast, saying
how everybody *knows* the world has changed a lot since the Second World War ended, and she was alive when Hitler was in
power, for God's sake, and she's lived through something, and it's
part of history.

"It wasn't *that* long ago," she says, and flips her honey hair again
and lights a cigarette. "Besides, you'd have to talk to somebody
from Europe about all that. They lived through it." Once she told
me that in high school she'd had an assignment to write an essay

about why Hitler was good for Germany. "Personally, I never liked him," she said. "We were always Democrats. But we had that assignment."

So I go over to visit, and we talk and I ask all these questions and she says, "You sound like one of those oral-history projects," and I say, "No, really, I'm interested." I'm always telling her, anything you can remember, any detail — it's really important. Everybody's life is important, I say. I'm interested. I can't even explain why.

Sometimes she says things like "You know, I bet you won't believe this, but we girls, way back — and this wasn't in the country, either — we used to use cotton strips all bundled up, instead of Kotex. And we'd wash them out and use them over again." Or, "The first pair of nylon stockings I bought, they lasted two years. Then stockings started not lasting." Once, she looked across the kitchen table at me and said, almost experimentally, as if she wanted to hear how it would sound aloud, "You know, one time your father came home, just an ordinary day, and I looked up and I wasn't even thinking, it just darted into my head: Someday he'll walk in and I just won't be here, I'll just leave. But it never happened."

None of it amounts to anything, though. Her details don't add up to a life story. Maybe that's why she's been giving me all these things the past few years — her possessions, everything she bought in 1939, the year of her marriage. This teacup, which I look at closely, for a long time, sitting at my own white-and-yellow kitchen table, alone, across the city from her.

The teacup was made in a country far away, of which other countries knew little. An English politician (but you can't go just blaming *him,* my mother says) shook a nation away as he tightly furled his black umbrella. A country lost its absorption in peaceful work, lost its pure science of flinging flowers onto the sides of teacups.

I tell her I believe that something could have been different. What would have happened if someone with an important black umbrella had considered the future of teacups, if powerful men bowed their heads at the difficulties of implanting the waxy tulip on porcelain? Old questions — certain people have tried to answer them, there are books. But many of us still live with the details; the souvenirs of some places are never broken. This cup is a detail, a small uncharred finger from the mid-century bonfire.

I visit my mother. We sit in her blue-and-white kitchen. My mother stands up for the future. "Life goes on, you can't keep going over things," she says. "It's the *flow* of life that counts." She wants me to ride forward into the golden light that she says is the future and all its possibility. "Look ahead," she tells me.

I try, but everything drives me into the past that she insists is safely gone. How can I ride forward on her errand when all the world, even the smallest object, sends me back, sets me wondering over and over about our own strange life and country, always trying to understand history and sexuality. Details, however small, get sorted into their appropriate stories, all right, but I am always holding out for the past and thinking how it keeps coming back at us. No details are disparate, I tell her. Mother, the cups were discontinued because a country was discontinued.

"Oh, but now you're talking politics," she says, and clears off the kitchen table. "Over my head, over my head," she says.

But it's not. That's what makes me mad. She *knows*. They all do, those brides who chose their china in 1939. Many things fell that year, for those brides — not only flowers into teacups. Their bodies fell, paired with other bodies, on beds together for the first time. "But that was no tragedy," she says, smiling, with her hands on the back of a chair. Smiling because she knows after all our talks that I think something was wasted when she first fell. Because I have refused to fall. "Some people just don't want to get married — I know that," she says broadmindedly. But she knows I'm saying marriage isn't *there* anymore; the flowered flannel nightgown isn't being hung on a peg in a closet next to a pair of striped drawstring pajamas anymore. We don't get married anymore, Mother. Don't blame me; I didn't think it up.

"Don't talk like a sausage," she'll say. "Some people — there are always some people who do not *want* to get married. I understand this. I understand you. You don't want to get married. Fine. That's just fine. It's fine. Many people live . . . that way."

Her own marriage, I agree, was no tragedy. It was the old bow pulled across the cello, making its first sexual sound again. Another generation joining the long, low moan. The falling of flowers down the sides of teacups, the plunging bodies on white sheets. I know people could take any amount of this pain. But the falling of the other bodies, the rain of bodies in Europe, that happened that year too, Mother.

Marriage, that's one thing; we agree that for her it was no tragedy, wasn't the end, really. But Europe was already broken, broken for good; there was no replacing a nation of glassblowers. Bodies fell that year in Madrid, too. In the cities of Spain, women looked up at the sky in terror. In Barcelona, almost for the first time in history, a woman carrying home a branch of forsythia wrapped in waxed paper ran for cover, hiding from the air. In that war, bombs fell on women from the air, and it was planned.

My mother says she can't get over how I'm always connecting things.

"Everybody I know talks this way," I say. "Does it embarrass you?"

"No. Just — well, tell the truth."

"I will. I'll try to."

The only real difference between us, between my mother and me, is all the talking I do. Her cello voice was drowned somewhere in the sound of falling flowers, in marriage, in the new thought of bombs falling on women with flowers, with teacups. But this particular teacup and its golden shoreline escaped, and she and I have both sat with it in our kitchens. She gave it to me.

Mothers know their daughters go to their bedrooms and try on the strange clothes women wear and look at themselves in the full-length mirror, trying to understand the future, the lipstick, the bras. Is there a mother who gives a daughter a teacup and thinks it is not also inspected?

"Mother," I said last week when I was over to visit and she was putting red tulips in a vase, talking about how everybody she knew smoked and how she was glad I'd never taken it up. "Mother, everybody I know, they're always talking about their parents, trying to figure out their mothers. Did you do that? My friends, we all do that."

"No," she said. "We didn't, I guess. We didn't talk the way you do. We didn't, you know, have *relationships*." Then she remembered about the teacups, and we changed the conversation.

If she were alone having a cup of tea, as I am now, she would be smoking a cigarette, staring dreamily out the kitchen window, absently rubbing her index finger over the nail of her thumb (she still uses nail polish) in circle after circle. The smoke would be circling around her head of honey-and-smoke hair. Just sitting. I can see her.

This afternoon, though, it is my finger looped in the ear of this European cup. She is not the only submerged figure I see — she and this buoyant cabbage-head rose. There is so much sinking, no hand can hold all that has happened.

We sit around a kitchen table, my friends and I, and try to describe even one thing, but it flies apart in words. Whole afternoons go. Women often waste time this way. But history has to get written somehow. There are all these souvenirs in our houses. We have to wash and dust them. They get handed down when there's no way of explaining things. It's as if my mother has always been saying, Darling, look at the teacup. It has more to say.

BAINE KERR

Rider

(FROM THE DENVER QUARTERLY)

1. Trees

ANYONE DRIVING between California and the Rockies for the first time will realize he has been lied to all his life: the country has not been settled, the West not won. A huge unvanquished heartland remains, called the Great Basin. Its dry riven bowl engulfs parts of Idaho, Oregon, California, Arizona, and Utah. Its massed center is the wilderness known as the state of Nevada. It is a place like nothing else in the world. Within it, water — and thus the flow of valley, mountain, plain; the configuration of life — does not drain to the sea, but inward upon itself, toward some ephemeral and finally nonexistent midpoint.

Driving across, it feels like an emptied ocean, restless, bereft of the tidal patterns of seas, and those of land, where rivers organize geography toward an oceanic destination. Ghosts of glaciers and wide water haunt the great heat and aridity. Epochs intermingle. Limestone shoulders granite. Life zones, from Sonoran to Arctic, tiered across 2000 miles from south to north, can occur in the Basin with minute accuracy in a five-mile span. Causal principles are left to the absolute rhythm of sun and night and the recklessness of wind. Wind facets everything, from pebbles to mountains' faces. Dunes swell from nothing and advance in crescent ranks directionless across the desert. There is rarely a blue day in the Basin unconvulsed somewhere by the isolated rage of a thunderstorm — a spasm of entropy trapped in the limitlessness of the place.

Diastrophism — the wrenching of the earth's crust into faults, mountains, basins — is what happened here, though no one is quite sure how. Irresistible energies still play upon the land without purpose; the land turns, subsides, protean in all its aspects except the greatest heights, the Basin Ranges. These are the mountains no one knows, the massively beautiful peaks between the Rockies and the Sierra Nevada. Instead of composing an uplifted continental ridge, they follow the sinuous confusions of fault lines, jutting from ruptures in the Basin's blasted bowl, angling crookedly for one, two hundred miles, stopping precipitous in the desert again. Most fascinating of central Basin mountains is 13,000-foot Wheeler Peak in the Snake Range of eastern Nevada. Wheeler intercedes between two utterly barren 30-mile flats as a sharp, slate-blue and ice-white verticality above the boneless, panting desert. Shapes and attitudes — rocks, trees, Wheeler's mass venting through clouds — all are jagged, oblique, bewitchingly irregular, especially the sheer northeast face, a ragged semicircle of 2000-foot cliffs gnawed by glaciers, called "Wheeler's cirque."

In prehistory, Frémont Indians hammered petroglyphs into the mountain's lower boulders, invoking its spirit. Centuries later Shoshone, Goshute, and Paiute survived on the pinyon nuts of its foothills. John Muir wandered there in 1878, stunned by the structure of the cirque. And there, wondering at the savagery of rock and ice, and at the past, he never suspected the extraordinary secret the cirque held.

Above ancient Lehman Caves, hidden within a boulder field and a grove of Englemann spruce, is the one entrance to the glacial flats at the foot of the cirque's walls. From the flats, climb to timberline, just before the still-breathing ice field that seals the base of the streaked cliffs, and you might once have found the oldest thing alive on this planet. The hills surrounding Wheeler Peak are forested with Great Basin bristlecone pine, the strange dwarf trees that are unmatched even by giant sequoia in longevity. And somehow *above* timberline on the mountain, at 11,400 feet, a small bristlecone, the oldest of its ancient kind, had been growing 5000 years within a ruck of quartzite boulders, enclosed by the towering broken cup of the cirque. The pine's twisted body was almost entirely deadwood, fretted by wind and ice, polished by Arctic weather to a gloss that shined silver, ivory, yellow, and a bleeding red — dead but for one tiny curling strip of bark feeding the one still-green branch.

The Forest Service came across this tree in the 1950s and named it *Prometheus*. In 1964 a young geologist, a Ph.D. candidate doing field work near the glacier, attempted to measure its age. His coring tool sheared in two inside the incredibly dense wood of the tree, and, whether only frustrated and stupid, or suddenly — alone within the cirque — berserk, he sawed it down, cut it into chunks, and removed it from the mountain.

2. Kevin

There are two ways to travel. Like hummingbirds, who zing five hundred miles without touching ground, fasting in flight. Or like geese, who investigate lakes, fields, city parks, everything en route, and gorge themselves constantly. On this migration from San Francisco to Colorado, Kevin was the hummingbird, I the goose. Finally arranging a breakfast stop at Frenchman's Café in Nevada had been the first victory for goose travel since we left the afternoon before.

This first leg — the 240 miles from The City and the sea, through full spring in the Sacramento valley, up into winter on the Sierra Nevada, down past Reno's lights through the vacant black desert to Frenchman's Café — had been marked by a quietly festering discord, the grudging coexistence of rival species. It was my car, my trip to Colorado. He came as a rider, to share driving and gas, on his way to Cleveland. We'd never met before and, from the very first, our differences showed little promise of moderating with the comradeship of the road.

For one thing, that Kevin didn't like to stop and eat along the way began to irritate me beyond reason. Originally, in the first hours of the trip it had only irritated me within reason, I think, as I've always needed to pause periodically for coffee and trash food while traveling. Kevin scorns all stimulants and foods prepared in public kitchens; also, he's a compulsive believer in "making good time." He had carried aboard a supermarket bag brimming with what he considered ample staples for the journey: cheeses, apples, crumbly home-baked wheat bread, pounds of dried fruit — expensive apricots, muscatels, Chinese salted plums — and nuts of every variety. I can't tolerate dried fruit or nuts. Even raisins. Even peanut butter.

At first he was generous, offering to divvy the health bag half and half, but generosity soon turned to condescension. I'd need coffee and he'd suggest cashews. I'd be driving, eyes fixed on the road's white lines in the Sierra midnight, and perceive, near the rear-view mirror, Kevin's thumb and forefinger proffering a withered fig like some semiprecious gem, saying softly, "Try this. It's good for you."

In San Francisco I'd picked him up at Burns's house, Burns being the mutual friend who'd arranged the ride. Unfolding the map, I explained our initial, crucial decision. Two routes proceed from San Francisco east eventually to Denver, my destination. I-80, a little faster, but oppressively dull and beset with two hugely enervating obstacles: Salt Lake City and 500 miles of Wyoming. U.S. 50, slower, riskier regarding availability of gas, but a scenic delight following the old storied route of the Wells Fargo line. Either way would advance Kevin usefully toward Cleveland, his goal. But, as this trip was kind of my valedictory to California, I'd really prefer taking 50. After Reno, it goes through the heart of the Great Basin, through the silver-mining and hot-spring country of Nevada, by the Utah canyonlands, over the Colorado Rockies. Besides, outside of Ely, Nevada, the magnificent valley beneath Wheeler Peak alone justifies taking the road less traveled by.

Kevin had nodded.

We boarded my brand-new Pontiac Ventura, buckled up, and soon were tugging the basketball-orange U-Haul beast up the first of a hundred mountain inclines — like two lawmen bringing in a caged brute for bounty. The trailer did hold outlaw booty of a sort: detritus salvaged from a disastrous decade-long encounter with the State of California. Things hadn't gone well there; not quite ruin, but rack enough for a while — divorce, disintegration, teeterings on the edge of madness, that kind of thing. At last I was leaving The City, its insanities, my failures. Bringing to a close the years of my twenties not with a bang, but a shudder. San Francisco in March of 1974 had gotten a little edgy, to say the least. The Symbionese Liberation Army had just swallowed up Hearst's daughter, and the random murders called "Zebra killings" had stirred the old foul pot that always simmers there somewhere. The City's buoyance had caved in, as it regularly does, to a kind of manic gloom. One thinks of The Earthquake at times like those, and of leaving town.

As Kevin and I and my U-Hauled past set out, my mind

teemed, conflicted with thoughts of transit. There were two preoccupations: making this last trip a "memorable" exodus, rife with symbols, lousy with epiphanies, thus coming away from the Golden State with something to show for it; and then *getting there*, to Colorado, and, presumably, a new life. A wonderful change of fortune I still couldn't quite believe had saved me, that winter in San Francisco, from drowning in my accumulated fecklessness. Chris, with whom I'd lived two years after divorcing my first wife, had become pregnant, we'd decided to marry, and I'd gotten a great offer in Denver. *Denver:* landlocked, as safe as you could be from The Earthquake. I flew Chris there the week before the trip, to begin house-hunting, and she'd called that morning to describe the little gingerbread Victorian she'd found. When I reached Denver we would get married, in Glenwood Springs, just the two of us. This trip with Kevin was the last transcontinental step, the thread between a bootless past and a solid future. Even more than a good job, a new wife, a first birth waited at its conclusion. Across the Great Basin, just over the Continental Divide, a pellucid wholeness beckoned: concentric glowing rings — Colorado, the house there, the woman, Chris, inside, the child inside her — an aurora 1300 miles to the east . . . "an orbed drop of light, and this is love." I couldn't begin to talk to Kevin of these things as I drove — of love and the urgency of what to *do* with it (like fire when first discovered: Shall we boil beans and dry socks with it? Or put it to kindling forests and ravaging worlds? Or simply sit wonderingly, rapt with its beauty?). I did try to tell him about Wheeler Peak.

I babbled, in fact, of that mountain, its breathtaking cirque, its ancient trees, the grotesque forest of bristlecone pine that populates that place where other spirits must also reside. I babbled, while driving, to the point of strange obsession with this subject, until late in the night when, straining in the underpowered, overloaded car up Donner summit, I stopped midsentence, having gained audible evidence that Kevin was asleep. I was tired myself, set on stopping in Reno for slots and coffee. But some hours later Kevin awoke and produced the dispiriting dessicated fig. I was undone. We left Reno behind, sparkling in the cold crystal night. Dawn rose near Fallon and with it my mighty resolve to pause at Frenchman's Café, after which Kevin would take the wheel.

I shook him awake. "Time for breakfast, Kevin. A mug of coffee, and ham and eggs. Nothing improves scenery like ham and eggs, as Mark Twain put it. He loved Nevada too."

About Kevin. Burns had called asking if I wanted a rider, and of course I did. I didn't much fancy pulling that trailer alone across the mountains; the trip promised to be slow, tortuous, expensive. A rider would cut costs, enable us to drive straight through, and perhaps make the journey more a pleasure than a chore. Burns seemed anxious, for some reason, that Kevin be delivered into good hands on his way to Cleveland, and I owed Burns a sizable favor, for a sizable loan a few years back I still hadn't completely paid off. Burns didn't know Kevin very well — the younger brother of a good friend of his, a shy kid, twenty-one, twenty-two years old, worked odd jobs in The City. And I learned very little more about him than that, in the forty hours we were almost constantly together. There's nothing objectionable about his appearance. Long blond hair in a ponytail, clean-shaven, glasses, about six feet tall. A well-kept hippie. In addition to gobbling dried fruits, he smoked dope, joint after joint after joint — a practice that began to bother me once he started driving.

Most striking about Kevin was his silence. I don't hear very well and at most he barely whispered. At first I was afraid he couldn't talk at all. We'd conduct rather difficult conversations. For example:

"So you're going to Cleveland?"

Nod.

"Your folks there?"

Nod.

"So you're just headed back for a visit with your folks?"

Nod.

"What's Cleveland like?"

Shrug.

"I hear the Cuyahoga River is so polluted it caught on fire once."

Nothing.

It wasn't that he seemed especially bashful; I don't know what it was. San Francisco then had gotten, as they said, "heavy into ego-loss," a matter of large metaphysical consequence I've never understood. (I imagine it was an effort to dissociate from L.A., which has always been, as we know, heavy into ego-projection.) I figured that Kevin, being younger, was probably on top of this currently hippest phenomenon of San Francisco hipness. He was certainly beyond "far out"; he'd gotten down to the mellow mumble, and seemingly had lost his ego (somewhere in the Mission District, I'd guess) irretrievably. Ego-loss, as I've indicated, did not interest me at the time. What interested me was more like ego-gain, or ego-salvage: Chris, family, house, job, and so on.

Near Auburn, about three hours into the trip, as the sun lowered behind us into the gauzy-green March of the Central Valley, we did have a two-way conversation of sorts, but it didn't go much better; what Kevin said was so unsatisfactory.

We talked about San Francisco. I mentioned the Zebra killings (a group of black men had been corking off whites at random — housewives, delivery boys, pigeon feeders in the park), which I'd found fairly unsettling. Downright terrifying in fact. I asked Kevin if he felt any relief now that the Motherlode hills lay between us and the violence of the Bay Area.

"I love San Francisco," he murmured.

Well, yes, no doubt. And a great city it is. Very European, as they say. But, my God, there was weirdness rolling through that fog of late. Wasn't there?

"Just the goddam pigs."

Hmmmm. The reference here was to police, not the murderers. The possibility of a very fundamental rift yawned between us. And I wanted this trip, my valedictory, to be a success.

"Have you traveled much cross-country before?" I shifted subject.

"Once."

"When?"

"Two years ago."

"That was when you and your brother came out from Cleveland." I filled in his information for him. He nodded.

"Which way did you come?"

"I don't know."

"Did you come through Wyoming and Salt Lake?"

"I don't remember," Kevin said, turning to me. "I don't remember anything between Cleveland and the coast."

He leaned into the back seat to delve in his health bag, coming up, like a diver, with a handful of macadamia nuts. Meantime I pondered what had been Kevin's longest spoken sentence. Nothing, *nothing* in all that magnificence between Ohio and California, impressed him; that unspeakable magnitude of geography, which ought to reduce a born-and-bred American to humble study of his land, failed to nick Kevin's memory. This struck me as very bizarre. I, on the trip, would illuminate the Great West for this deprived soul.

I turned on the radio, twirled the tuner, landing fortuitously on a C&W station. Within a half-minute Kevin had jerked out his arm and snapped the radio off. "God I hate that shit," he muttered.

"You do?" I stared at him, amazed at his incivility.

He nodded, grinding his molars on macadamia nuts.

"Well, you're going to have to put up with it." I clicked the radio back on. And I was going to have to put up with him. Besides needing his help driving and splitting expenses, I was obliged to Burns. No matter. We reeled along into the numinous twilight of the Sierras banked like hooded giants before us, and I began to babble of Wheeler Peak. Kevin smoked a joint, graciously regularly passing it my way, though I continued to refuse. I lit a cigarette; a look of mild horror crossed Kevin's face, and he rolled down the window. The importunate little beggar. No matter. I turned up the heater and kept talking. Kevin rolled and smoked, rolled and smoked, and, by all appearances, listened throughout the evening.

I felt great. We were a hundred miles into Nevada with three hundred more to go — one good full fine day of Great Basin. The sky was immaculate as my daughter's eye is now; my stomach pleased as she after draining the breast. There were likely to be few if any cars on U.S. 50 all day long. I could sleep as I wished, but I had no wish to sleep.

At Frenchman's Café, which we'd just left, we'd seen one of those strikingly peculiar sights that occur nowhere but in the maverick state of Nevada. I was sopping up the last of my overeasies (while Kevin nursed a glass of undrinkably sulfurous water), when a van, lettered TRANS-NEVADA BUS LINES, pulled up outside and the uniformed driver plus four ladies, three black, one white, wearing diminutive amounts of leather and lace, got out. They yawned and stretched, silhouetted against the cracked bed of a dry saline lake across the highway, and, behind that, shimmering, featureless, monochromatic distances of desert. They stood there as desultory as if passing time in some gilt and scarlet lobby on the Vegas strip. Inside, a rancher, looking up from the pool table, announced, "Here's Sammy with a load of *hoo*ers." Evidently the sole service of the Trans-Nevada Bus Line was to shuttle hookers cross-state from Reno to Ely and back, and the driver always stopped for coffee at Frenchman's Café.

"How about that?" I remarked to Kevin. Kevin looked both puzzled, and uncaring to be unpuzzled. "Whores!" I said. "Right dead in the middle of nowhere." Kevin nodded, and suggested that we better get moving.

He drove, and I tried to sleep and couldn't. I couldn't sleep, I realized after we'd ventured twenty miles beyond Frenchman's, because I'd contracted a case of Traveler's Lust, an odd kind of horniness resulting from being up all night driving and thinking, triggered no doubt by the whores at the café. But the same feverous complaint had struck other times when I was strung out from traveling in that part of Nevada. Could be something in the place itself, in the wild freedom of unbroken horizons and brilliant light, that disputes thoughts of destination and confuses a linear imagination. Somehow passion haunts these spare wastes; the wind blows voluptuous visions across your mind and engorges your lower heart. I wondered if Kevin could possibly sense it.

He drove, I thought, very poorly. He'd mentioned, when we switched places, that he hated American cars but could handle them all right as he'd driven a cab for a while in San Francisco. I found that hard to believe. Kevin of the mellow mumble as a garrulous cabby? But I knew it was true as soon as he began manhandling my car — taking first gear to 45 mph, steering, stopping, careening downhill without the least regard for the 2000-pound buffalo hitched to the rear bumper and fighting us all the way. A radical change came over Kevin as soon as he took the wheel. Even as a passenger he'd never made peace with the infamous seat-belt interlock system that encumbers my Pontiac, mumbling with increasing ill humor each time, after stopping, he forgot to latch himself in place. But now the mumble became a decided mutter. At every pothole he cursed my car's suspension; at every incline he damned its miserable six-cylinder engine. He began rolling and smoking again. That calmed him down, but not me.

As we topped the crest of Railroad Pass between Fallon and Austin, engine puling under its burden, rods, I was sure, about to be hurled through the hood straight up into the bright eye of the sun, we were abruptly confronted with an enormous black hole in the sky. Immediately it was upon us — the classic Basin banzai squall. The blue sky shuttered to an inky gloom, reticulated with lightning. Gusts nudged us side to side like a cat with a mouse, and as Kevin roared down the tail of the pass, the trailer began to whip. Hailstones the size of dried figs suddenly polka-dotted the enveloping darkness.

"SLOW DOWN!" I hollered, hastily adding, "SLOWLY! Slow down *slowly!*"

Kevin looked terrified. As we neared the foot of the pass, the hail quit, the gloom lifted a few hundred feet, and soon we cruised almost sanely. I suggested that Kevin turn on the head-lights. He did. "Take it easy," he said, and I tried.

We were passing through hot-spring country, I informed Kevin, thinking a little conversation might ease the tension. Miraculously, a few seconds after I said this, through the mists to the front right a pale elongation of steam gathered shape — Antelope Hot Springs — expending its heat from the center of the earth into an ice-bitten lunar world smoking with fog, in mid-Nevada. It was almost as a vision called forth by my suggestion of it, and by my memory of stopping in the next valley south, a year ago, with Chris.

It had been June 1973, the first of our four trips investigating possibilities east of California. Traveler's Lust smote us both out-side of Austin; fortunately we were together and near a hot spring. Veering with abandon from the straight and narrow ma-cadam, we toiled through the billows of alkaline dust for twelve miles. Emigrant Spring is a place of magic. It bubbles merrily square in the center of an enormous cratered basin, a ruthlessly barren concavity zoned entirely by 11,000-foot mountains. Some-one has built a small rectangular concrete pool to catch the hot turquoise water; someone had left a picnic table, with benches bolted to it, oddly floating in the pool. We arrived wrapped in dust, stripped, swam, and made love in those amniotic waters. We chased each other naked across stretches of tufa and sand, screamed into the echoless immensity, and returned to the bene-diction of the anabaptismal pool. We sat face to face on the benches, drinking beer on the floating table, spinning slowly counterclockwise, half in hot water, half in alpine air, beneath the noon sun and cobalt sky, rotating slowly eye to eye in the primal torque of the girdling ring of snow-topped peaks. We left transformed, in the Basin's spell.

This time, of course, things went much differently, with a tongue-tied idiot, not Chris, my companion. Kevin drove with two-fisted fixation, and lust seized a less wholesome focus as I closed my eyes and drifted into a waking dream of oily, black-skinned *hoo*ers sprawled on hot white sand. I hadn't really slept, but I had to.

Not far from Austin in mid-Nevada the storm rose, literally rose a couple of miles into the air, and we could watch its unabated fury, its long curls of rain evaporating before they reached the earth, stray steadily to the south in an otherwise empty sky. I suggested to Kevin that we stop for beer in Austin. He didn't respond and I felt obliged to explain. I'd be driving next and I'd gotten too wired up to get any sleep. Beer would relax me.

Kevin frowned. He was silent for fifteen or twenty minutes. He appeared to be deep in thought.

"It wouldn't be cool," he finally said quietly.

"What?"

"Juicing."

"WHAT!"

"I don't like it," Kevin said. "Drinking and driving."

I couldn't believe it. This dumb doper who'd been risking my life and ruining my car all morning become a moralist over a can of beer.

"I'd rather hitch," he said.

"Go ahead. Of course we haven't even *seen* a car for the last hundred and fifty miles. And if you saw one they wouldn't stop." I snorted. The bitch of it was that I needed him now, after no sleep for nearly thirty hours; I needed someone to drive.

Kevin grumbled and within a few minutes we ascended the curving approach into the crumbling little silver-town of Austin. At my direction he pulled in front of the Austin Hotel's palely glowing Oly sign. He got out to prepare and selfishly consume a Gouda and wheat bread sandwich. I sidled a bit nervously into the hotel — one of Nevada's oldest whorehouses — and returned untempted with a six-pack.

I could see it coming as we prepared to press on. Kevin, absorbed in his teetotalism, outraged at my abuse of privilege — a *six*-pack — forgot what one must not forget in a 1974 Pontiac. He turned the key, the damnable buzzer rang, red lights flashed. He grabbed the loose seat belt, ripped it toward him, flung it away, jamming his elbow against the door and evidently injuring his funny bone.

"GODDAM this fucking piece of tin," he yelled.

"SHUT UP," I yelled back.

I circled the car, opened his door, and told him to get out. Either stick out your thumb, I said, or move over and keep your bullshit to yourself, because I was going to drive. He moved over; I drove. From Austin to Eureka, to Ely, where the sun set in lurid flames behind the vapors of Kennecott Copper, throughout the afternoon, I drank beer upon beer, Kevin smoked joint upon joint, both of us in silence, neither thinking about the land we passed, both thinking very separate thoughts.

There are few contiguities more dissimilar than the states of Nevada and Utah. They share nothing but an overlapping Basin geography. Utah is sanctimonious, shrill, and suspicious. Strangers are treated not merely as curiosities but as contaminants. Nevada is open, free, the most lawless place in the land — sublimely, profoundly profane. Nevada is, consequently, somehow the more vital and beautiful place. Strangers there are everyone.

Wheeler Peak stands thirty miles east of Ely; thirty more miles past the mountains is the Utah line. On the outskirts of Ely, I irrevocably balked at the prospect of contending with the long and treacherous Mormon night. I knew Kevin would be hard to convince. Since Mormons, I said, trying to put it rationally, go to bed at nine o'clock, gasoline is hard to come by afterward in Utah. With that in mind, and considering my own fatigue, and considering that, should we proceed, we'd miss seeing Wheeler by day — something we both, I trusted, looked forward to — prudence remained in laying over this evening in Ely and breaking camp early enough to catch dawn behind the mountain.

Kevin, as usual, said nothing, which I chose to regard as compliance. With a beery, weary purposefulness, I negotiated town, and parked behind the Eldorado Hotel and Casino. I walked inside and booked a room for two. Above the desk hung a short, crookbacked branch, like a piece of driftwood, pranked out with a

sequined inscription: *Ely, Nevada   Home of Bristlecone Pine*
WORLD'S OLDEST LIVING THING! The lobby opened on a
casino, deserted but for five old-timers in bolo ties, playing cards.
    Undismayed, I returned outside for my dop kit and Kevin, but
Kevin, his health bag and backpack, were gone. On the dash I
found a $20 bill and a note: "Hitching on. Can't afford the time
and money for room. Here's my share for gas. Good luck, Kev."
    Kev? The fool. I locked the car, went inside, arranged a
cheaper room, and brooded at the bar. An hour passed, and still
I sat glumly, lacking even the energy to pull on any of the
hundred glittering slots. I considered, as thoughtfully as I could,
calling Chris in Colorado, but couldn't muster the will for that. I
didn't want to talk to her just then. I didn't want to talk to the
bartender or anybody; I'd talked myself out.
    I couldn't call Chris, I realized, because, alone now in this
bright little town, I had to resolve things myself. A beer-soaked
thought occurred, that even here, beached in Ely, 600 miles from
The City, halfway *home,* I still hadn't been able to shake loose
from California (The Earthquake's tremors range far beyond its
epicenter . . .).
    There were two alternatives: sleep long and deep, and face
Wheeler and Utah fresh in the morning — follow the vision of
Emigrant Spring back to Chris, pregnant in Colorado — keep it
whole; or cave in to entropy in Ely, indulge my Last Chance before our private wedding next week in Glenwood. It wouldn't be
hard; Ely sports four or five casino-whorehouses where hundreds
of miners lavish their money and seed nightly on those most compelling of passions, gambler's greed and wanton love. So the
choices were clear: recklessness or responsibility. Keep it, or lose
it.
    Dark desire began to well up again, almost as a pent-up re-
sponse to Kevin's purities. Now that he had left, it was as though
Kevin had been, oddly, a restraining, *responsible* influence. Yet
there seemed a kind of crude intent in his $20 bill: the standard
price of an Ely trick. I wandered undecided through the colorful,
now-vacant casino to the front door, like a cat drawn to a fish
market. Outside, incredibly, enchantingly, in the arcs of neon
aureoles, snow dropped densely and gently like millions of tiny
parachutes. A good two inches already quilted the highway, and
the way it was sticking it had to be cold. The next town was 140
miles, and no one would be out tonight. The fool.

I scraped the windshield, unlocked the door, latched in, and turned the car into town, leaving curlicue tracks in the parking lot, slewing smoothly back onto U.S. 50. I passed through the dazzling, silent place east toward the wilderness. I couldn't leave him alone in a snowstorm in the dead center of the Great Basin. He might, he actually might, die. But he might by then already be in Utah, happily headed for Cleveland in someone's VW bus, or in a semi, offering a bewildered trucker a toke. Still I kept driving stupidly, ever more slowly, inexorably toward Wheeler Peak. I had to find him; I *needed* to find him.

After no more than a few hundred yards the lights of Ely vanished, as though the town, and all humanity, had suddenly disappeared. The highway dissolved with the desert into one white surface. It was coldly quiet except for the purling of the car's slow tread, tires grinding at the icy crust like rowels. I began to lose sight of the object of the quest though the sense of quest grew more and more intense. I was fully aware of the almost laughably bizarre situation I dragged myself toward: driving alone, obsessively, at no more than 10 mph, sedulously combing the roadside for Kevin, though there was nothing, *nothing* to see in the whirling chaos outside, and surely no one, not even an empty ranch house for God knew how far. Still I kept tracking into no man's land with an increasingly strange image of myself: a car towing an orange steel box stuffed with my past, struggling across the white lifeless face of the earth, across a planet drowning in unceasing tides of snow — an image of the absurd and saving will of the solitary Family Man, searching for something, a purpose to keep his life of a piece.

The odds were against us. I wouldn't find him, would have to turn back — a disturbing thought: trying to wheel the car and trailer around the other way on an invisible road. Then I'd have to report him lost. Missing person — an apt identity for Kevin, with his fogged brain, his wholesome snacks, his uncomprehending remove from everything, mumbling out alone into the swarming brutality of the night. They might not find the body for days, if ever. If they never found him, what then? He might somehow have made it through; he might have vanished, just vanished, subsumed into the wanton desert. I would have to call Cleveland: "Your son may have frozen to death in the Great Basin."

And if they did find him, it would be like . . . like the Face in the Glacier? Tyndal Glacier in Colorado, where decades ago a woman, climbing at its rim, had fallen. Rangers never located the body at the base, for good reason. The glacier had swallowed it up. But every seven years, the story goes, she appears, four or five feet down in transparent ice, as the glacier's slow heave lifts her for a few days near the surface, clearly visible from the rim above. Nothing short of a backhoe could chip her out, so she will stay there, rising and sinking in the ponderous, aching flow of ice. The face, they say, looks puzzled. The lips are parted, brow intent, eyes wide, ice-brightened, staring in perpetual mystification. The fingers stretch taut, the arms twist up at the sky.

I shuddered. It might happen to both of us, the Family Man and the Missing Person, the two lone fools in the storm. It might happen just to *me*, piled in a drift, or skidding clean off the road, tumbling and rolling, car and trailer, down to some raw death. And no one was looking for *me*.

It seemed like I'd driven for hours, though I couldn't have covered more than five miles. I was ready to quit, if only I could turn around. But there he was. Stock-still, an apparition behind the flowing curtain of snow — stiff and caked white, awkwardly holding his bag of cheeses, nuts, and fruits, arm and thumb extended rigid as bone toward the car's two cones of light.

I rolled to a stop alongside him. He fumbled furiously at the door, set down the health bag, and went at it with both hands — obviously numb and useless. He finally pried the door, dumped his bag and pack in the back, and sat down on the unbuckled seat belt. The buzzer rang like a siren in the hush of the night, and Kevin raised up, startled. I helped him strap on the belt. He sighed and let out a lugubrious snuffle, clearly frozen half-through.

"Thanks," he said. "For stopping."

"You better believe it. What in hell did you think you were doing? Walking out into a blizzard in the middle of the night in the desert! Did you actually think anyone would be driving tonight? Why didn't you go back to town? What's *wrong* with you?"

He snuffled again, rubbed his hands in front of the heater fan.

"Are you suicidal?"

"No."

"Then you're hopeless," I said, and he appeared to nod his head. "You're inhuman. Do you realize that I saved your life?"

Kevin looked puzzled — like the pure, solitary bewilderment of the face trapped in ice. Unreachable helplessness.

"Forget it," I said. "You'll thaw out."

"I left you some money for gas." He stuttered from the cold.

"Yes. Thanks." So we'd settled accounts. We sat quiet in the warm idling car for a few minutes. The snow was thinning, and the indistinct glow of the moon began showing through to the east. "Well," I said, and Kevin looked up expectantly. He seemed adequately abashed — nothing like a little exposure to the elements for that. He was probably chastened enough to be a competent driver now, if not companion. "Well, we might as well keep going. I'll drive us over the pass. You'll warm up by then and we can stop for coffee in Delta."

He nodded.

Once the night cleared and the three-quarter moon marked out terrain, the boundaries of the road, it wasn't too bad. Fairly soon the bristlecone forest began — two trees on the right, one farther up on the left, then, around a curve, thick ranks of the stubby, man-sized, convoluted, primeval pines, lining the roadside, interpreting the highway's turns, depth, and grade, like guides with arms and fingers pointing the way over the pass.

As we climbed a hill, Wheeler Peak rose, gigantic and luminous, from behind a gray ridge. The bleak formless night had resolved into an exquisite mountain, caparisoned with new snow, glowing under a gem-clear moon. Above its clean white shanks the cirque gaped, a deep black rictus fringed with light. Magnificent, lovely, terrifying. Desolation had reared up into menace. It wholly dominated the world of the Basin; it made, almost, nothing else matter. It seemed to consolidate . . . what? This trip, this passage, bulked up in one swelling, indomitable form?

I'd stupidly strayed onto a glistening patch of ice, and more stupidly braked; the car and trailer began to fishtail out of control. It was exhilarating, the danger, the loose, gliding grace of the skid, the anarchy of ice. The mountain oscillated in the windshield. If it swung clear off to the side, that would be it: we'd be spinning off the road. But it stayed, steadied to the front. Tires hit pavement and I could steer again, dead on toward Wheeler Peak, like a huge lodestone, attracting, ordering the wayward energies of the night.

Behind it lay black Utah, through which I'd sleep, and above Utah in the east the flat-sided orb of the moon. I would dream that night of cities, subside into the world of women and men, where life resides, where in a few months my daughter would be born. And the first human gesture would not be a scream, but the unfolding of a tiny red hand, inch-long fingers touching at the unfamiliar air. We passed around and away from the mountain, behind us, in the west now. It lowered slowly, some ancient, living glacial creature, keeper of secrets I'd rather not know. Or, only a mammoth, austere, indifferent fist of rock. Just past the border, we switched places. Kevin drove, and we made good time.

JACK MATTHEWS

A Questionnaire for Rudolph Gordon

(FROM THE MALAHAT REVIEW)

1) How many times was this questionnaire forwarded through the mail before it caught up with you?
2) List the various things that had occupied your mind during the morning before it arrived.
3) How many of your father's paintings have you now sold?
4) Do you sense that you are nearing the end of your "resources"?
5) Do you still dream of that little boat, nosing at the dock as if it were alive and waiting for you?
6) Did you sell the painting in which your father had put the boat?
7) This painting also showed a woman, leaning over and scooping up sand; who was the little boy she was facing?
8) Do you remember that heavy cloth bathing suit, with its straps and the heavy, scratchy wool against your skin?
9) What was your mother saying as your father painted the picture?
10) Why had you been crying?
11) Were you aware of his sitting back there, farther up the bank, painting as your mother talked to you?
12) The woman had been singing a song to calm you down; what was this song?
13) Was the woman truly your mother?

14) What if she lied to you; what if all your life she merely *pretended* to be your mother?

15) What if the man painting the picture with both of you in it (not to mention the little rowboat) was also a Pretender?

16) Why would they want to deceive you like that?

17) Why were you crying before your "mother" sang the little song to calm you down and amuse you?

18) Can you remember times when they talked to you lovingly, and you felt totally secure with them . . . only to see her eyes slip nervously to the side, to look at *him* . . . and only for him to look troubled, worried, as if they had both gotten beyond their depth?

19) Can you remember the woman saying, "No, we shouldn't have done it," and the man answering, "Anyway, it's too late now to change"?

20) The little beach cottage you stayed in was painted blood red; its porch and shutters were painted white; what was behind the little cottage?

21) Do you remember climbing this steep hill one day, and having the woman cry out in fear that you would fall and hurt yourself?

22) Can you remember the smell of the pine needles and the rough warmth of the stones as you climbed steadily upward, and then turned to look into the wind, at the bay?

23) She was smaller than you, down below; and the man was smaller, too, because they existed far beneath your feet; what did you say when they begged for you to come down?

24) Why did you say "never," instead of "no"?

25) Why were you not afraid?

26) What did you see in the bay?

27) What was the name of the great ship that lay like a shadow in the haze of water?

28) Are you certain you cannot remember the shapes of the letters of her name, so that *now* you can read what was then only the mystery of print?

29) Why is the name of this ship unimportant?

30) Were you surprised when you looked down and saw that he had climbed so near, without your being aware?

31) Can you remember the dark expression of anger on his face as he reached out to clasp your ankle?

32) Did he hurt you, carrying you so roughly down through the rocks and pine trees to the back of the cottage?

33) What was the song you could hear so faintly from the cabin next door?

34) Was this the first phonograph you can remember ever hearing?

35) Was this the song the woman sang to you later, after you were taken down to the shore?

36) Were you crying because of the scolding you received for climbing the steep hill in back?

37) Do you remember the old smell of salt and dead fish that drifted in the air?

38) Where were your real parents?

39) Had you been kidnapped?

40) Has this thought ever occurred to you before?

41) Do you remember the toy revolver and holster you wore?

42) Do you remember the little suitcase they let you carry?

43) Do you remember the photograph of a man and woman smiling out at you in your bedroom?

44) What was written on the photograph?

45) Did the man and woman read it to you, so that you are certain it said, "From Mom and Dad with Love"?

46) Why can't you remember the faces in the photograph?

47) Was your *real* father a painter?

48) Was this man . . . *could* this man have been your real father?

49) Could the woman have been your real mother?

50) But how can you be certain they lied to you in other matters?

51) Don't we all lie to one another?

52) Isn't the lie we tell our children one expression of love?

53) Isn't it also an expression of our fear?

54) Can there be love without fear?

55) Is it possible that this man and this woman, even though they remember the specific moment you came out of *her* body, are still not certain that you are *their son*?

56) What is a father?

57) What is a mother?

58) What is a son?

59) Why have you refused to answer these questions?

60) Why have you sold so many of your father's paintings?

61) Why do you need so much money to live?
62) Why can't you find a job?
63) When did the woman die?
64) Were you there when her eyes clouded over?
65) Were you present when your father was run down by the trolley car in the city?
66) Did you know that his legs and back were terribly mutilated in the accident, and he was dead before the ambulance arrived, hemorrhaging brilliant red streams against the black asphalt of the street?
67) In your opinion, did he think of you as he was dying?
68) Did your mother think of you as she was dying?
69) Why do you think you cannot answer such questions?
70) Do you see yourself in the painting with the little boy, and the mother scooping sand up in her hand, and the rowboat nudging at the dock, like a small hungry animal desiring suck?
71) What color is the sky in the painting?
72) Why is it darker than the land?
73) Why is it darker than the water?
74) Have you sold this painting yet?
75) Is it the last of your father's paintings in your possession?
76) When you do sell it, will something break loose and drift away?
77) Will the hand be seized by a spasm, and will sand spill from it?
78) Will the child cry again, staring out upon an empty scene, while the ship fades into pale gray, leaking color out of the letters of its name?
79) Who is in the red cottage now?
80) Why do you think it is empty or torn down?
81) If your father were alive, could he reach you now and carry you back to safety?
82) Could the blood on the asphalt be thought of as your father's last and most original composition?
83) Were your father and mother as lonely as children in those last moments?
84) Would you have helped them in some way *if you could have been sure?*
85) Why do you pretend you don't know *sure of what?*

86) Have you never doubted their authenticity before?
87) Aren't there other reasons than kidnapping for stealing a child?
88) Perhaps they didn't know how you came about, and felt guilty?
89) Who can say where these things all begin?
90) Don't you understand that "these things" are the cabin, the steep hill, the boat, the sand, the man, the woman, the child?
91) Were you aware that the painting was omitted in 90?
92) If you sell it, finally, will you have enough money?
93) Don't you have the pride and the skill to make your own way in life?
94) Why does that expression remind you of him?
95) If you sell it finally, will you ever sleep again?
96) Why do you think there is no one now to sing a song to you and dry your tears and pretend to be your mother?
97) When will you stop lying in your answers?
98) Do you think even *this* would turn us away, if our hands and hearts and mouths were not packed with earth?
99) Do you truly believe that some things do not abide, beyond the habit and way of the world?
100) Truly, this is enough for now, and somehow you must rest content with this personal questionnaire.

Love always,
Mom and Dad

STEPHEN MINOT

A Passion for History

(FROM THE SEWANEE REVIEW)

PICTURE: On the shore where the river joins the sea, a lobster-man's boathouse-home, gray-shingled and trim, morning dew drifting in vapor from the roof, a column of smoke rising from the chimney, flower boxes with petunias.

It's enough to turn the stomach.

He is not naive. He will not be trapped by sentimentality. He will not be seduced by those Currier and Ives virtues — thrift, honesty, piety, and hard work. These are slogans devised by the rich, by landholders and factory owners. There is no beauty in poverty.

Picture: On the ledge next to the lobsterman's home stands a couple. She wears a dress only a country girl would buy. Tall, long-boned, graceful, she would be beautiful if she had any notion of style. Beauty is there, hidden.

He has rumpled white pants and a blue polo shirt, the costume of a man consciously trying to be informal but not quite succeeding. He is older than she. But they are not father and daughter or brother and sister. As they look out on the glisten of the river which blends into the sea beyond, his right hand rests ever so gently on her right buttock.

They are mismatched, these two. It is more than her mail-order dress and his rumpled elegance, though that is a part of it. There is some deeper aberration here. Like a parent, he can sense something wrong without being able to describe it. But he is not the man's parent. He is the man himself.

It is Kraft himself who is standing there. The woman beside

him is Thea. The cottage where she lives is to their left. He is
conscious now where his right hand is and can, in fact, feel the
warmth of her body. This kind of thing has been happening to Kraft lately. He can't
be sure whether some microcircuit in his brain is loose, blacking
out certain periods of time, allowing him to stand on a bank *planning* to take a walk with someone and then skipping ahead to the
actual event, or whether it works the other way around — being
in the middle of an experience and suddenly viewing it from a
distance, with historical perspective, as it were.

"Brooding?" she asks.

"Me? No. I don't brood. That's an indulgence. Thinking,
maybe. Sorry. I was just thinking."

"Perhaps you miss teaching. Miss students and all that."

"No, not in the least. I'm not that kind of teacher, you know.
A course here, a lecture series there. Not regular teaching. Not
in my field."

He always underrates his academic work, he being a radical and
teaching being a bourgeois profession and history departments
generally being elitist and unenlightened. He prefers to think of
himself as a political organizer, though he has done little of that
since the 1960s. He hopes that, now in his forties, he is better
known for his articles and his recent volume on the radical movement in America. But Thea, his lovely Thea, has read nothing,
heard nothing. She has lived her life here in rural Nova Scotia,
and as everyone knows, rural Nova Scotia is nowhere. She has
never heard of him. He is for her just what he tells her about
himself. No less and no more.

"I'd love to learn history," she says.

"Never mind that," he says. "You've got history in you. That's
enough."

"No, I really would."

"Not the way *they* teach it you wouldn't. All dates and kings."

"And you?"

"Me? I teach about people. History is people. Little people.
The way they live. Know how one person lives and you know a
whole period. Not kings. People. Do you understand?"

"Of course," she says, taking half a step back and turning just
slightly to the right as if to search the treetops, checking to see if
an osprey nest had been built during the night, and incidentally,

innocently, pressing ever so gently against the palm of his hand with the curve of her bottom.

Picture: On the smooth gray ledge which forms the bank of the Worwich River at the point where it flows into the sea, a man in white pants embraces a long limber girl, kissing her and now beginning to undo the first of one hundred and two tiny, cloth-covered buttons which run down the back of her dress, she laughing, the sound drifting up like a loon's call.

From this height one can see not only the little boathouse-home but the marshy estuaries formed by the meeting of river and sea and farther, on the sea side, a great gray rectangle of a house surrounded by tall grass, ledge outcroppings, and a scattering of overturned tombstones.

This large rectangle is the house Kraft has bought for himself and his family as a summer home — house and barn and outhouse and woodsheds and 953 acres of land. This is what he has bought with the royalties from his book on the radical movement in America.

Like a mistress it is an embarrassment and a pleasure. He makes a point of keeping it out of the press. His name *is* mentioned in the press from time to time since he is known to liberals as "the guru of radicals" and to hard radicals as "a running-dog revisionist." Thus he has no following whatever but he is read.

When interviewers press him, he refers to his property as his "rural retreat" or his "wilderness camp." Once a Maoist sheet — a sloppy mimeographed affair — reported scathingly that he had bought up a thousand acres of land in Nova Scotia. This, of course, he brands as a total fabrication. They have exaggerated by forty-seven acres.

His house up on the high land is in a permanent state of disrepair. He has not allowed one can of paint to be used inside or out. It is a weathered gray. There is no electricity and water must be lifted bucketful by bucketful from an open well. The plaster was half gone when he bought it, so they removed the other half, leaving the horizontal laths as semi-partitions between the rooms. It is, he reminds his family from time to time, their rural slum.

But this spring there is no family. He came up alone in mid-April, leaving his wife and three children in New Haven by mutual agreement. He was to have two and a half absolutely clear months to type the final draft of his most recent book, this one on the *liberal* tradition.

It was a perfect arrangement. No meetings to attend, no speeches to present, no teaching, no family to sap his energies. So of course he has done no writing.

There are times when he can't stand the clutter and filth of his own house — clutter, filth, and whispering deadlines. Those are the times when he comes here to the neat little boathouse-home on the river, the little Currier-and-Ives home Thea shares with her father.

Right now he is walking beside Thea, walking back to that perfect little place, his arm around her and hers around him. Seven of the one hundred and two tiny cloth-covered buttons down her back are undone. Ninety-five to go.

Kraft is not entirely certain that this is right. His wife, a sure and competent and rational woman with a law degree and a practice of her own, would consider this a serious malady. Worse than the flu. Akin to income-tax evasion. And of course she would be right.

With these thoughts passing through his mind he sees in the far distance, inland, just coming out of the woods and beginning to cross the rocky field, approaching the boathouse-home, old Mr. McKnight.

"Oh," Kraft says, noticing for the first time that the barrow which the old man pushes has a wooden wheel. Involuntarily Kraft's mind provides a parenthetical notation. *(Hand-fashioned oak wheels disappeared from each county at the point when mail-order houses reached that district.)*

"Oh," Thea says, not hearing his unspoken observation. "It's Father."

Kraft likes the old man — his courtly, country way. But he has mixed feelings about delaying what he and Thea had been heading toward.

"Well," she says, "no matter. He'll stay for a while and we'll talk. But then it'll be time for his scavenging."

Every day at low tide the old man scours the beaches for usable items — timbers, orange crates, even nails, which can be pried out and ground smooth on the whetstone. *(Recycling has been an economic necessity until the last half of the twentieth century.)* Clearly old McKnight lives in the previous century.

"I don't mind," Kraft says. Actually he does and he doesn't mind. Both. But that is too complicated to explain. Even to himself. "I don't mind," he says again. They are on the front

stoop — a simple porch with no roof. She sits in the big rocker
and he is perched on a nail keg old Mr. McKnight has salvaged
from the sea. It would be a time before the old man put the wood
in the shed and came around to suggest a cup of coffee. Nothing
whatever moves rapidly in rural Nova Scotia. Especially time.

"I don't mind," Kraft says, thinking that the last time he said it
to himself in his own head. "It's good talking with the old man.
Just this morning I wrote in my journal, 'I hope I see old Mr.
McKnight today. He is my link with the region. I like hearing his
voice. I learn a lot from him.' "

"Are you perhaps spending too much time with that journal of
yours?" It is exactly the question his wife asked by letter the week
before. Unsettling.

"I've kept that going ever since I was ten. I'm not going to stop
now." He is, though, spending too much time writing in his journal and she knows it just as clearly as he does, so it is essential that
he defend himself. "It's an act of survival, writing that journal."

"Survival?"

"Did you know that shipwrecked sailors rowing a lifeboat are
taught to study their own wake? Otherwise they turn in great
circles. Did you know that?" She shakes her head. "I wrote
about that last week, as a matter of fact. 'Sheepherders,' I pointed
out, 'talk to themselves and address their members with obscene
endearments.' Well, I mean, here I am living in an ark of a house
up there without electricity or running water miles from anywhere, adrift for two months with only a rough draft and a set of
correction notes to work with and a publisher's deadline for navi-
gation. Did you know that mermaids are an optical illusion
caused by solitude and malnutrition?"

"I didn't know you believed in mermaids."

"I don't. You don't have to believe in them to know that they
exist. I've got an entry about that too."

"Those entries," she says, shaking her head. He notices that
she is shelling lima beans. Where did they come from? "You
spend too much time with them," she says.

"It's just a trail of where my thoughts have been."

She shrugs. She is no lawyer and never argues. She makes
commentary on his thoughts, but she never presses her point.
"All that looking back," she says gently. "It'll turn you to salt."
She smiles and a loon laughs. Either that or a loon smiles and she
laughs. "Time to do up the dishes," she says. "He'll be coming in

and he'll want a cup of coffee right soon. Come sit with me while I fix up."

Picture in sepia: A woman stands by the soapstone sink, her hand on the pump. There is little light in the room because the windows are small. *(Large windows were avoided not only because of expense but because of a strong sense of nocturnal dangers. Except in cities police protection was practically unknown.)* There is no view of the river or the sea.

The kitchen walls are made of the narrow tongue-in-groove boarding, a poor man's substitute for plaster. Open shelves rather than cupboards — the price of a hinge saved. Kitchen table bare pine, unvarnished, scrubbed with salt — to be replaced in the 1920s with white enamel. Kraft can glance at a photograph of an American kitchen and date it within a decade and can lecture without notes on its impact on the status of women, the institution of marriage, and the hierarchy within the family. Here in Worwich he has found a lost valley. Time has moved on like a great flock of geese, leaving a strange silence and sepia prints.

"He's been cutting wood," Thea says, pumping cold water into the dishpan and adding hot from the aluminum teakettle. Kraft's mind flashes a notation. *(The shift from the heavy cast-iron kettle to the aluminum was as significant for women as the replacement of the wood range by gas.)* "I imagine on your land."

"He's welcome to it. I've got enough problems without clearing my own woodlots." He has a quick vision of his study, the upper room in the big house on the bluff, his papers scattered about like leaves after a storm. His manuscript, the one on the American liberal movement, in cluttered piles; and in addition to his own journals there are his *father's* journals, which he has foolishly brought. One more distraction. One more bit of clutter. So if old Mr. McKnight wants to poach, wants to clear land, he is welcome to it. Perhaps Kraft can persuade the old man to steal unfinished manuscripts as well.

Simplicity. Order. He looks at Thea there at the sink. She is both. Her cottage, her life is harmony. His own place is a shambles. How can a man, he wonders, pick a summer home so far from the complexities of contemporary society, so painstakingly distant, and work so hard to keep the place unimproved, simple, true to Thoreau, and still end up with such an enormous rubbish heap in his own study?

Thea has finished washing. She rinses the plates and mugs with one more spurt from the pump, dries each item, places each on open shelves, each in the correct place. He feels a great wave of envy for her life, a passionate and agonized longing which he mistakes for healthy sexual desire.

"It is madness to romanticize the nineteenth-century rural life," he had written in his journal only that morning. "Even a cursory examination of the McKnight family reveals a history of backbreaking work, sickness, and early death."

He silently recites his observation verbatim, cursed with total recall. No, blessed. Without some kind of historical sense of reality this recent affair with Thea will turn into a nightmare of complications.

There is nothing to envy in Thea's life, he tells himself, and the affair is only a passing sexual fancy, a mildly comic sample of male menopause.

The evidence of brutish living is all around him, after all. Abandoned houses, cellar holes where families were burned out in midwinter; private cemetery plots grown over with chokecherry, no one left to tend them. One such is right on the rocky scrub grass he calls his front lawn. McKnights. Half of them children. A family shattered by the brutality of what they had hoped would be their New Scotland.

They came from Scotland, looking for the good life, and they hung on for more than two hundred years. But now as a clan they are broken and scattered, beaten by isolation, by madness, by sudden death, the younger ones fleeing to Montreal, to Toronto, to the States, the survivors selling the last remaining house and most of the land to this American historian and his family, who come north as summer residents, looking for the good life.

"Find it?" she asks.

"What?"

"Find it?" For an instant he thinks she has a witch's ability to read minds. (*Statements made about witches in the eighteenth century closely resemble fantasies of present-day patients described as paranoid; thus our diagnosis of mental illness depends from the outset on our current view of reality.*) But she has asked him for a pitcher of milk she has left on the windowsill to keep cool.

He sees it, hands it to her. She smiles. "If you don't want him cutting your wood," she says, "you should tell him."

Kraft shakes his head. "I'll never get around to clearing up

those woodlots," he says. "There was a time when all the fixing
up around the place went well. We really got a lot done. The
boys and me working outside clearing fields and cutting back
chokecherry. Good, honest work. And Tammy and my daughter
working inside, making the place livable. Like a bunch of
colonists."

"But then . . ." His voice fades out. Why tell her all that? The
second and the third summer, complaints from the children about
the isolation; excuses to avoid the work; wry jokes about the lack
of plumbing, the lack of electricity, the enforced intimacy; wise-
cracks growing sharper, less funny each summer. He finds this
embarrassing. It is not the way he likes to think of his family.
There is no need to share this with Thea.

She has finished the dishes and dries her hands on the roller
towel, looking at him. Just the touch of a smile.

"They don't understand," she says. He wonders whether he
has just voiced some of his disappointments or whether, again,
she is reading his mind. "They don't understand, but I do."

"I don't know what I'd do without you," he says. Actually he
does know. It is unutterable. Everything would fall to pieces
without her around to listen, to be his lover. It is not just sexual;
it is human contact. He depends on both her and her father.
Their presence. Both of them.

And there, suddenly, is old Mr. McKnight. He is standing at
the kitchen door. Gray-bearded but with no mustache — a tintype. No smile but not unfriendly. *(It is a significant comment on
the impact of the Industrial Revolution that from the introduction of the
camera in the mid-nineteenth century until after the First World War it
was not customary to smile when having one's picture taken.)* Old Mr.
McKnight gives just the ghost of a nod of recognition and extends
his hand in an Old World handshake.

"I couldn't seem to get any work done this morning," Kraft
says. He doesn't want to seem like a summer resident. He *isn't* a
summer resident.

"All that work with your head," Mr. McKnight says. "It can't be
good."

"Right."

"Come look at this," the old man says. Kraft follows him into
the workroom, where there is a skeleton of ribs fashioned to a
backbone. It is the beginnings of a rowboat upside down, raised

on two sawhorses. Mr. McKnight builds one a year, shaping the oak ribs in a crude boiler out back.

"Here," Mr. McKnight says, seizing Kraft's wrist. The old man's fingers are armored, rough plates joined. He takes Kraft's hand as if it were a plane and slides the palm along the oak keel. Kraft winces, expecting splinters from any unpainted surface. But of course it is perfectly sanded. Needlessly sanded.

"A filly's ass," the old man says.

"She's beautiful," Kraft says. "Like everything of yours."

"Ha!" Mr. McKnight smiles for the first time. The two men share their chauvinistic joke like a brotherhood — the younger one uneasily. "Time for a cup of coffee," the old one says just loud enough for it to become an order for Thea. "Tide's not about to wait for me or you."

Kraft nods, thinking: When the tide's out for you it will be high for Thea and me. He smiles to himself but Mr. McKnight casts a quick questioning look. Does the old man read thoughts too?

Thea has placed three mugs of coffee on the kitchen table and beside each a cloth napkin and a spoon. They sit down. (*Informal eating was considered bad taste well into the 1920s and still is frowned on in rural Ireland and Scotland. The eating of food even under picnic circumstances was invested with ritual significance and required sitting correctly at a table.*)

"That skiff," old Mr. McKnight says, "is as fine as you can find here to Boston." (Boston *became a Nova Scotian term for all of New England by the 1780s.*) "Not one bit of metal in her, you know. No nails. All pegged. Even the cleat is cedar heart. Hard as brass and it won't tarnish." He nods to himself in full agreement with himself. "Gives pleasure twice, it does — once in the building and again in the owning."

"In Halifax," Thea says, "they make them out of plywood."

They all three smile. "Imagine that," the old man says. Kraft does not mention fiber glass. For the McKnights it doesn't exist yet. "Halifax skiffs are nailed too. Full of nails. Rust out on you sooner or later. Ten, fifteen years they'll rust out on you. Drown you sooner or later. Like putting a metal wheel on a barrow. Takes me a winter to shape a wooden wheel. Eight pieces glued and pegged. It's work, but it'll last a lifetime. Two, with luck. Same for lobster traps. Pegged and laced. You can't find a better trap."

Kraft nods, letting the old man continue, though he knows that in the States they are using a plastic lobster trap which is in every way superior. Ugly and indestructible as the aluminum beer can. "I build the best traps around here," the old man says. "The very best." They all nod, a part of the ritual. "Well, can't sit here all day. Tide's calling me," he says and abruptly he is gone. Quick as that.

And now, oddly, when the two of them are free, Kraft is hesitant. The room seems small, airless. Enclosing. Warily he looks to the window, to the door. He hears again the old man's proclamation — "I build the best traps."

He looks at her sitting there opposite him. For an instant she is in sepia again, posed there, a tall woman, high cheekboned. She is an image which would startle young readers browsing through an old photo album. "Who was that?" — the patronizing surprise of moderns who cannot imagine passion cloaked in formality. A sepia print. Colorless. How does such a lovely person stand a colorless life? How does she exist?

"What's wrong?" she asks. "You're having dark thoughts again."

"You're the one who should be having dark thoughts," he says.

"Why?"

"Cooped up here, trapped."

"I'm not trapped."

"With nothing to read."

"I'm not much for reading."

"No profession."

"I keep the place neat. I mend. Grow things."

"The monotony — it must be suffocating. I should think the isolation would drive you crazy."

"I'm not alone now."

"Now." She has no conception of future time. "*Now.*" He stands up. He needs motion. "You know, don't you, that Tammy is coming up in ten days. Tammy and the children. And the dog. The whole bit. Did you forget that?"

"That's in a week. Now is now."

She floats in an eternal present. He can't imagine how that would be. He feels rage and envy. For him the present is the peak of a slippery hummock; he is forever sliding down one side or the other — either counting the days to something out there ahead of him or slithering back into the past.

He is standing behind her, his hands on her shoulders. She reaches up and takes both his hands and draws them down and around to her breasts. There is only the cotton fabric between his palms and the softness of her flesh. He feels her nipples. He stops thinking for an instant about past and future. I am holding the present in my hands, he thinks.

He is undoing the buttons down the back of her dress. She has leaned her head back so that it is against him, rocking gently.

"You're right," he says softly in her ear. "I'm not even going to think about Tammy."

Mistake! Mistake! The very word *Tammy* jars the mood, breaks his hold on the present. What is he doing? Somehow the action goes on, but he has floated up. The overview, the damned overview.

Picture: A man embraces a woman in an old-fashioned kitchen, her dress is loosened at the back, is down over one shoulder. The man is not at ease; he is harried by his passion, planning the next move, thinking ahead. He leads her up the stairs and into a simple, unadorned room: walls of vertical boarding, varnished dark. An iron bed, a rocking chair, a bureau with a wavy mirror attached, and a commode on which stand a kerosene lamp and a wash basin. Two books, a Bible and a copy of *Pilgrim's Progress,* both old. Perfect neatness. Perfect order.

Ninety-five tiny buttons open in a ripple and she stands bare-breasted in her petticoat. She shakes her hair down and it is long. Her petticoat slips to the floor at her feet. He has seen this image somewhere before, standing this way in the palm of an enormous seashell. But this is no time for art. She is with him on the bed. Her skin radiates warmth.

"Fast," he says. "Quickly." He is on an anxious schedule, racing to meet a sudden departure. The bed cries out like a flock of frantic gulls.

Then silence. Perfect silence.

That, one might imagine, was the climax of the day for him. But it was only the first of two. The second came after leaving.

He headed up the path toward his own house, not looking forward to returning, and he made the terrible mistake of looking back. A part of him knew that he shouldn't. But he had been living in the present and was careless. "Don't," he said to himself just as he turned, but it was too late.

There was the McKnight boathouse, the one he had just left, chimney smokeless, cracked, and leaning; the roof rotted through, sagging beams exposed, skeletal; windows all broken, flower boxes gone, holes black as empty eye sockets. Even the porch was gone, wrenched off by the grinding ice of winter storms years ago. Dead. All dead and gone. All history.

CHARLES NEWMAN

The Woman Who Thought Like a Man

(FROM PARTISAN REVIEW)

> Then how should I revenge myself?
> — *Cymbeline*

CORINNE L. HUFF had a cold. The air nozzle above her seat was locked full on, coursing a chill upon her forehead for the entire flight. The gentleman beside her had no more luck with it than the purser or the stewardess. "Nothing seems to work right anymore," he said, "even in first class." Corinne could only shrug assent and sniffle.

She had waited a half an hour for her luggage as the men with their carry-ons streamed by her. The strap of her cosmetic case spread a dull pain along her collarbone. Gusts of sourceless wind through the half-completed terminal pimpled her legs. A college girl in jeans, breasts banging her sweatshirt about, strode by, her suitcase on roller skates. The fluorescent corridors are slippery with disinfectant. They shine but issue neither reflection nor shadow. A porter sits disconsolately on the edge of the conveyor belt, and lowers his gaze as Corinne catches him eyeing her. Not one to pull rank gratuitously, she walks over to make talk.

"You guys really working up a sweat today, huh?" His dark face became friendlier, puffier.

"No ma'am. Nobody got much baggage anymore. They don't care for waitin' on it, carr'in' it, or packin' it."

"Well, I have my samples in mine," Corinne said curtly, handing him her stub. "The whole trip's wasted without them."

"You better check with the desk then, ma'am. This here flight's all through," said the colored man.

Corinne patiently explained to the towheaded, heavily forearmed airline official that her samples were in the bag, and he brought out a chart with drawings of different types of bags.

"Which one does yours look like?"

"None of them."

"Not a one?"

"Not even close. It's custom-made."

Then Corinne reached over, and plucking his pen from his shirt pocket, drew the official a picture. Then she pushed the pen back behind his ear. "You have a blue pen too, officer?" He shook his head. "Well, the bag's blue. Color it in when you have a chance. I've got a presentation first thing in the morning, so you better get it to the hotel before I hit the sack . . . and don't try to make up to me, kiddo. I know that custom blue bag is stacked up above this goddamn airport somewhere, and I want you to bring it in, sweet and low, like the young ensign that you are, just like you were bringing in a riddled fighter to your carrier in the Coral Sea."

"Look, ma'am. I'm no pilot."

"Well, be a hero once, anyway. It's good for the economy," and as Corinne disembarked for the cab rank, kicking her cosmetic case ahead of her across the marble floor, the official turned to his countermates in disbelief.

Outside in the terrible wind, Corinne pushed five dollars at the starter.

"Can't bust the rank, Miss, I gotta live with these guys every day."

The cabs continued to arrive desultorily in the slush. Twenty minutes later, three conventioneers ahead of Corinne piled into a Checker, the starter yelling, "Four to a cab," then lapsed into a mumble as he regarded her.

"That's quite all right," Corinne said sweetly if somewhat nasally, and grabbing the knee of one conventioneer, hauled herself onto a jump seat, her thick dark hair fanning out along the mesh which protected the driver.

The three conventioneers were wedged against one another like pickled vegetables, fedoras high on their foreheads, sweating even in the zero weather. Corinne's classic knees decorated either side of an enormous thigh of a paralyzed middleman, who desperately tried to avoid her eyes. But then she giggled mercifully, and everyone relaxed.

The men all had on heavy college rings, wedding bands, and nameplates; Harold, Dick, and Fitz. Corinne had the same, except hers were a bit smaller. In fact, everybody on the entire plane seemed to have on rings and nameplates, from the Jewish rear stewardess, T. Rich, to the imperturbable Scandinavian Captain Anderson.

The men were talking a highly technical language, perhaps out of some long-forgotten embarrassment. They were not your everyday salesmen, but some kind of engineers, probably petrochemical or geomorphological. Corinne winced out of the window. New Jersey appeared like a load of soiled, forgotten diapers. The men were elbowing each other, fighting for breathing room, the cabbie was talking about getting mugged, the windows were steaming up. Somebody said, "Well, what the hell do they expect me to do? Start over at forty-two?"

Then they were above the city on a spiral ramp, with the cabbie calling out for hotels; the Sheraton for Dick, the Hilton for Harold, and the St. Regis for Fitz, the latter of which they now approached. Fitz, who had crushed his legs into a corner for the entire trip to avoid touching Corinne, now tapped her on the knee with *U.S. News & World Report* and asked her if she were free for dinner. Freed from the anonymous bulk of his fellows, he appeared not at all badly put together.

About the only unattractive thing about Corinne Huff was her laugh, or rather the lack of one. Her jubilation had been so unabashed and full-throated, and her school friends had teased her about it so severely, that she had taken to stopping it by opening her mouth so theatrically wide as to cut off the epiglottis, and it was this noiseless guffaw at his odd, officious approach, which now spent itself upon Fitz, furrowing his clear brow.

"Look," he stammered, "I didn't mean . . ."

Corinne didn't know whether she was ashamed of belittling his casualness or put off by his ultimate tentativeness; she had told herself recently and repeatedly that women's greatest foolishness was their overconcern about how they were treated initially and their circumspection at how they were treated eventually. She closed her mouth on this thought.

"I'm sorry," she said, "but I've other plans."

"Of course. I just thought . . ."

"Why don't you give me your card, though? Perhaps I'll be free tomorrow."

Fitz said something into his lapels as he fumbled for his wallet. His face was quite red, and he handed his credentials over, and Corinne was relieved as the cab began to rev.

"Bye, Fitz."

He nodded rather too fast and hurriedly entered the St. Regis without overseeing his baggage.

"Hellew, Mrs. Huff," the Plaza's deskman greeted her. "Good to have you in the city again."

"I think I've got the flu, Jan," Corinne said as she signed in, putting "Buyer" under "Profession."

"There's a lot of it around, surely," Jan said, "but you look quite well all the same." She winked at him and smiled the bellboy into a trot.

Up in the suite, Corinne found that her bag had somehow preceded her, and the maid had already unpacked her swatches. They lay on the bed, a pointlessly organized mélange of hue and texture, those samples of which she was to locate carloads.

"The sweet n' stupid is coming back into fashion," Corinne muttered and then fell backward onto her products. This cold will do me in yet, was all she could think.

She was in the tub when Geoff rang. "Same old Four-twenty-seven, honey. C'mon up. I'll leave the door ajar."

She slipped and very nearly killed herself getting back into the tub.

Geoff soon emerged from the mirrored door, a fifth of Dewar's White Label in hand, and bending over from the waist, kissed the dark and massy islet rising from the water.

Geoff was a buyer for the same chain as Corinne, and they had met on a flight to Phoenix four years ago. They had become absolutely comfortable with one another. Corinne once told him that they fit as a mountain pine to a boulder, which Geoff liked, though he didn't know who was rock and who was tree. He carried her from the tub to the canopied bed and lay her down

among her swatches, which like all innocent goods brought to the
city, required nothing save their own multiplication. She had only
breath to say, "Watch the swatches," and then the portrait of their
avalanche was painstakingly painted. Pines and boulders, boulders and pines, end over end.

"Why are we so good together, Geoff? Just because we don't
see each other much?"

"Because we've got nothing to prove, I guess."

"It's odd you should say that. It's just lately that I've wanted to
prove something."

"With me?"

"Not exactly . . . with everybody," she said very softly.

Geoff seemed distracted. He sat on the edge of the bed, elbows
on knees, rubbing his eyes. Then Corinne's knees were on the
red spots his elbows had left, her arms wound about his head,
nipping his nape. Geoff steadied himself on his palms, blowing
her hair aside so he could see.

"You know," she said, from over his shoulder, "from the back
you don't look more than twenty-one."

"It's a bad back, though. Inside, I mean. I have to sit down to
urinate now."

"This is not a problem," Corinne said, but the phone rang
sharply, and Corinne's hands went to her heart. Geoff dropped
the receiver twice then handed it over to her.

"Mommy," it crackled.

"Oh Christ, Brucie, what's wrong!"

"When are you coming home, Mommy?"

"Tomorrow, honey, just like I told you."

"Well . . . uh," Corinne's husband, Fred, broke in. "Nothing's
wrong here dear. We just wanted to call before bed. I didn't see
the harm . . ."

"Of course. You're sure there's nothing . . ."

"Not a thing. How's your cold?"

"About the same, Fred."

"All right, Brucie?" Fred said.

There was no answer from the child, and Corinne's husband
told her he'd meet the plane.

Geoff was smoking a small cigar. "How's everything?"

"Fine. Just fine."

"Is what you're trying to prove have to do with him?"

"Not exactly."

"We've never talked about our families. I'll bet you have a nice family."

"Sure, Geoff. I'll bet you do too."

"So it's not the family then."

"Not exactly. Not mine anyway."

"I guess you don't want to talk. That's all right."

"Dammit," yelled Corinne, pounding her fists together, Geoff dropping ashes all over his chest, and then flailing madly at the sparks, "Dammit Geoff, don't you know what's happening with *women?*"

Geoff was looking around for an ashtray, both hands cupped with ashes. His chest was smeared with charcoal, his parts become very small. "You mean . . . women in general?"

"If you like. In America."

"You mean that they're more . . . aggressive . . . and everything?"

"Go on."

"No, I don't know much about it, I guess. It's a lot easier to get laid, of course."

"So *that's* how you think about it."

"Look, Corinne. Were you saving this number for me? I'm not your . . ."

"Because you are a sane, strong, and decent man, Geoff, who ought to know better. Who ought to know what's going on."

"Know what?" Geoff had absentmindedly slipped on his crimson acetate briefs.

"Don't you ever talk about this with your wife?"

"No, I mean, we're very open . . . but . . . anyway, what business is it of yours?"

"She doesn't tell you what it's like to be a woman?"

"She doesn't complain much, if that's what you mean."

"She has her life and you have yours. Is that what you mean?"

"This isn't like you, Corinne."

"I suppose I'm the exception that proves the rule."

"Which rule?"

"Geoff, don't you believe there are some things that people can't express, but they can feel them happening all around them? That we're on the edge of things?"

"Personally or politically?"

"In between."

"I guess. So what's coming?"

"You're not going to like it."

"I'm not liking it right now much, Corinne."

"Well, put it this way. Why are you attracted to me?"

Geoff thought for a while, and as if it were a prerequisite for reflection, slipped on his cavalry twill slacks and angora socks.

"Well, Corinne, you're sure smart and pretty enough, but what I think I like best about you is that you're tough but don't have to show it all the time."

"*Very* disarming," she said desperately.

"Hey, let's go catch some dinner."

"I can't bear the thought of getting dressed again."

"OK, let's have some sent up."

"I'm not hungry, and that's it, Geoff, that's what's happening. Women are getting tougher and they're going to show it more."

Geoff paused. "I don't think that's what you meant to say."

Corinne lay back, and wrapping an ice cube from her drink in a washcloth, lay it on her sinuses.

"You know, Corinne, I just don't get it. If you just could say what you wanted you'd probably get it."

"How could you know what I want?"

"That's what I just said."

"Look, I just can't decide whether I want to throw off everything inessential or get more of everything. Can't you understand that?"

"Oh Corinne, that's just how a man feels."

"Go get some dinner, Geoff. I've got to beat this cold before tomorrow."

"You want me to come back tonight?"

"Suit yourself."

"I will *not*," Geoff said with some dignity, "take the onus for this snafu!"

"You know, Geoff, you are beginning to smell like my husband."

"Oh?"

"Yeah. Scotch."

Geoff thought for a minute as he half-knotted his tie.

"Well then," he said, "you smell like your husband too."

Then he left without another word, for some reason carrying his loafers on his two longest fingers like a part-time fisherman with two incredible champion trout.

Corinne woke to moans. She reached out to embrace Geoff but found only slick sheet. Then she thought she was dreaming, not awake in a dead city, that her difficult breathing had startled her, and that this was somehow indicative of her life, forever being shaken out of real release, prevented from dreaming by her own banal breathing. But slowly the inventory of the room took stock of her: the dirty Degas prints, stiff crinoline drapes, the dry whine of the radiator enforced themselves. The moans reached a crescendo. A woman's moans, and not three feet from her through the wall, that conventionally rhythmic cry, somewhere between ecstasy and pain, a wordlessness refined to the point where it could be taken in whatever way its interpreter wished, named by every man to suit his fashion. It was the first time Corinne had heard it from another, and she lay rigid, nearly comatose, waiting anxiously for the silences to come.

What happened after that can only be related by the numbers, very much as in Kindergarten where all experiences are supposed to be of the same duration and intensity, utterly undifferentiated. At any rate, Corinne found herself in her robe in the hall, standing before room 427, where moaning had given way to the low squabble of a late-night talk show. She was startled by a stunning black maid in a pinafore, at least six-feet-two with the face of a West Indian goddess, who strode peremptorily down the hall and disappeared through double swinging doors into the Help's respite room. Corinne watched the doors until they ceased shuffling against one another, and then she heard voices again, charmingly accented, then tearful, and finally, the sobbing. From behind every door, the voices of women, whispering, sighing, weeping.

Back in her room, Corinne bolted the door, then unlocked it, realizing Geoff would misinterpret if he chose to return. Then she turned on the TV and spun the dial — news, weather, sports, Charlton Heston, moonshot reruns — snapped it off, then, her lungs crackling with dehydration, she tried to open the window. She got it up about an inch, and the fearful whine of Fifty-eighth

Street entered with a few toxic snowflakes. She tried the other window which gave off to a gray airshaft, but it was nailed shut. Corinne then poured a water tumbler full of Geoff's Scotch and traced with her finger the paisley pattern which flung itself from the drapes to the cornices and reappeared in the tassels of the bedspread. She tried the lyre-back chair at the writing desk; through the glass top, a card garlanded with puppies and rhododendrons announced: "We shall do our utmost to please you." Above the desk, she reached for a book but found that the spines of the leather editions had been sawn off and glued to a board. And then in the mirror she caught sight of her tousled bed, the swatches scattered about the pillows and the floor, exploded as artificially as in a store-window display, a buyer's market, and then she found herself fumbling in her purse for . . . Fitz's card. But when a cloudy voice in room 818 at the St. Regis answered, Corinne banged the receiver down and felt, for the first time in her thirty-two years, that she was perfectly capable of both inconsequence and betrayal.

It was close to midnight. Corinne Huff sat crosslegged in her chair, eyeing herself in the mirror in a way that she hadn't since she was sixteen. She began to slowly open her robe, then let it fall back. She touched her stomach, ran her hands over her crispness, as if it were a stranger's pet, and then lay back, strangely calm. She had not at all suddenly come to that irrefragably momentous American knowledge, contracted the nation's most recent humor. Corinne was "simply" fed up. She didn't want to go home. She didn't want to stay in New York and live it up. She didn't want to apologize to Geoff even though he perhaps deserved it. She didn't want to take the night flight to Acapulco, she didn't want to buy one more single thing, she didn't want to be anybody else, or with anybody else, and she didn't want to be alone. Corinne knew then that no person, group, idea, option, feeling, or law would ever solve the common problem of this slightly overheated, overdecorated room.

She put the night latch on the door, instructed the desk to cancel her next morning's appointments on account of illness, left a heavy tip for the maid, who would have to somehow dispose of the swatches, and after a large dose of antihistamine and the last of Geoff's Scotch, watched the room close about her, a foot at each blink.

*

On the plane again. We are patient only at incredible speeds. Corinne, pale, without makeup, hair tied severely back, on the aisle this time, the bulkhead seat facing the galley. Beyond, the controls. Each time the stewardess passes, her elbow brushes Corinne's hair, and with a couple of bloody Marys under her belt, this is all right. Everybody on the flight is drunk. The cockpit door is open, the navigator is reclining and reading a comic, welded in the curve of his brown hands. The pilot and co-pilot's heads are bathed in the Caribbean light of their incredible instrumentation. A tight-lipped woman emerges from the forward toilet. Her eyes are also red and wet. Garbage is mounting about them: discarded newspapers, cups and napkins, gutted macadamia-nut sacks, Corinne's Kleenex. The cold has gone to her chest. Why do they give you a menu when there's no choice, she thinks. Why do they build the shore so close to the sea? The man next to her is singing something to himself. When their elbows brush he jerks an unspoken, involuntary apology. Corinne has no more questions, so she watches the stews. In the toilet, they exchange their pumps for flats, their slacks for culottes, their jackets for blouses and apronettes. Their epaulettes and braid are piled in the corner with sanitary napkins and airsickness bags. They slam everything, even the tiniest doors in the galley. All the little doors and windows have made them crass. Girls without grace, but this is impossible between takeoff and landing, a good plane with no blood on it. The intercom has been found defective. The primary stew coils the microphone's impotence about her wrist, grinding her teeth. Another holds the yellow scrotum of an oxygen bag above her head, blowing on a tube, while yet another reads the prepared text as best she can without amplification. She knows no one can see her and no one listens to her, except perhaps one random inspector. To their everlasting credit, they are laughing at themselves. The eggs are under radar, the baby's milk is being boiled. Shit, they say. Another baby. The champagne has been broken out. And the clouds, the cirrus, are becoming themselves as we cannot.

Corinne has resolved to worry no more about herself and releases her chairback. But as she does so, strange and constant pressure exerts itself upon her kidneys. She glances over her shoulder and sees a little boy behind her, clutching his mother's wrist, his legs stiffened in fear against her chairback. The woman is about her age, but puffier and paler; nothing, clearly, but a mother. But then Corinne hears her own voice, if not exactly her choice of words, as well as that of Brucie and them all.

"Don't kick the seat. Didn't you see the lady turn around?"

"I'm scared, Mama."

"Look. Here're the directions. It says sit straight up and fasten seat belts. Are we doing it right? Fine."

"Wouldn't he like some breakfast?" A stew leans over. "Or maybe even a hot dog?"

"I want to go down," the child whines and squirms.

"Sit back and shut up!"

"The engines went off. We stopped," he says, without a quaver.

"That always happens when we're through climbing," the stew says. "Don't you watch television?"

"I always thought that too when I first flew," the mother said.

"I can't see the lights anymore," the boy says.

"Look out the window," says the stew. "See, we're not stopped."

"Do what the nice lady says, and wave to Daddy and Aunt Ella and Chipper."

Corinne felt the child's feet relax just for an instant but then thrust forward with redoubled force.

"There's a hole in the wing!" he yelled.

"Those are just flaps, honey," the stew said. "We're leveling off now."

"He got *that* from television," Mother says.

"Hello Aunt Ella!"

"Don't yell, child. Aunt Ella can't hear you. She's deaf."

"Daddy?"

"You promised your daddy you'd be good. Now read the instructions again. Out loud this time. Come on, how about a hot dog, honey?"

The other stews were passing up and down the aisle, absorbing the leers and fears, relating the captain's anticipation of turbulence. "Please stay seated," they were saying. Corinne saw it was getting darker. They were going faster than the sun. It wasn't good enough.

"We're going down now, Mama."

"Yes, dear, we're going down."

"Where to?"

"When we get home, we'll go to the filling station and get some steaks."

"I don't want to go down."

"You can't fly all day. You can't fly any more than to home."

"But I don't want to go down."

"You didn't want to go *up* before. Maybe you'll grow up to be an astronaut."

"Are we down now, Mama?"

"Not yet." The stew passed a hot dog to the kid.

"Oh, now you've got mustard all over. Wipe it off."

"No."

"Shut up or I'll leave you here . . . you want to be left here?"

"No."

"You want to take the bus home all by yourself?"

"Will Daddy be there?"

"We just said goodbye to Daddy. He's in Newark. Be a big boy. Be a man now. Or you'll have to find your own way home."

Corinne lay back. There wasn't much she would have added to that bit. What man had ever forgotten it? It wasn't the sort of thing one could be intelligent about. Well, there was something nice about flying, really, about the futility of giving contrary directions at such a height, etc., where fear and toughness were all of a piece. Not at all like coming back from a party with Fred, grinding your teeth in the swerving car, wearing out an imaginary brake pedal with a toeless pump from the death seat. The trees which line the road in Fred's wandering lights are the same color as our fuselage. . .

The child was stamping now. And the man beside her had evidently succeeded in singing himself to sleep, for he was slouched heavily on her shoulder, an enormous two-tone brogue like a fallen plinth against her calf.

She was just about to request a change in seating when the cockpit door opened and the Captain emerged. He was exceptionally handsome in a stereotyped way, tanned, with silvered temples and golden eyes. The Captain touched the bill of his cap over a half-supine Corinne, but did not look down.

"We have an announcement. There will be increasing turbulence the rest of the way. Please keep your belts on. Also, we're stacked up in an indefinite holding pattern. But if you look out the window," he finished, "you can see the lights of Akron."

Then as the plane suddenly broke its plane, the Captain smiled self-consciously and braced himself against Corinne's seatback.

His manicured nails were an inch from her mouth. The child's feet were relentless at her hams. The gentleman to her left had begun to snore. The Captain's hand was ringless, whorled with golden hair and large veins. Large light-blue veins. Also, a raised scar, like Akron from the air, another ganglia of strangulated energy. Like what lay in her lap. Like what kicked her back. Like what drove the plane. Like what lit the clouds. Though not enough alike.

The Captain thought the lady was about to scream or vomit. But it was only Corinne's suppressed laughter again. Pretty lips drawn up from pretty teeth, offense she was taught not to commit, defense against the tears she would not permit.

"Too many," she was thinking, "just too many damn people to love."

JOYCE CAROL OATES

Gay

(FROM PLAYBOY)

UNFORTUNATELY for Hilberry University, the first murder of this new year involved one of the most distinguished newer members of the English department.

Clark Pembroke Austen III came to Hilberry by way of a circuitous and rather puzzling route: Harvard, Oxford (where he was a Rhodes Scholar), Amherst, the University of Pennsylvania and Youngstown State University. With his graceful, rather shy good manners, his impeccable credits and the slightly British intonation of his speech, he was something of a catch for Hilberry — an unpretentious university in southwestern Ontario, not far from Niagara Falls, with an enrollment of about 5000 and a very modest budget, much of which seemed to be directed toward physical education, here called Human Kinetics.

Much speculation centered on Clark; his colleagues were fascinated by him and queried students about his teaching: Did he lecture, was he able to communicate, was he — well, in any way — *unusual?* He was a bachelor, of course. There were several other bachelors in the department and all of them, except a young instructor with the reputation of being popular with his girl students, were quite eccentric. They existed on the fringes of the department, however, and caused little trouble; one of them was possibly insane — but in a mild, harmless way, and he had, even, a small coterie of students who supported him. Clark Austen was another case entirely. Not only had he published his doctoral dissertation — *Stagecraft and Costume Design in Ford's " 'Tis Pity She's a Whore"* — at one of the top Ivy League schools, and a respectable scattering of scholarly critical essays in excellent journals, but he seemed to be on a casual, first-name basis with eminent scholars in the Ivy League, at Oxford and Cambridge and even at various European universities. He dressed beautifully, though rather formally — in suits with vests, blazers with gold buttons, dress shirts and ties. It was evident that his nails were manicured regularly, his neckties were in exquisite taste and his hair razor-styled so that its rather youthful length was not inappropriate for a man in his late forties. Rumor had it that Clark's shoes were custom-made, sent to him from a Bond Street shop in London. In any case, he carried himself well, as if constantly aware of an audience; he was always friendly, always good-natured, though sometimes his conversations were strained, even abstract and perfunctory, and members of the English department remarked to one another that there was something "remote" and "mysterious" about him. Frank Ambrose, the department's only black man, and one of the few men in the entire university who dressed with the quiet and expensive good taste with which Clark dressed, said that he liked Clark very much, they had had a lively discussion about the staging of Addison's *The Drummer* one afternoon, but, still, there was something quite secretive about the man. "Anyone from the Ivy League who winds up at a university like Hilberry has got to have some reason for it," Frank said soberly.

From the first, however, Clark was popular with his colleagues. He had a certain style, having been born in Boston of evidently quite well-to-do parents, and he was a delightful conversationalist when relaxed, after a few drinks; moreover, he showed his gratitude profusely — and even a kind of sweet humility — by complimenting his hosts on their lovely homes and charming children and delicious food. Sometimes he took a dozen roses, sometimes a bottle of Scotch or an excellent wine. "He's really very attractive," the wives said, as if arguing a subtle point. Indeed, he had a sort of ruined beauty, striking green-gray eyes and a noble nose and mouth rather eroded in the fattish contours of his face.

It was noted that he could drink a remarkable quantity of alcohol before he started to show any effects. Basil May, the department's new head, had an open house in September at which, it was estimated, Clark drank at least five martinis before his speech became slurred; and even then, he grew more and more gracious, more courtly. He complimented his hostess at great length, as if he'd never seen anyone so beautiful. "That dress is so becoming,

Mrs. May. I've never seen such lustrous, healthy hair — such an exquisite auburn shade! — it's impossible to believe that you're really the mother of three growing boys, it's just wonderful, just . . . just surpassingly wonderful!" The poor woman stood there by the buffet table, plain Joanna May, blushing, confused, embarrassed. Clark took another drink and self-consciously joined a small group of men who were discussing the phenomenon of popular culture and its consequences for English studies: Were *King Lear* and *Peanuts* mutually exclusive or were they, perhaps, part of the same creative expression, the "human essence"? Clark appeared to be listening politely, but he said nothing; he finished his drink quickly. It was said afterward by Jake Hanley, who stood nearest him, that his skin had gone dead-white in a matter of seconds. He interrupted the intellectual discussion by pointing to Eunice Ambrose and Marcella Blass, on the far side of the room, both of whom wore long dresses with floral prints and ropes of pearls. "Flowered skirts . . . flowered skirts and pearls and . . . and perfume," Clark said very slowly. "What does it mean? *What does it mean?*" When no one answered, he narrowed his eyes to slits, puffed out his cheeks and made a face that could only be called — so everyone said who happened to see it — incredulous. He waited a moment, then said, in an even slower voice, gesturing with his forefinger, "I say flowered skirts and pearls and perfume and open-toed shoes and shaved legs and shaved armpits and . . . I say, *What do they mean? What . . . what do they mean?*"

Then he staggered, set his glass down, complained of being suddenly dizzy. Of course, everyone came forward to help. Mrs. May asked if he might like to lie down for a few minutes, in one of the upstairs bedrooms; Brian Packer offered to drive him back to his apartment, since he and his wife were about to leave anyway. "Yes, thank you very much, thank you very, very much," Clark whispered. "I do think it's time for me to go home . . ."

After the Packers drove off with Clark, everyone talked about what an extraordinary thing to have happened — Clark Austen suddenly so drunk, his skin lardish-pale, his eyes glassy and tiny and somehow — this was most terrifying of all — somehow *not quite human.* Dr. May had been out of the room at the time of Clark's peculiar metamorphosis, so it had to be demonstrated for him. Jake Hanley tried but was too grossly melodramatic; Frank

Ambrose, himself a little drunk, but nerved up and witty, did a much better imitation. Everyone laughed, though of course it wasn't a laughing matter; it was really very strange, very unfortunate. Very *sad*.

They talked of little else but Clark Austen for the rest of the evening. The last persons to leave were the Ambroses. Saying good night to the Mays, Frank Ambrose suddenly ran a hand over his head, as if he had just thought of something incredible. "Do you suppose — look, do you suppose that poor bastard doesn't *know* he's queer?" Frank cried.

Almost immediately, Brian and Natalie Packer took up Clark's cause. Because the Packers were from Toronto, and therefore supposed themselves sophisticated, they were eager to befriend Clark; he was a remarkable man, Natalie insisted, far more sensitive than most. And he was lonely. Very lonely. Large groups upset him, Natalie said, but he was very much at home with the Packers; they were, after all, the only people in the department to have permanent orders at a downtown newsstand for the Sunday *New York Times*. Clark loved the ballet as much as the Packers did, and he was ecstatic over Natalie's cooking and genuinely fond of the Packer's twin poodles —large, rather flabby white dogs in late middle age — so it came about, quite naturally, that the three of them, in Natalie's words, constituted an "oasis" of sorts in the midst of Hilberry's general mediocrity.

Brian Packer was a tall, frail man in his early thirties, with a wistful, sweet, cherubic look; a specialist in seventeenth-century literature. He did not mind that Natalie governed both of their lives and tried to inspire him to write critical essays — so that, someday, they could return to Toronto and civilization. Everyone liked Brian. It was Natalie who claimed attention: hardly five feet tall, chirrupy, assertive, with a loud, abrasive, lusty laugh, she was five years Brian's senior and always caught up in special projects. One year it was harp lessons; another year, pottery; still another year, she decided to enroll in the master's program in sociology at the university but dropped out midway because of a violent quarrel she had with one of her professors, in front of an entire class. "The man is an idiot! A total idiot!" she cried. For months she went about, to faculty wives' meetings, to parties, telling everyone who would listen, including friends of the professor, what an idiot he was. "A creature like that should be fired immediately," she declared. She wrote letters to the dean of humanities and to the president of the university, but naturally, nothing was done: Hilberry was such a mediocre place, what else could she and Brian expect?

Natalie insisted that Clark come for dinner two or three times a week. She insisted that he bring things to be mended, if he had any; and she sent him back to his apartment — in a cold, regal, expensive high-rise north of the campus — with plastic containers filled with leftovers. She was convinced he didn't eat right, being a bachelor. He drank too much, she said bluntly — bluntness was one of Natalie's deliberately cultivated virtues — and he had poor eating habits and at times his shoulders slumped, as if he were very unhappy. While Brian corrected student papers at the dining room table, Natalie and Clark sat in the living room, sipping espresso and talking earnestly about innumerable important things: Clark's childhood, Clark's education, Clark's sensitivity and disappointments, his successes, his failures, his sickly father and his ignorant mother and his four vain, selfish sisters, his frank opinion of Hilberry — it was truly mediocre, wasn't it? — and of various individuals in the department: They were so lazy and pathetic, weren't they? And, of course, these people gossiped. Constantly. Natalie had been amazed at the amount of gossiping and backbiting that went on at Hilberry; it was so contrary to her own nature, and foreign to her own experience, that she had had difficulty adjusting to life here. Even now, six years after Brian's appointment, she could not quite believe how vicious her husband's colleagues and their smug, dowdy wives could be.

"Don't let them hurt you," she said warmly. "Don't *ever* let those small-minded people hurt you, Clark."

"Why, how would they hurt me?" Clark asked, surprised.

"Well — you know."

"I do . . . ?"

"They're narrow-minded, they're hopelessly bourgeois," she said. Though she was a small woman, her face was rather large; it had, somehow, a creased, muscular look, as if she were continually tensing her forehead and cheeks. When she was especially excited, as she was now, her glasses began to ride down her nose. Clark liked her — he was sure he liked her. She was so intense, so intelligent, so different from the other faculty wives . . . He was sure he liked her, though at times she intimidated him. *"They simply can't tolerate people who are different from them; they're right-wing prigs, believe me. So don't ever let those fools get you down."*

Clark tried to smile. His forehead was damp, his toes and fingers were twitching helplessly. What on earth was this awful woman saying . . . ?

"I'm not sure I understand," he said rather stiffly.

"Oh, Clark, for Christ's sake," Natalie laughed. "You needn't pretend with us. We're your friends, aren't we? You know we are! . . . Look, it's perfectly all right; Brian and I lived in Toronto for years. We quite approve of alternate lifestyles. We've always been totally liberal. And I mean liberal! It doesn't matter to *us*, Clark, not one bit."

"What doesn't matter to you . . . ?"

It was at that point, Natalie said afterward, that Clark fixed her with such a strange, malevolent look . . . so coldly vicious a look . . . that she faltered and could not speak. He had had only two drinks, and yet his eyes were glazed; there was a frightening, almost demonic air about him. And how quickly it had happened. . .

"Why, why . . . Clark, you look so angry . . ." she stammered.

"You horrible squat creature," Clark whispered. "You . . . you runtish little . . . ugly little runtish little *sow*."

He rose from the sofa. He got his coat. He left.

For days afterward, Natalie talked of nothing else. She went to visit other faculty wives, she made telephone calls, she dramatized again and again Clark Austen's terrifying metamorphosis, sometimes breaking into tears. How awful it had been, how totally unexpected! They had been such warm, intimate friends, and then he had turned on her! For no reason! No reason! Brian tried to calm her, but she refused to be calmed. "I have never in my life been so *frightened*," she told Joanna May, whom she met in the A&P. "The man looked at me as if he was about to strangle me. I'm not exaggerating! His face was twisted, his voice was guttural and inhuman . . ." While walking the poodles, she saw Eunice Ambrose driving by and shouted after her, waving her arms so energetically that Eunice had no choice but to stop; she told Eunice all about Clark, stressing the rapidity of his change, the totally unexpected nature of his hostility. "He hates women, of course. I should have known that. In a way, I *did* know. But I

was trying to be generous, trying to be liberal. It was such a
shock! Such a blow! One minute we were the best of friends and
the next, he had turned on me . . . called me an ugly little runtish
sow, can you imagine?"

"Natalie, he *didn't!* A what?"

"Brian and I stayed up all night afterward, literally shaking.
Shaking with fear that he might come back. Brian isn't very
strong, you know. These things upset him. When we looked
back over our relationship, we could see how Clark was primarily
interested in Brian: He was always asking Brian about his classes,
about his students, about where he bought his clothes. That sort
of thing." Natalie shivered dramatically. "I have absolutely nothing against homosexuals. I never have. Some dislike women —
are afraid of us, I suppose — but I sympathize with them. I'm as
understanding as can be. But, you see — and this is something I
worked out for myself, and Brian agrees that I'm right — the
freakish thing about Clark Austen is that while he knows very well
he isn't a normal man, he imagines — the poor fool imagines! —
that the rest of us are deceived. *That* is his secret."

"He thinks . . . ?"

"He thinks no one knows he's queer," Natalie said angrily.

By midwinter, Clark had gained at least ten pounds and his
stylish clothes were tight on him, and rumpled-looking, and he
seemed to have a perpetual cold. Frank Ambrose, whose office
was next to his, complained that the man was always snuffling and
wheezing and clearing his throat. Though it was said that his
students liked him — he was evidently quite a good lecturer and
had a beautiful reading voice for Shakespeare — he seemed
rather unhappy at Hilberry. He sent a note of apology to Natalie
Packer, but it was so absurdly hypocritical, Natalie said, so falsely
obsequious and groveling, that she'd ripped it up immediately.
"God, how I abhor effeminate men!" Natalie said.

Her stories about Clark involved now not only the ugly circumstances of their last evening as friends but other matters entirely:
Clark's miserable childhood, his envy and hatred of his four beautiful sisters, the probability — she would swear to it, really — that
he had been fired from his previous teaching positions, and his
truly shocking opinion of the Hilberry faculty (the place was a
"hotbed of mediocrity," in Clark's own words). Worst of all, in

Natalie's opinion, was the man's pathetic self-deception: as if
everyone didn't know fully well what he was!

"I thought you didn't mind homosexuals," Frank Ambrose said.

"Of course I don't *mind*. I certainly don't. But Clark Austen is
a hypocrite," Natalie said hotly. "And he's sick; the man is really
sick."

Nearly everyone detested Natalie, however much they liked
Brian; they repeated to one another, in scandalized delight, *ugly
little runtish sow!* Didn't that describe their Natalie perfectly? By
contrast, poor Clark seemed quite harmless. And he was lonely.
It was pathetic, really, how lonely he was. Taking pity on him,
Frank Ambrose stopped by his office late one afternoon. He was
conscious of the man's transparent gratitude that someone should
say hello; Clark's face actually seemed to light up. He asked
Frank to have a seat, please. Please do! Would he like some
coffee! Some tea?

Frank declined; he told people afterward that he'd been a little
afraid of sitting that close to Clark. After all . . . ! But the man
was so pathetic, and really quite nice, that he decided to invite him
out to the house that weekend. A few friends were getting together, nothing fancy. How would Clark like to join them?

Despite Frank's charity, however, the evening was doomed
from the start.

Clark arrived fifteen minutes early. He was wearing a handsome navy-blue blazer, gun-metal-gray trousers, a pale-blue shirt
and a yellow knit tie; he looked quite good, except for the fact
that his face was slightly flushed and it was evident that he'd had a
few drinks before coming to the Ambroses'.

Some five or six couples had gathered in the Ambroses' basement recreation room and though Clark knew them all, he didn't
mix very well but sat on the American Colonial sofa, staring at the
linoleum floor, or at the simulated-knotty-pine wall, or at the port-
able television set on its aluminum cart, though, of course, the set
was turned off and the screen was a featureless leaden-gray blank.
It was February now: Talk dwelt upon the overcast skies, the
streets that were so inadequately plowed, grocery prices, taxes, the
university's disappointing budget allotment from the legislature,
various children's ailments and hobbies and difficulties with or
successes in various schools, a rapid cascade of names that whirled
about Clark's head but left him untouched.

Then one of the Ambroses' little boys appeared in his pajamas, to pass Cheez-bits and cashews and tiny spicy hot dogs around to the guests, and it was generally noted how Clark, sitting there on the sofa with his drink on his knee and his hair rather loose and disheveled about his face, stared at the boy. Frank Ambrose was a good-looking black man, amazingly slender, with a lithe, graceful, almost boyish body, though he was well into his late thirties; his wife, Eunice, was a very pale woman with dull red hair and a sweet, patient, sometimes rather strained smile. Their children, all boys, were very light-skinned, with large dark eyes that were thickly lashed, and very dark, somewhat frizzy hair. They were beautiful children, everyone proclaimed. Really beautiful. So it was no wonder that Clark should be staring at little Marty with that peculiar half-smile, as if he had never seen anything quite like the child.

Approaching Clark, however, the boy hesitated; he began to giggle.

"What's wrong, Marty?" Eunice said. "Pass the hors d'oeuvres around. Go on."

But the child shied away, giggling.

"Marty, stop being so silly. You're being a naughty boy."

"It's really quite all right," Clark said quickly. He tried to laugh. "I'm not . . . I don't really . . . You see, I'm on a diet, anyway, and I mustn't have . . . It looks delicious, really, but I . . ."

"Marty!" Eunice said sharply. "What *is* wrong with you? I told you to pass those hors d'oeuvres around and stop being so silly, or I'll let Bobbie do it. Aren't you bad? Aren't you silly?"

The boy turned to his mother and motioned for her to bend down to him. He whispered something in her ear. "*What?*" Eunice said. "What on earth are you talking about?"

"Looks like a *witch*," the boy said, cupping his hands to his mouth and peering back over his shoulder at Clark. "Like on the *Monster Show* . . ."

"Why, Marty!" Eunice said. "Isn't that *bad* of you! Give those plates here and go right upstairs to bed. Isn't that bad, isn't that silly . . . ?"

Marty gave his mother the dishes and ran out of the room, still giggling.

Frank Ambrose cleared his throat nervously and said something about children's being so unpredictable, so irrational. They were likely to say anything without the slightest sense of —

"Exactly," Jake Hanley said. "And they don't mean it, of course."

"They don't *know* what they mean," Marcella Blass said.

"It's the influence of television . . ." someone else said.

"Not at all, not at all," Clark said slowly. "I understand. I . . . I was a child once myself."

There was another uncomfortable silence, as if the group doubted Clark's statement but was too polite to comment.

Talk leaped eagerly onto other, similar topics. But Clark remained oddly stiff, staring at the linoleum. It was a bright, cheerful design, swirls of green, orange, beige and red; it was meant to complement the dark-green-and-beige furniture. He sat there, beside Joanna May, who was talking animatedly with Eunice Ambrose and Jake Hanley and Sid Trainor about the latest fiasco in the drama department — and gradually it came to Joanna's attention, and then to the attention of the others, that Clark was muttering under his breath.

At first they tried to ignore him. Then it became more difficult. "What does it mean . . . ? What does it . . . mean? Shouldn't wear short skirts; knees bunchy and fat. Pizza. Henna rinse. Horrid old granny: the bitch! Pickaninny. Cute. Eyes, rosebud mouth. Won't you have another drink? Clark? Yes, thank you, thank you very much, yes, damn nigger, get me that drink fast, damn show-off, you'll see, you'll regret it . . ." He seemed oblivious of them, muttering, shaking his head from side to side. The entire sofa shook; he was six-two or -three and by no means a light man. His eyes were nearly shut as he spoke in that slow, painfully slow, almost meticulous way. Everyone stared in astonishment. The man's entire personality seemed to have changed within a few seconds. His face was chalky, a comic monster's face, ugly and creased and lined and worn; his mouth shaped itself into absurd, sinister contortions, as if he were a child before a mirror, trying to frighten himself. "Does it mean? What? Don't you touch me, you nigger. Don't you come near! I want another drink. I'm thirsty. Hairpiece. Knitted right into hair: five hundred dollars. Fraud! Crooks! Oh, my God, my God . . ."

It seemed that he was about to burst into tears. Frank Ambrose stood over him, trying to calm him down. "Clark? Look, Clark, are you all right?"

"Don't you touch me!" he said murderously.

He shoved poor Frank backward, moving so quickly that everyone was taken by surprise. Frank staggered a few steps, fell into Marcella Blass's lap, then onto the floor. The women began uttering short, faint, astonished cries. Clark himself tried to get to his feet but failed. He was so drunk that, it was said, the lower half of his face seemed dislodged somehow from the upper half; his jaw ground maniacally back and forth. "Lower-class bastards. I wasn't destined for this. Not on your goddamn life I wasn't! Clark Pembroke Austen the Third. Lower-class bastards, bags, bitches, cows, scum, *canaille* . . . Cheez-bits. Oh, my God! Wasn't destined for this. Call me a cab. Don't touch me, niggers. This is not *my* life, this is someone else's. Ugly ugly ugly. You'll regret your audacity. You ugly, ugly creatures . . . !"

"Now, Clark, please," Jake Hanley said earnestly. "You —"

Clark struggled massively to his feet. He swayed, stumbled across Joanna May's feet and threw his martini glass at Jake. Only the ice-cube fragments struck Jake, fortunately; the glass itself smashed against the simulated-knotty-pine wall.

"Ugly, ugly! Oh, my God! It cannot be, it cannot *be*. Forty-nine years old. Harvard, Oxford, Amherst . . . Somewhere in Canada? *Monster Show*. Call me a cab, you niggers! I don't want to eat your fucking tuna casseroles, I don't want to drink your cheap liquor, I want to go home, I hate you all, oh, my God, you'll regret it, bags, bitches, cows, goggle-eyed scum, little nigger brats prancing around in pajamas . . . This isn't my life, I swear." He began shrieking. "It isn't! *Isn't!*"

The following week, at least a half dozen variants of the story of the Ambroses' party made the rounds, not only of the English department but of the entire university. People laughed uproariously, then wiped their eyes and said, solemnly, "It's a shame, isn't it? So intelligent and gifted a man. Is he seeing a psychiatrist? . . . At least he shouldn't *drink*, if he's an alcoholic." Ron Blass was excellent at demonstrating Frank's backward stagger and his look of utter incredulity; Jake Hanley was perfect at imitating Clark's glowering, sneering, mad expression and his wail *This isn't my life! It isn't! Isn't!* In some versions of the story, Clark threw his martini glass at Eunice Ambrose, having accused her of marrying a "nigger"; in other versions, he attempted to fondle the Ambrose child and Frank intervened and a scuffle resulted; in still other versions, repeated as far away as the civil-engineering department and the Human Kinetics School, one of the new English professors had gone berserk over the weekend, attempted to rape a small child, was beaten by someone — the child's father, perhaps, or police — and had been committed to the Harris Clinic, the area's hospital for mentally disturbed people.

Clark himself was absent from classes for a week. When he returned, he still looked rather sick. His skin was slack, lifeless; his eyes were red-rimmed. When he met colleagues in the hall, he whispered greetings in a formal, embarrassed way. Everyone who had attended the fateful party received notes of apology shortly after he returned to classes. Each note was written in long-hand, begging forgiveness, expressing his sincere regrets for the "unfortunate incident." He was very, very sorry. He was ashamed of himself, he said, and though he could only barely remember what had happened, he knew he had behaved disgracefully and it would never, never happen again. He knew he must not drink; and he was not going to drink. He could understand anyone's wish not to see him again — he *knew* he had behaved in a beastly way. He intended to begin afresh and he begged their forgiveness and understanding, as far as they were capable of granting it to him . . .

"The poor bastard," Jake Hanley said, scanning the note Clark had written to the Ambroses. His own was quite moving but not so lengthy as the Ambroses; both, however, were longer and better phrased than the notes sent to the Mays and the Blasses and the Trainors. "He's really contrite, isn't he? Asked me how much he owed me for the cab — so he *did* remember I was the one who helped him out to the street — and said he was sorry if he'd insulted me in any way . . . You really should forgive him, Frank."

"You know what he called me. You heard him."

"He was drunk."

"That broken-down fag," Frank whispered. He was hot-blooded: That was Frank's particular reputation at Hilberry. A few years ago, in his early thirties, he had been something of a rake himself; he had drunk quite a bit, had attended student parties, had been involved in romantic escapades with various girl students — nothing serious, of course — and, of course, Eunice had forgiven him; on several occasions, he had gotten very drunk and had fought with friends and even with a patrolman. But that was years ago. Years ago. And he had never, so far as he knew, really insulted anyone; he had never called anyone a *nigger*.

"You should forgive and forget, Frank," Jake said. One of the department's two or three poets, Jake was a stocky, sandy-haired, easygoing man in his forties. He smiled a good deal. He smiled now, noting the black man's pouty expression; he was thinking of how surprised poor Frank had been, insulted in his own basement recreation room, sent staggering backward into Marcella Blass's lap. Jake laughed aloud, thinking of it.

"What the hell is so funny?" Frank asked.

"I was just thinking of Clark trying to get into the cab," Jake said, wiping at his eyes. "He slipped on the ice. He sprained his wrist, but nobody knew it at the time. The poor bastard! But the expression on that taxi driver's face . . . ! Jesus, did he look worried. It's such a shame, really."

"The son of a bitch needs to see a psychiatrist," Frank said. "One of these days he's going to kill somebody or kill himself. The first time I had a look at him I said —"

"I wonder if the administration will fire him," Jake said.

That spring, Clark met his classes regularly and attended departmental meetings and was courteous, as always, though rather abashed, and even a little timid, when he encountered his colleagues in the halls or in the men's washroom. Rumor had it that he was, at last, seeing a psychiatrist in the city; and he was evidently on a rigorous diet, slowly losing weight, so that by the end of the term, he looked fairly healthy. Something had been done to his hair: It was styled in the same way, but there were vivid red-brown glints to it. He was sometimes seen downtown, wearing sunglasses, smoking cigarettes in a black cigarette holder, dressed in quite fashionable clothes. People forgave him, gradually. Even Natalie Packer was inclined to express her sympathetic pity for him; and Frank Ambrose, meeting him one day in the library, believed he saw tears of contrition in the man's eyes, and grumbled hello, and made the necessary gesture of forgiveness by offering to shake hands. They did shake hands. Frank winced a little, remembering it, remembering the clammy touch of the man's hand. But he was happy he'd made the gesture. "After all," he said afterward, "the poor son of a bitch is *human.*"

Clark Austen spent the summer in Europe and rumor had it that he wouldn't be back to Hilberry in the fall. He had resigned, some said: or he had been secretly fired by the board of trustees. Someone told Frank Ambrose that Clark had been admitted to a Swiss hospital, having had a nervous breakdown while traveling in the Alps. Frank, who had received a postcard from Clark, from Italy, didn't know what to believe. He felt some relief, then, when Clark returned in September, as trim as he'd been the spring before, looking good, courteous, as always, though not quite so nervous. He had had a marvelous vacation, he told everyone.

There were a few parties in the autumn and Clark was invited, accepting with his usual gratitude. At the first, he drank nothing at all. At the second, he consented — since his host seemed to insist — to have a glass of red wine. At the third party, he drank two martinis but showed no effect, though he did leave early, with the excuse that a young nephew of his was a house guest that weekend. "He seems to be perfectly adjusted now," his friends said. "He *is* a very nice person, isn't he?"

It was sometime in late October that Clark was first seen — by a neighbor of the Trainors', herself the wife of a physics professor — in the company of a strange-looking young man. The young man was in his early twenties, had shoulder-length blond hair and very pale skin, a somewhat blemished forehead and long, narrow hands and feet. He wore a denim outfit and cowboy boots. At first, it was thought that he might be a student.

Jake Hanley saw him leaning against a wall in the Toronto-Dominion Bank, while Clark waited in one of the lines to make a withdrawal. The boy was smiling at nothing. He smiled into the air — dreamily, lazily. He was tall, even taller than Clark, but very thin; in fact, he looked sickly. His teeth were grayish-green, Jake said, and he certainly was not a student at Hilberry. "Frankly, he looked diseased," Jake said.

"Was he good-looking?" Frank asked.

Jake shrugged his shoulders and colored slightly. "How would I know? . . . I doubt it."

Ron Blass thought it was an unfortunate development in Clark's private life. His wife seemed very embarrassed about the subject and had no opinion at all. "It's a shame that poor Clark should have to stoop to *that*," Basil May said irritably. Since becoming head of the English department, he was acquiring, like his predecessor, who had had some emotional problems during his term of office and who had, in fact, retired two years early, a certain nervousness about nearly everything his faculty did. The pending publication of an article, the pending birth of a child, the latest rash of poems by Ron Blass or Jake Hanley, the newest idea put forth by anyone at all — and Dr. May began to feel jumpy and apprehensive. As an ordinary faculty member, he had been quite vocal, and even rather critical of the administration; now that he was an administrator, he distrusted such persons. He had begun to think that the university had drifted too far into democracy. But his wife, Joanna, surprisingly, thought that it might be a "good thing" for Clark to have a friend, even if it was a boy so much younger than he.

"All human beings want companionship," Joanna said bravely. Brian Packer looked grave when told about the boy, but Natalie said she wasn't surprised at all. "I wouldn't even be surprised to hear that Clark is handing most of his paycheck over to the boy, and that he's made him the beneficiary of his will. Men like him do things like that."

Sid Trainor said that, in his opinion, Clark Austen really yearned for a son, for a way into the "human community." "This might be his salvation, you know."

Love was one thing, friendship was one thing, but this relationship, Frank Ambrose said, was something quite different. They all knew what it was, there was no use denying it. "The man is sick. Next he'll be propositioning our students," Frank said.

"But if they were girl students . . . ?" Jake Hanley said.

It was possible that Frank blushed; his skin tone seemed to cloud.

"Anyway," Jake said, "Clark can't help it — he's the way he is and it isn't a disease, they say; it's just a behavioral matter, really nothing that unusual. Times have changed, Frank. The world is very experimental now."

It was true enough: The little Hilberry community had to confess that styles of living were vastly different now than they had been, say, twenty years ago. Students openly roomed together, not just girls and boys but threesomes, strange mixed groups, ragamuffin families that smoked marijuana together and ate only brown rice — or was it white rice? — and none of this was done with an air of defiance, as it had been in the 60s: It was quite ordinary, even conventional. "Boys and girls do anything they like now," Sid Trainor said slowly. "Anything we can imagine they probably do . . . and a lot we can't imagine."

"Still," it was pointed out, "Clark Austen is a member of the faculty. He must exercise responsibility and restraint . . . "

But nothing happened, time passed, and though Clark had the good sense never to bring the boy to campus, he was often sighted elsewhere with him. They went to movies together downtown, they ate at the Chinese Villa and the Blue Danube Hungarian Inn, they were seen one night at Si's, a pub near the university, both rather drunk — a reckless thing to do, everyone agreed, since Clark's students might very well have seen them there. Someone said that Clark had bought the boy a Yamaha, or that, at least, the two of them had been pricing motorcycles at a downtown dealer's. There was even a story — unsubstantiated, of course — that the two of them quarreled frequently and that, one cold, rainy night in November, the boy had shoved Clark out onto the balcony of his apartment and locked the door on him, and wouldn't let him in for over an hour. (Clark had been wearing nothing but a flannel bathrobe at the time.)

But nothing extraordinary happened, though everyone worried. Then, just before Christmas recess, Clark sent invitations to his colleagues for a New Year's Eve party.

At first they hesitated. Then, one by one, they accepted. It was a very friendly gesture on his part; he certainly did mean well. Natalie Packer was especially moved by the warmth of the invitation. She halfway regretted the things she had been saying about Clark. They *had* been friends, after all, until the evening of his strange breakdown. *We'll be happy to come to your party,* Natalie wrote Clark. *We've missed you very much.*

Clark's large, handsome apartment was on the eleventh floor of a high-rise building; entering it, his guests were impressed by gleaming surfaces, marble-topped tables, a brushed-velvet love seat, gilt-edged mirrors, prints of Constable in costly frames, fussy, striped silk wallpaper, a lavish oatmeal-colored rug, statues of Negroid-looking women carved in stone, brocade, lamps with fluted shades, a nonfunctional marble fireplace with luxurious brass andirons, a cherrywood dining set, dainty little cigarette boxes and ashtrays . . . a kaleidoscope of shapes and colors and textures, dizzying in its variety. "I'm so glad you like it," Clark

said, obviously flattered by their compliments. "It will take me
years to pay it off!"

He was pleased, too, by the cordiality with which they greeted
his nephew Carlie. All the men shook hands. Carlie flicked his
long, stringy hair out of his eyes, mumbled something and made a
grimace that resembled a smile. He seemed a little sullen. His
outfit for the evening was a buckskin shirt with fringes, tight-
fitting suede trousers, boots with three-inch heels, an identifica-
tion bracelet that was too loose for his bony wrist and a number of
rings on each hand. Clark introduced him as the son of his
brother who lived in Philadelphia, where he was "in banking."
Carlie was visiting Clark for an indefinable period of time, he
said; and they were taking the opportunity to improve Carlie's
writing. He wrote a theme a day and Clark went over it with him
and then he revised it and, in that way, he was gradually develop-
ing writing skills. Carlie listened, nodding without much interest.
He belched. He flicked his hair out of his eyes. Clark beamed at
him, and in that instant, Frank Ambrose experienced an odd
insight — he saw that, for the first time since coming to Hilberry,
Clark Austen was part of a couple. He was no longer a single individual, no longer a bachelor in the midst of couples.

But though the evening began well, it slid downhill quickly.
Clark was drinking too much and Carlie sat on the armrest of the
love seat, a beer bottle in hand, his expression remote, vacuous.
He was clearly stupefied with boredom. The hi-fi played Vivaldi,
turned too high. The food was delicious — liver *pâté*, caviar, an
entire ham, cold sliced roast beef, several delicatessen salads and
breads — but neither Clark nor Carlie was eating at all. Clark
kept hurrying into the kitchen, muttering under his breath, fussing like a demented old woman. He wore a dinner jacket and a
ruffled shirt of pale-blue silk, but there were stains on the jacket
sleeves, and as time passed, he grew increasingly flushed and confused. Frank and most of the others were standing around the
buffet, eating heartily. The food was of a much higher quality
than they served at their own parties: the Scotch was unquestion-
ably superior. Natalie Packer, whose appetite was legendary, stood
off by herself, a plate clutched in one hand and pressed against
her firm little tummy, her fork busy in the other hand. A small
trembling pyramid of food lay before her.

The trouble started when Marcella Blass, prettier than usual in

a floor-length blue dress, and a little drunk from the Scotch, began questioning Carlie in a warm, maternal voice. He was so thin,
she said, almost scolding. Why didn't he join them at the buffet,
why didn't he have some of this delicious food? The boy scowled,
then giggled. Marcella offered to prepare a plate for him. "I
don't want noner that shit," he said, drawing his arm swiftly beneath his nose. For some reason, Marcella giggled. At that moment, Clark reappeared, carrying a crab-meat-and-lobster casserole in what must have been a particularly heavy stoneware dish.
He bumped his hip against the sharp edge of the table, seemingly
distracted by something, staring toward Carlie; as if in a dream,
while everyone watched, the casserole dish tipped out of his
hands, a potholder fell with it, and there was a sickening crash.
Clark shrieked; he must have been burned.

It took a good ten minutes for the mess to be cleaned up. Clark
was very confused now, mumbling as if he were alone, actually
pushing people aside when they got in his way. Jake Hanley had
the mop and was energetically using it, and Clark simply yanked it
from him, stooped over, his hair loose about his face. Frank
poured himself another Scotch, straight, appearing to sense that
the party would be ending soon.

"Get your ass over here," Clark said to Carlie. "Do you hear
me, boy? Layin' there all evening, goddamned slut . . . There's
some stuff under the table there, some crab meat or mushrooms
or something, d'you hear me? — crawl under and get it, and
hurry up!"

Carlie set his bottle down, as if he were going to obey. Then
he giggled shrilly. "Crawl under and get it your*self,* Clark," he
said.

"Layin' there all evening," Clark said in a peculiar singsong
voice, one side of his face twisted into a kind of grin. Frank had
never seen Clark look like *that:* He was both playful and vicious,
clowning and demonic. He seemed unaware of the other guests.
A kind of skit had begun, a melodramatic comedy, which had the
air of being familiar to the two actors and yet exciting. "Goddamned lazy tart," Clark crooned.

"Who's calling who *what?*"

Clark strode over to Carlie and gripped his shoulder. He might
have misjudged his strength; Carlie cried out in pain and anger.
There was a brief scuffle. Frank looked around at the others,
searching for Eunice, wanting to catch her eye — or someone's

eye — before it was too late. But everyone was staring at Clark and Carlie. No one spoke. "Don't you touch *me*, I told you never to lay hands on *me*," the boy cried. He leaped to his feet and pushed Clark back against the wall, his eyes enormous. Somehow, his fist smashed against Clark's face; Clark's lower lip was split and bleeding. "I told you! I told you!" Carlie cried. His voice rose in terror. "It ain't my fault what happens!"

Droplets of blood had splashed onto Clark's ruffled shirt front. He moved his head slowly from side to side, as if trying to clear it. "Won't let me alone. Eh? I'll show you. Why are you all gaping at me? Who invited you? Goggle-eyed fools. Must be punished. You'll see: Six bullets and then reload. Spying on me. Carlie, get rid of them. Spies. Aren't we pretty, all fixed up for New Year's Eve! Flowered skirts and pearls and perfume, what does it mean? . . . Must be punished. Murderers."

"You're drunk, you stinking old fag," Carlie said, giving him another shove. "Shut up!"

"Filthy little beast," Clark said, wiping his mouth with his coat sleeve. He giggled softly. "Filthy, filthy little beast . . . should gargle with mouthwash, your breath is fetid . . . always has been . . ." His chest rose and fell. He was clearly winded, on the verge of collapsing. Yet he stood there, swaying, grinning, until the boy yelled something in despair and ran past him, back toward the bedroom.

Frank and the others exchanged incredulous looks. Clark wiped his mouth again, and again shook his head as if to clear it. He stared at Frank without seeing him. Frank started to say something, but the malevolent look in Clark's face discouraged him. Then, making a low wailing sound, Clark followed the boy back along the corridor. The boy had locked himself in the bedroom; Clark pounded on the door and commanded him to open it.

"Let's get the hell out of here," Basil May said.

There was a scramble to get to the hall closet, where their coats were hanging. Frank was saying, "Yes, but maybe we should — Maybe we owe it to — Don't you think we'd better do something?" But no one listened. Eunice was shivering violently and could hardly get her arms into her coat sleeves.

"Hurry up, hurry, for Christ's sake!" Jake Hanley muttered. "Where's my coat? Is this it? Let's get out of here before we're witnesses —"

At the other end of the apartment, Clark was calling to the boy in a peculiar wailing voice, partly cajoling, partly commanding. He was again pounding on the door.

"At least let's tell Clark we're leaving," Frank protested.

"Tell him yourself; nobody's stopping you."

They were leaving. Frank pulled at Basil May's arm. "Look, Dr. May, we can't just walk out on him, can we? I mean — what if something happens? Isn't that kid his beneficiary or something? — Where did we hear that? They're both drunk, they're both crazy, I've never seen anyone look so maniacal —"

"Frank, for God's sake. You've been drinking too much yourself. It's only a lover's spat; let's have the decency to leave them alone."

"But —"

Frank followed his friends out into the corridor, carrying his coat. Excited, frightened, like children, they ran down to the elevator, and he found himself running after them. Joanna May was in such a strange keyed-up state that her teeth were actually chattering. Frank, panting, said once again that he really thought they should stay a while longer, because something terrible might happen. But the elevator arrived and everyone crowded into it. The women made faint little squealing noises and Jake Hanley, who was a bit overweight, was wheezing.

On the way down, Brian Packer said, his voice trembling: "What could we have possibly done? It's a family squabble."

"We could notify the police," Marcella Blass said doubtfully.

"Oh, no! Like hell! And get sued for false arrest or something?" Ron Blass said. His voice slid up and down; he must have been very drunk. " 'S got a right to his own life, goddamn it. Everybody's got a right to his own life. See? No cops."

"What if something happens up there?" Frank asked. His heart was pumping absurdly. He knew that his eyes were enormous now and that the whites were glittering, but he could not help his fear.

"Frank, for Christ's sake!" Natalie Packer snorted. She had brought a roast-beef sandwich with her, pieces of rye bread clutched tight in her small plump hand. "Calm down, will you? You look like something in a minstrel show. Clark is old enough and big enough to choose his own playmates, isn't he? *What business is it of yours?*"

In the foyer of the apartment building, they felt much safer; they spoke in normal voices, hurrying to the front door.

Joanna May hurried alongside her husband, holding his arm. She said, laughing breathlessly, "Sometimes I think I've got a lot of catching up to do . . . I mean, the way the world is now." She giggled. She hiccuped. "Freedom, experimentation, lifestyles, alternative . . . alternate . . . whatdyacallit? . . . Got a lot of catching up to do."

"Joanna, really!" Basil said in disgust. "You're drunk."

Frank helped his wife down the icy steps. The others were going to their cars, breaking into couples, eager to be off. He wanted to shout after them. But there they went, breath steaming in the frigid air, and who was he to call them back . . . ? "It's such a shame, such a shame," Eunice mumbled. "That nice apartment and the delicious food and Clark trying to be so nice . . . I do hope that boy doesn't hurt him. What if somebody bashes in somebody's skull with one of those ugly statues? Oh, my God, Frank, I'm dizzy, I don't feel well . . ."

"Shut up and get in the car," Frank said.

From across the street, someone called over, "Happy New Year!" It was Ron Blass, or maybe Jake Hanley. Frank, pushing his wife into the car rather impatiently, hardly looked up to see.

"Happy New Year!" he shouted back.

TIM O'BRIEN

Going After Cacciato

(FROM PLOUGHSHARES)

IT WAS A BAD TIME. Billy Boy Watkins was dead, and so was
Frenchie Tucker. Billy Boy had died of fright, scared to death on
the field of battle, and Frenchie Tucker had been shot through the
neck. Lieutenants Sidney Martin and Walter Gleason had died in
tunnels. Pederson was dead and Bernie Lynn was dead. Buff
was dead. They were all among the dead. The war was always
the same, and the rain was part of the war. The rain fed fungus
that grew in the men's socks and boots, and their socks rotted, and
their feet turned white and soft so that the skin could be scraped
off with a fingernail, and Stink Harris woke up screaming one
night with a leech on his tongue. When it was not raining, a low
mist moved like sleep across the paddies, blending the elements
into a single gray element, and the war was cold and pasty and
rotten. Lieutenant Corson, who came to replace Lieutenant Martin, contracted the dysentery. The tripflares were useless. The
ammunition corroded and the foxholes filled with mud and water
during the nights and in the mornings there was always the next
village and the war was always the same. In early September
Vaught caught an infection. He'd been showing Oscar Johnson
the sharp edge on his bayonet, drawing it swiftly along his forearm and peeling off a layer of mushy skin. "Like a Gillette
Blueblade." Vaught had grinned. It did not bleed, but in a few
days the bacteria soaked in and the arm turned yellow, and
Vaught was carried aboard a Huey that dipped perpendicular,
blades clutching at granite air, rising in its own wet wind and
taking Vaught away. He never returned to the war. Later they
had a letter from him that described Japan as smoky and full of
bedbugs, but in the enclosed snapshot Vaught looked happy

enough, posing with two sightly nurses, a long-stemmed bottle of wine rising from between his thighs. It was a shock to learn that he'd lost the arm. Soon afterward Ben Nystrom shot himself in the foot, but he did not die, and he wrote no letters. These were all things to talk about. The rain, too. Oscar said it made him think of Detroit in the month of May. "Not the rain," he liked to say. "Just the dark and gloom. It's Number One weather for rape and looting. The fact is, I do ninety-eight percent of my total rape and looting in weather just like this." Then somebody would say that Oscar had a pretty decent imagination for a nigger.

That was one of the jokes. There was a joke about Oscar. There were many jokes about Billy Boy Watkins, the way he'd collapsed in fright on the field of glorious battle. Another joke was about the lieutenant's dysentery, and another was about Paul Berlin's purple boils. Some of the jokes were about Cacciato, who was as dumb, Stink said, as a bullet, or, Harold Murphy said, as an oyster fart.

In October, at the end of the month, in the rain, Cacciato left the war.

"He's gone away," said Doc Peret. "Split for parts unknown."

The lieutenant didn't seem to hear. He was too old to be a lieutenant, anyway. The veins in his nose and cheeks were shattered by booze. Once he had been a captain on the way to being a major, but whiskey and the fourteen dull years between Korea and Vietnam had ended all that, and now he was just an old lieutenant with the dysentery. He lay on his back in the pagoda, naked except for green socks and green undershorts.

"Cacciato," Doc Peret repeated. "He's gone away. Split, departed."

The lieutenant did not sit up. He held his belly with both hands as if to contain the disease.

"He's gone to Paris," Doc said. "That's what he tells Paul Berlin, anyhow, and Paul Berlin tells me, so I'm telling you. He's gone, packed up and gone."

"Paree," the lieutenant said softly. "In France, Paree? *Gay* Paree?"

"Yes, sir. That's what he says. That's what he told Paul Berlin, and that's what I'm telling you. You ought to cover up, sir."

The lieutenant sighed. He pushed himself up, breathing loud,

then sat stiffly before a can of Sterno. He lit the Sterno and
cupped his hands around the flame and bent down, drawing in
the heat. Outside, the rain was steady. "Paree," he said wearily.
"You're saying Cacciato's left for gay Paree, is that right?"

"That's what he said, sir. I'm just relaying what he told to Paul
Berlin. Hey, really, you better cover yourself up."

"Who's Paul Berlin?"

"Right here, sir. This is Paul Berlin."

The lieutenant looked up. His eyes were bright blue, oddly out
of place in the sallow face. "You Paul Berlin?"

"Yes, sir," said Paul Berlin. He pretended to smile.

"Geez, I thought you were Vaught."

"Vaught's the one who cut himself, sir."

"I thought that was you. How do you like that?"

"Fine, sir."

The lieutenant sighed and shook his head sadly. He held a
boot to dry over the burning Sterno. Behind him in the shadows
sat the crosslegged, roundfaced Buddha, smiling benignly from
its elevated perch. The pagoda was cold. Dank and soggy from a
month of rain, the place smelled of clays and silicates and old
incense. It was a single square room, built like a pillbox, with a
flat ceiling that forced the soldiers to stoop and kneel. Once it
might have been an elegant house of worship, neatly tiled and
painted and clean, candles burning in holders at the Buddha's
feet, but now it was bombed-out junk. Sandbags blocked the windows. Bits of broken pottery lay under chipped pedestals. The
Buddha's right arm was missing and his fat groin was gouged with
shrapnel. Still, the smile was intact. Head cocked, he seemed
interested in the lieutenant's long sigh. "So. Cacciato's gone
away, is that it?"

"There it is," Doc Peret said. "You've got it now."

Paul Berlin smiled and nodded.

"To gay Paree," the lieutenant said. "Old Cacciato's going to
Paree in France." He giggled, then shook his head gravely. "Still
raining?"

"A bitch, sir."

"You ever seen rain like this? I mean, ever?"

"No, sir," Paul Berlin said.

"You Cacciato's buddy, I suppose?"

"No, sir," Paul Berlin said. "Sometimes he'd tag along, but not
really."

"Who's his buddy?"

"Vaught, sir. I guess Vaught was, sometime."

"Well," the lieutenant said, dropping his nose inside the boot to smell the sweaty leather, "well, I guess we should just get Mister Vaught in here."

"Vaught's gone, sir. He's the one who cut himself — gangrene, remember?"

"Mother of Mercy."

Doc Peret draped a poncho over the lieutenant's shoulders. The rain was steady and thunderless and undramatic. Though it was mid-morning, the feeling was of endless dusk.

"Paree," the lieutenant murmured. "Cacciato's going to gay Paree — pretty girls and bare ass and Frogs everywhere. What's wrong with him?"

"Just dumb, sir. He's just awful dumb, that's all."

"And he's walking? He says he's walking to gay Paree?"

"That's what he says, sir, but you know how Cacciato can be."

"Does he know how far it is?"

"Six thousand eight hundred statute miles, sir. That's what he told me — six thousand eight hundred miles on the nose. He had it down pretty well. He had a compass and fresh water and maps and stuff."

"Maps," the lieutenant said. "Maps, flaps, schnaps. I guess those maps will help him cross the oceans, right? I guess he can just rig up a canoe out of those maps, no problem."

"Well, no," said Paul Berlin. He looked at Doc Peret, who shrugged. "No, sir. He showed me on the maps. See, he says he's going through Laos, then into Thailand and Burma, and then India, and then some other country, I forget, and then into Iran and Iraq, and then Turkey, and then Greece, and the rest is easy. That's exactly what he said. The rest is easy, he said. He had it all doped out."

"In other words," the lieutenant said, lying back, "in other words, fuckin AWOL."

"There it is," said Doc Peret. "There it is."

The lieutenant rubbed his eyes. His face was sallow and he needed a shave. For a time he lay very still, listening to the rain, hands on his belly, then he giggled and shook his head and laughed. "What for? Tell me — what the fuck for?"

"Easy," Doc said. "Really, you got to stay covered up, sir. I told you that."

"What for? I mean, what for?"

"Shhhhhhh, he's just dumb, that's all."

The lieutenant's face was yellow. He laughed, rolling onto his side and dropping the boot. "I mean, why? What sort of shit is this — walking to fucking gay Paree? What kind of bloody war is this, tell me, what's wrong with you people? Tell me — what's *wrong* with you?"

"Shhhhhh," Doc purred, covering him up and putting a hand on his forehead. "Easy does it."

"Angel of Mercy, Mother of Virgins, what's wrong with you guys? Walking to gay Paree, what's *wrong?*"

"Nothing, sir. It's just Cacciato. You know how Cacciato can be when he puts his head to it. Relax now and it'll be all fine. Fine. It's just that rockhead, Cacciato."

The lieutenant giggled. Without rising, he pulled on his pants and boots and a shirt, then rocked miserably before the blue Sterno flame. The pagoda smelled like the earth, and the rain was unending. "Shoot." The lieutenant sighed. He kept shaking his head, grinning, then looked at Paul Berlin. "What squad you in?"

"Third, sir."

"That's Cacciato's squad?"

"Yes, sir."

"Who else?"

"Me and Doc and Eddie Lazzutti and Stink and Oscar Johnson and Harold Murphy. That's all, except for Cacciato."

"What about Pederson and Buff?"

"They're the dead ones, sir."

"Shoot." The lieutenant rocked before the flame. He did not look well. "Okay." He sighed, getting up. "Third Squad goes after Cacciato."

Leading to the mountains were four clicks of level paddy. The mountains jerked straight out of the rice, and beyond those mountains and other mountains was Paris.

The tops of the mountains could not be seen for the mist and clouds. The rain was glue that stuck the sky to the land.

The squad spent the night camped at the base of the first mountain, then in the morning they began the ascent. At midday Paul Berlin spotted Cacciato. He was half a mile up, bent low

and moving patiently, steadily. He was not wearing a helmet —
surprising, because Cacciato always took great care to cover the
pink bald spot at the crown of his skull. Paul Berlin spotted him,
but it was Stink Harris who spoke up.

Lieutenant Corson took out the binoculars.

"Him, sir?"

The lieutenant watched while Cacciato climbed toward the
clouds.

"That him?"

"It's him. Bald as an eagle's ass."

Stink giggled. "Bald as Friar Tuck — it's Cacciato, all right.
Dumb as a dink."

They watched until Cacciato was swallowed in the rain and
clouds.

"Dumb-dumb." Stink giggled.

They walked fast, staying in a loose column. First the lieutenant, then Oscar Johnson, then Stink, then Eddie Luzzutti, then
Harold Murphy, then Doc, then, at the rear, Paul Berlin. Who
walked slowly, head down. He had nothing against Cacciato.
The whole episode was silly, of course, a dumb and immature
thing typical of Cacciato, but even so he had nothing special
against him. It was just too bad. A waste of time in the midst of
infinitely wider waste.

Climbing, he tried to picture Cacciato's face. The image came
out fuzzed and amorphous and bland — entirely compatible with
the boy's personality. Doc Peret, an acute observer of such things,
hypothesized that Cacciato had missed Mongolian idiocy by the
breadth of a single, wispy genetic hair. "Could have gone either
way," Doc had said confidentially. "You see the slanting eyes?
The pasty flesh, just like jelly, right? The odd-shaped head? I
mean, hey, let's face it — the guy's fucking ugly. It's only a theory, mind you, but I'd wager big money that old Cacciato has
more than a smidgen of the Mongol in him."

There may have been truth to it. Cacciato looked curiously
unfinished, as though nature had struggled long and heroically
but finally jettisoned him as a hopeless cause, not worth the di-
minishing returns. Open-faced, round, naive, plump, tender-
complected, and boyish, Cacciato lacked the fine detail, the refine-
ments and final touches that maturity ordinarily marks on a boy
of seventeen years. All this, the men concluded, added up to a

case of simple gross stupidity. He wasn't positively disliked — except perhaps by Stink Harris, who took instant displeasure with anything vaguely his inferior — but at the same time Cacciato was no one's friend. Vaught, maybe. But Vaught was dumb, too, and he was gone from the war. At best, Cacciato was tolerated. The way men will sometimes tolerate a pesky dog.

It was just too bad. Walking to Paris; it was one of those ridiculous things Cacciato would do. Like winning the Bronze Star for shooting a dink in the face. Dumb. The way he was forever whistling. Too blunt-headed to know better, blind to the bodily and spiritual dangers of human combat. In some ways this made him a good soldier. He walked point like a boy at his first county fair. He didn't mind the tunnel work. And his smile, more decoration than an expression of emotion, stayed with him in the most lethal of moments — when Billy Boy turned his last card, when Pederson floated face-up in a summer day's paddy, when Buff's helmet overflowed with an excess of red and gray fluids.

It was sad, a real pity.

Climbing the mountain, Paul Berlin felt an odd affection for the kid. Not friendship, exactly, but — real pity.

Not friendship. Not exactly. Pity, pity plus wonder. It was all silly, walking away in the rain, but it was something to think about.

They did not reach the summit of the mountain until mid-afternoon. The climb was hard, the rain sweeping down, the mountain oozing from beneath their feet. Below, the clouds were expansive, hiding the paddies and the war. Above, in more clouds, were more mountains.

Oscar Johnson found where Cacciato had spent the first night, a rock formation with an outcropping ledge as a roof, a can of burned-out Sterno, a chocolate wrapper, and a partly burned map. On the map, traced in red ink, was a dotted line that ran through the paddyland and up the first small mountain of the Annamese Cordillera. The dotted line ended there, apparently to be continued on another map.

"He's serious," the lieutenant said softly. "The blockhead's serious." He held the map as if it had a bad smell.

Stink and Oscar and Eddie Lazzutti nodded.

They rested in Cacciato's snug rock nest. Tucked away, looking out on the slate rain toward the next mountain, the men were quiet. Paul Berlin laid out a game of solitaire. Harold Murphy rolled a joint, inhaled, then passed it along, and they smoked and watched the rain and clouds and wilderness. It was peaceful. The rain was nice.

No one spoke until the ritual was complete.

Then, in a hush, all the lieutenant could say was, "Mercy."

"Shit" was what Stink Harris said.

The rain was unending.

"We could just go back," Doc Peret finally said. "You know, sir? Just head on back and forget him."

Stink Harris giggled.

"Seriously," Doc kept on, "we could just let the poor kid go. Make him M.I.A., strayed in battle, the lost lamb. Sooner or later he'll wake up, you know, and he'll see how insane it is and he'll come back."

The lieutenant stared into the rain. His face was yellow except for the network of broken veins.

"So what say you, sir? Let him go?"

"Dumber than a rock." Stink giggled.

"And smarter than Stink Harris."

"You know *what*, Doc."

"Pickle it."

"Who's saying to pickle it?"

"Just pickle it," said Doc Peret. "That's what."

Stink giggled but he shut up.

"What do you say, sir? Turn back?"

The lieutenant was quiet. At last he shivered and went into the rain with a wad of toilet paper. Paul Berlin sat alone, playing solitaire in the style of Las Vegas. Pretending, of course. Pretending to pay thirty thousand dollars for the deck, pretending ways to spend his earnings.

When the lieutenant returned he told the men to saddle up.

"We turning back?" Doc asked.

The lieutenant shook his head. He looked sick.

"I knew it!" Stink crowed. "Damn straight, I knew it! Can't hump away from a war, isn't that right, sir? The dummy has got to learn you can't just hump your way out of a war." Stink grinned and flicked his eyebrows at Doc Peret. "I knew it. By golly, I knew it!"

Cacciato had reached the top of the second mountain. Standing bareheaded, hands loosely at his sides, he was looking down

on them through a blur of rain. Lieutenant Corson had the
binoculars on him.

"Maybe he don't see us," Oscar said. "Maybe he's lost."

"Oh, he sees us. He sees us fine. Sees us real fine. And he's
not lost. Believe me, he's not."

"Throw out smoke, sir?"

"Why not?" the lieutenant said. "Sure, why not throw out
pretty smoke, why not?" He watched Cacciato through the glasses
while Oscar threw out the smoke. It fizzled for a time and then
puffed up in a heavy cloud of lavender. "Oh, he sees us," the
lieutenant whispered. "He sees us fine."

"The bastard's *waving!*"

"I can see that, thank you. Mother of Saints."

As if stricken, the lieutenant suddenly sat down in a puddle, put
his head in his hands and began to rock as the lavender smoke
drifted up the face of the mountain. Cacciato was waving both
arms. Not quite waving. The arms were flapping. Paul Berlin
watched through the glasses. Cacciato's head was huge, floating
like a balloon in the high fog, and he did not look at all
frightened. He looked young and stupid. His face was shiny.
He was smiling, and he looked happy.

"I'm sick," the lieutenant said. He kept rocking. "I tell you,
I'm a sick, sick man."

"Should I shout up to him?"

"Sick." The lieutenant moaned. "Sick, sick. It wasn't this way
on Pusan, I'll tell you that. Sure, call up to him — I'm sick."

Oscar Johnson cupped his hands and hollered, and Paul Berlin
watched through the glasses. For a moment Cacciato stopped
waving. He spread his arms wide, as if to show them empty,
slowly spreading them out like wings, palms up. Then his mouth
opened wide, and in the mountains there was thunder.

"What'd he say?" The lieutenant rocked on his haunches. He
was clutching himself and shivering. "Tell me what he said."

"Can't hear, sir. Oscar —?"

There was more thunder, long-lasting thunder that came in
waves from deep in the mountains. It rolled down and moved
the trees and grasses.

"Shut the shit up!" The lieutenant was rocking and shouting at
the rain and wind and thunder. "What'd the dumb fucker say?"

Paul Berlin watched through the glasses, and Cacciato's mouth opened and closed and opened, but there was only more thunder. Then his arms began flapping again. Flying, Paul Berlin suddenly realized. The poor kid was perched up there, arms flapping, trying to fly. Fly! Incredibly, the flapping motion was smooth and practiced and graceful.

"A chicken!" Stink squealed. "Look it! A squawking chicken!"

"Mother of Children."

"Look it!"

"A miserable chicken, you see that? A chicken!"

The thunder came again, breaking like Elephant Feet across the mountains, and the lieutenant rocked and held himself.

"For Christ sake." He moaned. "What'd he say? Tell me."

Paul Berlin could not hear. But he saw Cacciato's lips move, and the happy smile.

"Tell me."

So Paul Berlin, watching Cacciato fly, repeated it. "He said goodbye."

In the night the rain hardened into fog, and the fog was cold. They camped in the fog, near the top of the mountain, and the thunder stayed through the night. The lieutenant vomited. Then he radioed that he was in pursuit of the enemy.

"Gunships, Papa Two-Niner?" came the answer from far away.

"Negative," said the old lieutenant.

"Arty? Tell you what. You got a real sweet voice, Papa Two-Niner. No shit, a lovely voice." The radio voice paused. "So, here's what I'll do, I'll give you a bargain on the arty — two for the price of one, no strings and a warranty to boot. How's that? See, we got this terrific batch of new one–fifty-five in, first-class ordinance, I promise you, and what we do, what we do is this. What we do is we go heavy on volume here, you know? Keeps the prices low."

"Negative," the lieutenant said.

"Well, geez. Hard to please, right? Maybe some nice illum, then? Willie Peter, real boomers with some genuine sparkles mixed in. We're having this close-out sale, one time only."

"Negative. Negative, negative, negative."

"You'll be missing out on some fine shit."

"Negative, you monster."

"Okay," the radio voice said, disappointed-sounding, "but you'll

wish . . . No offense, Papa Two-Niner. Have some happy
hunting."

"Mercy," said the lieutenant into a blaze of static.

The night fog was worse than the rain, colder and more sad-
dening. They lay under a sagging lean-to that seemed to catch
and hold the fog like a net. Oscar and Harold Murphy and Stink
and Eddie Lazzutti slept anyway, curled around one another like
lovers. They could sleep and sleep.

"I hope he's moving," Paul Berlin whispered to Doc Peret. "I
just hope he keeps moving. He does that, we'll never get him."

"Then they'll chase him with choppers. Or planes or
something."

"Not if he gets himself lost," Paul Berlin said. "Not if he hides."

"What time is it?"

"Don't know."

"What time you got, sir?"

"Very lousy late," said the lieutenant from the bushes.

"Come on."

"Four o'clock. O-four-hundred, which is to say A.M. Got it?"

"Thanks."

"Charmed." His ass, hanging six inches from the earth, made a
soft warm glow in the dark.

"You okay, sir?"

"I'm wonderful. Can't you see how wonderful I am?"

"I just hope Cacciato keeps moving," Paul Berlin whispered.
"That's all I hope — I hope he uses his head and keeps moving."

"It won't get him anywhere."

"Get him to Paris maybe."

"Maybe." Doc sighed, turning onto his side. "And where is he
then?"

"In Paris."

"No way. I like adventure, too, but, see, you can't walk to Paris
from here. You just can't."

"He's smarter than you think," Paul Berlin said, not quite be-
lieving it. "He's not all that dumb."

"I know," the lieutenant said. He came from the bushes. "I
know all about that."

"Impossible. None of the roads go to Paris."

"Can we light a Sterno, sir?"

"No," the lieutenant said, crawling under the lean-to and lying flat on his back. His breath came hard. "No, you can't light a fucking Sterno, and no, you can't go out to play without your mufflers and galoshes, and no, kiddies and combatants, no, you can't have chocolate sauce on your broccoli. No."

"All right."

"No!"

"You saying no, sir?"

"No." The lieutenant sighed with doom. "It's still a war, isn't it?"

"I guess."

"There you have it. It's still a war."

The rain resumed. It started with thunder, then lightning lighted the valley deep below in green and mystery, then more thunder, then it was just the rain. They lay quietly and listened. Paul Berlin, who considered himself abnormally sane, uncluttered by high ideas or lofty ambitions or philosophy, was suddenly struck between the eyes by a vision of murder. Butchery, no less. Cacciato's right temple caving inward, a moment of black silence, then the enormous explosion of outward-going brains. It was no metaphor; he didn't think in metaphors. No, it was a simple scary vision. He tried to reconstruct the thoughts that had led to it, but there was nothing to be found — the rain, the discomfort of mushy flesh. Nothing to justify such a bloody image, no origins. Just Cacciato's round head suddenly exploding like a pricked bag of helium: boom.

Where, he thought, was all this taking him, and where would it end? Murder was the logical circuit-stopper, of course; it was Cacciato's rightful, maybe inevitable due. Nobody can get away with stupidity forever, and in war the final price for it is always paid in purely biological currency, hunks of toe or pieces of femur or bits of exploded brain. And it *was* still a war, wasn't it?

Pitying Cacciato with wee-hour tenderness, and pitying himself for the affliction that produced such visions, Paul Berlin hoped for a miracle. He was tired of murder. Not scared by it — not at that particular moment — and not awed by it, just fatigued.

"He did some awfully brave things," he whispered. Then realized that Doc was listening. "He did. The time he dragged that dink out of his bunker, remember that."

"Yeah."

"The time he shot the kid in the kisser."

"I remember."

"At least you can't call him a coward, can you? You can't say he ran away because he was scared."

"You can say a lot of other shit, though."

"True. But you can't say he wasn't brave. You can't say that."

"Fair enough," Doc said. He sounded sleepy.

"I wonder if he talks French."

"You kidding, partner?"

"Just wondering. You think it's hard to learn French, Doc?"

"Cacciato?"

"Yeah, I guess not. It's a neat thing to think about, though, old Cacciato walking to Paris."

"Go to sleep," Doc Peret advised. "Remember, pal, you got your own health to think of."

They were in the high country.

It was country far from the war, high and peaceful country with trees and thick grass, no people and no dogs and no lowland drudgery. Real wilderness, through which a single trail, liquid and shiny, kept taking them up.

The men walked with their heads down. Stink at point, then Eddie Lazzutti and Oscar, next Harold Murphy with the machine gun, then Doc, then the lieutenant, and last Paul Berlin.

They were tired and did not talk. Their thoughts were in their legs and feet, and their legs and feet were heavy with blood, for they'd been on the march many hours and the day was soggy with the endless rain. There was nothing symbolic, or melancholy, about the rain. It was simple rain, everywhere.

They camped that night beside the trail, then in the morning continued the climb. Though there were no signs of Cacciato, the mountain had only one trail and they were on it, the only way west.

Paul Berlin marched mechanically. At his sides, balancing him evenly and keeping him upright, two canteens of Kool-Aid lifted and fell with his hips, and the hips rolled in their ball-and-socket joints. He respired and sweated. His heart hard, his back strong, up the high country.

They did not see Cacciato, and for a time Paul Berlin thought they might have lost him forever. It made him feel better, and he climbed the trail and enjoyed the scenery and the sensations of being high and far from the real war, and then Oscar found the second map.

The red dotted line crossed the border into Laos.

Farther ahead they found Cacciato's helmet and armored vest, then his dogtags, then his entrenching tool and knife.

"Dummy just keeps to the trail." The lieutenant moaned. "Tell me why? Why doesn't he leave the trail?"

"It's the only way to Paris," Paul Berlin said.

"A rockhead," said Stink Harris. "That's why."

Liquid and shiny, a mix of rain and red clay, the trail took them higher.

Cacciato eluded them but he left behind the wastes of his march — empty tins, bits of bread, a belt of golden ammo dangling from a dwarf pine, a leaking canteen, candy wrappers, and worn rope. Clues that kept them going. Tantalizing them on, one step then the next — a glimpse of his bald head, the hot ash of a breakfast fire, a handkerchief dropped coyly along the path.

So they kept after him, following the trails that linked one to the next westward in a simple linear direction without deception. It was deep, jagged, complex country, dark with the elements of the season, and ahead was the frontier.

"He makes it that far," Doc Peret said, pointing to the next line of mountains, "and we can't touch him."

"How now?"

"The border," Doc said. The trail had leveled out and the march was easier. "He makes it to the border and it's bye-bye Cacciato."

"How far?"

"Two clicks maybe. Not far."

"Then he's made it," whispered Paul Berlin.

"Maybe so."

"By God!"

"Maybe so," Doc said.

"Boy, lunch at Tour d'Argent! A night at the old opera!"

"Maybe so."

The trail narrowed, then climbed, and a half hour later they saw him.

He stood at the top of a small grassy hill, two hundred meters ahead. Loose and at ease, smiling, Cacciato already looked like a civilian. His hands were in his pockets and he was not trying to hide himself. He might have been waiting for a bus, patient and serene and not at all frightened.

"Got him!" Stink yelped. "I knew it! Now we got him!"

The lieutenant came forward with the glasses.

"I knew it," Stink crowed, pressing forward. "The blockhead's finally giving it up — giving up the old ghost, I knew it!"

"What do we do, sir?"

The lieutenant shrugged and stared through the glasses.

"Fire a shot?" Stink held his rifle up and before the lieutenant could speak he squeezed off two quick rounds, one a tracer that turned like a corkscrew through the mist. Cacciato smiled and waved.

"Look at him," Oscar Johnson said. "I do think we got ourselves a predicament. Truly a predicament."

"There it is," Eddie said, and they both laughed, and Cacciato kept smiling and waving.

"A true predicament."

Stink Harris took the point, walking fast and chattering, and Cacciato stopped waving and watched him come, arms folded and his big head cocked as if listening for something. He looked amused.

There was no avoiding it.

Stink saw the wire as he tripped it, but there was no avoiding it.

The first sound was that of a zipper suddenly yanked up; next, a popping noise, the spoon releasing and primer detonating; then the sound of the grenade dropping; then the fizzling sound. The sounds came separately but quickly.

Stink knew it as it happened. With the next step, in one fuzzed motion, he flung himself down and away, rolling, covering his skull, mouth open, yelping a funny, trivial little yelp.

They all knew it.

Eddie and Oscar and Doc Peret dropped flat, and Harold Murphy bent double and did an oddly graceful jackknife for a man of his size, and the lieutenant coughed and collapsed, and Paul Berlin, seeing purple, closed his eyes and fists and mouth, brought his knees to his belly, coiling, and let himself fall.

Count, he thought, but the numbers came in a tangle without sequence.

His belly hurt. That was where it started. First the belly, a release of fluids in the bowels next, a shitting feeling, a draining of all the pretensions and silly hopes for himself, and he was back where he started, writhing. The lieutenant was beside him. The air was windless — just the misty rain. His teeth hurt. Count, he thought, but his teeth hurt and no numbers came. I don't want to die, he thought lucidly, with hurting teeth.

There was no explosion. His teeth kept hurting and his belly was floating in funny ways.

He was ready, steeled. His lungs hurt now. He was ready, but there was no explosion. Then came a fragile pop. Smoke, he thought without thinking, smoke.

"Smoke." The lieutenant moaned, then repeated it. "Fucking smoke."

Paul Berlin smelled it. He imagined its velvet color, purple, but he could not open his eyes. He tried, but he could not open his eyes or unclench his fists or uncoil his legs, and the heavy fluids in his stomach were holding him down, and he could not wiggle or run to escape. There was no explosion.

"Smoke," Doc said softly. "Just smoke."

It was red smoke, and the message seemed clear. It was all over them. Brilliant red, thick, acid-tasting. It spread out over the earth like paint, then began to climb against gravity in a lazy red spiral.

"Smoke," Doc said. "Smoke."

Stink Harris was crying. He was on his hands and knees, chin against his throat, bawling and bawling. Oscar and Eddie had not moved.

"He had us," the lieutenant whispered. His voice was hollowed out, senile-sounding, almost a reminiscence. "He could've had all of us."

"Just smoke," Doc said. "Lousy smoke is all."

"The dumb fucker could've had us."

Paul Berlin could not move. He felt entirely conscious, a little embarrassed but not yet humiliated, and he heard their voices, heard Stink weeping and saw him beside the trail on his hands and knees, and he saw the red smoke everywhere, but he could not move.

"He won't come," said Oscar Johnson, returning under a white flag. "Believe me, I tried, but the dude just won't play her cool."

It was dusk and the seven soldiers sat in pow-wow.

"I told him all the right stuff, but he won't give it up. Told him it was crazy as shit and he'd probably end up dead, and I told him how he'd end up court-martialed at the best, and I told him how his old man would shit when he heard about it. Told him maybe things wouldn't go so hard if he just gave up and came back right now. I went through the whole spiel, top to bottom. The dude just don't listen."

The lieutenant was lying prone, Doc's thermometer in his mouth, sick-looking. It wasn't his war. The skin on his arms and neck was loose around deteriorating muscle.

"I told him — I told him all that good shit. Told him it's ridiculous, dig? I told him it won't work, no matter what, and I told him we're fed up. Fed up."

"You tell him we're out of rations?"

"Shit, yes, I told him that. And I told him he's gonna starve his own ass if he keeps going, and I told him we'd have to call in gunships if it came to it."

"You tell him he can't walk to France?"

Oscar grinned. He was black enough to be indistinct in the dusk. "Maybe I forgot to tell him that."

"You should've told him."

The lieutenant slid a hand behind his neck and pushed against it as if to relieve some spinal pressure. "What else?" he asked. "What else did he say?"

"Nothing, sir. He said he's doing okay. Said he was sorry to scare us with the smoke."

"The bastard." Stink kept rubbing his hands against the black stock of his rifle.

"What else?"

"Nothing. You know how he is, sir. Just a lot of smiles and stupid stuff. He asked how everybody was, so I said we're fine, except for the scare with the smoke boobytrap, and then he said he was sorry about that, so I told him it was okay. What can you say to a dude like that?"

The lieutenant nodded, pushing against his neck. He was quiet a while. He seemed to be making up his mind. "All right." He finally sighed. "What'd he have with him?"

"Sir?"

"Musketry," the lieutenant said. "What kind of weapons?"

"His rifle. That's all, his rifle and some bullets. I didn't get much of a look."

"Claymores?"

Oscar shook his head. "I didn't see none. Maybe so."

"Grenades?"

"I don't know. Maybe a couple."

"Beautiful recon job, Oscar. Real pretty."

"Sorry, sir. He had his stuff tight, though."

"I'm sick."

"Yes, sir."

"Dysentery's going through me like coffee. What you got for me, Doc?"

Doc Peret shook his head. "Nothing, sir. Rest."

"That's it," the lieutenant said. "What I need is rest."

"Why not let him go, sir?"

"Rest," the lieutenant said, "is what I need."

Paul Berlin did not sleep. Instead he watched Cacciato's small hill and tried to imagine a proper ending.

There were only a few possibilities remaining, and after what had happened it was hard to see a happy end to it. Not impossible, of course. It could still be done. With skill and boldness, Cacciato might slip away and cross the frontier mountains and be gone. He tried to picture it. Many new places. Villages at night with barking dogs, people whose eyes and skins would change in slow evolution and counterevolution as Cacciato moved westward with whole continents before him and the war far behind him and all the trails connecting and leading toward Paris. It could be done. He imagined the many dangers of Cacciato's march, treachery and deceit at every turn, but he also imagined the many good times ahead, the stinging feel of aloneness, and new leanness and knowledge of strange places. The rains would end and the trails would go dry and be baked to dust, and there would be changing foliage and great expanses of silence and songs and pretty girls in straw huts and, finally, Paris.

It could be done. The odds were like poison, but it could be done.

Later, as if a mask had been peeled off, the rain ended and the sky cleared and Paul Berlin woke to see the stars.

They were in their familiar places. It wasn't so cold. He lay on his back and counted the stars and named those that he knew, named the constellations and the valleys of the moon. It was just too bad. Crazy, but still sad. He should've kept going — left the trails and waded through streams to rinse away the scent, buried his feces, swung from the trees branch to branch; he should've slept through the days and ran through the nights. It might have been done.

Toward dawn he saw Cacciato's breakfast fire. He heard Stink playing with the safety catch on his M-16, a clicking noise like a slow morning cricket. The sky lit itself in patches.

"Let's do it," the lieutenant whispered.

Eddie Lazzutti and Oscar and Harold Murphy crept away toward the south. Doc and the lieutenant waited a time then began to circle west to block a retreat. Stink Harris and Paul Berlin were to continue up the trail.

Waiting, trying to imagine a rightful and still happy ending, Paul Berlin found himself pretending, in a vague sort of way, that before long the war would reach a climax beyond which everything else would become completely commonplace. At that point he would stop being afraid. All the bad things, the painful and grotesque things, would be in the past, and the things ahead, if not lovely, would at least be tolerable. He pretended he had crossed that threshold.

When the sky was half-light, Doc and the lieutenant fired a red flare that streaked high over Cacciato's grassy hill, hung there, then exploded in a fanning starburst like the start of a celebration. Cacciato Day, it might have been called. October something, in the year 1968, the Year of the Pig.

In the trees at the southern slope of the hill Oscar and Eddie and Harold Murphy each fired red flares to signal their advance.

Stink went into the weeds and hurried back, zipping up his trousers. He was very excited and happy. Deftly, he released the bolt on his weapon and it slammed hard into place.

"Fire the flare," he said, "and let's go."

Paul Berlin took a long time opening his pack.

But he found the flare, unscrewed its lid, laid the firing pin against the primer, then jammed it in.

The flare jumped away from him. It went high and fast, rocketing upward and taking a smooth arc that followed the course of the trail, leaving behind a dirty wake of smoke.

At its apex, with barely a sound, the flare exploded in a green dazzle over Cacciato's hill. It was a fine, brilliant shade of green.

"Go," whispered Paul Berlin. It did not seem enough. "Go," he said, and then he shouted, "Go."

TOM ROBBINS

The Chink and the Clock People

(FROM THE AMERICAN REVIEW)

To NEITHER THE SIWASH nor the Chinese does the Chink belong. As are many of the best and worse contributions to the human race, the Chink is Japanese. With their flair for inventive imitation, the Japanese made the Chink.

He was born on an island in the Ryukyu chain. It was called an island, but in actuality it was a volcano, a half-submerged dunce cap that Nature had once placed on the noggin of the sea for forgetting which had come first, land or water. For centuries this volcano had sent shock after shock of purple smoke into the sky. It was a chain smoker. A Ryukyu chain smoker.

Upon the sides of this smoking volcanic cone the Chink's parents had raised yams, and the little Chink had played. Once, when he was six, he climbed to the top of the volcano. His sister found him there, on the edge of the crater, unconscious from the fumes, his hair and eyebrows singed. He had been looking in.

When he was eight, he emigrated to the United States of America, where his uncle tended gardens in San Francisco. The Chink picked up English and other bad habits. He went to high school and other dangerous places. He earned American citizenship and other dubious distinctions.

When asked what he wished to do with his life, he answered (although he had learned to appreciate movies, jukebox music, and cheerleaders) that he wanted to grow yams on the side of a volcano — but as that was impractical in the city of San Francisco, he became, like Uncle, a gardener. For more than a dozen years he made the grass greener and the flowers flowerier on the campus of the University of California at Berkeley.

By special arrangement with his employers, the Chink attended one class a day at the university. Over a twelve-year span he completed a good many courses. He was never graduated, but it would be a mistake to assume he did not receive an education.

He was astute enough to warn his relatives, on December 8, 1941, the day after Pearl Harbor, "We'd better get our yellow asses back to some safe volcano and eat yams till this blows over." They didn't listen. After all, they were patriotic, property-owning, tax-paying American citizens.

The Chink wasn't anxious to flee, either. He was in love again. Camping on the rim of a different volcano.

On February 20, 1942, came the order. Two weeks later, the army took steps. In March, evacuation was in full swing. Some 110,000 people of Japanese ancestry were moved out of their homes in "strategic" areas of the West Coast and settled in ten "relocation" camps farther inland. They could bring to camp only what they could carry. Left behind were houses, businesses, farms, home furnishings, personal treasures, liberty. Americans of non-Nip ancestry bought up their farmland at ten cents on the dollar (the crops failed). Seventy percent of the relocated people had been born and reared in the U.S.

"Loyal" Japanese were separated from "disloyal." If one would swear allegiance to the American war effort — and could pass an FBI investigation — one had the choice of remaining in a relocation camp or finding employment in some nonstrategic area. The camps were militaristic formations of tarpaper barracks, supplied with canvas cots and pot-bellied stoves. Six to nine families lived in a barracks. Partitions between "apartments" were as thin as crackers and did not reach the ceiling (even so, there were an average of twenty-five births per month in most camps). There was no great rush to leave the camps: a loyal family that had been relocated on an Arkansas farm had been killed by an irate anti-Jap mob.

Disloyal Japanese-Americans — those who expressed excessive bitterness over the loss of their property and the disruption of their lives, or who for various other reasons were suspected of being dangerous to national security — were given the pleasure of one another's company at a special camp, the Tule Lake Segregation Center in Siskiyou County, California. The Chink had been asked if he supported the American war effort. "Hell, no!" he

replied. "Ha ha ho ho and hee hee." He waited for the logical
next question, did he support the Japanese war effort, to which
he would have given the same negative response. He was still
waiting when the military police shoved him on the train to Tule
Lake.

Tule was even less of a lake than Siwash. It had been drained
so that land could be "reclaimed" for farming.

The detention camp had been built on that part of the dry lake
bottom that was unsuitable for cultivation. However, the inmates
(or "segregees," as the War Relocation Authority preferred to label them) were put to work on surrounding farmland, building
dikes, digging irrigation ditches, and producing crops that proved
once again that the greenest thumbs are often yellow.

(Perhaps the author is telling you more about Tule Lake than
you want to know. But the camp, in northern California near the
Oregon border, still exists, and while time, that ultimate diet pill,
has reduced its 1032 buildings to their concrete foundations, the
government may have plans for them which may someday be
your concern.)

Baked in summer, dust-blinded in fall, frozen in winter and
mud-up-to-elbows in spring, the Tule Lake camp was surrounded
by a high barbed fence. Soldiers in lookout towers kept constant
watch on — kids swimming in ditches, adolescents hunting rattle-
snakes, old men playing Go, and women shopping for notions in a
commissary where the latest issues of *True Confessions* were always
on the racks. It was reported that even if the guards were removed, the segregees would not try to escape. They were afraid
of Tule Lake farmers.

The Chink petitioned to be allowed to join his family in a less
restrictive camp. But his FBI check disclosed that he had, over a
period of years, pursued such heathen practices as jujitsu, ike-
bana, Sanskrit, mushroom magic, and Zen archery; that at UC he
had written academic papers which suggested anarchist leanings;
and that he had had repeated intimate relations with Caucasian
women, including the niece of an admiral in the U.S. Navy.
Please to remain at Tule Lake.

In early November of 1943, there was trouble at Tule Lake. A
careless GI truckdriver accidentally killed a Japanese farm
worker. Angered, the segregees refused to complete the harvest.
There followed a confrontation which army spokesmen identified

as a "riot." Among the 155 ringleader troublemakers who were beaten and imprisoned in the stockade was the man we now call the Chink. The Chink had not participated in the "riot," had, in fact, been looking forward to the rhythm of harvest, but camp authorities claimed that his notorious insubordinate attitude (not to mention the crazed way he had of venerating plants, vegetables, and other men's wives) contributed to unrest at the camp.

If he liked the segregation center little, he liked the stockade less. For several days and nights he meditated upon the yam, that tuber that while remaining sweet to the taste and soft to the touch is so tough it will thrive on the sides of live volcanos. "Yam" became his mantra. *Om mani padme yam. Hare yam-a. Wham, bam, thank-you yam. Hellfire and yam nation.* Then, like the yam, he went underground. He tunneled out of the stockade, out of the camp.

He headed for the proverbial hills. The Cascade Mountains lay to the west, across twenty or more miles of lava beds. The lava felt sharply familiar. Each rip in his shoes brought him closer to his childhood. All night, he jogged, walked, rested, jogged. At sunrise, Mt. Shasta, a cone of diamond ice cream, a volcano on a sabbatical, adorned (like the whooping cranes) with the power of white, was waiting. Encouraging him. An hour after dawn he was in tree-cover.

His plan was to follow the crest trail through the Cascades, down the full length of the Sierra Nevada, and into Mexico. In the spring, perhaps, he would wetback into the U.S. again and work the crops. There weren't many farmers who could distinguish a Nip from a Spick, not under a straw hat, not with spine bent to the rutabagas. Alas, Mexico was a thousand miles away, the month was November, there was already snow at the higher altitudes, flop flap was the song of his shoes.

Fortunately, the Chink knew which plants to chomp, which nuts and mushrooms to toast over tiny minimum-smoke fires. As best he could, he patched his shoes with bark. His journey went well for a week or more. Then, out of the mysterious dwelling place of weather, there rode an abrupt and burly storm. For a while it toyed with him, blowing in his ears, aging his normally black hair, hanging flakes artfully from the tip of his nose. But the storm was on serious business, and soon the Chink, crouched though he was in the lee of a cliff, realized that, by comparison, the passion of this storm to storm made puny his own desire to reach Mexico. Snow snow snow snow snow snow. The last thing a person sees before he dies he will be obliged to carry with him through all the baggage rooms of lasting death. The Chink strained to squint a sequoia or at least a huckleberry bush, but all his freezing eyes saw was snow. And the snow wanted to lie atop him as badly as any male ever wanted to lie on female.

The storm had its way with him. He lost consciousness trying to think of God, but thinking instead of a radiant woman cooking yams.

Of course, he was rescued. He was rescued by the only people who possibly could have rescued him. He was discovered, hauled in, bedded down, and thawed out by members of an American Indian culture that, for several reasons, cannot be identified beyond this fanciful description: the Clock People.

It is not easy, perhaps, to accept the fact of the Clock People's existence. You might read through every issue of the *National Geographic* since the Year One and not find an exact parallel to the Clock People's particular distinctions. However, if you think about it for a while — the way the author has — it becomes obvious that the civilizing process has left pockets of vacuum which only Clock People could have filled.

The room in which the fugitive regained consciousness was large and well-heated, draped with crude blankets and the skins of animals. Whether it was a cave, a camouflaged cabin, or an elaborate tepee/hogan-type dwelling, the Chink would never say. He was careful not to disclose any details that might aid in pinpointing the location of his hosts.

As has been written, the Clock People are an American Indian culture. Ethnically speaking, however, they are not a tribe. Rather, they are a gathering of Indians from various tribes. They have lived together since 1906.

At the dawning of April 18, 1906, the city of San Francisco awakened to a terrible roar, mounting in intensity. For sixty-five seconds the city shook like a rubber meatball in the jaws of Teddy Roosevelt. There followed a silence almost as terrible as the roar. The heart of San Francisco lay in ruins. Buildings had tumbled into creviced streets, twisted bodies of humans and horses colored the rubble, gas hissed like the Snake of All Bad Dreams from dozens of broken mains. During the next three days, flames enveloped 490 blocks, unquenched by the teardrops of the homeless and lame.

History knows the catastrophe as the Great San Francisco Earthquake. That is not how the Clock People know it, but, then, the Clock People don't believe in earthquakes.

Among the crowds who watched the blazing devastation from surrounding hills was a scattering of American Indians. Largely from California tribes, though including folk from Nevada and Oregon, and in whose midst there moved representatives of the few but notorious Siwash, they were the first of the urbanized Indians. Poor, generally, they held jobs of menial or disreputable stature along the Barbary Coast (it should be emphasized, however, that they had been drawn into the city, each and every one of them, not by desire for money — they needed no money where they came from — but by *curiosity* alone). The white San Franciscans camping on the smoky hilltops surveyed the ruins in a state of shock. Perhaps the Indians, too, were overwhelmed by the spectacle, but they, as always, appeared as inscrutable as the other side of a nickel. Yet, the Indians were to display shock aplenty. It was when the fires were at last controlled and the citizens began to rush back into the still-warm ashes, singing, praising the Lord, and shouting to one another their plans for rebuilding their metropolis, that Indian eyes widened in disbelief. They simply could not comprehend what they were witnessing. They realized that the White Man lacked wisdom, but was he completely goofy? Couldn't he read the largest and most lurid of signs? Even those Indians who had grown to trust the White Man were grievously disappointed. Rebuild the city? They shook their heads and muttered.

For several weeks they remained on the hill, strangers united by shock and disappointment as well as by a common cultural comprehension of what had transpired below. Then, through communications the nature of which is known best to them, several of the Indians led a migration of a small band of souls into the Sierras, where, in a period of thirteen full moons, they generated the stalk of a new culture. (Or, should we say, under their impetus, the ancient stalk of Life Religion put forth unexpected and portentous shoots.)

On behalf of the Susquehanna, the Winnebago, the Kickapoo, the Chickasaw, the Kwakiutl, the Potawatomi, and all the other splendidly appellated aborigines who came to be labeled "Indians" through the ignorance of an Italian sailor with a taste for oranges, it is only fitting that "Indians" misnamed our Japanese-American hero "Chink."

There were very few Japanese in San Francisco in 1906, but Chinese were plentiful. Already there was a Chinatown, and its exotic trappings were a lure to tourists. Drugs, gambling, and prostitution abounded in the Chinese quarter, just as they did on the Barbary Coast, and the Indians often had overheard their employers speaking of the competition from the "Chinks."

In the years between 1906 and 1943, the Clock People had, naturally, discussed on many occasions the circumstances of their Sierra migration. More than once, they had wondered aloud why the yellow people had been so unenlightened as to join the whites in resurrecting San Francisco. It had been astonishing enough to watch the White Man set about to repeat his mistake, but to watch the Orientals follow him . . . !

Their curiosity about yellow men probably had influenced their decision to rescue this near-frozen outsider. During his days of recuperation, the storm victim had heard various of his hosts inquire about the condition of "the Chink." His sense of irony was not so frost-bitten that he could refrain from perpetuating, once he had recovered, the misnomer.

Eventually, perhaps, he confessed to his Japanese ancestry. Certainly and soon, he confessed to being a fugitive. The Clock People elected to harbor him, and were never to regret it. In the years that followed, the Chink performed them many services. In return, he was accepted as one of them, and gained privity to all of the secrets of the clockworks.

The pivotal function of the Clock People is the keeping and observing of the clockworks. The clockworks is a real thing. It is kept at the center, at the soul, of the Great Burrow.

The Great Burrow is a maze or labyrinthine sequence of tunnels, partly manmade, partly of geological origin. More specifically, a natural network of narrow caves, lying beneath a large knoll in the Sierra wilderness, was lengthened and elaborated upon by the Indians who exiled themselves from San Francisco in 1906. Many, if not most, of the tunnels are dead ends.

The Clock People, as we now know them, divided themselves into 13 families, not necessarily along tribal lines. (What is the numerical significance of the Clock People's taking 13 months to structure their ritual, then separating into 13 families? Well, briefly, they consider 13 a more natural number than 12. To the Babylonians, 13 was unlucky. That is why, when they invented astrology, they willfully overlooked a major constellation, erroneously assigning to the zodiac only 12 houses. The Clock People knew nothing of Babylonian superstition, but they knew the stars, and it was partly in an effort to override the unnatural 12-mindedness of Western culture that they chose to give 13 its due.) To each family was assigned the responsibility for one section of the Great Burrow. Each family knows one section inch by inch, but is completely ignorant of the other 12 sections. So, no family nor no individual knows the Way. The Way, of course, being the true path that takes one through the Great Burrow maze to the clockworks. Moreover, it is not possible for the families to compile a map of the Way, for each family holds as a sacred secret its knowledge of its burrow or section of the Way.

(In naming these tunnel sections "burrows," the Clock People were not particularly identifying with animals — no more so than were the Indians in whose culture totems played such a large and vivid role. Totemically-oriented Indians utilized the characteristics of certain animals *metaphorically*. It was simply a form of poetic symbolism. They used animals to think with.)

Okay. Who gets to the clockworks, how, and when? Each morning at sunrise, that day's designated guides — one from each of the 13 families — gather at the portal, or entrance, to the Great Burrow. Then, they are all blindfolded except for the guide representing the Family of the First Burrow. The blindfolded 12 link hands and are led by the first guide through any of several routes he or she may take to reach the beginning of the Second Burrow. A guide will purposefully attempt never to use the same route twice. Often a guide will backtrack, and sometimes he or she will instruct the others in the party to let go of each other's hands and spin. Since, by this date, there are around 20 members in each family, an individual acts as guide only about 13 times a year.

Now, when the first guide reaches the terminus of his burrow and the beginning of the next, he instructs the guide for the Second Burrow to remove his blindfold, while binding his own eyes. And so it goes until the group is at the large central chamber, which contains the clockworks. There, they go about "keeping the time" until the hour for the return trip. Theoretically, the 13 daily guides emerge from the Great Burrow at sunset, although this occurs in actuality only upon those days when there are 13 hours of daylight.

Occasionally, other people accompany the guides on their mission. An aged or sickly person who is about to die or a pregnant woman commencing labor is led, blindfolded, to the central burrow, for insomuch as it is possible, all Clock People deaths and births occur in the presence of the clockworks. Aside from birthing or dying, the reason for the daily visits to the clockworks is to check the time.

Maybe we should say "check the *times*," for the clockworks is really two clocks and the sort of time each one measures is quite distinct.

First, there is a huge hourglass, at least 7 feet in diameter and 13 feet tall, made from the finely stitched and tightly stretched internal membranes of large beasts (elk, bears, mountain lions). The hourglass is filled with acorns, enough so that it takes them approximately 13 hours to pour, or funnel, one by one, through the slender passage in the waist of the transparent device. When the daily guides enter the soul burrow, the hourglass is turned upon its opposite end. When they depart — in approximately 13 hours — they flip it again. So, "checking the time," or "keeping the time" is, in the 26-hour day of the Clock People, the same as "making time," or, more generally, "making history." The Clock People believe that they are making history and that the end of history will come with the destruction of the clockworks.

Please do not construe the "end of history" or the "end of time" to mean "the end of life" or what is normally meant by the apocalyptically-minded when they speak (almost wishfully, it seems) of the "end of the world." That is paranoiac rubbish, and however one may finally evaluate the Clock People, their philosophy must be appreciated on a higher plane than doomsday drivel.

Well, then, what do the Clock People mean by the "end of history" and how will the clockworks be destroyed?

Zoom in on this: these people, these clandestinely exiled Indians, have no other ritual than this one: THE CHECKING OF THE

CLOCKWORKS — the keeping/making of history. Likewise, they have but one legend or cultural myth: that of a continuum they call the Eternity of Joy. It is the Eternity of Joy that they believe all men will pass into once the clockworks is destroyed. They look forward to a state of timelessness, when bored, frustrated, and unfulfilled people will no longer have to "kill time" for time will be finally dead.

They are preparing for timelessness by eliminating from their culture all rules, schedules, and moral standards other than those that are directly involved with the keeping of the clockworks. The Clock People may be the most completely anarchistic community that has ever existed. Rather, they may be the first community so far in which anarchy has come close to working. That is impressive in itself and should fan with peacock tails of optimism all those who dream of the ideal social condition.

The Clock People manage their anarchism (if that is not a contradiction) simply because they have channeled all of their authoritarian compulsions and control mania into a single ritual. It is clearly understood by all members of the community that there is no other ritual, no other required belief than this ONE — and, furthermore, that they themselves created the ritual: they have no silly superstitions about gods or ancestor spirits who hold this ritual over their heads in return for homage and/or "good" conduct.

Ritual, usually, is an action or ceremony employed to create a unity of mind among a congregation or community. The Clock People see the keeping of the clockworks as the *last* of the *communal* rituals. With the destruction of the clockworks, i.e., at the end of time, all rituals will be personal and idiosyncratic, serving not to unify a community/cult in a common cause but to link each single individual with the universe in whatever manner suits him or her best. Unity will give way to plurality in the Eternity of Joy, although, since the universe is simultaneously Many and One, whatever links the individual to the universe will automatically link him or her to all others, even while it enhances his or her completely separate identity in an eternal milkshake unclabbered by time. Thus, paradoxically, the replacement of societal with individual rituals will bring about an ultimate unity vastly more universal than the plexus of communal rites which presently divides peoples into unwieldy, agitating, and competing groups.

Now, the Clock People, being visionaries, are not content with their time-checking ritual. After all, it is the lone authoritarian, compulsive action which binds them. They chafe to dispense with it. If it could be eliminated, they could pass out of history and into the Eternity of Joy. Timeless, they could bear their children and bury their dead wherever they chose. However, they understand that at this evolutionary stage they still require the ritual, even as they realize that destroying the clockworks is entirely within their power.

They will not destroy it. They have agreed — and this is central to their mythos — that the destruction must come from the outside, must come by natural means, must come at the will (whim is more like it) of that gesticulating planet whose more acute stirrings thoughtless people call "earthquakes."

Here, we can understand a bit more about the origins of their culture. The great rumble of 1906, which destroyed practically the whole of San Francisco, was taken by the Indians as a sign. They had left the land and gone to the city. That the city could be destroyed by the land in 65 seconds gave them a clue as to where the real power lay.

Within a natural context the phenomenon would never have appeared as a holocaust. Away from the herding centers we prize as cities, an "earthquake" would only manifest itself as a surface quickening of the globe's protoplastic movements, which, at various depths and various intensities, are occurring all of the time, and so not in time but all over time. Being "all over time" is the same as being out of time, because the notion of time is welded inseparably to the notion of progression, but what is already everywhere cannot possibly progress.

From there, it is a short leap to the ledge of the dream: the Eternity of Joy (a continuous present in which everything, including the dance of aging which we mistake as a chronological unfolding rather than a fixed posture of deepening cellular awareness, is taken together and always).

When the citizens of San Francisco began immediately to rebuild their city, the Indians were understandably very disappointed. The white (and yellow) San Franciscans hadn't learned a thing. They had been given a sign — a powerful, lucid sign — that urban herding and its concomitant technologies are not the proper way to partake of this planet's hospitality. Actually, there are countless ways to live upon this tremorous sphere in mirth and good health, and probably only one way — the industrialized, urbanized, herding way — to live here stupidly, and man has hit upon that one wrong way. The people of San Francisco failed to heed the sign. They capitulated, opting to stay in time and so out of eternity.

Readers may wonder why the Indians, who recognized the "earthquake" for what it really was, did not simply usher in the Eternity of Joy then and there. Well, they had both a realistic view and a sense of humor regarding their situation. They understood that it would take at least three or four generations to cleanse themselves of previous cultural deposits. The patriarchs — only two or three of whom are still alive — reasoned that if they could channel all of their fellows' frustrations and self-destructive compulsions into a single, simple ritual, then two things would follow. One, outside of that ritual, the community could experiment freely with styles of life instead of the attractions of death. Two, sooner or later, the Earth would issue another potent sign, one powerful enough to destroy their last icon of time-bound culture, the clockworks, ending the ritual even while it was reshaping much of American civilization.

Which brings us, ticking, to the matter of the second clock. The first clock in the original clockworks, the membrane hourglass, sits in a pool of water. The Great Burrow is situated upon a deep fracture, a major branch of the San Andreas Fault. The Sierra fault is clearly shown on geological maps of northern California (which does hint at the location of the original clockworks, doesn't it? even though the fracture is very long). In addition, the underground stream that feeds the Great Burrow pool flows directly into the San Andreas Fault. That pool of water is the second clock in the clockworks system. Consider its components.

Moments prior to an earthquake, certain sensitive persons experience nausea. Animals, such as cattle, are even more sensitive to prequake vibrations, feeling them earlier and more strongly. By far the most quake-sensitive creatures in existence are catfish. Readers, this is scientific fact; the dubious among you should not hesitate to check it out. Catfish.

Now, there is a species of catfish, hereditarily sightless, that dwells exclusively in subterranean streams. Its Latin name is *Satan eurystomus,* again for the skeptical, but spelunkers know these fish as blindcats. Relatively rare in California, blindcats are quite common in the caverns and caves of the Ozark states and Texas.

The clockworks pool is inhabited by such catfish. Their innate catfish earthquake sensitivity is compounded by the fact that they are tuned in, fin and whisker, to the vibrations of one of the globe's largest and most frenetic fault systems. When a tremor of any Richterian passion is building, the catfish go into a state of shock. They cease feeding, and when they move at all, it is erratically. By constantly monitoring changes in the Earth's magnetic field or the tilt of the Earth's surface or the rate of movement and intensity of stress where faults are slowly creeping, seismologists have correctly predicted a handful of minor tremors, though with no great exactitude. The clockworks catfish, on the other hand, have registered upcoming quakes as far away as Los Angeles (in 1971) and as early as four weeks in advance.

On the earthen walls of the Central Burrow, the Clock People have marked in sequence the dates and intensities of all tremors, mad or mild, that have occurred along the 2000 miles of West Coast faults since 1908. The whole pattern, transcribed from the catfish clock, reveals a rhythmic structure that indicates to the rhythmic minds of the Indians that something emphatic is going to be coming along any week now.

This peek on destruction is Pythagorean only in the sense that with the cataclysmic konking of the last vestige of cultural ritual will come the kind of complete social and psychic freedom that only natural, timeless anarchy can offer, the birth of a new people into the Eternity of Joy.

The Clock People regard civilization as an insanely complex set of symbols that obscure natural processes and encumber free movement. The Earth is alive. She burns inside with the heat of cosmic longing. She longs to be with her husband again. She moans. She turns softly in her sleep. When the symbologies of civilization are destroyed, there will be no more "earthquakes." Earthquakes are a manifestation of man's consciousness. Without manmade follies, there could not be earthquakes. In the Eternity of Joy, pluralized, deurbanized man, at ease with his gentle technologies, will smile and sigh when the Earth begins to shake. "She is restless tonight," they will say.

"She dreams of loving."

"She has the blues."

Among the Clock People, who never had tasted a yam, the Chink dwelt for 26 years.

For the first eight of those years, he lived virtually as a Clock Person himself, an honorary member of the Family of the Thirteenth Burrow, sharing their food, lodging, and women. (Being an anarchistic, or more precisely, a pluralistic society, some of the Clock People were monogamous, some, perhaps most, practitioners of free love. In a pluralistic society, love quickly shows all of its many smeared and smiling faces, and it should be noted that the term "family" was relevant only to the clockworks ritual, outside of which there was uninhibited intermingling. For example, a man from the Family of the Fifth Burrow might impregnate an Eleventh Burrow lady, and the resulting child, once of age, might be assigned to the Family of the Ninth Burrow.)

In 1951, the war now only a glint in the American Legion's shell-popped eye, the Chink moved into a shack that he built some nine or ten miles from the Great Burrow. The shack was strategically erected at the narrow entrance to the valley which, with a creek as its racing stripe, totaled out against the base of the tunnel-filled knoll. In the other direction, a couple of miles farther beyond the shack, was a trail that led to a dirt road that led to a paved highway that led past, eventually, a combination gas station, café, and general store. The Chink began to take fortnightly hikes to that store, where, among other supplies, he picked up newspapers and magazines. These he read to those Clock People (all spoke English but few could read it) who were interested, which was mainly the younger ones, the older Indians regarding that "news" that did not have to do with quakes, hurricanes, floods, and other geophysical shenanigans as trivia. The belch of civilization, they called it. Maybe the older Indians were right. It was the Eisenhower Years, remember, and the news read as if it had been washed out of a Pentagon desk commander's golf socks.

The Chink also linked the older Indians with the rest of the world, but in a different manner. Throughout the decades, the Clock People had mysteriously maintained periodic contact with certain Indians on the outside. These outside contacts were medicine men, or shamans, although exactly what was their relationship to the clockworks ritual and Eternity of Joy legend the Chink was never to ascertain. However, in the mid-50s, one or more of these outsiders took to showing up at the Sierra store at the precise hours of the Chink's unannounced visits. They'd drink a beer with him, and give him a piece or two of seemingly insignificant gossip which he would feel compelled to pass along once he was back at the Great Burrow. Thus, he functioned as a medium, like the air is the medium for drumbeats, connecting Clock People, young and old, with distant drummers.

He also functioned as an agent of diversion. When hunters, hikers, or prospectors entered the area, the Chink used his wiles to guide them away from the vicinity of the Great Burrow. Often, studding conversation with tips about game, scenic waterfalls, or ore deposits was enough to divert the intruders, but occasionally a small rockslide or other mishap would have to be arranged. Even so, a few interlopers, especially rangers of the U.S. Forest Service, slipped through the Chink's net. Those who got too close were slain by the Clock People. From 1965 to 1969, seven outsiders took arrows through their breasts and were buried inside the Great Burrow.

These slayings were a source of contention between the Chink and the Clock People, the latter regarding them as the regrettable but necessary price of protection, the former declaring: "There are many things worth living for, there are a few things worth dying for, but there is nothing worth killing for."

The Chink tried to impress upon the Clock People that, with the increase in air traffic over the mountains, as well as in the number of outdoorsmen whom civilization was driving into the wilderness, it was only a matter of "time" before their culture was exposed. What would they do then? Obviously, the System would not be gracious enough to leave them alone. "We will hide in the tunnels," answered some of the middle-aged. "We will defend ourselves to the death," answered some of the youth. "The movements of the Earth will take care of all that," answered the elders, smiling enigmatically.

If the killings upset him, the Chink accepted other contradictions in the Clock People's philosophy with ease. When faced with a contradiction, as he was — as we all are — daily if not hourly, it seemed only fair to him to take both sides.

Yet, he grew increasingly impatient with the Clock People's notions, and toward the end of his Sierra stay his hickory-dickory mouse of mockery ran frequently up their clock.

Now, a number of the young men of the Great Burrow had lost patience, too. Through the Chink's news broadcasts they had learned of mushrooming militancy among American Indians.

They learned of "Red Power" and of proud reservations whose residents were freshly painted — and armed to the teeth. In early spring of 1969, a quartet of bucks slipped away from the Great Burrow, venturing into the strange world beyond the still snowy mountains to see for themselves. A couple of months later, they returned, excited, feathered, beaded, buzzing of revolution. Two comrades threw in with them, and they deserted the Clock People to go face the White Man on his own terms — and in his own time. The bucks called at the Chink's shack on their way down the mountains. "You're as tired as we are of sitting around waiting for a motherfucking earthquake," they said in the idiom they had recently adopted. "You're strong and smart and have taught us much. Come with us and join the movement."

"This movement of yours, does it have slogans?" inquired the Chink.

"Right on!" they cried, and they quoted him some.

"Your movement, does it have a flag?" asked the Chink.

"You bet," and they described their emblem.

"And does your movement have leaders?"

"Great leaders."

"Then shove it up your butts," said the Chink. "I have taught you nothing." He skipped down to the creek to gather watercress.

A few weeks later, he accepted the invitation of an aged Siwash chief, who was the principal outside confederate of the Clock People, a degenerated warlock who could turn urine into beer, to be initiated as a shaman, an honor which gave him rights of occupancy in the sacred cave on faraway Siwash Ridge. At once he left for the Dakota hills to construct a clockworks whose ticks might more accurately echo the ticks of the universe, which, as he listened, sounded more and more like "ha ha ho ho and hee hee."

WILLIAM SAROYAN

A Fresno Fable

(FROM THE NEW YORKER)

KEROPE ANTOYAN, the grocer, ran into Aram Pashmanian, the lawyer, in the street one day and said, "Aram, you are the very man I have been looking for. It is a miracle that I find you this way at this time, because there is only one man in this world I want to talk to, and you are that man, Aram."

"Very well, Kerope," the lawyer said. "Here I am."

"This morning," the grocer said, "when I got up I said to myself, 'If there is anybody in this whole world I can trust, it is Aram,' and here you are before my eyes — my salvation, the restorer of peace to my soul. If I had hoped to see an angel in the street, I would not have been half so pleased as I am to see you, Aram."

"Well, of course I can always be found in my office," Aram said, "but I'm glad we have met in the street. What is it, Kerope?"

"Aram, we are from Bitlis. We understand all too well that before one speaks, one thinks. Before the cat tastes the fish, his whiskers must feel the head. A prudent man does not open an umbrella for one drop of rain. Caution with strangers, care with friends, trust in one's very own — as *you* are my very own, Aram. I thank God for bringing you to me at this moment of crisis."

"What is it, Kerope?"

"Aram, every eye has a brow, every lip a mustache, the foot wants its shoe, the hand its glove, what is a tailor without his needle, even a lost dog remembers having had a bone, until a candle is lighted a prayer for a friend cannot be said, one man's ruin is another man's reward."

"Yes, of course, but what is the crisis, Kerope?"

"A good song in the mouth of a bad singer is more painful to the ear than a small man's sneeze," the grocer said.

"Kerope," the lawyer said. "How can I help you?"

"You are like a brother to me, Aram — a younger brother whose wisdom is far greater than my own, far greater than any man's."

"Well, thank you, Kerope," Aram said, "but *please* tell me what's the matter, so I can try to help you."

In the end, though, Kerope refused to tell Aram his problem.

MORAL: If you're really smart, you won't trust even an angel.

JOHN SAYLES

Breed

(FROM THE ATLANTIC)

BRIAN WOKE on the lee side of a hill with a buffalo licking his face. At first he was only aware of the tongue, sticky and thick as a baby's arm, lapping down to sample his ears and cheeks. He had laid his sleeping bag out in the dark, snuggling it at the foot of what he took to be a drift fence, to have at least some shelter from the grit-blasting Wyoming wind. If it *was* still Wyoming; he hadn't been awake enough during the last part of the ride to look out for signs.

As he squirmed away from whatever the big thing mopping at his face was he glimpsed through half-sleep that each of the posts in the fence was painted a different color. Cherry-red, lime-green, lemon-yellow. He was in a carny-colored corral with a live bull bison.

No.

He tried to go back under, thinking it was only the effects of the three-day power-hitch across the country from New Jersey, all that coffee and all those miles talking with strangers. But then the rich brown smell dawned on him and he knew. He knew. He had never seen a live buffalo before but he was sure this was what they smelled like. It smelled like The West.

The buffalo retreated a few steps when Brian sat up, fixing him with swimming brown walleyes. There were bare patches worn in the wool of its flanks and hump, shiny black leather showing through. Its beard was sugared with dust and meal of some kind, and Brian could hear the flop of its tail chasing flies.

"Morning, Buffalo."

The animal snorted through its flat nose for an answer, made munching quivers with its jaw. Brian fingered matter from his eyes and peered out over the fence to where he remembered the road. There were cut-out letters hung from a crossbar like the ranches he'd seen in southern Wyoming had. Brian read them backward. CODY SPRAGUE'S WILD WEST BUCKIN' BISON RIDE, it said, FOOD — GAS — SOUVENIRS. Brian didn't understand how he could have missed the sign and the flapping pennants strung from it, even in the dark. The buffalo licked its nose.

Brian pulled on his sweat-funky road clothes and packed his sleeping bag away. The buffalo had lowered its eyelids to half-mast, no longer interested. Brian stood and walked around it. A shifting cloud of tiny black flies shadowed its ass, an ass cracked and black as old inner-tube rubber. There was something not quite real about the thing, Brian felt as if stuffing or springs would pop out of the seams any moment. He eased his hands into the hump wool. Coarse and greasy, like a mat for scuffing your feet clean on. The buffalo didn't move but for the twitching of its rump skin as insects lit on it. Brian gave it a couple of gentle, open-palmed thumps on the side, feeling the solid weight like a great warm tree stump.

"Reach for the sky!"

Brian nearly jumped on the animal's back as a cold cylinder pressed the base of his neck.

"Take your mitts off my buffalo and turn around."

Brian turned himself around slowly and there was a little chicken-necked man pointing an empty Coke bottle level with his heart. "One false move and I'll fizz you to pieces." The little man cackled, showing chipped brown teeth and goosing Brian with the bottle. "Scared the piss outa *you*, young fella. I seen you there this morning, laid out. Didn't figure I should bother to wake you till you woke yourself, but Ishmael, he thought you was a bag a meal. He's kind of slow, Ishmael."

The buffalo swung its head around to give the man a tentative whiff, then swung back. The man was wearing a fringed buck-skin jacket so stained it looked freshly ripped off the buck. He had a wrinkle-ring every other inch of his long neck, a crooked beak of a nose, and dirty white hair that shot out in little clumps. Of the three of them, the buffalo seemed to have had the best sleep.

Brian introduced himself and stated his business, which was to make his way to whatever passed for a major highway out here on the lone prairie. Thumbing from East Orange to the West Coast.

He had gotten a bum steer from a drunken oil-rigger the other night and was dumped out here.

"Cody Sprague," said the little man, extending his hand. "I offer my condolences and the use of my privy. Usually don't open till nine or ten," he said, "but it don't seem to make a difference either whichway."

He led Brian across the road to where there was a metal outhouse and an orange-and-black painted shack about the size of a Tastee-Freeze.

"People don't want to come," he said. "They don't want to come. Just blow by on that Interstate. That's what you'll be wantin to get to, isn't but five miles or so down the way. They finished that last stretch a couple years back and made me obsolete. That's what they want me. Obsolete."

Sprague clucked away at Brian's elbow, trotting a little to stay close as if his visitor would bolt for freedom any second. He called through the door of the little Sani-Port as Brian went in to wash and change to fresh clothes.

"You got any idee what it costs to keep a full-grown American bison in top running condition? Not just a matter of set im loose to graze, oh no, not when you've got a herd of one. Got to protect your investment, the same with any small businessman. Dropping like flies they are. That's an endangered species, the small businessman. Anyhow, you don't let him out there to graze. Don't know *what* he might pick up. You got five hundred head, you can afford to lose a few to poisnin, a few to varmint holes, a few to snakes and whatnot. Don't make a dent. But me, I got everything I own riding on Ishmael. He don't dine on nothin but the highest-protein feed. He's eaten up all my savings and most of the last bank loan I'm likely to get. You ever ridden a buffalo?"

"No," said Brian over the running water inside, "I've never even been on a horse."

"Then you got a treat coming, free a charge. You'll be my icebreaker for the weekend, bring me luck. I'd offer you breakfast, but confidentially speakin, the grill over here is out of commission. They turned off my lectricity. You might of noticed the lamp in there don't work. How they expect a buffalo to keep up its health without lectricity I'll never understand. It's that kind of thinking put the species on the brink of extinction."

*

Brian came out with fresh clothes and his teeth finger-brushed, and Cody Sprague hustled him back into the corral with Ishmael.

"Is there a saddle or anything? Or do I just get on?"

"Well, I got a blanket I use for the little girls with bare legs if it makes them nervous, but no, you don't need a thing. Like sitting on a rug. Just don't climb up too high on the hump is all, kind of unsteady there. Attaboy, hop aboard."

The buffalo didn't seem to mind, didn't seem to notice Brian crawling up on its back. Instead it lifted its head toward a bucket nailed to a post on the far side of the corral.

"How do I make him go?" asked Brian. There was no natural seat on a buffalo's back, he dug his fingers deep in the wool and pressed his knees to its flanks.

"That's my job, making him go, you just sit tight." Sprague scooted out of the corral, then returned with a half-empty sack of meal. He poured some in the far bucket, then clanged it with a stone. Ishmael began to move. He was in no hurry.

"Ridem cowboy!" yelled Sprague.

Brian felt some movement under him, distantly, a vague roll of muscle and bone. He tried to imagine himself as an eight-year-old kid instead of seventeen, and that helped a little. He tried to look pleased as the animal reached the bucket and buried its nose in the feed.

"This part of the ride," said Cody apologetically, "is where I usually give them my little educational spiel about the history of the buffalo and how the Indians depended on it and all. Got it from the library up to Rapid. Got to have something to keep them entertained at the halfway point while he's cleaning out that bucket. You know the Indian used every part of the beast. Meat for food, hide for clothes and blankets, bone for tools, even the waste product, dried into buffalo chips, they used that for fuel. There was a real — real *affi*nity between the buffalo and the Plains Indian. Their souls were tied together." He looked to Brian and waited.

"He sure is big." Brian threw a little extra enthusiasm into it. "I didn't realize they were this big."

Sprague spat on the ground, sighing, then looked up to see what was left in the bucket. "Pretty sorry attraction, that's what you mean, isn't it?"

"Well, I wouldn't say —"

"I mean *is*n't it? If he don't eat he don't move." Cody shook his head. "The kids, well, they pick up on it right away. Least they used to before that Interstate swept them all off. What kind of ride is it where the animal stops and chows down for five minutes at a time? Got so bad he'd commence to drool every time he seen a human under twelve years of age. Feed, that's all they understand. Won't mind kindness and he won't mind cruelty but you talk straight to his belly and oh Lord will he listen. That's how they got extincted in the first place, they seen their colleagues droppin all around them but they were too involved with feeding their faces to put two and two together. They'd rather be shot and scalped than miss the next mouthful. Plain stupid is all." He gave Ishmael a thump in the side. "You'd just as soon name a rock or a lump of clay as give a title to this old pile of gristle." He squatted slightly to look the buffalo in the face. "A damn sorry attraction, aren't you? A damn sorry fleabag of an attraction."

He straightened and hefted the meal. "Might as well be stuffed, I figure. Put him on wheels. The few people I get anymore all want to snip a tuft of wool offen him for a souvenir. I had to put a stop to it, wouldn't of been a thing left. Cody Sprague's Bald Buckin Bison."

Ishmael lifted his head and flapped his tongue in the air a couple of times.

"Got to fill the other bucket now. He expects it. Took me the longest time to figure the right distance, long enough so it's two bits' worth of ride but not so long that the thoroughbred here thinks it's not worth the hike. The kids can tell though. I never been able to fool them. They feel left out of it, feel gypped. Um, if you don't mind, would you stay on him for the rest of the ride?" Cody was hustling across the corral toward another hanging bucket, with Ishmael swinging a liquid eye after him. "He needs the exercise."

Brian sat out the slow plod across the corral and slid off when it reached the bucket. He brushed his pants and got a stick to scrape his sneakers clean of the buffalo stool he'd stepped in. The rich brown smell was losing its charm.

"You'll be going now, I suppose," said Sprague coming up behind him.

"Uh, yeah. Guess so." It was a little creepy, the multicolored corral in the middle of all that open range. "Thanks for the ride, though."

"Nothing to keep you here, Lord knows." He was forcing a

smile. "S'almost nine now, business should pick up. Ought to build a fire, case anybody stops for a hot dog." He gave a weak cackle. "I could use it for part of my pitch — frankfurters cowboy style. Call em prairie dogs."

"Yuh."

"You'll be wantin that Interstate I suppose, get you out of here. Five miles or so north on the road and you'll smack right into it."

"Thanks." Brian shouldered his duffel bag. "Hope the trade improves for you."

"Oh, no worry, no worry. I'll make out. Oh, and here, take one of these." He fished an aluminum star from his pocket and presented it to Brian. "Souvenir for you and good advertising for me."

"Deputy Sheriff," said the badge. "Issued at Cody Sprague's Wild West Buckin' Bison Ride." There was a picture of a cowboy tossed high off the back of an angrily kicking buffalo. Brian pinned it on his shirt and Cody brightened a bit.

"Who knows," he said, "maybe today's the day. Maybe we'll get discovered by the tourist office today and be written up. You get your attraction in one of those guidebooks and you got a gold mine. Wall-to-wall customers, turn em away at the gate. I could save up an maybe afford an opposite number for Ishmael. Don't know if or what buffalo feel but I suppose everything gets lonely for its own kind, don't you?"

"I suppose."

"Say, I wasn't kidding about that fire. If you're hungry I could whip us up a late breakfast in no time. There's stock I got to use before it goes bad so it'd be on the house."

"I really got to get going. Sorry."

"Well, maybe you brought me luck. Yessir, maybe today will be the day."

Brian left him waving from the middle of the corral, buckskin fringes blowing in the quickening breeze. When he was out of sight around the bend he unpinned the aluminum star and tossed it away, it dug into his chest too much. Then the signs appeared, the backs of them first, then the messages as he passed by and looked behind. Every thousand yards there was another, starting with WHOA! HERE IT IS! and progressing to more distant warnings. When Brian got to FOR THE RIDE OF YOUR LIFE, STOP AT CODY SPRAGUE'S he couldn't hold out anymore, he dropped his

bag and trotted back to where he'd chucked the star. He found it
without too much trouble and put it in his back pocket.

He went through the land of blue-green sage clumps, leaning
into the wind whipping over low hills, walking alone. There
weren't any cars or people. More sage, more hills, more wind, but
no human trace but the road beneath him like a main street of
some vanished civilization. Open range, there were no fences or
water tanks. He looked at his Road Atlas and guessed that he was
a little ways up into South Dakota, a little below the Bear in the
Lodge River with the Rosebud Indian Reservation to the east and
the Pine Ridge to the north. He tried to remember who it was
he'd seen in the same situation. Randolph Scott? Audie Murphy?
Brian checked the sun's position to reassure himself that he was
heading in the right direction. There was nothing else to tell by.
A patch of hill suddenly broke free into a butternut cluster of
high-rumped antelope, springing away from him. He was in The
West.

He had been walking on the road for over an hour when an old
Ford pickup clattered to a halt next to him. A swarthy, smooth-
faced man wearing a green John Deere cap stuck his head out.

"Who you workin for?" he called.

"Huh?"

"Who you workin for? Whose place you headed?"

"I'm not working for anybody," said Brian. "I'm trying to hitch
west."

"Oh, I thought you were a hand. S'gonna give you a ride over
to whatever outfit you're headed for."

Brian tried not to look too pleased. Thought he was a hand.
"No, I'm just hitching. I was walking up to the Interstate."

"You got a hell of a walk. That's twenty miles up."

"But the guy said it was only five."

"What guy?"

"The old guy back there. He's got a buffalo."

"Sprague? You can't listen to him, son. A nice fella, but he's a
little bit touched. Got a sign up on Ninety, says it's only five miles
to his place. Figured nobody's gonna bother, they know the real
story, and he's right. Guess he's started to believe his own
publicity."

"Oh."

"But you hop in anyway. I'm goin up that area in a while." Brian tossed his duffel bag in the back and got in with the man. "J. C. Shangreau," he said, offering his hand. "I'll get you north surer than most anything else you're likely to catch on this road. If you don't mind a few side trips."

Brian had to kick a shotgun wrapped in burlap under the seat to make room for his legs. "Don't mind at all."

"Got to pick up some hands to help me work my horses." Shangreau had quite a few gold teeth in his mouth and very bloodshot eyes. "Got me a couple sections up there, I run seventy-five head. Gonna have ourselves a cuttin bee if I can roust out enough of these boys."

They turned off left on one of the access roads and began to pass clusters of small trailer houses propped on cinder block. Shangreau stopped at one, went to the door and talked a bit, then came back alone.

"Hasn't recovered from last night yet. Can't say as I have either. There was nothing to celebrate, cept it being another Friday, but I did a job of it. You know when your teeth feel rubbery in the morning?"

Brian wasn't used to adults asking him hangover questions. "Yeah."

"That's the kind of bag I got on. Rubber-toothed."

He stopped at another trailer with no luck. This one hadn't come home overnight.

"Hope he's feelin good now, cause there's an ambush waitin at home for him. I had a big one like that in the kitchen I'd think twice about carryin on. She'll just squeeze all the good time right out of that man."

"Many of these people around here Indian?" Brian asked it noncommittally, fishing. The drill-rigger the night before had gone on and on about how the Indians and the coyotes should have been wiped out long ago.

"Oh sure," said Shangreau, "most of em. Not many purebred though, things being what they are. Most of these boys I'm after is at least half or more Indian. You got your Ogalala around here, your Hunkpapa and the rest. I'm a good quarter Sioux myself. Old Jim Crow who we're headin after now is maybe seven-eighths, fifteen-sixteenths, something like that. It's hard to keep count. Jim has got three or four tribes to start with, his mother was part Flathead as I recall, and then he's got white and I wouldn't be surprised if one of them buffalo soldiers didn't slip in a little black blood way back when. But you won't see too many purebred, less we catch Bad Heart at home, and he's another story altogether. What are you?"

"Irish."

"Me too, a good quarter. Monaghans."

They came to a pair of trailer houses that had been butted up together. A dozen fat little children wearing glasses ran barefoot out front. An older fat boy with extra-thick glasses and a silver-sprayed cowboy hat chased them, tossing a lasso at their legs. Brian got out of the pickup with Shangreau and a round, sad-looking man met them at the door to the first trailer.

"I see you're bright-eyed an bushy-tailed as everone else is this mornin," said J. C. "Them horses don't have much competition today, it looks like. Jim Crow, this here's Brian."

"Hey."

Jim Crow nodded. He was wearing nothing but flannel pajama bottoms and his belly hung over. His slant eyes and mournful expression made him kind of Mongoloid-looking.

"You know anyone else could join us? Couple of my possibilities crapped out on me."

"My brother-law's here from over the Rosebud. Sam. I'll ask him. And Raymond could come along. Raymond!"

The boy in the silver cowboy hat turned from where he had just cut a little sister out from the herd.

"You're coming along with us to work J. C.'s horses. Go tell your ma."

Raymond left the little sister to untie herself and ran off looking happy.

Sam was a little older and a little heavier than Jim Crow and had blue eyes. Brian sat in front between J. C. and Crow while Raymond and Sam were open in the back. Raymond's hat blew off almost immediately and they had to stop for him to run get it. His father told him to sit on it till they got to J. C.'s.

They stopped next at a lone trailer still on its wheels to pick up a young man called Jackson Blackroot. All the men got out and went to the door to try to catch a glimpse of Blackroot's new wife, who was supposed to be a looker. She obliged by coming out to say Hello boys and offer to make coffee. They turned it down, suddenly shy. She was dark and thin and reasonably pretty though Brian didn't see anything outstanding. Jackson was a friendly young guy with a big white smile who looked like an Italian. He shook Brian's hand and said he was pleased to meet him.

Bad Heart's trailer was alone too, a little box of a thing sitting on a hill. J. C. stopped out front and honked once.

"Be surprised if he's there," whispered Crow.

"If he is I be surprised if he shows himself."

They waited for a few minutes with the motor running and Shangreau had the pickup in gear when a short, pock-scarred man emerged from the trailer and hopped in the rear without a greeting.

It was a long bumpy way up to Shangreau's ranch and he did most of what little talking went on. The other men seemed to know each other and about each other but weren't particularly comfortable riding together.

"Brian," asked J. C., "you in any big hurry to get up there?"

Brian shrugged.

"I mean if you're not you might's well stop for lunch with us, look on when we work the horses. Hell, you can join the party if you're careful, can always use an extra hand when we're cuttin'."

"Sure." Brian was willing to follow just about anything at this point if there was food in it. He hadn't eaten since yesterday morning. He wondered exactly what cutting was going to be.

The J. C. Ranch wasn't much. A side-listing barn surrounded by a wood-and-wire corral and a medium-sized unpainted shack in a couple of thousand acres of dry-looking open range. The shack squatted on a wood platform, there was a gas tank and a hot water heater on the front porch. J. C. explained that this was the working house, they had another aluminum-sided place farther west on the property. There were wide cracks in the floorboard inside, blankets hung to separate the rooms. Shangreau's broad-faced wife grunted a hello and went back to pouring cornstarch into her stewpot. She had the biggest arms Brian had ever seen on a woman.

The men took turns washing their hands in a pail and sat around the kitchen table. Lunch was a tasteless boiled beef and potato stew that the men loaded with salt and shoveled down. There was little talk at the table.

"Well now," said J. C., pushing back in his chair when everyone seemed finished, "let's get at them horses."

The men broke free into work. They readied their ropes and other gear while Brian and Raymond collected wood, old shack boards, and dead scrub for the branding fire. They built up the fire in a far corner of the corral, Jim Crow nursing it with a scuffed old hand bellows. When there were bright orange coals at the bottom and the irons were all laid out, the men spread with ropes in hand, forming a rough circle around the narrow chute that led into the corral from the barn, what Shangreau called the squeezer.

"And now, pilgrim," he said waving Brian back a little, "you gonna see some *masc*ulatin."

Raymond went up and started the first horse out through the squeezer and things began to happen fast, Brian struggling to keep up. The horse was not so huge, its back about chin-high to Brian, but it was thick and barrel-chested, its mottled gray sides working fast with suspicion. Raymond flapped his hat and clucked along the chute rail beside it till it was in the open and the men were swinging rope at its hooves, not picture-book lassoing but dropping open nooses on the ground and jerking up when it stepped in or near them. It took a while, plenty of near misses and times when the horse kicked free or the rope just slipped away, and Bad Heart was closest to Brian cursing a constant chant low on his breath, fuckin horse, goddamn horse, hold im, bust the fucker, and Raymond was in the corral trying to get his rope untangled and join the fun and Brian was hustling not to be trampled or roped.

"Bust im! Bust im!" J. C. was yelling and the stocky horse wheeled and crow-hopped but was met in every direction by another snapping rope. Finally Sam forefooted him cleanly and Jim jumped in quick to slip one over the head and jumped back to be clear as they hauled the animal crashing down onto its side.

"Choke im down! Choke im down!" yelled J. C. and they held its head into the ground with the rope while Bad Heart, cursing louder now and grimacing, wrestled its hind legs bent, one at a time, and strapped them back against its belly. They held it on its back now, writhing and lathered, eyes bugged hugely and nostrils wide, the men adding a rope here and there to help them muscle it still. Shangreau motioned Brian up with his head and handed him a rope end.

"Choke im," he said, "don't let him jerk. You let him jerk he's gonna hurt himself."

J. C. went to where the tools were laid out on a tarp and returned with a long, mean-looking jack-knifey thing. The horse rested between spurts of resistance now, its huge chest heaving, playing out in flurries like a hooked fish. The men used the pauses to dig in their heels and get a stronger grip. J. C. waved the blade through the branding fire a few times, then knelt between the stallion's pinioned legs.

"Hold him tight, boys, they're comin off!"

The horse farted and screamed and shot a wad of snot into the blanket Bad Heart held its head with all at once, its spine arched clear off the ground and whumped back down, but J. C. had them in his fist and wouldn't be shook. He aimed and he hacked and blood covered his wrists till they cut free in his hands, a loose, sticky mess that he heaved into the far corner of the corral. He wasn't through. The horse rested quivering and Brian shifted the rope from where it had scored its image in his palms and J. C. brought what he had pointed out before as the masculator, a pair of hedge clippers that gripped at the end instead of cut.

"Ready?" he called, and when they were straining against the horse he worked the masculator inside and grabbed it onto what he wanted and yanked. There was blood spurting then, flecking the horse and the men and staining solid one leg of J. C.'s work pants. The rest was relatively easy, the branding and the tail-bobbing, the horse too drained to do much more than try to wave its head under Bad Heart's knee. With the smell of burned flesh and fear around them, the men shortened their holds, worked in toward the horse, quiet now, Bad Heart's stream of abuse almost soothing. Each man grabbed a rope at some strategic point on the horse, J. C. taking over for Brian, and when each nodded that he was ready, they unlooped and jumped back in one quick motion. The horse lay still on its back for a moment, as if it had fallen asleep or died, then slowly rolled to its side and worked its legs underneath. It stood woozily at first, snorted and shook its head a few times, groin dripping thinly into the dirt, and then Raymond opened the corral gate to the range beyond and hat-flapped it out. It trotted a hundred yards off and began to graze.

"Forget he ever had em in a couple minutes," said J. C. He

thumped Brian on the back, his hand sticking for a moment. "Gonna make a cowboy out of you in no time."

The men sat near each other, leaning on the corral slats, resting. "What's it for?" Brian decided there was no cause to try to seem to know any more than he did. "Why can't you leave them like they are?"

"It's a matter of breed." J. C. was working a little piece of horse from the masculator jaws. "You leave them stallions be, they don't want a thing but fight and fuck all day long. You don't want your herd to inbreed. Let them inbreed and whatever it is strange in them comes to the surface, gets to be the rule rather than the exception."

Bad Heart sat alone across the corral from them, over by where the genitals had been thrown. Raymond tried to do tricks with his rope.

"Don't want em too wild," said Jackson Blackroot.

"Or too stunted and mean," said Sam. "Or too high-strung."

"And you don't want any candy-assed little lap ponies. Like I said, it's a matter of breed. We keep one, maybe two stallions isolated, and trade them between outfits to crossbreed. You stud my herd, I'll stud yours. What we want is what you call your hybrid vigor. Like all the different stock I've got in me. Irish and Indian and whatnot. Keeps one strain from takin over and going bad."

"But you do keep a stud horse?"

"Oh yeah. Now I know what you're thinking, these sod-pounders up here haven't heard of artificial insemination. We know all right, it's a matter of choice. I been up to county fairs and whatnot, seen the machines they got. The mechanical jack-off machine and the dock syringe and all that. If that's your modern rancher, well you can have him. If God meant beasts to fuck machines he would of given em batteries. It's like that A.S.P.C.A. bunch, always on our backs about the modern rancher and the proper way to masculate. Now there isn't but one way to do it. Ours. Horses know they been *cut*."

Cutting and branding and bobbing took about a half hour per horse. It was tense, hard work and Brian got numbed to where only the burned-hair smell when the brand was seared on both-

ered him. He liked the shouting and sweating and the physical
pull against the animals, and supposed the rest, the cutting and
all, was necessary. They didn't seem to mind much after it was
done.

The men seemed to loosen and touch more often as they got
deeper into work, breaks between cuttings grew longer and more
frequent. They sat on a little rise to the side of the corral passing
dripping ice-chest beers and a bottle of Johnnie Walker J. C. had
provided, gazing over at the string of fresh-cut geldings. Gimme
a hit a that coffin varnish, they would say, and the bottle would be
passed down, bloody hand to bloody hand, all of them half-shot
with liquor but soon to work it off on the next horse.

"Must be some connection with their minds," said Sam. "Once
you lop their balls off, whatever part of their mind that takes care
of thinkin on the fillies must turn off too. So they don't even
remember, don't even think like a stallion anymore. They forget
the old ways."

"They turn into cows, is what. Just strong and dumb."

"But you got to do it," said J. C. "Otherwise you might's well let
them run wild, run and fuck whenever they want, tear down all
the fences and keep territory all to themselves. Nosir, it's got to
be done."

The afternoon wore on in tugs and whinnies. Raymond forefooted a big roan all by himself and Brian caught a stray hoof in
his thigh that spun him around. One of the horses, a little scab-
colored animal, turned out to be a real bad one, kicking all red-
eyed and salty, running at the men instead of away until Bad
Heart up with a branding iron, swinging at its head and spitting
oaths but only managing to herd it right on out of the half-open
corral door. It scampered up the rise with the others, kicking its
heels and snorting.

"Raymond, dammit!" yelled Jim Crow. "You sposed to latch
that damn gate shut!"

"I *did!*" Raymond had the look of the falsely accused. He took
his silver hat off to plead his innocence. "I closed it right after
that last one."

"Then how'd it get open?"

"It wasn't me."

"Don't worry about it," said J. C. "We'll have to go catch him
tomorra. He's a tricky sumbitch to bring in. Just a wrong-headed

animal, is all. That's the one you give me," he said to Bad Heart, "pay back that loan."

Bad Heart grunted.

It was turning to evening when they finished. A cloud of fat black flies gloated over the heap of testicles in the corner. Brian had a charley-horse limp where he'd been kicked. They sprawled on the rise and pulled their boots off, wiggled red, sick-looking toes in the air, and sucked down beer in gasping pulls. Still-warm sweat came tangy through their denim, they knocked shoulders and knees, compared injuries, and debated over who would be sorest in the morning. Bad Heart coiled the rope he had brought and lay down alone in the back of the pickup. They pondered on what they should do next.

"The way I see it," said Jim Crow, "it's a choice between more of Minnie's cooking and goin out for some serious drinking."

They were silent then, it was up to J. C. to pass the verdict on his wife's cooking.

"Sheeit," he said, "if that's all that's keepin us here let's roll. What's open?"

"Not much. Not much legal, anyways. There is that whatsisname's place, up to Interior."

"Then let's get on the stick. Brian, you a drinkin man?"

"I suppose."

"Well you will be after tonight. Interior, what's that, fifty mile or so? Should be able to get there afore dark and then it's every man for himself. No need to change but we'll have to go round and tell the women. Let's ride, fellas."

In the pickup they talked about horses and farm machinery and who used to be a bad hat when they were young and who was still capable of some orneriness on a full tank and about drunks they'd had and horses they'd owned and about poor old Roger DuPree whose woman had the roving eye. They passed liquor front seat to truck-bed, taking careful, fair pulls of the remaining Johnnie Walker and the half-bottle of Mogen David J. C. had stashed under the barn floor. Brian closed one eye the way he did when he drank so they wouldn't cross and Bad Heart carefully wiped the neck when it was his turn. They banged over the yellow-brown land in the long plains twilight, holding the bottles below sight-line as they stopped at each trailer to say they wouldn't be out too

late. Raymond started to protest when it was time for him to be
left off, but Jim Crow said a few growling words and his mournful
face darkened even sadder; it would just *kill* him if he had to
smack the boy. Raymond didn't want a scene in front of the guys
and scooted off flapping the rump of an imaginary mount with
his silver hat. The liquor ran out and Sam's belly began to rumble
so they turned out of their way to hunt some food.

They reached a little kitchen emporium just before it closed up
and J. C. sprang for a loaf of Wonder Bread and some deviled
ham spread. The old woman in the store wore a crucifix nearly
half her size and wouldn't sell alcoholic beverages. FOR PEACE OF
MIND, said a faded sign over the door, INVESTIGATE THE CATHOLIC
FAITH.

"Sonsabitches damnwell ought to be investigated," said Jim
Crow. "Gotten so I can't but give a little peep of colorful language around the house and she's off in the bedroom on her
knees mumbling an hour's worth of nonsense to save my soul.
What makes her think I'd trust that bunch with my soul escapes
me."

"Now they mean well enough, Jim, it's just they don't understand Indian ways. Think they dealin with a bunch of savages up
here that haven't ever heard of religion. Think that somebody's
got to get theirselves nailed to a tree before you got a religion."

"Fuck religion!" shouted Bad Heart from the back, and that
ended the conversation.

A sudden rain hit them with a loud furious slap, drenching the
men in the back instantly and smearing the windshield so thick
that J. C. lost sight and the pickup sloughed sideways into the
shoulder ditch. It only added to their spirits, rain soothing them
where the sweat had caked itchy, not cold enough to soak through
their layer of alcohol. It gave them a chance to show they didn't
give a fart in a windstorm how the weather blew, to pile out and
hunker down in the mud and slog and heave and be splattered by
the tires when the pickup finally scrambled up onto the road.
The flash downpour cut dead almost the moment the truck was
free, just to make its point clear. J. C. spread a blanket over the
hood and the men stood together at the side of the road waiting
for Jackson Blackroot to slap them down a sandwich with his
brand-new Bowie knife. The ham spread was a bit watery but nobody kicked, they hurried to stuff a little wadding down to soak

up more liquor. They pulled wet jeans away from their skin and stomped their boots free of mud on the road pavement. J. C. came over to Brian.

"Don't you worry about the delay, son. We'll show you a real cowboy drunk soon enough."

"No rush."

"Damn right there's no rush. Got time to burn out here. Time grows on trees. Well, bushes anyway, we're a little short on trees. There isn't a picture show or a place with live music in some hundred miles, the Roman Church is about the only organization has regular meetings and you can have that. Isn't much cause for people to get together. Workin horses like we done is something though. A little excitement, even if it is work. Hell, it's better that it is work, you feel good about it even after it's over, not like a drunk where it takes a couple years of selective memory to make it into something you like to talk about."

"Doesn't seem so bad."

"Oh, there's worse, I'm sure. But I see you're passing through, not staying. Nobody lives here unless they were born here and can't hack it anywhere else. It's why most of the land around here was made into reservation, nobody else wanted it. Oh, the Badlands, up by Interior, they're striking to look at so the Park Service took them for the tourists, but the rest — hell, even the migrating birds don't come back anymore."

"Where you traveling to, Brian?" It was old Sam that asked.

"California."

He frowned. "You best be careful. That California is wild. Had a brother was killed there."

"I'll watch myself."

"I'd steer clear of it if it was me. They say it's wild."

J. C. laughed. "When was this brother killed, Sam?"

"Just around the start of the war. Got himself caught in something called the Zoot Suit Riots and that was all she wrote. Just plain wild."

"You know where I found Brian?" said J. C. "He was walkin up Six-Hat Road there by Petrie's, sayin he's gonna walk to the Innerstate. Seems he got his directions from old Cody Sprague there."

The men laughed. "Be better off gettin em from the buffalo," said Jackson Blackroot, "at least he's a native."

"Sprague isn't from around here?"

"He come out from some city back east, what was it, Philadelphia — ?"

"Pittsburgh."

"Right. He come out from Pittsburgh on his vacation one summer and he sees all these roadside attractions up there on Ninety,
the prairie dog village, reptile farms, Wall Drug Store, all that,
and he thinks he's found his calling. He worked in some factory
all his life and always had something about bein his own boss,
owning his own business. So he takes his savings, which couldn't
of been much, and buys himself two acres down on Six-Hat, the
most worthless two acres in the whole state probly, and somewhere he gets ahold of that animal. Gonna build a dude ranch
with the money he makes selling rides. Well it's been six, seven
years now and I don't know how the hell he survives but he still
hasn't got but them two acres and that animal."

"He's a nice old guy though," said J. C. "Talk your ear off, a
little crazy, but a nice old guy."

"He's a character all right," said Jackson.

"He's an asshole." Bad Heart climbed into the rear of the
pickup.

They had eaten all the bread and were talking about Sam's
brother getting killed in Los Angeles when Jackson remembered
something.

"Hey," he said, "what we gonna do about that wake they're
having over there for Honda Joe? Suppose we ought to go?"

"Just slipped my mind," said J. C. "Live just five mile away from
us, no way I can't make an appearance, and it slipped my mind.
Listen, as long as there's all of us together and we got the
truck —"

"I suppose we ought to go."

"Damn shame it is, young kid like that. Goes through all that
Vietnam business with hardly a scratch, gets himself a Silver Star,
then comes back to smash hisself up on a goddamn motorsickle.
Young kids like that seem bent on it. I remember I couldn't talk
my brother out of his plan for all the world, nosir, he had to have
his California."

"It wasn't this it would of been some other," said Jackson.

"If it wasn't the bike maybe he would of drunk hisself to death
like some others around here."

"No, I don't think so. Honda Joe was always in a hurry to get there."

"Well he got there all right. In a couple pieces maybe, but he got there."

"We ought to go look in on him, for his mother's sake. What say, fellas?"

"I never liked Honda Joe," said Bad Heart.

"Well then, dammit, you can stay in the truck."

"If there's one thing I can't stand," said Jim Crow very quietly when they were on their way to Honda Joe's wake, "it's a sulky Indian."

It was still twilight when they passed by the access road to J. C.'s place again. He didn't offer to drop Bad Heart home before they went on. They crossed Six-Hat Road, Brian was just able to make out one of Cody Sprague's signs to the right, and then a half mile farther along they were stopped by a horse standing in the middle of the road, facing them.

J. C. turned on the headlights and they saw it was the scab-colored one that had escaped in the afternoon.

"The hell's he doin out here?" said J. C. He turned the engine off and got out quietly. He left the door open and walked slowly toward the horse, talking soft. "Good horse," he said, "nice horse. Come to papa. Attaboy."

The horse stood for a moment, nostrils wide open, then bolted off the road and out of sight. J. C. slammed back into the truck. Only Bad Heart dared laugh.

The trailer was alone and far away from the blacktop, far even from the oiled road that serviced most of the other places around. It sat as if run aground next to the dry streambed that cut through a gently sloping basin. Young men's cars, Pintos and Mavericks, Mustangs and Broncos, surrounded it, parked every whichway. To the rear was an orderly block where the family men had pulled in their Jeeps and pickups. J. C. slipped in among these and the men eased out. They had sobered, what with the food and the surprise rain and the knowledge of the work cut out ahead of them. They shuffled and stuffed their hands in their pockets, waiting for J. C. to lead. The mud and blood had stiffened again on their clothes, they tried to get all their scratching done before they had to go in. Bad Heart stretched out in the rear, glaring out into space. J. C. sighed and fished under the seat, behind the shotgun, and came out with a pint of gin. "I was saving this for an emergency," he said, and tossed it to Bad Heart. "Entertain yourself."

They were met at the door by two dark old Indians wearing VFW hats. Evening, gentlemen, glad you could come. There was a visitor's book to sign and no place to sit, the trailer was crammed to its aluminum gills. There were nods and hullos from the men already inside, crop and stock and weather conversations to drift into, and woman-noise coming from back in the bedrooms. Drink was offered and declined, for the moment anyway. A knot of angry-looking young men leaned together against one wall, planning to make yet another wine-run up to Interior and back. Suspicious eyes lingered on Brian, coming hardest and hairiest from the young men. Brian felt extra uncomfortable in his sun-lightened hair and three-day road stubble in the midst of all the smooth, dark people. He was glad for the stains of horse-cutting left on him, as if having shared that gave him some right of entry.

Mrs. Pierce was on them before they could get their bearings. She smelled of tears and Four Roses and clutched at their elbows like she was drowning.

"J. C.," she said, "you come, I knew you would. And Jim. Boys. I knew you'd all come, I knew everybody'd come for my Joey."

She closed one eye when she had to focus on somebody. She squinted up to Brian. "Do I know you?"

"This is Brian, Mrs. Pierce," said J. C. "He's been working horses over to my place."

"Well Brian," she said sober-faced, talking slow as if explaining house rules to a new kid in the neighborhood, "you just make yourself at home. Joey had him a lot of white friends, he was in the Army."

The woman had straight black hair with streaks of iron-gray, she stood up to Brian's shoulders, her face flat and unwrinkled. She could have been anywhere from thirty-five to fifty. She was beautiful. Brian told her not to worry about him.

"You come to stay a while, J. C.? You have something to drink? We got plenty, everybody brang for my Joey. We'll go right through the night into tomorrow with him. Will you stay, J. C.?"

"Well, now, Mrs. Pierce, we'd really like to, we all thought high of young Joseph there, but like I said we been working horses all day and these boys are just all *in*. I promised their women I'd get them home early and in one piece. You know how it is."

The woman gave a little laugh. "Oh, I do, I surely do. We'll get him home in one piece, that's what the recruiters said, come onto Rosebud when we were over there. Make a man of him and send him back in better shape than when he left. Well, he's back, I suppose. Least I know where he is, not like some that are missing or buried over there. Don't figure anyone'll want to borrow him anymore." She stopped a moment and turned something over in her mind with great effort, then looked to J. C. again. "We're havin a service Tuesday over to the Roman. Appreciate it if you all could be there."

"We'll make every effort, Ma'am. And if there's anything you need help with in the coming weeks —"

"Oh no, J. C., save your help. Won't need it. After the service I'll just hitch up and drive on out of here. Go up north, I got people. I put two husbands and four sons in this country now and I'll be damned if it gets a drop more outen me. No, I'm to go up north."

"It's hard livin up there, Mrs. Pierce."

"Well it aint no bed a goddamn roses down here neither, is it?"

The men hung on in the main room a bit more for courtesy, swapping small talk and trying to remember which of the wild Pierce boys had been responsible for which piece of mischief, trying to keep out of the way of the women, who seemed to know what they were there for. Mrs. Pierce weaved her way through the somber crowd assuring and being assured that her poor Joey was a good boy and would be sorely missed by all. Brian noticed she was wearing the boy's Silver Star on a chain around her neck.

It took a good hour to get through the crowd, the people didn't seem to see much of each other and there was a lot of catching up to do, but they were herded steadily, inevitably, toward the bedroom where they knew Honda Joe would be laid out. They shied and shuffled at the doorway a little, but there was no avoiding it. A steady, humming moan came from within, surrounded by other, soothing sounds. J. C. took a deep breath and led the way.

Whoever did the postmortem on Honda Joe must have learned the trade by mail. The corpse, tucked to the chin under an American flag, looked more like it should have been leaning against a stuffed pony at the Wall Drug Store than like something that had lived and breathed. The skin had a thick look to it and a sheen like new leather, and even under the flag you could tell everything hadn't been put back where it belonged. The men went past the Murphy bed on both sides, up on their toes as if someone was sleeping. They clasped their hands in front of them and tried to look properly mournful. Jackson Blackroot muttered a few words to the corpse. Brian took his turn and concentrated on a spot on the boy's hairline till he felt he'd put in his time. He was moving away when he heard the whooping from outside.

"Yee-haaaaa!" somebody was yelling. "Yipyipyeeeeee!"

There was the sound of hooves then, and the whooping grew distant. The men emptied out into the night range to see what it was.

"Yeow! Yeow! Yeow!" called a voice over to the left. Someone was riding a horse out there in the pitch black, someone pretty loaded from the sound of him.

"Goddamn Indians," grumbled one of the old men wearing a VFW hat. "Got no sense a dignity."

"Yee-hahaaaaa!" called the rider as a gray shape galloped by on the right.

"Sounds a bit like Bad Heart," said J. C. "Sounds a whole lot like him."

They went to J. C.'s pickup and Bad Heart was gone. There was some gear missing too, some rope, a bridle. They checked in the front. J. C.'s shotgun was still there but Jackson's bowie knife was gone.

"He loses it I'll wring his goddamn neck," said Jackson.

The men all got in their cars and pickups then and put their headlights on. The beams crisscrossed out across the little basin, making eerie pockets of dark and light.

"Yah-haaaaa!"

A horse and rider appeared at the far edge of the light, disappeared into shadow, then came into view again. It was Bad Heart, bareback on the little scab-colored stallion. It strained forward as if it were trying to race right out from under him. There was something tied with rope to its tail, dragging and flopping behind, kicking up dust that hung in the headlights' arc. Bad Heart whacked its ribs and kneed it straight for the dry streambed. It gathered and leaped, stretching out in the air, and landed in perfect stride on the far bank.

"Fucker can ride," said Jim Crow.

"Fucker could always ride," said J. C. "Nobody ever denied that. Like he's born on horseback."

Bad Heart lay close to the line of the stallion's back, seemed to flow with its every muscle. With the day's blood staining his old tan Levis and the scabby red-brown of the horse it was hard to tell where one began and the other left off.

"Yee-yeeheeeeeeee!"

Bad Heart circled the trailer a few more times before a couple of the young men commandeered Jeeps and lit out after him. It was a good chase for a while, the Jeeps having more speed but the little stallion being able to cut and turn quicker. They honked and flicked their lights and kept Bad Heart pinned in view of the trailer but couldn't land him till he tried to make the horse jump the streambed one time too many. It just pulled up short and ducked its head, sending him flying over, tumbling through the air till he hit halfway up the opposite bank.

The horse trotted off out of all the lights and Bad Heart lay wailing.

He was pretty scraped up when they got to him, one side of his face all skinned and his left leg bent crooked from midway up the thigh. He cursed as they made a splint from a rake handle, cursed as they carried him in on a blanket, cursed when they laid him out on the Murphy bed next to Honda Joe.

"Wait'll the fucker wakes up in the mornin," he kept saying while they tried to calm him down. "Gonna have a big surprise. Wait'll he wakes up. Big fuckin surprise."

Jackson found his bowie knife tucked in Bad Heart's boot when they pulled it off. The knife was bloody up to the hilt.

Brian went out with J. C. and Jackson to see about the horse. Everyone had turned their headlights off so J. C. got his flashlight from the pickup. They walked out in the dark a bit and then they heard whuffing up ahead and J. C. shined at it.

The stallion held its head up high, eyes shining back amber in the beam, bridle dangling, chest and sides lathered and heaving. It stood and looked at them as Jackson whispered his way up and took the bridle.

J. C. came up and took the bowie knife from Jackson. He cut the rope free from the stallion's tail. Brian went back with him to see what had been dragging behind.

It was a blood-sticky hide. The hair coarse and greasy, like something you'd scuff your feet clean on. It had a sad, lonely smell. It smelled like The West.

J. C. played the light off away from it. "I suppose we best take this thing over, break the news to old Sprague. You wanna come along for the ride?"

"Sure."

"Spose we'll call it a night after that. Get you up to Ninety in the morning." He turned the flashlight on the stallion, limping a bit as it followed Jackson toward the trailer. "There isn't all that much to do in Interior anyways."

ANNE TYLER

Your Place is Empty

(FROM THE NEW YORKER)

EARLY in October, Hassan Ardavi invited his mother to come from Iran for a visit. His mother accepted immediately. It wasn't clear how long the visit was to last. Hassan's wife thought three months would be a good length of time. Hassan himself had planned on six months, and said so in his letter of invitation. But his mother felt that after such a long trip six months would be too short, and she was counting on staying a year. Hassan's little girl, who wasn't yet two, had no idea of time at all. She was told that her grandmother was coming but she soon forgot about it.

Hassan's wife was named Elizabeth, not an easy word for Iranians to pronounce. She would have been recognized as American the world over — a blond, pretty girl with long bones and an ungraceful way of walking. One of her strong points was an ability to pick up foreign languages, and before her mother-in-law's arrival she bought a textbook and taught herself Persian. *"Salaam aleikum,"* she told the mirror every morning. Her daughter watched, startled, from her place on the potty-chair. Elizabeth ran through possible situations in her mind and looked up the words for them. "Would you like more tea? Do you take sugar?" At suppertime she spoke Persian to her husband, who looked amused at the new tone she gave his language, with her flat, factual American voice. He wrote his mother and told her Elizabeth had a surprise for her.

Their house was a three-story brick Colonial, but only the first two stories were in use. Now they cleared the third of its trunks and china barrels and *National Geographics*, and they moved in a few pieces of furniture. Elizabeth sewed flowered curtains for the window. She was unusually careful with them; to a foreign mother-in-law, fine seams might matter. Also, Hassan bought a pocket compass, which he placed in the top dresser drawer. "For her prayers," he said. "She'll want to face Mecca. She prays three times a day."

"But which direction is Mecca from here?" Elizabeth asked.

Hassan only shrugged. He had never said the prayers himself, not even as a child. His earliest memory was of tickling the soles of his mother's feet while she prayed steadfastly on; everyone knew it was forbidden to pause once you'd started.

Mrs. Ardavi felt nervous about the descent from the plane. She inched down the staircase sideways, one hand tight on the railing, the other clutching her shawl. It was night, and cold. The air seemed curiously opaque. She arrived on solid ground and stood collecting herself — a small, stocky woman in black, with a kerchief over her smooth gray hair. She held her back very straight, as if she had just had her feelings hurt. In picturing this moment she had always thought Hassan would be waiting beside the plane, but there was no sign of him. Blue lights dotted the darkness behind her, an angular terminal loomed ahead, and an official was herding the passengers toward a plate-glass door. She followed, entangled in a web of meaningless sounds such as those you might hear in a fever dream.

Immigration. Baggage Claims. Customs. To all she spread her hands and beamed and shrugged, showing she spoke no English. Meanwhile her fellow-passengers waved to a blur of faces beyond a glass wall. It seemed they all knew people here; she was the only one who didn't. She had issued from the plane like a newborn baby, speechless and friendless. And the customs official didn't seem pleased with her. She had brought too many gifts. She had stuffed her bags with them, discarding all but the most necessary pieces of her clothing so that she would have more room. There were silver tea sets and gold jewelry for her daughter-in-law, and for her granddaughter a doll dressed in the complicated costume of a nomad tribe, an embroidered sheepskin vest, and two religious medals on chains — one a disc inscribed with the name of Allah, the other a tiny gold Koran, with a very effective prayer for long life folded up within it. The customs official sifted gold through his fingers like sand and frowned at the Koran. "Have I done something wrong?" she asked. But of course he didn't understand her. Though you'd think, really, that if he would just *listen* hard enough, just meet her eyes once . . . it was a very simple language, there was no reason why it shouldn't come through to him.

For Hassan, she'd brought food. She had gathered all his favorite foods and put them in a drawstring bag embroidered with peacocks. When the official opened the bag he said something under his breath and called another man over. Together they unwrapped tiny newspaper packets and sniffed at various herbs. "Sumac," she told them. "Powder of lemons. Shambahleh." They gazed at her blankly. They untied a small cloth sack and rummaged through the kashk she had brought for soup. It rolled beneath their fingers and across the counter — hard white balls of yogurt curd, stuck with bits of sheep hair and manure. Some peasant had labored for hours to make that kashk. Mrs. Ardavi picked up one piece and replaced it firmly in the sack. Maybe the official understood her meaning: she was running out of patience. He threw up his hands. He slid her belongings down the counter. She was free to go.

Free to go where?

Dazed and stumbling, a pyramid of knobby parcels and bags, scraps of velvet and brocade and tapestry, she made her way to the glass wall. A door opened out of nowhere and a stranger blocked her path. "Khanom Jun," he said. It was a name that only her children would use, but she passed him blindly and he had to touch her arm before she would look up.

He had put on weight. She didn't know him. The last time she'd seen him he was a thin, stoop-shouldered medical student disappearing into an Air France jet without a backward glance. "Khanom Jun, it's me," this stranger said, but she went on searching his face with cloudy eyes. No doubt he was a bearer of bad news. Was that it? A recurrent dream had warned her that she would never see her son again — that he would die on his way to the airport, or had already been dead for months but no one wanted to break the news; some second or third cousin in America had continued signing Hassan's name to his cheerful, anonymous letters. Now here was this man with graying hair and a thick mustache, his clothes American but his face Iranian, his eyes sadly familiar, as if they belonged to someone else. "Don't you believe me?" he said. He kissed her on both cheeks. It was his smell she recognized first — a pleasantly bitter, herblike smell that brought her the image of Hassan as a child, reaching thin arms around her neck. "It's you, Hassan," she said, and then she started crying against his gray tweed shoulder.

They were quiet during the long drive home. Once she reached over to touch his face, having wanted to do so for miles. None of the out-of-focus snapshots he'd sent had prepared her for the way he had aged. "How long has it been?" she asked. "Twelve years?" But both of them knew to the day how long it had been. All those letters of hers: "My dear Hassan, ten years now and still your place is empty." "Eleven years and still . . ."

Hassan squinted through the windshield at the oncoming headlights. His mother started fretting over her kerchief, which she knew she ought not to have worn. She'd been told so by her youngest sister, who had been to America twice. "It marks you," her sister had said. But that square of silk was the last, shrunken reminder of the veil she used to hide beneath, before the previous Shah had banished such things. At her age, how could she expose herself? And then her teeth; her teeth were a problem too. Her youngest sister had said, "You ought to get dentures made, I'm sure there aren't three whole teeth in your head." But Mrs. Ardavi was scared of dentists. Now she covered her mouth with one hand and looked sideways at Hassan, though so far he hadn't seemed to notice. He was busy maneuvering his car into the right-hand lane.

This silence was the last thing she had expected. For weeks she'd been saving up stray bits of gossip, weaving together the family stories she would tell him. There were three hundred people in her family — most of them related to each other in three or four different ways, all leading intricate and scandalous lives she had planned to discuss in detail, but instead she stared sadly out the window. You'd think Hassan would ask. You'd think they could have a better conversation than this, after such a long time. Disappointment made her cross, and now she stubbornly refused to speak even when she saw something she wanted to comment on, some imposing building or unfamiliar brand of car sliding past her into the darkness.

By the time they arrived it was nearly midnight. None of the houses were lit but Hassan's — worn brick, older than she would have expected. "Here we are," said Hassan. The competence with which he parked the car, fitting it neatly into a small space by the curb, put him firmly on the other side of the fence, the American side. She would have to face her daughter-in-law alone. As they climbed the front steps she whispered, "How do you say it again?" "Say what?" Hassan asked. "Her name. Lizabet?" "Elizabeth. Like Elizabeth Taylor. *You* know." "Yes, yes, of course," said his mother. Then she lifted her chin, holding tight to the straps of her purse.

Elizabeth was wearing bluejeans and a pair of fluffy slippers. Her hair was blond as corn silk, cut short and straight, and her face had the grave, sleepy look of a child's. As soon as she had opened the door she said, "*Salaam aleikum.*" Mrs. Ardavi, overcome with relief at the Persian greeting, threw her arms around her and kissed both cheeks. Then they led her into the living room, which looked comfortable but a little too plain. The furniture was straight-edged, the rugs uninteresting, though the curtains had a nice figured pattern that caught her eye. In one corner sat a shiny red kiddie car complete with license plates. "Is that the child's?" she asked. "Hilary's?" She hesitated over the name. "Could I see her?"

"*Now?*" said Hassan.

But Elizabeth told him, "That's all right." (Women understood these things.) She beckoned to her mother-in-law. They climbed the stairs together, up to the second floor, into a little room that smelled of milk and rubber and talcum powder, smells she would know anywhere. Even in the half-light from the hallway, she could tell that Hilary was beautiful. She had black, tumbling hair, long black lashes, and skin of a tone they called wheat-colored, lighter than Hassan's. "There," said Elizabeth. "Thank you," said Mrs. Ardavi. Her voice was formal, but this was her first grandchild and it took her a moment to recover herself. Then they stepped back into the hallway. "I brought her some medals," she whispered. "I hope you don't mind."

"Medals?" said Elizabeth. She repeated the word anxiously, mispronouncing it.

"Only an Allah and a Koran, both very tiny. You'll hardly know they're there. I'm not used to seeing a child without a medal. It worries me."

Automatically her fingers traced a chain around her neck, end-

ing in the hollow of her collarbone. Elizabeth nodded, looking
relieved. "*Oh* yes. Medals," she said.

"Is that all right?"

"Yes, of course."

Mrs. Ardavi took heart. "Hassan laughs," she said. "He doesn't
believe in these things. But when he left I put a prayer in his
suitcase pocket, and you see he's been protected. Now if Hilary
wore a medal, I could sleep nights."

"Of course," Elizabeth said again.

When they re-entered the living room, Mrs. Ardavi was smiling,
and she kissed Hassan on the top of his head before she sat down.

American days were tightly scheduled, divided not into morning and afternoon but into 9:00, 9:30, and so forth, each half
hour possessing its own set activity. It was marvellous. Mrs. Ardavi wrote her sisters: "They're more organized here. My daughter-in-law never wastes a minute." How terrible, her sisters wrote
back. They were all in Teheran, drinking cup after cup of tea
and idly guessing who might come and visit. "No, you misunder-
stand," Mrs. Ardavi protested. "I like it this way. I'm fitting in
wonderfully." And to her youngest sister she wrote, "You'd think
I was American. No one guesses otherwise." This wasn't true, of
course, but she hoped it would be true in the future.

Hassan was a doctor. He worked long hours, from six in the
morning until six at night. While she was still washing for her
morning prayers she could hear him tiptoe down the stairs and
out the front door. His car would start up, a distant rumble far
below her, and from her bathroom window she could watch it
swing out from beneath a tatter of red leaves and round the corner and disappear. Then she would sigh and return to her sink.
Before prayers she had to wash her face, her hands, and the soles
of her feet. She had to draw her wet fingers down the part in her
hair. After that she returned to her room, where she swathed
herself tightly in her long black veil and knelt on a beaded velvet
prayer mat. East was where the window was, curtained by chintz
and misted over. On the east wall she hung a lithograph of the
Caliph Ali and a color snapshot of her third son, Babak, whose
marriage she had arranged just a few months before this visit. If
Babak hadn't married, she never could have come. He was the
youngest, spoiled by being the only son at home. It had taken her

three years to find a wife for him. (One was too modern, one too lazy, one so perfect she had been suspicious.) But finally the proper girl had turned up, modest and well-mannered and sufficiently wide of hip, and Mrs. Ardavi and the bridal couple had settled in a fine new house on the outskirts of Teheran. Now every time she prayed, she added a word of thanks that at last she had a home for her old age. After that, she unwound her veil and laid it carefully in a drawer. From another drawer she took thick cotton stockings and elastic garters; she stuffed her swollen feet into open-toed vinyl sandals. Unless she was going out, she wore a housecoat. It amazed her how wasteful Americans were with their clothing.

Downstairs, Elizabeth would have started her tea and buttered a piece of toast for her. Elizabeth and Hilary ate bacon and eggs, but bacon of course was unclean and Mrs. Ardavi never accepted any. Nor had it even been offered to her, except once, jokingly, by Hassan. The distinctive, smoky smell rose to meet her as she descended the stairs. "What does it taste like?" she always asked. She was dying to know. But Elizabeth's vocabulary didn't cover the taste of bacon; she only said it was salty and then laughed and gave up. They had learned very early to travel a well-worn conversational path, avoiding the dead ends caused by unfamiliar words. "Did you sleep well?" Elizabeth always asked in her funny, childish accent, and Mrs. Ardavi answered, "So-so." Then they would turn and watch Hilary, who sat on a booster seat eating scrambled eggs, a thin chain of Persian gold crossing the back of her neck. Conversation was easier, or even unnecessary, as long as Hilary was there.

In the mornings Elizabeth cleaned house. Mrs. Ardavi used that time for letter writing. She had dozens of letters to write, to all her aunts and uncles and her thirteen sisters. (Her father had had three wives, and a surprising number of children even for that day and age.) Then there was Babak. His wife was in her second month of pregnancy, so Mrs. Ardavi wrote long accounts of the American child-rearing methods. "There are some things I don't agree with," she wrote. "They let Hilary play outdoors by herself, with not even a servant to keep an eye on her." Then she would trail off and gaze thoughtfully at Hilary, who sat on the floor watching a television program called "Captain Kangaroo."

Mrs. Ardavi's own childhood had been murky and grim. From the age of nine she was wrapped in a veil, one corner of it clenched in her teeth to hide her face whenever she appeared on the streets. Her father, a respected man high up in public life, used to chase servant girls through the halls and trap them, giggling, in vacant bedrooms. At the age of ten she was forced to watch her mother bleed to death in childbirth, and when she screamed the midwife had struck her across the face and held her down till she had properly kissed her mother goodbye. There seemed no connection at all between her and this little overalled American. At times, when Hilary had one of her temper tantrums, Mrs. Ardavi waited in horror for Elizabeth to slap her and then, when no slap came, felt a mixture of relief and anger. "In Iran —" she would begin, and if Hassan was there he always said, "But this is not Iran, remember?"

After lunch Hilary took a nap, and Mrs. Ardavi went upstairs to say her noontime prayers and take a nap as well. Then she might do a little laundry in her bathtub. Laundry was a problem here. Although she liked Elizabeth, the fact was that the girl was a Christian, and therefore unclean; it would never do to have a Christian wash a Moslem's clothes. The automatic dryer was also unclean, having contained, at some point, a Christian's underwear. So she had to ask Hassan to buy her a drying rack. It came unassembled. Elizabeth put it together for her, stick by stick, and then Mrs. Ardavi held it under her shower and rinsed it off, hoping that would be enough to remove any taint. The Koran didn't cover this sort of situation.

When Hilary was up from her nap they walked her to the park — Elizabeth in her eternal bluejeans and Mrs. Ardavi in her kerchief and shawl, taking short painful steps in small shoes that bulged over her bunions. They still hadn't seen to her teeth, although by now Hassan had noticed them. She was hoping he might forget about the dentist, but then she saw him remembering every time she laughed and revealed her five brown teeth set wide apart.

At the park she laughed a great deal. It was her only way of communicating with the other women. They sat on the benches ringing the playground, and while Elizabeth translated their questions Mrs. Ardavi laughed and nodded at them over and over. "They want to know if you like it here," Elizabeth said. Mrs.

Ardavi answered at length, but Elizabeth's translation was very short. Then gradually the other women forgot her, and conversation rattled on while she sat silent and watched each speaker's lips. The few recognizable words — "telephone," "television" "radio" — gave her the impression that American conversations were largely technical, even among women. Their gestures were wide and slow, disproving her youngest sister's statement that in America everyone was in a hurry. On the contrary, these women were dreamlike, moving singly or in twos across wide flat spaces beneath white November skies when they departed.

Later, at home, Mrs. Ardavi would say, "The red-haired girl, is she pregnant? She looked it, I thought. Is the fat girl happy in her marriage?" She asked with some urgency, plucking Elizabeth's sleeve when she was slow to answer. People's private lives fascinated her. On Saturday trips to the supermarket she liked to single out some interesting stranger. "What's the matter with that *jerky*-moving man? That girl, is she one of your dark-skinned people?" Elizabeth answered too softly, and never seemed to follow Mrs. Ardavi's pointing finger.

Supper was difficult; Mrs. Ardavi didn't like American food. Even when Elizabeth made something Iranian, it had an American taste to it — the vegetables still faintly crisp, the onions transparent rather than nicely blackened. "Vegetables not thoroughly cooked retain a certain acidity," Mrs. Ardavi said, laying down her fork. "This is a cause of constipation and stomach aches. At night I often have heartburn. It's been three full days since I moved my bowels." Elizabeth merely bent over her plate, offering no symptoms of her own in return. Hassan said, "At the table, Khanom? At the table?"

Eventually she decided to cook supper herself. Over Elizabeth's protests she began at three every afternoon, filling the house with the smell of dillweed and arranging pots on counters and cabinets and finally, when there was no more space, on the floor. She squatted on the floor with her skirt tucked between her knees and stirred great bowls of minced greens while behind her, on the gas range, four different pots of food bubbled and steamed. The kitchen was becoming more homelike, she thought. A bowl of yogurt brewed beside the stove, a kettle of rice soaked in the sink, and the top of the dishwasher was curlicued with the yellow dye from saffron. In one corner sat the pudding pan, black on the bottom from the times she had cooked down sugar to make a sweet for her intestines. "Now, this is your rest period," she always told Elizabeth. "Come to the table in three hours and be surprised." But Elizabeth only hovered around the kitchen, disturbing the serene, steam-filled air with clatter and slams as she put away pots, or pacing between stove and sink, her arms folded across her chest. At supper she ate little; Mrs. Ardavi wondered how Americans got so tall on such small suppers. Hassan, on the other hand, had second and third helpings. "I must be gaining five pounds a week," he said. "None of my clothes fit."

"That's good to hear," said his mother. And Elizabeth added something but in English, which Hassan answered in English also. Often now they broke into English for paragraphs at a time — Elizabeth speaking softly, looking at her plate, and Hassan answering at length and sometimes reaching across the table to cover her hand.

At night, after her evening prayers, Mrs. Ardavi watched television on the living-room couch. She brought her veil downstairs and wrapped it around her to keep the drafts away. Her shoes lay on the rug beneath her, and scattered down the length of the couch were her knitting bag, her sack of burned sugar, her magnifying glass, and *My First Golden Dictionary*. Elizabeth read novels in an easy chair, and Hassan watched TV so that he could translate the difficult parts of the plot. Not that Mrs. Ardavi had much trouble. American plots were easy to guess at, particularly the Westerns. And when the program was boring — a documentary or a special news feature — she could pass the time by talking to Hassan. "Your cousin Farah wrote," she said. "Do you remember her? A homely girl, too dark. She's getting a divorce and in my opinion it's fortunate; he's from a lower class. Do you remember Farah?"

Hassan only grunted, his eyes on the screen. He was interested in American politics. So was she, for that matter. She had wept for President Kennedy, and carried Jackie's picture in her purse. But these news programs were long and dry, and if Hassan wouldn't talk she was forced to turn at last to her *Golden Dictionary*.

In her childhood, she had been taught by expensive foreign tutors. Her mind was her great gift, the compensation for a large, plain face and a stocky figure. But now what she had

learned seemed lost, forgotten utterly or fogged by years, so that
Hassan gave a snort whenever she told him some fact that she had
dredged up from her memory. It seemed that everything she
studied now had to penetrate through a great thick layer before it
reached her mind. "Tonk you," she practiced. "Tonk you. Tonk
you." "Thank you," Hassan corrected her. He pointed out useful
words in her dictionary — grocery-store words, household words
— but she grew impatient with their woodenness. What she
wanted was the language to display her personality, her famous
courtesy, and her magical intuition about the inside lives of other
people. Nightly she learned "salt," "bread," "spoon," but with an
inner sense of dullness, and every morning when she woke her
English was once again confined to "thank you" and "NBC."

Elizabeth, meanwhile, read on, finishing one book and reaching
for the next without even glancing up. Hassan chewed a thumb-
nail and watched a senator. He shouldn't be disturbed, of course,
but time after time his mother felt the silence and the whispery
turning of pages stretching her nerves until she had to speak.
"Hassan?"

"Hmm."

"My chest seems tight. I'm sure a cold is coming on. Don't you
have a tonic?"

"No," said Hassan.

He dispensed medicines all day; he listened to complaints.
Common sense told her to stop, but she persisted, encouraged by
some demon that wouldn't let her tongue lie still. "Don't you
have some syrup? What about that liquid you gave me for constipation? Would that help?"

"No, it wouldn't," said Hassan.

He drove her on, somehow. The less he gave, the more she
had to ask. "Well, aspirin? Vitamins?" Until Hassan said, "Will
you just let me *watch?*" Then she could lapse into silence again, or
even gather up the clutter of her belongings and bid the two of
them good night.

She slept badly. Often she lay awake for hours, fingering the
edge of the sheet and staring at the ceiling. Memories crowded in
on her, old grievances and fears, injustices that had never been
righted. For the first time in years she thought of her husband, a
gentle, weak man given to surprising outbursts of temper. She
hadn't loved him when she married him, and at his death from a

liver ailment six years later her main feeling had been resentment. Was it fair to be widowed so young, while other women were supported and protected? She had moved from her husband's home back to the old family estate, where five of her sisters still lived. There she had stayed till Babak's wedding, drinking tea all day with her sisters and pulling the strings by which the rest of the family was attached. Marriages were arranged, funerals attended, childbirth discussed in fine detail; servants' disputes were settled, and feuds patched up and then restarted. Her husband's face had quickly faded, leaving only a vacant spot in her mind. But now she could see him so clearly — a wasted figure on his deathbed, beard untrimmed, turban coming loose, eyes imploring her for something more than an absentminded pat on the cheek as she passed through his room on her way to check the children.

She saw the thin faces of her three small boys as they sat on the rug eating rice. Hassan was the stubborn, mischievous one, with perpetual scabs on his knees. Babak was the cuddly one. Ali was the oldest, who had caused so much worry — weak, like his father, demanding, but capable of turning suddenly charming. Four years ago he had died of a brain hemorrhage, slumping over a dinner table in faraway Shīrāz, where he'd gone to be free of his wife, who was also his double first cousin. Ever since he was born he had disturbed his mother's sleep, first because she worried over what he would amount to and now, after his death, because she lay awake listing all she had done wrong with him. She had been too lenient. No, too harsh. There was no telling. Mistakes she had made floated on the ceiling like ghosts — allowances she'd made when she knew she shouldn't have, protections he had not deserved, blows which perhaps he had not deserved either.

She would have liked to talk to Hassan about it, but any time she tried he changed the subject. Maybe he was angry about the way he had heard of Ali's death. It was customary to break such news gradually. She had started a series of tactful letters, beginning by saying that Ali was seriously ill when in truth he was already buried. Something in the letter had given her away — perhaps her plans for a rest cure by the seaside, which she never would have considered if she'd had an ailing son at home. Hassan had telephoned overseas, taking three nights to reach her. "Tell me what's wrong," he said. "I know there's something. When her tears kept her from answering, he asked, "Is he dead?"

His voice sounded angry, but that might have been due to a poor connection. And when he hung up, cutting her off before she could say all she wanted, she thought, I should have told him straight out. I had forgotten that about him. Now when she spoke of Ali he listened politely, with his face frozen. She would have told him anything, all about the death and burial and that witch of a wife throwing herself, too late, into the grave; but Hassan never asked.

Death was moving in on her. Oh, not on her personally (the women in her family lived a century or longer, burying the men one by one) but on everybody around her, all the cousins and uncles and brothers-in-law. No sooner had she laid away her mourning clothes than it was time to bring them out again. Recently she had begun to feel she would outlive her two other sons as well, and she fought off sleep because of the dreams it brought — Babak lying stiff and cold in his grave, Hassan crumpled over in some dark American alley. Terrifying images would zoom at her out of the night. In the end she had to wrap herself in her veil and sleep instead on the Persian rug, which had the dusty smell of home and was, anyway, more comfortable than her unsteady foreign mattress.

At Christmas time, Hassan and Elizabeth gave Mrs. Ardavi a brightly colored American dress with short sleeves. She wore it to an Iranian party, even leaving off her kerchief in a sudden fit of daring. Everyone commented on how nice she looked. "Really you fit right in," a girl told her. "May I write to my mother about you? She was over here for a year and a half and never once stepped out of the house without her kerchief." Mrs. Ardavi beamed. It was true she would never have associated with these people at home — children of civil servants and bank clerks, newly rich now they'd finished medical school. The wives called their husbands "Doctor" even in direct address. But still it felt good to be speaking so much Persian; her tongue nearly ran away with her. "I see you're expecting a baby," she said to one of the wives. "Is it your first? I could tell by your eyes. Now don't be nervous. I had three myself; my mother had seven and never felt a pain in her life. She would squat down to serve my father's breakfast and 'Eh?' she would say. 'Aga Jun, it's the baby!' and there it would be on the floor between her feet, waiting for her to cut the cord and finish pouring the tea." She neglected to mention how her mother had died. All her natural tact came back to her, her gift with words and her knowledge of how to hold an audience. She bubbled and sparkled like a girl, and her face fell when it was time to go home.

After the party, she spent two or three days noticing more keenly than ever the loss of her language, and talking more feverishly when Hassan came home in the evening. This business of being a foreigner was something changeable. Boundaries kept shifting, and sometimes it was she who was the foreigner but other times Elizabeth, or even Hassan. (Wasn't it true, she often wondered, that there was a greater distance between men and women than between Americans and Iranians, or even *Eskimos* and Iranians?) Hassan was the foreigner when she and Elizabeth conspired to hide a miniature Koran in his glove compartment; he would have laughed at them. "You see," she told Elizabeth, "I know there's nothing to it, but it makes me feel better. When my sons were born I took them all to the bath attendant to have their blood let. People say it brings long life. I know that's superstition, but whenever afterward I saw those ridges down their backs I felt safe. Don't you understand?" And Elizabeth said, "Of course." She smuggled the Koran into the car herself, and hid it beneath the Texaco maps. Hassan saw nothing.

Hilary was a foreigner forever. She dodged her grandmother's yearning hands, and when the grownups spoke Persian she fretted and misbehaved and pulled on Elizabeth's sleeve. Mrs. Ardavi had to remind herself constantly not to kiss the child too much, not to reach out for a hug, not to offer her lap. In this country people kept more separate. They kept so separate that at times she felt hurt. They tried to be so subtle, so undemonstrative. She would never understand this place.

In January they took her to a dentist, who made clucking noises when he looked in her mouth. "What does he say?" she asked. "Tell me the worst." But Hassan was talking in a low voice to Elizabeth, and he waved her aside. They seemed to be having a misunderstanding of some sort. "What does he *say*, Hassan?"

"Just a minute."

She craned around in the high-backed chair, fighting off the dentist's little mirror. "I have to know," she told Hassan.

"He says your teeth are terrible. They have to be extracted and the gums surgically smoothed. He wants to know if you'll be here for another few months; he can't schedule you till later."

A cold lump of fear swelled in her stomach. Unfortunately she *would* be here; it had only been three months so far and she was planning to stay a year. So she had to watch numbly while her life was signed away, whole strings of appointments made, and little white cards filled out. And Hassan didn't even look sympathetic. He was still involved in whatever this argument was with Elizabeth. The two of them failed to notice how her hands were shaking.

It snowed all of January, the worst snow they had had in years. When she came downstairs in the mornings she found the kitchen icy cold, crisscrossed by drafts. "The sort of cold enters your bones," she told Elizabeth. "I'm sure to fall sick." Elizabeth only nodded. Some mornings now her face was pale and puffy, as if she had a secret worry, but Mrs. Ardavi had learned that it was better not to ask about it.

Early in February there was a sudden warm spell. Snow melted and all the trees dripped in the sunshine. "We're going for a walk," Elizabeth said, and Mrs. Ardavi said, "I'll come too." In spite of the warmth, she toiled upstairs for her woolen shawl. She didn't like to take chances. And she worried over Hilary's bare ears. "Won't she catch cold?" she asked. "I think we should cover her head."

"She'll be all right," said Elizabeth, and then shut her face in a certain stubborn way she had.

In the park, Elizabeth and Hilary made snowballs from the last of the snow and threw them at each other, narrowly missing Mrs. Ardavi, who stood watching with her arms folded and her hands tucked in her sleeves.

The next morning, something was wrong with Hilary. She sat at the breakfast table and cried steadily, refusing all food. "Now, now," her grandmother said, "won't you tell old Ka Jun what's wrong?" But when she came close Hilary screamed louder. By noon she was worse. Elizabeth called Hassan, and he came home immediately and laid a hand on Hilary's forehead and said she should go to the pediatrician. He drove them there himself. "It's her ears, I'm sure of it," Mrs. Ardavi said in the waiting room.

For some reason Hassan grew angry. "Do you always know better than the experts?" he asked her. "What are we coming to the doctor for? We could have talked to you and saved the trip." His mother lowered her eyes and examined her purse straps. She understood that he was anxious, but all the same her feelings were hurt and when they rose to go into the office she stayed behind.

Later Hassan came back and sat down again. "There's an infection in her middle ear," he told her. "The doctor's going to give her a shot of penicillin." His mother nodded, careful not to annoy him by reminding him she had thought as much. Then Hilary started crying. She must be getting her shot now. Mrs. Ardavi herself was terrified of needles, and she sat gripping her purse until her fingers turned white, staring around the waiting room, which seemed pathetically cheerful, with its worn wooden toys and nursery-school paintings. Her own ear ached in sympathy. She thought of a time when she had boxed Ali's ears too hard and he had wept all that day and gone to sleep sucking his thumb.

While Hassan was there she was careful not to say anything, but the following morning at breakfast she said, "Elizabeth dear, do you remember that walk we took day before yesterday?"

"Yes," said Elizabeth. She was squeezing oranges for Hilary, who'd grown cheerful again and was eating a huge breakfast.

"Remember I said Hilary should wear a hat? Now you see you should have been more careful. Because of you she fell sick; she could have died. Do you see that now?"

"No," said Elizabeth.

Was her Persian that scanty? Lately it seemed to have shrunk and hardened, like a stale piece of bread. Mrs. Ardavi sighed and tried again. "Without a hat, you see —" she began. But Elizabeth had set down her orange, picked up Hilary, and walked out of the room. Mrs. Ardavi stared after her, wondering if she'd said something wrong.

For the rest of the day, Elizabeth was busy in her room. She was cleaning out bureaus and closets. A couple of times Mrs. Ardavi advanced as far as the doorway, where she stood awkwardly watching. Hilary sat on the floor playing with a discarded perfume bottle. Everything, it seemed, was about to be thrown away — buttonless blouses and stretched-out sweaters, stockings and combs and empty lipstick tubes. "Could I be of any help?" Mrs. Ardavi asked, but Elizabeth said, "Oh, no. Thank you very much." Her voice was cheerful. Yet when Hassan came home he went upstairs and stayed a long time, and the door remained shut behind him.

Supper that night was an especially fine stew, Hassan's favorite ever since childhood, but he didn't say a word about it. He hardly spoke at all, in fact. Then later, when Elizabeth was upstairs putting Hilary to bed, he said, "Khanoum Jun, I want to talk to you."

"Yes, Hassan," she said, laying aside her knitting. She was frightened by his seriousness, the black weight of his mustache, and her own father's deep black eyes. But what had she done? She knotted her hands and looked up at him, swallowing.

"I understand you've been interfering," he said.

"I, Hassan?"

"Elizabeth isn't the kind you can do that with. And she's raising the child just fine on her own."

"Well, of course she is," said his mother. "Did I ever say otherwise?"

"Show it, then. Don't offer criticisms."

"Very well," she said. She picked up her knitting and began counting stitches, as if she'd forgotten the conversation entirely. But that evening she was unusually quiet, and at nine o'clock she excused herself to go to bed. "So early?" Hassan asked.

"I'm tired," she told him, and left with her back very straight.

Her room surrounded her like a nest. She had built up layers of herself on every surface — tapestries and bits of lace and lengths of Paisley. The bureau was covered with gilt-framed pictures of the saints, and snapshots of her sisters at family gatherings. On the windowsill were little plants in orange and aqua plastic pots — her favorite American colors. Her bedside table held bottles of medicine, ivory prayer beads, and a tiny brick of holy earth. The rest of the house was bare and shiny, impersonal; this room was as comforting as her shawl.

Still, she didn't sleep well. Ghosts rose up again, tugging at her thoughts. Why did things turn out so badly for her? Her father had preferred her brothers, a fact that crushed her even after all these years. Her husband had had three children by her and then complained that she was cold. And what comfort were children? If she had stayed in Iran any longer Babak would have asked her to move; she'd seen it coming. There'd been some disrespect creeping into his bride's behavior, some unwillingness to take advice, which Babak had overlooked even when his mother pointed it out to him. And Hassan was worse — always so stubborn, much too independent. She had offered him anything if he would just stay in Iran but he had said no; he was set on leaving her. And he had flatly refused to take along his cousin Shora as his wife, though everyone pointed out how lonely he would be. He was so anxious to break away, to get *going*, to come to this hardhearted country and take up with a Christian girl. Oh, she should have laughed when he left, and saved her tears for someone more deserving. She never should have come here, she never should have asked anything of him again. When finally she went to sleep it seemed that her eyes remained open, burning large and dry beneath her lids.

In the morning she had a toothache. She could hardly walk for the pain. It was only Friday (the first of her dental appointments was for Monday), but the dentist made time for her during the afternoon and pulled the tooth. Elizabeth said it wouldn't hurt, but it did. Elizabeth treated it as something insignificant, merely a small break in her schedule, which required the hiring of a baby-sitter. She wouldn't even call Hassan home from work. "What could he do?" she asked.

So when Hassan returned that evening it was all a surprise to him — the sight of his mother with a bloody cotton cylinder hanging out over her lower lip like a long tooth. "What *happened* to you?" he asked. To make it worse, Hilary was screaming and had been all afternoon. Mrs. Ardavi put her hands over her ears, wincing. "Will you make that child hush?" Hassan told Elizabeth. "I think we should get my mother to bed." He guided her toward the stairs, and she allowed herself to lean on him. "It's mainly my heart," she said. "You know how scared I am of dentists." When he had folded back her bedspread and helped her to lie down she closed her eyes gratefully, resting one arm across her forehead. Even the comfort of hot tea was denied her; she had to stay on cold foods for twelve hours. Hassan fixed her a glass of ice water. He was very considerate, she thought. He seemed as shaken at the sight of her as Hilary had been. All during the evening he kept coming to check on her, and twice in the night she heard him climbing the stairs to listen at her door. When she moaned he called, "Are you awake?"

"Of course," she said.

"Can I get you anything?"

"No, no."

In the morning she descended the stairs with slow, groping feet, keeping a tight hold on the railing. "It was a very hard night," she said. "At four my gum started throbbing. Is that normal? I think these American pain pills are constipating. Maybe a little prune juice would restore my regularity."

"I'll get it," Hassan said. "You sit down. Did you take the milk of magnesia?"

"Oh, yes, but I'm afraid it wasn't enough," she said.

Elizabeth handed Hassan a platter of bacon, not looking at him.

After breakfast, while Hassan and his mother were still sitting over their tea, Elizabeth started cleaning the kitchen. She made quite a bit of noise. She sorted the silverware and then went through a tangle of utensils, discarding bent spatulas and rusty tongs. "May I help?" asked Mrs. Ardavi. Elizabeth shook her head. She seemed to have these fits of throwing things away. Now she was standing on the counter to take everything from the upper cabinets — crackers, cereals, half-empty bottles of spices. On the very top shelf was a flowered tin confectioner's box with Persian lettering on it, forgotten since the day Mrs. Ardavi had brought it. "My!" said Mrs. Ardavi. "Won't Hilary be surprised!" Elizabeth pried the lid off. Out flew a cloud of insects, grayish-brown with V-shaped wings. They brushed past Elizabeth's face and fluttered through her hair and swarmed toward the ceiling, where they dimmed the light fixture. Elizabeth flung the box as far from her as possible and climbed down from the counter. "Goodness!" said Mrs. Ardavi. "Why, *we* have those at home!" Hassan lowered his teacup. Mixed nuts and dried currants rolled every which way on the floor; more insects swung toward the ceiling. Elizabeth sat on the nearest chair and buried her head in her hands. "Elizabeth?" said Hassan.

But she wouldn't look at him. In the end she simply rose and went upstairs, shutting the bedroom door with a gentle, definite click, which they heard all the way down in the kitchen because they were listening so hard.

"Excuse me," Hassan said to his mother.

She nodded and stared into her tea.

After he was gone she went to find Hilary, and she set her on her knee, babbling various folk rhymes to her while straining her ears toward the silence overhead. But Hilary squirmed off her lap and went to play with a truck. Then Hassan came downstairs again. He didn't say a word about Elizabeth.

On the following day, when Mrs. Ardavi's tooth was better, she and Hassan had a little talk upstairs in her room. They were very polite with each other. Hassan asked his mother how long they could hope for her to stay. His mother said she hadn't really thought about it. Hassan said that in America it was the custom to have house guests for three months only. After that they moved to a separate apartment nearby, which he'd be glad to provide for her as soon as he could find one, maybe next week. "Ah, an apartment," said his mother, looking impressed. But she had never lived alone a day in her life, and so after a suitable pause she said that she would hate to put him to so much expense. "Especially," she said, "when I'm going in such a short time anyway, since I'm homesick for my sisters."

"Well, then," said Hassan.

At supper that night, Hassan announced that his mother was missing her sisters and would like to leave. Elizabeth lowered her glass. "Leave?" she said.

Mrs. Ardavi said, "And Babak's wife, of course, will be asking for me when the baby arrives."

"Well . . . but what about the dentist? You were supposed to start your appointments on Monday."

"It's not important," Mrs. Ardavi said.

"But we set up all those —"

"There are plenty of dentists she can see at home," Hassan told Elizabeth. "We have dentists in Iran, for God's sake. Do you imagine we're barbarians?"

"No," Elizabeth said.

On the evening of the third of March, Hassan drove his mother to the airport. He was worrying about the road, which was slippery after a snowfall. He couldn't find much to say to his mother. And once they had arrived, he deliberately kept the conversation to trivia — the verifying of tickets, checking of departure times, weighing of baggage. Her baggage was fourteen pounds overweight. It didn't make sense; all she had were her clothes and a few small gifts for her sisters. "Why is it so heavy?" Hassan asked. "What have you got in there?" But his mother only said, "I don't know," and straightened her shawl, looking elsewhere. Hassan bent to open a tooled-leather suitcase. Inside he found three empty urn-shaped wine bottles, the permanent-press sheets from her bed, and a sample box of detergent that had come in yesterday's mail. "Listen," said Hassan, "do you know how much I'd have to pay to fly these things over? What's the matter with you?"

"I wanted to show my sisters," his mother said.

"Well, forget it. Now, what else have you got?"

But something about her — the vague, childlike eyes set upon some faraway object — made him give in. He opened no more bags. He even regretted his sharpness, and when her flight was announced he hugged her closely and kissed the top of her head. "Go with God," he said.

"Goodbye, Hassan."

She set off down the corridor by herself, straggling behind a line of businessmen. They all wore hats. His mother wore her scarf, and of all the travelers she alone, securely kerchiefed and shawled, setting her small shoes resolutely on the gleaming tiles, seemed undeniably a foreigner.

WILLIAM S. WILSON

Anthropology: What is Lost in Rotation

(FROM ANTAEUS)

> . . . we take it that:
> mouth : ear : : vagina : anus
> — LÉVI-STRAUSS,
> *The Raw and the Cooked*
>
> *bouche : oreille : : vagin : anus*
> —*Le Cru et le Cuit*

THAT YOU WANT to give me pleasure gives me as much pleasure as what you do to give me pleasure.

Translation: you don't feel satisfied.

No, I don't.

Don't tell me what you think I want to hear.

I am pleased by your desire to please me.

But you are unsatisfied.

Yes, I am.

Now you have told me the truth, and I realize that I prefer the truth, at least the truth I would have suspected anyway, to what I think I want to hear, and I am proud of myself again, and forgive you as I respect myself, and now I love you again. But you are still unsatisfied.

You weren't thinking about me when you were inside me. You were trying to distract me so that you could be alone. So don't complain that I wasn't with you.

When I married an Englishwoman studying English literature

at the Sorbonne I underestimated the difficulties. Don't under-estimate yourself. Actually I was thinking about an Indian boy I want to arrest for murder.

Yes, you made love to me as though you were looking for a clue.

I think the accused is entitled to one quotation: "Men owe us what we imagine they will give us. We must forgive them this debt." Simone Weil.

I have a quotation too. "I also am other than what I imagine myself to be. To know this is forgiveness." *"Moi aussi, je suis autre que ce que je m'imagine être. Le savoir, c'est le pardon."*

But then you can't arrest him, you have no evidence.

The evidence is that four structural anthropologists have died, apparently poisoned, and each of them had done field work in his village.

But you say they worked there a decade ago, when he was a child. Where is the motive?

The motive is mine. I can't leave the mystery of four similar simultaneous deaths.

Why do you think the murderer is this Indian?

Why do you think this Indian lives in Paris?

He has told you. He worked his way to Paris translating for anthropologists and missionaries in an attempt to discover his father, the anthropologist who left him with nothing but the name Emile. You need a criminal, and out of that need you have con-structed Emile.

I have many needs besides the need for a criminal. These four victims were once a model team of anthropologists, two husbands and two wives, able to study both the men and the women inti-mately. A great loss to the Sorbonne. Emile intends to study their book for patterns to use when he returns to rebuild his society.

Where is he going to study anthropology, in prison?

No, Emile is not going to prison. We don't have enough evi-dence to hold him. He wants to find out who named him, that is, who his father was, and he wants to learn enough about his peo-ple to restore them to the rightness he thinks he remembers from his childhood. He may also solve the mystery of the murders.

You are letting him go free so that he can convict himself? The procedure sounds too literary to be legal.

He has chosen to play detective himself, searching for an anthropologist who left him a name, whether sardonically or tenderly, who knows? And why does he search for him? To understand himself? To kill his father? I don't know. I am too old to learn anthropology, yet someone has to find clues to the murders. Emile has come to Paris looking for the secret of himself. If he finds the murderer for us, and the murderer is himself, then we may be able to help him.

If he committed the murders, why doesn't he confess?

You have touched upon the mystery. Emile is capable of killing, but I'm not sure that he can be the murderer because so far he is incapable of understanding murder. The clue I look for in a homicide is the clue that tells me which suspect is capable of murder.

Yes, since I can hide nothing from you, I do almost nothing that I would have to hide from you except the doing of nothing that I would have to hide from you. I lie about nothing except why I never lie to you. I would not be able to conceal from you that I had killed a man, but I would try to conceal from you that I am capable of killing.

Perhaps you will help Emile to understand.

Me? What would I say to him?

He will be living in our apartment. The condition under which he can remain in Paris and attend the Sorbonne is that he be French. The government cannot hold him indefinitely without charges. You and I are adopting him as our son.

I wonder how he can trust you since you think he killed four people. Suppose he kills you?

I don't see that he would have a motive. He is not a savage.

I don't know. I don't think that anyone outside Paris can understand love and murder as we do.

But Emile loves Paris, and loving Paris is a murderous education.

Inspector Mirouet?

Yes, Emile?

I am writing a paper on anderology. Perhaps you would correct the grammar?

I don't know the word, Emile. *Anthropology*, perhaps?

No, Inspector. The question is the origins of cooking over a fire.

I thought that Lévi-Strauss had solved that forty years ago. Yes, of course, but I have some new materials coded for the computer. I am afraid that they will not seem polite. They will weather that shock at the Sorbonne, Emile. I understand that, Inspector. But my paper will seem rude to the English, perhaps. Then we will not show it to the English, Emile, unless you want my wife's help with it. Perhaps you should tell me first. The word for a hot coal carried to a fireplace to start a fire is *bitch*. The English will take that in stride, Emile. And the bitch is carried to the firedogs, just as the female is carried to the male dog to be lined. The French for firedog is *andier*, from the Gaulish *andero*, young bull. The origins of fire are shown in the image of carrying a bitch to a dog for breeding. The female comes to the male to start a fire. The male goes to the female to put out a fire. I will explain the story of Europa and the bull, and the scene on the Vaphio gold cup. Are you laughing at me, Inspector?

No, Emile. I am merely recalling how Madame Mirouet and I met.

Is it polite for me to ask how you met, Inspector?

Of course, Emile. Haven't I told you? I was a student of anderology doing field work at the Sorbonne.

Inspector Mirouet?

Yes, Emile?

I have found a curious gap in Professor Lévi-Strauss' information.

You know something that he didn't know?

I doubt that. But he professes not to know the meaning of the word *reyuno*. I have found the word in my memory, and also in the computer data bank. It is a rude word for penis.

I never heard the word, Emile. Perhaps Lévi-Strauss simply didn't know it.

I won't believe that, Inspector. Anyone who worked along the coast would have learned that meaning. The apparent ignorance of the word must be an example of upward displacement of ignorance. Not to understand the word, which seems to me impossible, is not to understand the thing, which is possible. When this upward displacement is redisplaced downward, and then upward again, something will be out of line, but the system will seek to preserve its coherence even if it loses correspondence with the facts.

Where did you learn to think like this, Emile?

At the Sorbonne, Inspector, reading Lévi-Strauss.

Inspector?

Yes, Emile?

I want to return to Brazil now.

That isn't possible, Emile. We aren't ready. Has anything frightened you?

I am going to hide it from you, Inspector.

What is it, Emile. Has someone hurt you?

I have hurt myself, Inspector. I will never be able to restore my people to their beautiful ways. I have found an upward displacement in the system of structural anthropology which I was going to use to rebuild my society with simplicity and symmetry, and the whole system is distorted by an error in rotation. I can use none of it.

Explain it, Emile. Perhaps it isn't as bad as you think.

I will be patient, but this spoils everything. Damn Rousseau.

What does Rousseau have to do with it, Emile? I can't keep up with you.

You know that Rousseau suffered from enuresis and hypospadias.

Enuresis I know, but what is hypospadias?

A deformity of the penis. The urethra opens on its under surface. I am afraid that after Rousseau's hypospadias subsequent upward displacements in French thought are rotated incorrectly.

This is a strong charge, Emile. Are you sure of the evidence?

I am afraid that I am.

Do not be reluctant to expose error, Emile. We will be pleased to learn our mistakes.

But I am not pleased to tell you. My people, my family, are scattered in hospitals and reservations, and I was going to reunite them.

You may yet, Emile. Perhaps the mistake can be corrected.

You are patriotic, Inspector, but this logical scandal is not easily mitigated. Lévi-Strauss knew it, too. In *From Honey to Ashes* he asks, "Which organ, then, can be defined as posterior and high in a system in which the posterior, low position is occupied by the anus, and the anterior, high position by the mouth? We have no choice: it can only be the ear . . ." He goes on to write that ". . . vomiting is the opposite correlative of coitus, and defecation the opposite correlative of auditory communications," but the ear is not in front, like the vagina, or behind, like the anus. My grandmother held me by the ears, or pulled my nose; sometimes she patted me on the crown of my head. We know the back of the head from an ear. The rest of mythologic is distorted by the translation of Rousseau's urethra, and I am afraid that I can be of no help here, and of no help to my people. But at least I know what I must do next.

What are you going to do?

With your permission, Inspector, have my occipital bone x-rayed and enroll in medical school.

Inspector?

Yes, Emile?

Let me read these x-rays with you. Notice this dark spot on the occipital. Here it is, from the left. And here, from the right. Do you see it?

Just a shadow, Emile. I can't tell if there is something there or something missing.

A scar, Inspector. Here, you can feel it on my head when you know where it is.

Yes, I feel something. What can you figure out from the scar, Emile?

The four anthropologists could not determine what occurred in the huts to which women retired for childbirth, where a mother and child stayed for a few weeks. The myths require a hole in the occipital region. When a male baby was born, the mother trephined a hole in the back of the head and removed some brain tissue.

How can you know this from Paris, Emile?

Because that is where the coroner's reports are. You think that I hid behind potted palms and blew poisoned darts at four professors. But the clues you needed to their deaths were there at the Sorbonne, in their behavior.

I did not see them, and the doctors did not recognize the symptoms of a disease.

They trembled, they swayed and spun around as though they

were doing a parody of a native dance, they became stiff, threw fits, and then went into comas and died.

Did any of your people die that way?

I trust my memory that the most powerful man in the village would start having seizures, and would think himself possessed by that spirit we named "the weather of elsewhere." Then he would die, and life would continue like a story about life until another man became boastful, and he would sicken and die. This happened so slowly that I don't know if it broke the rhythm of our lives or gave our lives their rhythm.

Have you figured out the cause?

I can only speculate. The highlanders of New Guinea were cannibals and suffered deaths similar to those of the anthropologists. The disease is called *kuru,* and is caused by a slow-acting virus. Research has been slow, for animals infected with the virus can take three or four years before they show any symptoms.

Your people are not cannibals, however.

No, but I have had the skulls of children from my tribe examined, and have received reports from laboratories and museums that have skulls of Indians. Lévi-Strauss was right. Logic requires an orifice high and posterior, and since one was not there, the mother, hidden in the hut after the birth of the baby, drilled a small hole in the back of the baby's head.

For God's sake why?

They could not know. I suppose they had to complete a pattern: "... *les mythes se pensent dans les hommes, et à leur insu."* They would extract some brain tissue, mix it in a dish, and serve it to certain men.

To kill them?

No, the women could not make that connection. After all, although the disease acts swiftly once it reveals itself, it can take years to develop.

Do you know how your people caught the disease?

I don't know that it is a disease. A virus that is benign is transferred from brain to brain and deteriorates into molecules of RNA without protein coats, or into naked strands of DNA. The virus may be innocent, but something can happen to it when it enters the host cell. The host cell seems to transform a virus into a viroid, and years later death ensues. So your four anthropologists . . .

Yes, Emile?

Your four anthropologists wanted to participate in the lives of my people in order to understand them. They might have told the men of my tribe that they were longing to taste some dish, and neither the men nor the anthropologists could have known that the women had mixed in the brains of children.

Why did no one figure this out?

The anthropologists were studying my people synchronically. They missed the narrative of disease, although they brought it with them here to Paris, where they created a mystery about my people and about me.

You seem to have solved the mystery, Emile.

I don't know, Inspector. When I return to Brazil I will do research. I think that there may be a transmissible canine encephalopathy, one that slowly destroys the cerebellum and the hypothalamus.

You are formidable, Emile. I accuse you of murder, and you solve a mystery and construct hypotheses about disease that might save other lives. Are you bitter, Emile? Do you seek revenge?

No, no revenge. My people are murdered, hospitalized, or thrown together on reservations. I would like to find them and kindle a family of families that would compose itself like a flame. I don't know the possibilities. But I remember a place that I will take them to where the water falls from a cliff into a pool. In the cave under the waterfall we will kindle a fire. And I will explain to them that our lives should, as the water and flame do, find their own patterns.

An ambitious program, Emile, inventing a society.

I don't intend to invent it. I mean only to be the improbable accident that starts the fire that continues to burn according to the probabilities of fire. I want to found a village in the forest. The nights are long under the waterfall around the fire, just as they are in Paris. I will tell stories of my journey to Paris, and I will tell them about Jean-Jacques Rousseau and the night a girl with a withered nipple tried to seduce him.

You hate us more than we hate ourselves, Emile.

No, Inspector. I was reading that story when I paused to think about asymmetry, and while scratching the back of my head, I felt the little scar that gave me an idea.

And your father, Emile? You came to Paris to find out who named you. The anthropologist who probably was your father. Have you found him?

No, Inspector. The stories of young men searching for their fathers are stories of young men who through their adventures father themselves by doing for themselves what they hoped a father would do for them. You adopted me, half-Indian, half-comprador, after you found me parading up and down waiting for someone to read me as a clue. I was not looking for my father. He died of a slow-acting virus, if I remember his death correctly. I named myself Emile. What would I need a father for?

Emile.

Yes, Madame.

What are you reading?

A book about Brazil. The unexplored parts are photographed by satellites. I am thinking about a place where my people will be safe.

I am married to an Inspector of Police in Paris, Emile, and I don't feel safe.

The case is somewhat different. Where is the Inspector tonight, Madame?

He has been called to Marseilles, Emile. I don't know why. He'll return tomorrow.

And what are you reading, Madame?

Actually I was looking for two passages I had thought to read aloud to you. They remind me of your descriptions of the life you hope to start in Brazil. Let me take off these earrings and then I'll read them to you.

Why do you remove your earrings?

Haven't you heard the Inspector say to me, "A Frenchwoman, after she has finished dressing, always removes one piece of jewelry."

But you are not French, Madame.

A point I invariably make to him, Emile. Let me read you the passages, and then I want you to tell me about the cave, the waterfall, and the fire.

I am ready to listen, Madame.

Coleridge wrote, "*Most of my readers will have observed a small water-insect on the surface of rivulets, which throws a cinque-spotted shadow fringed with prismatic colours on the sunny bottom of the brook; and will have noticed, how the little animal wins its way up against the stream, by alternate pulses of active and passive motion, now resisting the current, and now yielding to it in order to gather strength and a momentary* fulcrum *for a further propulsion. This is no unapt emblem of the mind's self-experience in the act of thinking.*"

I think, Madame, that you would make a creditable Indian.

I haven't found it easy being an Englishwoman in Paris, Emile.

Yet Paris is a seductive city.

Then you understand me, Emile?

Yes, Madame.

I have another passage to read to you first. It describes you. Coleridge wrote of a tree, "*At the same moment it strikes its roots and unfolds its leaves, absorbs and respires, steams forth its cooling vapor and finer fragrance, and breathes a repairing spirit, at once the food and tone of the atmosphere, into the atmosphere that feeds it.*"

I can't understand English when it is read aloud to me, Madame, but I will take the water-insect as my totem, and tell my people a story about an imaginative woman who seduces an Indian boy with metaphors.

Emile?

Don't turn around.

I want to hold you. With you I don't feel sensations; I feel you.

Look out the window at the lime tree. Have you decided who I am?

No, I don't recognize you, yet I know what you are. You are immediacy.

Don't turn around. Look out the window and tell me what you see.

I see a lime tree in the first light of a Parisian dawn. I see Paris filled to the brim.

Don't look back.

Your hands don't hesitate.

I don't look behind us.

Your hands on my hips. I know who you are now and why I'm not afraid. You aren't afraid of yourself.

Don't turn around. I am looking past your head at what you see through the window. I can feel that you enjoy my hands.

I do. I like your fingers across my hips and your kisses on my back.

Don't turn around.

I want to see you but I can wait. I want to feel your hands

there, yes, like that. I was going to forgive you for not giving me
this pleasure that I had imagined for myself. I no longer need to.
I have become as immediate to myself as you are to me, yet now
your immediacy equals your indeterminacy. Let me turn around
to see you.

No, I want to stand behind you, touching you with my fingers.

Do what I asked you to, Emile.

Only if you forgive yourself for imagining that you could live
there.

I forgive myself when your flesh touches mine. You know what
I want to hear.

You should ask.

I want to hear about the waterfalls and the streams and the
trees, and the families you will gather to lead into the jungle. I
want you to describe the splash of the falls, the deep cave, the
flames that are kindled and that flicker and waver and renew their
shape, and the skills you use, without bridges or boats, to help
each other across impassable streams.

. . . And not enough food, twenty exhausted people, crying
children, cold, damp.

Then what is it, Emile? I am not sentimental, I wear expensive
but sensible shoes, and I am not going to become an Indian.

What do you feel now?

Strange. The feeling is so vivid, yet it disappears when I reach
for it with words.

Don't reach. Let it surround you. Then you have it, when it
has you. Stand up to it.

You can leave now, Emile. I know enough not to turn around.

Are you satisfied with that?

Yes, strangely, I am. I wonder why you have done this for me.

That is the question I will leave you with, and then I'll never
have left you, and that will be to perform yet another act that
must make you wonder why I have done it, and thus you will
always feel me behind you, one hand over your *bouche*, like this,
with a finger on your teeth, and the other hand over your *vagin*,
like this, and me whispering into your hair *une pensée de derrière*,
that I could crush your skull against the window frame.

Biographical Notes

Biographical Notes

FREDERICK BUSCH was born in Brooklyn in 1941 and now lives in Pool-ville, New York, with his wife Judith and their two sons. His books are *I Wanted a Year Without Fall, Breathing Trouble, Hawkes: A Guide to His Fictions, Manual Labor, Domestic Particulars* and *The Mutual Friend*. He teaches literature at Colgate University.

PRICE CALDWELL holds a Ph.D. from Tulane University and teaches crea-tive writing and American literature courses at Mississippi State Uni-versity. He has published stories in *Georgia Review, New Orleans Review, Mississippi Review* and other magazines and an article on Wallace Ste-vens in the *Journal of English and Germanic Philology*. He is presently working on a book on Stevens and a novel.

JOHN CHEEVER was born in Quincy, Massachusetts, in 1912, received his only formal education at Thayer Academy, served four years in the army, and has published novels and collections of short stories. The story that appears in this volume is part of *Falconer*, his tenth book. He lives with his wife in an old farmhouse in the Hudson Valley.

ANN COPELAND holds a Ph.D. in English from Cornell and has taught English in several high schools and colleges in the United States and Canada. Her stories have appeared in *The Texas Quarterly, Canadian Fiction Magazine*, and *Western Humanities Review*. She presently lives in New Brunswick, Canada, and is completing a collection of short stories.

JOHN WILLIAM CORRINGTON took his D.Phil. at the University of Sussex in Brighton, England, and his J.D. at Tulane University School of Law. His work includes three novels, four volumes of poetry, and a collec-tion of stories. Last year, one of his stories, "The Actes and Monu-ments," appeared in *The Best American Short Stories 1976*, and in *Prize Stories: The O. Henry Awards*. He is presently working in political philos-ophy and jurisprudence. He practices law in New Orleans.

PHILIP DAMON was raised up and down the East Coast in the 1940's and 1950's. He was educated at Gettysburg College and later at the University of Iowa Writers' Workshop, where he was a Teaching and Writing Fellow. His stories have appeared in *Transatlantic Review, Antaeus, Ararat,* Ball State *Forum, Cimarron Review, The Iowa Review,* and other quarterlies. Since 1968 he has been a member of the creative writing faculty at the University of Hawaii.

LESLIE EPSTEIN is the author of the novel *P.D. Kimerakov* and a book of novellas and stories, *The Steinway Quintet: Plus Four,* from which "The Steinway Quintet" is taken. He is a Professor of English at Queens College, CUNY, though he is spending this year writing a novel on a Guggenheim Fellowship. He has also been a Rhodes Scholar, a Fulbright Fellow, and received a grant from the National Endowment of the Arts. He lives in New York with his wife and three children.

EUGENE K. GARBER is a former student and teacher at the University of Iowa Writers' Workshop and now teaches at Western Washington State College. He has published some thirty short stories that have appeared in such magazines as the *Hudson Review* and *The Iowa Review.* He is presently putting together a collection of his work.

PATRICIA HAMPL is a poet who has recently begun to write fiction. "Look at a Teacup" is her first published story. In 1976 she was awarded a National Endowment for the Arts Fellowship (for poetry) which she used to travel in the United States and Europe. She lives in her hometown, St. Paul, Minnesota.

BAINE KERR was born in 1946 in Houston. He has degrees in English from Stanford University and the University of Denver, and is completing a law degree at the University of Denver. His writing has been published in the *Denver Quarterly, Co-Evolution Quarterly, Big Rock Candy Mountain,* and *Place,* where he was an editor. An essay on N. Scott Momaday will appear soon in *Southwest Review.* Mr. Kerr lives with his wife, Cindy, and daughter, Dara, in Boulder, Colorado, precisely where the plains meet the Rockies.

JACK MATTHEWS is Professor of English at Ohio University and the author of more than one hundred published short stories as well as numerous poems, essays, articles, and reviews. He has also published eight books, the latest of which is *Collecting Rare Books for Pleasure and Profit.* His novel *Hanger Stout, Awake!* has just been reprinted in paperback. Mr. Matthews received a Guggenheim Fellowship in 1974–75.

STEPHEN MINOT is the author of *Chill of Dusk,* a novel, and *Crossings,* a collection of short stories. His work has appeared in fourteen periodicals, including *The Atlantic, Harper's, Playboy, The Virginia Quarterly Re-*

view, and *The North American Review*. They have been translated into German, French, and Flemish and have been reprinted in England. He is also the author of *Three Genres*, a college text on writing, and is co-editor with Robley Wilson, Jr., of *Three Stances of Modern Fiction*, a critical anthology. He has received a Saxton Memorial Fellowship, served as Writer in Residence at The Johns Hopkins University, 1974–75, and received a Fellowship from the National Endowment for the Arts for 1976–77. He has recently been promoted to Full Professor at Trinity College, Hartford, Connecticut, where he has taught since 1959. "A Passion for History" appears in modified form in his recently completed novel, *Ghost Images*.

CHARLES NEWMAN's publications include the novels *New Axis, The Promise-keeper*, and the three novellas *There Must Be More to Love Than Death*, as well as the autobiographical *Child's History of America*, which won the Zabel Award from the National Institute of Arts and Letters. He has also published short fiction and criticism in a number of periodicals and was founder and editor of the *TriQuarterly Review*, 1964–1974. He has received fellowships from the Rockefeller and Guggenheim foundations and the National Endowment for the Arts, and teaches at Johns Hopkins University. Currently he is breeding a new strain of hunting dog in the Blue Ridge Mountains and working on several novels.

JOYCE CAROL OATES was born in 1938 and grew up in the country outside Lockport, New York. She was graduated from Syracuse University in 1960 and received her Master's Degree in English from the University of Wisconsin. From the start of her writing career Miss Oates has earned high literary awards, among them a Guggenheim Fellowship, the Richard and Hinda Rosenthal Foundation Award of the National Institute of Arts and Letters, and the Lotos Club Award of Merit. For her novel *Them* she won the National Book Award in 1970. Her novel *Do With Me What You Will* was a major selection of the Literary Guild of America. Her latest novel, *Childwold*, was published in 1976, and a collection of stories, *Night-Side*, in the fall of 1977. Miss Oates already has had published, in addition to eight novels, nine volumes of short stories (many of which have been widely anthologized in literary and mass-circulation magazines), two volumes of critical essays, and four volumes of poetry. Four of her plays have been produced in New York.

TIM O'BRIEN is the author of *If I Die in a Combat Zone*, a war memoir, and *Northern Lights*, a novel. His work has appeared in *Shenandoah, Redbook, Denver Quarterly, Playboy, The Massachusetts Review*, and other magazines. He has received a National Endowment for the Arts Fellowship and a Massachusetts Arts and Humanities Foundation Award. The story in this volume is the opening passage of a novel, *Going After Cacciato,* to be published in 1978.

Tom Robbins is the author of two popular novels, *Another Roadside Attraction* and *Even Cowgirls Get the Blues,* and lots of love letters to women with names like Terrie, Holly, and Margy. He hoboes in and out of a small town in Washington State.

William Saroyan was born in Fresno, California, in 1908. His first book, *The Daring Young Man on the Flying Trapeze and Other Stories,* appeared in 1934, following publication of the title story in *Story* magazine. After forty-four years he is still devoted to the short story form, in all its inexhaustable variety. A recent work, *After Forty Years/The Daring Young Man on the Flying Trapeze,* contains in addition to the twenty-six stories in the original book, a daily journal covering seventy-four days, and seventy-four stories, literary larks, and fables, not unlike "A Fresno Fable."

John Sayles has written two novels, *Pride of the Bimbos* in 1975 and *Union Dues* in 1977. His stories have appeared in the *O. Henry Prize Stories* and *The Atlantic.* He presently lives in Santa Barbara, California, where he is at work on another novel, more stories, and screenplays.

William S. Wilson graduated from the University of Virginia, where he majored in the philosophy of science, and received a Ph.D. from Yale University in English literature. His numerous articles on painting and sculpture and his stories have appeared in *Antaeus, New Directions, Tri-Quarterly* and *Paris Review,* and he has just completed a collection of stories, *Why I Don't Write Like Franz Kafka.* He teaches in New York where he lives with his two daughters and one son.

Anne Tyler has recently published her seventh novel, *Earthly Possessions.* She lives in Baltimore with her husband and two children.

The Yearbook of the American Short Story

January 1 to December 31, 1976

Roll of Honor, 1976

DIXON, STEPHEN
Dog Days. South Carolina Review, April.
DUBUS, ANDRE
Contrition. North American Review, Winter.

EDMONDS, DALE
Crispus Attucks Falls.   Quartet, Winter.
EDWARDS, MARGARET
The Disappointment.   Virginia Quarterly, Winter.
ENGBERG, SUSAN
Pastorale.   Sewanee   Review, Summer.

FETLER, ANDREW
Shadows on the Water. American Review, 4, April.
FISCHER, DAVID
The Life of Elizabeth Danton. Carolina Quarterly, Spring–Summer.
FORD, RICHARD
In Desert Waters. Esquire, August.
FRANCIS, H. E.
A Circle of Light. Ascent, Vol. 2, No. 1.

GARLINGTON, JACK
Clinker. Southern Humanities Review, Fall.
GIBBONS, ROBERT
Slaves' Auction. Southern Review, Spring.
GOGGIN, MARGARET
Chiaroscuro. North American Review, Fall.
GOLDBERG, LESTER
The Survivor. Literary Review, Fall.
GORDON, CAROLINE
The Strangest Day in the Life of Captain Meriwether Lewis as Told to His Eighth Cousin, Once Removed. Southern Review, Spring.
GOTTLIEB, ELAINE
The Woman Who Was Absent. Southern Review, Spring.

GRAY, FRANCINE DU PLESSIX
Tribe. New Yorker, May 31.
GURGANUS, ALLAN
Communiqué. Atlantic, September.

HALL, JAMES BAKER
A Sense of the Blind Side. Western Humanities Review, Autumn.
HALLEY, ANNE
1937: Beatrice, the Blind Child, the Hope and Fear of Transformations. Shenandoah, Spring.
HASHIM, JAMES
The Party. Kansas Quarterly, Winter.
HEEGER, SUSAN
After Dark. Shenandoah, Spring.
HERRIN, LAMAR
The Rookie Season. Paris Review, Summer.
HORNE, LEWIS B.
What Do Ducks Do in Winter? Ascent, Vol. I, No. 3.

JOHNSON, CHARLES
Ox-Herding Tale. Antaeus, 24, Winter.
JUST, WARD
Honor Power Riches Fame & the Love of Women. Atlantic, October.

KANEMOTO, GAYLE
Expecting Amy. Hawaii Review, Spring.
KAPLAN, JOHANNA
Not All Jewish Families Are Alike. Commentary, June.
KOCH, MICHAEL
A Fine and Dandy Breakaway. Four Quarters, Spring.
KRANES, DAVID
Sight. North American Review, Summer.
KRAUSE, JO NEACE
Consumers' Wants. Yale Review, Spring.

LAVERS, NORMAN
  Process. Ohio Review, Winter.
LAVIN, MARY
  Eterna. New Yorker, March 8.
LEFFLAND, ELLA
  Last Courtesies. Harper's, July.
LEWIS, CLAYTON W.
  Children of Esau. Virginia Quarterly, Autumn.

MACLEOD, ALISTAIR
  The Closing Down of Summer. Fiddlehead, Fall.
MAJOR, J. W., JR.
  Friends and Lovers. Denver Quarterly, Spring.
MATTHEWS, JACK
  The Visionary Land. Michigan Quarterly Review, Spring.
MATYSHAK, STANLEY
  The Renaissance Man of Television. Kansas Quarterly, Spring.
MAXWELL, WILLIAM
  The Thistles in Sweden. New Yorker, June 21.
MAYHALL, JANE
  Islands. Yale Review, Summer.
MERWIN, W. S.
  The Element. New Yorker, October 4.
MILLER, J. L.
  Royce Simmons. South Dakota Review, Autumn.
MILLER, WARREN C.
  Fabricator. Quartet, Winter.
MILLMAN, JOAN
  The Effigy. Carolina Quarterly, Spring–Summer.
MURRAY, JOHN F.
  O'Phelan's Daemonium. New Yorker, March 24.

NELSON, KENT
  One Turned Wild. Cimarron Review, January.
  Spring Calf. Transatlantic Review, 57, October.

NEUGEBOREN, JAY
  An Orphan's Tale. Moment, May–June.
  Monkeys and Cowboys. Present Tense, Summer.
NIATUM, DUANE
  Crow's Sun. Transatlantic Review, Nos. 55/56, May.

OATES, JOYCE CAROL
  The Tryst. Atlantic, August.
O'BRIEN, TIM
  Speaking of Courage. Massachusetts Review, Summer.
O'NEILL, KEVIN
  The Pensioner. Carolina Quarterly, Spring–Summer.
OZICK, CYNTHIA
  Bloodshed. Esquire, January.

PERERA, VICTOR
  Don Chepe. Antioch Review, Vol. 34, Nos. 3 & 4.

RAHMANN, PAT
  The Comfort of Strangers. Transatlantic Review, 53/54.
RITTER, ERIKA
  A Quiet Little Dinner. Fiddlehead, Fall.
ROSENBERG, L. M.
  Memory. Atlantic, November.
ROTHBERG, ABRAHAM
  Under the El. Saturday Evening Post, November.

SAROYAN, WILLIAM
  The Duel. New Yorker, June 14.
  Fire. New Yorker, November 15.
SCHAEFFER, SUSAN FROMBERG
  Destinies. Denver Quarterly, Autumn.
SCHAFER, WILLIAM J.
  Rhythm and Blues. Carleton Miscellany, Spring–Summer.
SCHIFFMAN, CARL
  The Sweet Emily. Transatlantic Review, Nos. 55/56, May.

SCHROCK, GLADDEN
Fragments of a Killdeer. Massachusetts Review, Autumn.

SCHROEDER, ANDREAS
One Tide Over. Canadian Fiction,
Winter.

SCOTT, SYDNEY
Act of Love. Four Quarters, Spring.

SEABURG, ALAN
The Rape. Literary Review, Fall.

SHULMAN, SONDRA
Portrait of Plotkin. Antioch Review,
Vol. 34, Nos. 3 & 4.

SILMAN, ROBERTA
Debut. Atlantic, January.

SINGER, ISAAC BASHEVIS
The Power of Darkness. New
Yorker, February 2.

SLOMKA, ANNE
Down Elmyra's Road. Fiddlehead,
Fall.

STERN, RICHARD
The Ideal Address. Harper's,
September.

STREITER, AARON
Death Song: My Friends. South Dakota Review, Summer.

STUART, JESSE
Beginning and End of the Circle.
Kansas Quarterly, Summer–Fall.

TEILHET-WALDORF, SARAL
Fear. Commentary, June.

TEITEL, NATHAN
Adrift in J. Alfred Prufrock. Atlantic, March.

THOMAS, JAMES
Christmas in Calpe. Cimarron Review, Fall.

TOPEROFF, SAM
The Chinese Puzzle Race. Atlantic,
October.

TRENIN, MARINA
The Ordinary Day. North American
Review, Spring.

TRETHEWEY, ERIC
The Grammar of Silence. Fiddlehead, Spring.

TY-CASPER, LINDA
Triptych for a Ruined Altar. Univer-
sity of Windsor Review, Fall–
Winter.

UNDERWOOD, JERRY
Crossing Nebraska. Denver Quarterly, Summer.

VEDER, BOB
Father of the King. Literary Review,
Fall.

WEST, THOMAS A., JR.
Dreams and Wishes. Western Humanities Review, Spring.

YATES, RICHARD
Thieves. Ploughshares, Vol. 3, No.
1.

II. Foreign Authors

AICHINGER, ILSE
Herod. Trans. by Derk Wynand.
Malahat Review, January.

BEN-NER, YITCHAK
Alexander the Great. Trans. by
Richard Flantz. Antaeus, Winter.

BOULANGER, DANIEL
The Grand Turk. Trans. by Patsy
Southgate. Paris Review, Fall.

BUNIN, IVAN
Transfiguration. Trans. by Robert
L. Bowie. Colorado Quarterly,
Spring.

CORTÁZAR, JULIO
Silvia. Fiction, Vol. 4, No. 3.

KIELY, BENEDICT
Elm Valley Valerie. New Yorker, August 2.

MÁRQUES, GABRIEL GARCIA
The Autumn of the Patriarch. New Yorker, September 27.

NORRIS, LESLIE
Three Shots for Charlie Betson. Atlantic, September.

NYE, ROBERT
The Barber. Esquire, March.

PLUNKETT, JAMES
A Great Occasion. Sewanee Review, January–March.

RICARDOU, JEAN
Epitaph. Trans. by Erica Freiberg. Chicago Review, Winter.

ROSENAK, MICHAEL
The Blurred Letters. Response, Summer–Fall.

STEAD, CHRISTINA
Uncle Morgan at the Nats. Partisan Review, Vol. XLIII, No. 1.

Distinctive Short Stories, 1976

I. American Authors

ALFORD, EDNA
The Hoyer. Fiddlehead, Fall.
ANDERSON, JAMES E.
The Evil Seekers. Kansas Quarterly, Winter.
APPLE, MAX
My Real Estate. Georgia Review, Fall.
APRIMOZ, ALEXANDRE
Escargot. Fiddlehead, Winter.
ARDIZZONE, TONY
Idling. Carolina Quarterly, Fall.
ASCHER, SHEILA, and STRAUS, DENNIS
In Doubt. Chicago Review, Spring.

BANKS, RUSSELL
The New World. Ploughshares, Vol. 3, No. 2.
BARTHELME, DONALD
The Captured Woman. New Yorker, June 28.
BAUER, CHRISTOPHER
This Is Where I Work. Transatlantic Review, 57, October.
BEATTIE, ANN
The Lawn Party. New Yorker, July 5.
Secrets and Surprises. New Yorker, October 25.

BENNETT, JOHN
Conway and Blume. Remington Review, April.
BERGES, RUTH
Twilight Farewell. South Dakota Review, Autumn.
BIER, JESSIE
The Man on the Bicycle Machine. Virginia Quarterly, Autumn.
BRAZILLER, KAREN
He Didn't Seem to Have More Sense Than Patsy Gum. Fiction, Vol. 4, No. 3.
BREWSTER, ELIZABETH
Strangers. Fiddlehead, Spring.
BROUGHTON, T. ALLAN
The Harrowing. Four Quarters, Spring.
BROWNSON, CHARLES
The Student. Carolina Quarterly, Winter.
BUMPUS, JERRY
Lovers. Vagabond, Nos. 23–24.
BURT, DEIRDRE
An Old Apéritif. Ploughshares, Vol. 3, No. 1.

CARRIER, JEAN-GUY
No One's Fault. Canadian Fiction, Winter.

GOLDWATER, FRANCES
Burned Persons. Carolina Quarterly, Fall.
GREENBERG, ALVIN
The Origins of Life. Antioch Review, Vol. 34, Nos. 3 & 4.
GREENBERG, BARBARA
Settlements. Epoch, Spring.
GREENWOOD, ROBERT
Archetypes. Denver Quarterly, Winter.

HALPERIN, IRVING
The Restoration. South Dakota Review, Spring.
HAMMER, CHARLES
People Hell Bent. Kansas Quarterly, Winter.
HARDING, KATHERINE
Success Is Not a Destination but the Road to It. Atlantic, May.
HARNACK, CURTIS
Mentor. Southern Review, Summer.
HARPER, SUSAN
Time Out of Mind. North American Review, Spring.
HARTH, SYDNEY
Commanded to Love. Denver Quarterly, Autumn.
HAYES, GREGORY
Robert Johnson Sings the Blues, November 23, 1936. Kansas Quarterly, Summer–Fall.
HELPRIN, MARK
Letters From the Samantha. New Yorker, January 5.
HERMANN, RICK
The Sons of Porfirio Alonzo. Kansas Quarterly, Summer–Fall.
HORNE, LEWIS B.
A Doting Walk. Canadian Fiction Magazine, Spring.
HOWER, EDWARD
The Educated Billy Goats. Transatlantic Review, Nos. 55/56, May.
HUDDLE, DAVID
Gartley's Door. Carleton Miscellany, Spring–Summer.

JUDD, JOSEPH
Pupi. Antioch Review, Vol. 34, Nos. 3 & 4.
JUST, WARD
The Short War of Mr. and Mrs. Conner. Atlantic, June.

KALECHOFSKY, ROBERTA
Reflections From a Park Bench. Forum, Winter.
KINSELLA, W. P.
Caraway. Prism International, Spring.
KOMIE, LOWELL B.
The Butterfly. Kansas Quarterly, Winter.
KONECKY, EDITH
The Place. Aphra, Spring–Summer.
KRANES, DAVID
Hunt. North American Review, Summer.

LAMB, MARGARET
On the Edge of the Glacier. Yale Review, Autumn.
LA ROSA, PABLO
The Volunteer. Kansas Quarterly, Summer–Fall.
LAVIN, MARY
A House to Let. Ploughshares, Vol. 3, No. 1.
LEVIN, BOB
Open Man. Carolina Quarterly, Spring–Summer.
The Best Ride to New York. Massachusetts Review, Summer.
LONG, DAVID
The Flight of Hailstones. North American Review, Fall.
LUNDQUIST, RICHARD
Of Silence and Slow Time. Kansas Quarterly, Summer–Fall.

MCCLELLAND, KAY
Tabor's Pasture. Southern Review, Summer.
MCDONALD, WALTER R.
Snow Job. Quartet, Winter.

McNAMARA, EUGENE
    The Search for Sarah Grace. Canadian Fiction Magazine, Spring.
McNIECE, JAMES
    Toccata and Fugue for a Holiday. Chicago Review, Fall.
MALONE, MICHAEL PATRICK
    I Was Charlie Manson. Ascent, Vol. I, No. 3.
MARIN, DANIEL B.
    Winter's Tale. Carolina Quarterly, Winter.
MARSHALL, JOYCE
    The Accident. Fiddlehead, Winter.
    The Gradual Day. Canadian Fiction, Winter.
MARTINEZ, JOSÉ RAFAEL
    Rain. South Dakota Review, Summer.
MATANIE, STEPHEN
    Dancing. Chicago Review, Spring.
MESCHERY, JOAN
    The Daines' House. Western Humanities Review, Spring.
MIDWOOD, BART
    John O'Neill versus the Crown. Paris Review, Summer.
MINOT, STEPHEN
    Aye. Southern Review, Summer.
MOODY, R. BRUCE
    Primal Scene. Michigan Quarterly Review, Spring.

NELSON, KENT
    A Small Deception. Michigan Quarterly Review, Fall.
NIBBELINK, CYNTHIA
    Some Gangster. Green River Review, Vol. VII, No. 1.

OATES, JOYCE CAROL
    Hello Fine Day Isn't It. Malahat Review, April.
    The Giant Woman. Kansas Quarterly, Winter.
OBUCHOWSKI, PETER
    A Wisp of Roses. Kansas Quarterly, Winter.

ORR, JEAN
    Saturday Spring. Southern Review, Autumn.

PALEY, GRACE
    In the Garden. Fiction, Vol. 4, No. 2.
PAPALEO, JOE
    The Company. Epoch, Spring.
PETERSON, BRENDA
    Day Pass Away Like Smoke. Sewanee Review, Fall.
PETERSON, MARY
    Coming About. North American Review, Fall.
POPE, ROBERT
    The Pattern in the Blanket. Chicago Review, Fall.
POTREBENKO, HELEN
    Have a Nice Day. Prism International, Spring.

RATH, ROGER
    The Sportsman. Carleton Miscellany, Spring–Summer.
RAY, DAVID
    Under the Clock. Chariton Review, Spring.
REICH, DAVID
    The Puerto Rican Factory. Transatlantic Review, 53/54, February.
REID, BARBARA
    A Bird of Passage. Quartet, Spring–Summer.
RIMLER, WALTER
    Joaquin Murietta. Florida Quarterly, January.
ROBINSON, FRED MILLER
    The Infant Football Game. Massachusetts Review, Autumn.
ROBINSON, MARGARET A.
    Father's Day. Redbook, May.
ROBINSON, SONDRA
    The God of Snails. South Dakota Review, Winter.
ROGERS, THOMAS
    Prunes and Prisms. American Review, October.

ROOKE, CONSTANCE, and ROOKE, LEON
No Whistle Slow. Southern Review, Summer.

ROTHBERG, A. N.
A Funny Story to Be Told at Jeffrey's Wedding. Michigan Quarterly Review, Summer.

ROTHBERG, NAOMI
Family Life. North American Review, Spring.

SCHRAMM, D. G. H.
A Gallery of Castles. South Dakota Review, Autumn.

SCHWARTZ, LYNNE SHARON
Life Is An Adventure, with Risks. Transatlantic Review, No. 57, October.

SEABROOKE, DEBORAH S.
Late Crossing. Greensboro Review, Winter.

SELZ, THALIA
The Algerian Hook. Falcon, Spring.

SHAW, JOAN KATHERINE
The Bus Ride. Western Humanities Review, Spring

SHORT, DALE
Cider Apples. Southern Humanities Review, Spring.

SILBERT, LAYLE
The Dancing Lesson. Falcon, Spring.
Exotic Flies. South Dakota Review, Winter.

SILMAN, ROBERTA
For Reasons of Health. New Yorker, July 12.

SIMMONS, CHARLES
Certain Changes. American Review, 4, April.

SKEEN, PAMELA PAINTER
Sylvia. Ascent, Vol. 2, No. 1.
Knowing Is For Later. Southern Humanities Review, Winter.

SMITH, RAE-JOLENE
The Buried Self. Western Humanities Review, Summer.

SOBKOWSKY, FAYE
Mendel. Fiction, Vol. 4, No. 3.

SONG, CATHY
Beginnings. Hawaii Review, Spring.

SPEER, LAUREL
The Hundred Percent Black Steinway Piano. Remington Review, April.

SPENCER, ELIZABETH
Prelude to a Parking Lot. Southern Review, July.

SPINGARN, LAWRENCE P.
A Good Address. Colorado Quarterly, Autumn.

STAPLES, GEORGE
The Visit of the Djibli. Antaeus, Autumn.

STERLING, ABIGAIL
Eric. Transatlantic Review, 53/54.

STOCKANES, ANTHONY E.
Vandals. Ascent, Vol. 2, No. 1.

STOUT, ROBERT JOE
Bandol. Twigs, Spring.

SUMMERS, HOLLIS
A Hundred Paths. Epoch, Winter.

SUROWIECKI, JOHN
Finn in Sunset. Carolina Quarterly, Winter.

SWAN, MARY
Anna. Fiddlehead, Spring.

TAAFFE, GERALD
The Office Party. North American Review, Spring.

THOMAS, ANNABEL
The Pinning. Twigs, Fall.

THOMAS, JAMES
Paco and I at Sea. Esquire, September.

TRAPNELL, JUDSON B.
Evensong. Kansas Quarterly, Summer–Fall.

TRIVELPIECE, LAUREL
Good Works. Carleton Miscellany, Spring–Summer.

UPDIKE, JOHN
Love Song for a Mood Synthesizer. New Yorker, June 14.

VALE, KATHRYN
   First Fruits. Carleton Miscellany, Spring–Summer.
VALGARDSON, W. D.
   Celebration. University of Windsor Review, Spring–Summer.
   Trees. Ontario Review, Spring–Summer.
VIVANTE, ARTURO
   The Tenant. New Yorker, August 9.
VLASTOS, MARION
   Sea Story. Epoch, Fall.
VOGAN, SARA
   Mozart in the Afternoon. Cutbank, Spring.

WAIDNER, FREW
   Mise en Scene. South Dakota Review, Winter.
WAMPLER, MARTIN
   Rings on Her Toes. Transatlantic Review, 53/54.
WEAVER, GORDON
   The Engstrom Girls. Southern Review, Summer.
   Horse: Now. Quarterly West, Fall.
WEEKS, CARL S.
   A Process in the Weather of the Heart. Greensboro Review, Winter.

WHITE, JAMES P.
   Spread. Quartet, Winter.
WIEBE, DALLAS
   Jesse Graber. Falcon, Spring.
WILDMAN, JOHN HAZARD
   Under a Direct Demanding Sun. Southern Review, Winter.
WILLARD, NANCY
   Animals Running on a Windy Crown. American Review, October.
WILLIAMS, JOY
   The Trumpet Player. Antaeus, Spring.
   The Excursion. Partisan Review, Vol. XLIII, No. 2.
WILSON, DON
   The Tale of the Upright Man. Canadian Fiction Magazine, Spring.
WOLFF, TOBIAS
   Smokers. Atlantic, December.

YATES, RICHARD
   Thieves. Ploughshares, Vol. 3, No. 1.

ZAKARAS, PAUL
   But Someday You'll See. North American Review, Spring.
ZELVER, PATRICIA
   The Little Pub. Atlantic, June.

II. Foreign Authors

AKSENOV, VASILY
   Little Whale, A Varnisher of Reality. American Review, October.

BLANCHOT, MAURICE
   Death Sentence. Trans. by Lydia Davis. Georgia Review, Summer.
BODKER, CELIA
   Snow. Trans. by Nadia Christensen. South Dakota Review, Winter.

BOGUSLAVSKAYA, Z. B.
   The Change. Trans. by Terence Rickwood. Malahat Review, April.

FERRUCCI, FRANCO
   The Instructions of Desire. American Review, October.

GARSHIN, VSEVOLOD
   The Tale of the Rose and the Toad. Trans. by Eugene M. Kayden. Colorado Quarterly, Spring.

IK, KIM YONG
Village Wine. Harper's, May.

JHABVALA, R. PRAWER
A Very Special Fate. New Yorker,
March 29.

LISPECTOR, CLARICE
In Search of Dignity. Trans. by
Eloah F. Giacomelli. Malahat Re-
view, October.

LURIE, MORRIS
Repository. Antaeus, 24, Winter.

MATUTE, ANA MARIA
The Island. Trans. by Elaine Kerri-
gan Gurevitz. Malahat Review,
April.

MEACOCK, NORMA
Chun: Difficulty at the Beginning.
Transatlantic Review, Nos. 55/56,
May.

MORTIMER, PENELOPE
Granger's Life So Far. New Yorker,
March 22.

NARAYAN, R. K.
God and the Cobler. Playboy,
February.

NESCIO
Young Bucks. Trans. by Felix J.
Douma. Malahat Review, October.

O'BRIEN, FLANN
John Duffy's Brother. Antaeus,
Spring.

RHYS, JEAN
Goodbye Marcus, Goodbye Rose.
New Yorker, August 30.

SANSOM, WILLIAM
Windfall. Transatlantic Review 53/
54.

Addresses of American and Canadian Magazines Publishing Short Stories

Americas, Organization of American States, Washington, D.C. 20006

Ampersand Magazine, Ltd., 816 South Hancock Street, Philadelphia, Pennsylvania 19147

Antaeus, 1 West 30th Street, New York, New York 10001

Antioch Review, 212 Xenia Avenue, Yellow Springs, Ohio 45387

Apalachee Quarterly, P.O. Box 20106, Tallahassee, Florida 32304

Aphra, RFD, Box 355, Springtown, Pennsylvania 18081

Ararat, 109 East 40th Street, New York, New York 10016

Argosy, 205 East 42nd Street, New York, New York 10017

Arizona Quarterly, University of Arizona, Tucson, Arizona 85721

Arlington Quarterly, Box 366, University Station, Arlington, Texas 76010

Ascent, English Department, University of Illinois, Urbana, Illinois 61801

Aspen Leaves, Box 3185, Aspen, Colorado 81611

Atlantic Monthly, 8 Arlington Street, Boston, Massachusetts 02116

Aura, Box 348 NBSB, University Station, Birmingham, Alabama 35294

Bachy, 11317 Santa Monica Boulevard, West Los Angeles, California 90025

Boston University Journal, Box 357, Boston University Station, Boston, Massachusetts 02215

Brushfire, Box 9012 University Station, Reno, Nevada 89507

Canadian Fiction, 4248 Weisbrod Street, Prince George, British Columbia, Canada

Canadian Forum, 30 Front Street West, Toronto, Ontario, Canada

Capilano Review, 2055 Purcell Way, North Vancouver, British Columbia, Canada

Carleton Miscellany, Carleton College, Northfield, Minnesota 55057

Carolina Quarterly, P.O. Box 1117, Chapel Hill, North Carolina 27514

Chariton Review, Division of Language & Literature, Northeast Missouri State University, Kirksville, Missouri 63501

Chelsea, P.O. Box 5880, Grand Central Station, New York, New York 10017

Chicago Review, University of Chicago, Chicago, Illinois 60637

Cimmaron Review, 203B Morrill Hall, Oklahoma State University, Stillwater, Oklahoma 74074

Colorado Quarterly, University of Colorado, Boulder, Colorado 80303

Commentary, 165 East 56th Street, New York, New York 10022

Confrontation, English Department, Long Island University, Brooklyn, New York 11201

Connecticut Fireside, Box 5293, Hamden, Connecticut 06518

Contributor, 30 East Sprague, Spokane, Washington 99202

Cosmopolitan, 1775 Broadway, New York, New York 10019

The Critic, 180 North Wabash Avenue, Chicago, Illinois 60601

Cutbank, Department of English, University of Montana, Missoula, Montana 59801

Dark Horse, % Barnes, 47A Dana Street, Cambridge, Massachusetts 02138

December, Box 274, Western Springs, Illinois 60558

Denver Quarterly, University of Denver, Denver, Colorado 80210

Dogsoldier, East 323 Boone Street, Spokane, Washington 99202

Ellery Queen's Mystery Magazine, 229 Park Avenue South, New York, New York 10003

Epoch, 252 Goldwin Smith Hall, Cornell University, Ithaca, New York 14850

Esquire, 488 Madison Avenue, New York, New York 10022

Event (Canada), Doughlas College, P.O. Box 2503, New Westminster, British Columbia, Canada

Event (U.S.A.), 422 South Fifth Street, Minneapolis, Minnesota 55415

Falcon, Mansfield State College, Mansfield, Pennsylvania

Fantasy and Science Fiction, Box 271, Rockville Centre, New York 11571

The Fault, 41186 Alice Avenue, Fremont, California 94538

Fiction, Department of English, City College of New York, 138th Street and Convent Avenue, New York, New York 10031

Fiction International, Department of English, St. Lawrence University, Canton, New York 13617

Fiddlehead, Department of English, University of New Brunswick, New Brunswick, Canada

Forum, Ball State University, Muncie, Indiana 47302

Four Quarters, La Salle College, Philadelphia, Pennsylvania 19143

Gallery, 936 North Michigan Avenue, Chicago, Illinois 60611

Gallimaufry, 359 Frederick Street, San Francisco, California 94117

Georgia Review, University of Georgia, Athens, Georgia 30601
Gone Soft, Salem State College, Salem, Massachusetts 01970
Good Housekeeping, 959 Eighth Avenue, New York, New York 10019
Graffiti, Box 418, Lenoir Rhyne College, Hickory, North Carolina 28601
Green River Review, Box 594, Owensboro, Kentucky 42301
Greensboro Review, University of North Carolina, Box 96, McIver Building, Chapel Hill, North Carolina 27401
Harper's Bazaar, 572 Madison Avenue, New York, New York 10022
Harper's Magazine, 2 Park Avenue, New York, New York 10016
Hawaii Review, Hemenway Hall, University of Hawaii, Honolulu, Hawaii 96822
Hudson Review, 65 East 55th Street, New York, New York 10022
Husk, Cornell College, Mount Vernon, Iowa 52314
Intellectual Digest, 110 East 59th Street, New York, New York 10022
Iowa Review, University of Iowa, Iowa City, Iowa 52240
Jeffersonian Review, P.O. Box 3864, Charlottesville, Virginia 22903
Jesture Magazine, Thomas More College, Box 85, Covington, Kentucky 41017
Kansas Quarterly, Kansas State University, Manhattan, Kansas 66502
Ladies' Home Journal, 641 Lexington Avenue, New York, New York 10022
Laurel Review, West Virginia Wesleyan College, Buckbannon, West Virginia 26201
Lifestyle, 572 Madison Avenue, New York, New York 10022
Literary Review, Fairleigh Dickinson University, Teaneck, New Jersey 07666
Lotus, Department of English, Ohio University, Athens, Ohio 45701
Mademoiselle, 420 Lexington Avenue, New York, New York 10022
The Malahat Review, University of Victoria, Victoria, British Columbia, Canada
Massachusetts Review, University of Massachusetts, Amherst, Massachusetts 01002
Matrix, Box 510, Lennoxville, Quebec, Canada
McCall's, 230 Park Avenue, New York, New York 10017
MD, MD Publications, Inc., 30 East 60th Street, New York, New York 10022
Michigan Quarterly Review, University of Michigan, Ann Arbor, Michigan 48104
Mississippi Review, Box 37, Southern Station, University of Southern Mississippi, Hattiesburg, Mississippi 39401
Moment, 150 Fifth Avenue, New York, New York 10011
Mother Jones, 607 Market Street, San Francisco, California 94105
Ms., 370 Lexington Avenue, New York, New York 10017
Nantucket Review, P.O. Box 1444, Nantucket, Massachusetts 02554

National Jewish Monthly, 1640 Rhode Island Avenue, N.W., Washington, D.C. 20036

New Directions, 333 Sixth Avenue, New York, New York 10014

New Letters, University of Missouri, Kansas City, Missouri 64110

New Orleans Review, Loyola University, New Orleans, Louisiana 70118

New Renaissance, 9 Heath Road, Arlington, Massachusetts 02174

New River Review, Radford College Station, Radford, Virginia 24142

New Voices, P.O. Box 308, Clintondale, New York 12515

New Writers, 507 Fifth Avenue, New York, New York 10017

New Yorker, 25 West 43rd Street, New York, New York 10036

Nimrod, University of Tulsa, Tulsa, Oklahoma 74104

North American Review, University of Northern Iowa, Cedar Falls, Iowa 50613

Northern Minnesota Review, Bemidji State College, Bemidji, Minnesota 56601

Northwest Review, Erb Memorial Union, University of Oregon, Eugene, Oregon 97403

Occident, Eshleman Hall, University of California, Berkeley, California 94720

Ohio Journal, Department of English, Ohio State University, 164 West 17th Avenue, Columbus, Ohio 43210

Old Hickory Review, P.O. Box 1178, Jackson, Tennessee 38301

Ontario Review, 6000 Riverside Drive East, Windsor, Ontario, Canada

Paris Review, 45–39 171 Place, Flushing, New York 11358

Partisan Review, Rutgers University, 1 Richardson Street, New Brunswick, New Jersey 08903

Pathway Magazine, P.O. Box 1483, Charleston, West Virginia 25325

Penthouse, 909 Third Avenue, New York, New York 10022

Perspective, Washington University Post Office, St. Louis, Missouri 63130

Phylon, Atlanta University, Atlanta, Georgia 30314

Playboy, 232 East Ohio Street, Chicago, Illinois 60611

Ploughshares, P.O. Box 529, Cambridge, Massachusetts 02139

Prairie Schooner, Andrews Hall, University of Nebraska, Lincoln, Nebraska 68508

Present Tense, 165 East 56th Street, New York, New York 10022

Prism International, University of British Columbia, Vancouver, British Columbia, Canada

Quarry, College V, University of California, Santa Cruz, California 95060

Quarterly Review of Literature, 26 Haslet Avenue, Princeton, New Jersey 08540

Quarterly West, 141 Olpin Union, University of Utah, Salt Lake City, Utah 84112

Quartet, 1119 Neal Pickett Drive, College Station, Texas 77840

Queens Quarterly, Queens University, Kingston, Ontario, Canada

Re: Artes Liberales, School of Liberal Arts, Stephen F. Austin State University, Nacogdoches, Texas 75961

Redbook, 230 Park Avenue, New York, New York 10017

Remington Review, 505 Westfield Avenue, Elizabeth, New Jersey 07208

Response, Box 1496, Brandeis University, Waltham, Massachusetts 02154

Roanoke Review, Box 268, Roanoke College, Salem, Virginia 24513

Rocky Mountain Review, Box 1848, Durango, Colorado 81301

Salmagundi Magazine, Skidmore College, Saratoga Springs, New York 12866

San Francisco Review, P.O. Box 671, San Francisco, California 94100

San José Studies, 174 Administration Building, San José State University, San José, California 95192

Saturday Evening Post, 1100 Waterway Boulevard, Indianapolis, Indiana 46202

Seneca Review, Box 115, Hobart and William Smith College, Geneva, New York 14456

Sense of Humor, P.O. Box 3088, Grand Central Station, New York, New York 10017

Seventeen, 320 Park Avenue, New York, New York 10022

Sewanee Review, University of the South, Sewanee, Tennessee 37375

Shenandoah, Box 122, Lexington, Virginia 24450

Singles World, 121 Cedar Lane, Teaneck, New Jersey 07666

South Carolina Review, Box 28661, Furman University, Greenville, South Carolina 29613

South Dakota Review, Box 111, University Exchange, University of South Dakota, Vermillion, South Dakota 57069

Southern California Review, Bauer Center, Claremont Men's College, Claremont, California 91711

Southern Humanities Review, Auburn University, Auburn, Alabama 36830

Southern Review, Louisiana State University, Baton Rouge, Louisiana 70803

Southwest Review, Southern Methodist University, Dallas, Texas 75222

Spectrum, Box 14800, Santa Barbara, California 93107

St. Andrews Review, St. Andrews Presbyterian College, Laurinsburg, North Carolina 28352

Striver's Row, Department of English, Johns Hopkins University, Baltimore, Maryland 21218

Sumus, The Loom Press, 500 West Rosemary Street, Chapel Hill, North Carolina 27541

Sun & Moon, 4330 Hartwick Road, College Park, Maryland 20740

Sunday Clothes, Box 66, Hermosa, South Dakota 57701

Tamarack Review, Box 157, Postal Station K, Toronto, Canada

Texas Quarterly, Box 7527, University Station, Austin, Texas 78712

Transatlantic Review, P.O. Box 3348, Grand Central Station, New York, New York 10017

Transpacific, P.O. Box 486, Laporte, Colorado 80535

TriQuarterly, Northwestern University, Evanston, Illinois 60201

Twigs, Hilltop Editions, Pikeville College Press, Pikeville, New York 41501

Virginia Quarterly Review, 1 West Range, Charlottesville, Virginia 22903

Vis à Vis, Division of Library Science, California State University, Fullerton, Fullerton, California 92634

Viva, 909 Third Avenue, New York, New York 10022

Wascana Review, Wascana Parkway, Regina, Saskatchewan, Canada

Webster Review, Webster College, Webster Groves, Missouri 63119

Western Humanities Review, Building 41, University of Utah, Salt Lake City, Utah 84112

Western Review, Western New Mexico University, Silver City, New Mexico 88061

Windsor Review, University of Windsor, Windsor, Ontario, Canada

Yale Review, P.O. Box 1729, New Haven, Connecticut 06520

Yankee, Dublin, New Hampshire 03444